COVERT ACTION

DAVID BRUNS
J.R. OLSON

SEVERN RIVER
PUBLISHING

Severn River Publishing
www.SevernRiverBooks.com

ISBN: 978-1-64875-582-8 (Paperback)

ALSO BY BRUNS AND OLSON

The Command and Control Series

Command and Control

Counter Strike

Order of Battle

Threat Axis

Covert Action

Proxy War

Also by the Authors

Weapons of Mass Deception

Jihadi Apprentice

Rules of Engagement

The Pandora Deception

To Richard "Dick" David Bruns, Sr.
1940–2023

Lifelong reader
Beloved father

Central Asia

PROLOGUE

United States Code
Title 50 - WAR AND NATIONAL DEFENSE
Chapter 44 - NATIONAL SECURITY
Subchapter III - ACCOUNTABILITY FOR INTELLIGENCE ACTIVITIES
Sec. 3093 - Presidential approval and reporting of covert actions

50 USC § 3093 (e) - "Covert Action" defined
. . . the term "covert action" means an activity or activities of the United States Government to influence political, economic, or military conditions abroad, where it is intended that the role of the United States Government will not be apparent or acknowledged publicly . . .

1

Tashkent, Uzbekistan

Tim Trujillo clenched his eyes shut, then opened them again. The words on the laptop screen still ran together. He pulled off his reading glasses and rubbed his face with a callused hand. Tired and long past hungry, right now he was feeling every bit of his fifty years.

Tim checked his Tissot Seastar diver's watch, a gift from his wife on his retirement from the Army. When Jenny gave Tim the expensive timepiece, she made him promise to take her scuba diving. It was a promise he had yet to fulfill.

He focused on the dial. Five minutes after one in the morning.

Where in the hell was the shuttle? Tim got to his feet and stretched his arms skyward, feeling the vertebrae pop along his spine.

The temporary waiting room for the private air terminal of the Islam Karimov Tashkent International Airport was deserted. Ongoing construction at the growing public airport had forced yet another relocation of the exclusive terminal, this time to a remote corner of the property. There was nothing out here but a concrete apron for the planes to park, a single hangar, and the maintenance shed that had been repurposed as a waiting room. The holding area for passengers was two rows of low-slung, tattered vinyl chairs, a single desk with a heavy black phone, and a coffee pot.

Tim strode to the window facing the main terminal, a soaring modern structure of glass and steel looming in the distance across a pair of concrete runways. The design mirrored the mountain range hidden in the darkness beyond the terminal, making it seem as if the building was growing from the landscape.

Grand infrastructure projects like this were springing up all over Central Asia as part of the Belt and Road Initiative, the Chinese government's thirty-year plan to create a modern Silk Road reconnecting Asia and Europe. It seemed everywhere Tim went in this part of the world, China was building something new. And not just slapdash, get-it-done projects. These were massive ventures built for growth fifty years in the future. Four-lane highways, airports with a hundred gates, high-speed rail lines connecting regional cities.

Billions of dollars were being invested in sweetheart financing that the host countries would probably never be able to repay. And while he'd read dozens of articles lamenting this robber baron activity, Tim knew that nine out of ten Americans couldn't even find Uzbekistan on a map—if they'd ever even heard of it. He shook his head. Had he not seen this level of Chinese economic activity firsthand, he probably wouldn't believe it either.

His involvement in this part of the world changed nine months ago when Grand Surfan Oil and Gas, majority-owned by Chinese shareholders, hired him as a security consultant. With his background in Army intelligence and a career's worth of experience fighting non-state terrorist groups, he was just what the doctor ordered for the kinds of risk Grand Surfan was trying to protect against.

Tim went back to his laptop and tried to focus on the report he was writing.

The terrorist group known as the Seljuk Islamic Front, commonly abbreviated as SIF, is a regional insurgency that has gained rapid prominence in Central Asia over the last nine months. Although rumored to have ties to Uighur independence groups in western China, the SIF appears to limit its offensive activities to Chinese state-sponsored infrastructure projects in Central Asia. That said, just because Grand Surfan has not suffered any attacks yet does not mean the company is safe from future attacks. It is my recommendation that Grand Surfan effect an advanced security posture immediately...

He blinked again to clear his vision and ran his gaze down the list of recommended improvements to harden the company's field installations. The list was not short, or cheap. Oil fields were sprawling affairs, and in the vast spaces of the Central Asian steppes, every site was wide open to attack from all sides.

His report advocated for tripling the security forces, including a regional QRF with dedicated air transport capability. Specialized hardware to detect and defuse improvised explosive devices was a must. Surveillance camera networks needed to be upgraded at every facility. Tim wondered if he could ask for the latest Chinese government facial recognition software. He'd heard it was the best in the world, and the former intel officer in him wanted to see if it lived up to the hype.

Everything would be tied together on the brand-new Huawei 10G network. This part of the world welcomed the advanced telecommunications capability with open arms, even if the United States and much of Europe rejected the Huawei technology for security reasons. Tim had to admit the network was impressive. Nearly anywhere he went in the region, if he was able to access the Huawei network, he had blazingly fast internet. Mobile phone coverage in the mountainous region was spotty, but getting better all the time as the Chinese continued to build out the network. He knew more than a few of his former Army colleagues with cyber backgrounds who would love to see the inside of the latest Chinese communications network.

Tim grinned to himself. You can take the boy out of the Army, but you can't take the Army out of the boy.

He edited the list to spell out *quick reaction force* in place of the acronym *QRF*. That recommendation was probably overkill, but he decided to leave it. He was a consultant, after all. It was his job to make the best possible recommendations. His boss could figure out whether or not his proposal was worth the price tag. Hell, the company was pumping so much oil out of the region, they could afford everything on his wish list twice over.

He slapped the laptop lid shut and heaved a sigh.

This was his tenth day of visiting field installations for an on-the-ground security assessment. His whirlwind tour had taken him through Kazakhstan, Tajikistan, Kyrgyzstan, and Uzbekistan. His last stop before flying to Beijing to deliver his report in person was Ashgabat, Turkmenistan. One final series of inspections and his report would be complete.

Tim glared out the window at the empty tarmac. That assumed the damned shuttle ever showed up.

He rolled his shoulders. Every muscle ached and he smelled like he'd been on army field maneuvers for a week. The steppes were high desert country. Dusty and hot during the day and cold at night. He could feel grit in every crevice of his body, and he longed for a hot shower and a cold beer. His stomach rumbled. Maybe some barbecue, too.

He scratched at his stubbled chin. He'd quit shaving a week ago and his beard had reached the itchy stage of growth. Jenny hated him with a beard and always made him shave it off as soon as he got home.

A wave of homesickness swept over him at the thought of his wife. He did the mental math on the time zone difference between Tashkent and northern Virginia. One a.m. here, which meant it was three in the afternoon at home. Too early to call. Jenny would still be at work, and he knew she turned her cell phone off in the classroom.

He cradled his phone in his palm. Maybe just call anyway and leave her a message. A quick *I love you*. Tim smiled to himself as he pictured her listening to the voicemail. Her chestnut hair lit by the sun, the curve of her cheek, that secret smile she reserved only for him . . .

"Twenty-eight years and counting," he said out loud. Even his voice sounded dusty.

Call her, you idiot. Tell her you love her.

Facial recognition opened his phone to the home screen, a picture of him and Jenny flanked by their two kids. Emma, tall and slender with a mane of chestnut hair that rivaled her mother's, was on Tim's arm. Mark, a senior in high school and two years younger than his sister, took after his father. In the upper right of the screen, the icon for the Ironclad app he'd installed a few weeks ago pulsed three times, signaling that his secure backup was up to date.

He navigated to the list of recent calls. With his thumb poised over the line labeled *Sweet Jenny*, he heard the roar of a jet engine. He sat up just in time to see a small aircraft touch down on the runway and flash by the window.

Finally. He got to his feet and stowed the phone in the pocket of his cargo pants. From the window, Tim made out the form of a sleek Gulfstream G500 making the turn at the end of the runway and taxiing toward the private airfield apron.

A Gulfstream? That was new. Every Surfan shuttle he'd been on so far had been King Air 350 turboprops that had seen better days. This plane looked brand-new, but the tail number indicated it was a Chinese aircraft.

Across the concrete apron, the doors on the hangar slid open, spilling bright yellow light into the night. The jet made a ninety-degree turn and entered the hangar. The doors rolled closed behind it, but not before Tim spied a black Mercedes parked inside the building.

What the hell? Tim's eyes clocked to the whiteboard that served as the temporary flight schedule. Grand Surfan shuttle was listed for nine p.m., and he'd been waiting here since eight-thirty. There were no other flights listed. That plane *had* to be the Grand Surfan shuttle.

It's so late, he thought with a flash of irritation, they must assume there's no passengers waiting.

Tim headed for the door. He was not about to abandon his carefully planned itinerary without at least a discussion with the pilot.

The outside air was crisp and dry. Brilliant stars speckled the sky. He felt the skin of his bare forearms prickle with cold and realized he'd left his jacket back in the waiting room, along with his laptop and duffel.

He jogged across the dark tarmac to the passenger door at the corner of the hangar. The exterior lights on the building were out, which rankled the security consultant part of his brain. With all the construction going on, it was likely some contractor had messed up the wiring when they moved the private air terminal.

There was a one-foot square window set in the door at eye level. With one hand on the handle of the door, Tim peered into the window.

He froze. Then he moved away and flattened his back against the cold steel of the hangar wall. When Tim had his breathing under control, he slowly reapproached the window and looked into the hangar.

A Chinese man, slight of build with angular facial features, stood in full profile ten meters away. He held out his left hand parallel to the floor and slapped a closed fist into the open palm as if making a point.

A row of shelves crammed with spare parts and boxes blocked Tim's view of the person the Chinese man was speaking to with such vigor.

Tim returned to the wall, feeling the cold metal chill the sweat on his back. He swallowed.

Chinese Minister of State Security Yan Tao had flown into Tashkent in the middle of the night to have a clandestine meeting . . . but who was the other person?

Walk away, Tim. You're not an intelligence officer anymore. Report the meeting and get on with your life. Not your problem, dude.

But another part of his brain would not let it go. *Who is Yan talking to? At least find out that much.*

Tim went back to the window and tried to angle his line of sight so he could see who the Chinese spymaster was talking to, but it was no use. The storage shelves were in the way.

He pushed down gently on the door handle. It was unlocked. He eased the door open and slipped inside, allowing a full ten seconds for the door to close silently behind him.

Voices drifted toward him, speaking in English. The skin on the back of Tim's neck prickled. First data point: If the Minister had been meeting with another Chinese person, they'd be speaking Mandarin.

Three shelves ran parallel to the wall. Tim took two quick steps forward and slid into the space between the second and third shelves. He side-stepped gingerly along the aisle, trying to find a gap among the crowded shelves where he could see both men clearly.

"I need more resources," said the second voice. He spoke excellent English. The voice sounded vaguely familiar to Tim.

Minister Yan's flat response cracked like a whip. "You will get what you were promised. Nothing more."

In the gap between a cardboard box and an avionics rack, Tim finally found a clear view. The two men stood in the open, with the jet in the background. Minister Yan faced Tim, his posture rigid, his face twisted with annoyance.

The second man faced away from Tim. He was taller than the Minister and had thick, dark hair touched with gray. A tailored suit covered his broad shoulders.

"Do you understand?" Yan pressed.

"I am the one taking the risk here." The second man turned, and Tim saw his face for the first time.

Tim's mouth went dry. Of course he knew the voice. He'd heard it a hundred times on the radio and on TV. The question was, why was he *here*, and why was he meeting secretly with the head of Chinese clandestine services? Whatever Tim had stumbled into, this was explosive—and dangerous.

Get out now, you fool. Alarm bells clanged in his brain.

But he was here. He couldn't just ignore what he was seeing.

Tim removed his phone from his pocket and turned it on, cupping his hand over the glaring screen. He navigated to the video setting and extended the camera lens into the narrow opening. He tried to control his own breathing.

The Chinese man raised his voice, slashing his hand down again for emphasis. The second man's bearded face twisted in anger as he responded in kind.

"Without me, you have nothing!" he shouted.

Tim stopped the recording. That was enough. He put the phone back in his pocket and turned to retreat down the aisle. A wire hanging loose from the avionics box snagged on his shirt sleeve, emitting a *scritch* sound as it scraped along the edge of the metal rack.

The two men stopped speaking. Tim froze, holding his breath. A wave of sweaty nausea swept up his torso.

The figure of a man appeared at the end of the aisle, blocking his exit.

Tim charged. Lowering his shoulder, he plowed into the man, driving him back against the wall of the hangar. The guard was solidly built and quick on his feet. Even as Tim pistoned his fists into the man's midsection, he felt his opponent grappling him, swinging his body into the wall and using Tim's momentum against him.

Tim's hip crashed into a vertical steel support and a bolt of pain shot up his spine. He threw an elbow at the shorter man's face and felt a satisfying crunch of cartilage. Tim clapped his hands on both of the man's shoulders, pushed down, and drove his knee upward as hard as he could, catching the man on the point of his chin. The guard's head snapped back and he sagged to the floor.

Tim spun, throwing open the door. Crisp night air rolled over him. Bright stars signaled freedom.

A new form filled the doorway. Before Tim could react, a fist lashed out, catching him in the throat. Two more blows followed, pounding into the left side of his chest.

Tim's heart stuttered. His mouth gaped open, but no oxygen entered his body. His knees crashed to the floor. A final blow smashed into the side of his face with the force of a sledgehammer. His eardrum popped, his head whipped to the side, and the stars in the sky smeared into a blur.

A gentle vibration under Tim's cheek brought him back to consciousness. When he raised his head, his beard snagged in the close-cropped fibers of a royal blue carpet.

His eyes took in creamy leather seats, polished wood accents, a table, and the blade-like face of the Chinese Minister of State Security. Yan's dark eyes, like polished stones, regarded Tim the way a man might view an insect.

The Minister nodded at the chair opposite him. Tim's hands were bound behind his back, and he had to use his chin to push his torso off the floor. He settled onto his knees and surveyed the cabin.

Two men in dark suits sat in captain's chairs two rows behind the Minister. The shorter of the pair sported two black eyes and an obviously broken nose. The second security man was a giant, with not a scratch on him. Tim's face still ached where the man had coldcocked him and he couldn't hear anything from his left ear.

Tim got to his feet, moved to the chair opposite the Minister, and lowered himself into the cushioned seat. He did a quick self-assessment as he moved. Nothing broken, but the bindings on his hands were tight and his throat felt like it was on fire. His wristwatch was gone. The finger where he wore his West Point class ring was bloody, but the ring was still in place.

The raccoon eyes of the shorter security guy followed Tim's every movement, daring him to step out of line. Payback was going to be a bitch.

The Minister held up Tim's passport. "Timothy Ernesto Trujillo. Security consultant to Grand Surfan Oil"—he sniffed—"and a spy for the CIA."

"I'm—" Tim's voice caught in his dry throat. He looked meaningfully at the bottle of water on the table between them.

The Minister sighed and made a hand motion. The shorter guard twisted the cap off a bottle of water. He held it so Tim could drink, while allowing a good amount to spill down his chest. He held his wrist so that Tim's watch was on full display.

Time... what time was it?

Tim tried to focus on the face of the watch, but the guard turned his wrist away.

As Tim swallowed the last of the water, his mind went into overdrive analyzing the situation. He was probably headed back to China, where who knew what awaited him. His only chance at survival was to keep them talking, buy himself some time.

"I'm not a spy," Tim said. "I thought you were the Surfan shuttle."

"Hmm." The Minister pulled Tim's phone out of his inside jacket pocket and turned it on. The Minister studied the home screen.

"You have a beautiful family, Mr. Trujillo. Would you like to see them again?"

Tim nodded.

"Then I suggest you be truthful with me. Who else knows you were in that hangar?"

"No one." That much was true.

The Minister turned the phone screen toward Tim. It was unlocked. "Then why were you recording me?"

There was no good answer, so Tim stayed silent.

"Who told you about the meeting?"

"No one. I already said I was waiting for the shuttle."

The Minister's thin lips twisted in disgust. "You're a retired Army intelligence officer caught in an act of espionage on foreign soil."

Tim said nothing.

"Do you know what the penalty is in China for spies?" the Minister asked.

"We're not in China," Tim said.

A mocking smile. "You never know. The Chinese empire grows larger every year."

If there was a hand signal, Tim didn't see it, but the guards moved on him together. While Shorty went to the cabin door, the giant lifted Tim out of the chair like he was a child. He spun Tim around and marched him forward. Tim tried to struggle, but it was useless.

The door of the jet yawned open. The rush of wind filled the cabin. The giant security guard forced Tim toward the door.

"Wait!" he shouted.

The Minister appeared in front of him.

"Do you want to talk now?" he yelled back.

"Let me see my family first. On the phone, I mean."

The Minister shrugged and swiped his finger up the screen of Tim's phone. The image on his home screen sprang to life. He'd seen it a million times, but his eyes drank in the details like it was the very first time.

The fall of Emma's hair. He could almost feel his daughter's arm curving around his back. Mark needed a haircut, and he had the same lopsided smile that Tim saw when he looked in the mirror. And Jenny, sweet Jenny. She deserved so much better than this . . .

Tim's eyes tracked to the upper right corner. The shield icon pulsed three times.

He let his knees sag, and the man holding him leaned forward to compensate for the added weight.

When he felt the shift, Tim drove his body upward and snapped his head back into the giant's face. The man's teeth cut into Tim's scalp. He hoped he'd knocked a few out.

Tim lashed out with a foot and caught the shorter guard between the legs. He felt his toe sink deep into soft flesh. He pushed off the wall, trying to throw the giant off balance.

The man was just too strong. He surged Tim's body forward and launched him into space.

The deafening wind noise ceased. The roar of the jet faded and Tim was alone in the dark night sky.

Falling.

Jenny. Sweet Jenny.

2

Dushanbe, Tajikistan

Russian President Nikolay Sokolov leaned back in his chair at the head of the table. He tilted his glass, letting the vodka slide down his throat. It was an expensive brand, but it might as well have been battery acid. In fact, given how the last few days had unfolded, battery acid might have been preferable.

Because of the growing security threat in the city, the dinner for the principals had been hastily relocated from a downtown restaurant to a large conference room at the Ministry of Foreign Affairs building, where the three-day meeting of the CSTO had been held. The dinner, like everything else about his first visit to Central Asia as President, was a disappointment.

At least there was vodka. The silent waitress refilled his glass, and Nikolay studied the clear liquid in the light of the cheap chandelier.

To his right, Miras Karimov rambled on. Nikolay found it truly amazing that the man could spew forth so many words and yet say absolutely nothing. It was an act, Nikolay knew. The new President of Kazakhstan was a polished, intelligent man with a tremendous social media following and big plans for this country's future. Plans that may or may not include the Russian Federation.

No, Karimov's words were empty because he was buying time. The question Nikolay had tried to divine over the last three days was, buying time for what?

Kazakhstan and Russia shared a border of over 7700 kilometers. The country practically defined Russia's southern near-abroad. Under Nikolay's uncle, Kazakhstan had always been a stalwart ally, an important connection from the old Soviet days. But while Nikolay had been unseating Uncle Vitaly from his perch as President of Russia, Karimov had done the same in his own country. With a political skill that bordered on genius, this man nearly ten years Nikolay's junior had taken control over the largest landlocked nation in the world, including the massive oil, gas, and mining resources that spread across it. Resources that Nikolay not only wanted, but was historically entitled to.

But Karimov seemed to have other ideas.

Nikolay studied the man. Barely forty, with carefully styled dark hair and slim glasses that gave him a studious look, Karimov fancied himself a modern technocrat who was going to drag his homeland into the twenty-first century. There was so much common experience between them, they should be friends. Nikolay needed this man as his ally. And yet, at this moment, he struggled to tamp down the irritation he felt at the wall of words Karimov was erecting between them.

This entire trip was supposed to be a celebration, he mused. No, not just a celebration, a coronation. A recognition that Nikolay Sokolov was the undisputed leader of the Russian Federation. That the old ways were in the dustbin of history. He would treat his neighbors as valued partners. Not equals, but better than anything they'd had from Russia in the past.

In honor of the occasion, a new economic agreement had been carefully negotiated over the last six months. It was a fair document, Nikolay knew, with something in it for everyone. Kazakhstan got an increase in tariff rates, the other members of the CSTO were awarded Russian armaments and increased security commitments, and Russia received a fresh infusion into the lifeblood of her economy: oil and gas flowing into Russia's massive pipeline infrastructure. Signing this agreement was the only reason why he'd agreed to spend three days away from Moscow.

But when Nikolay arrived, the dream vanished like a mirage in the desert. The carefully crafted agreement sat unsigned in the next room. For three days he had questioned, cajoled, and negotiated with these men to no avail. No one, least of all this man of many words and no meaning prattling at his elbow, would tell him why he was not returning to Moscow this night with a signed agreement.

Karimov's carefully trimmed goatee moved rhythmically as he somehow managed to demolish his dessert without slowing down his verbal assault.

"Mr. President," he said around a mouthful of chocolate mousse. "We deeply value your commitment to the CSTO." He paused, spoon midway to his lips, and Nikolay pounced.

"But?" Nikolay said sharply. His glass was empty again.

I should stop drinking now, he thought. He could taste the burn of frustration on his tongue. Vodka never made a bad situation better.

Nikolay signaled the waitress to refill his glass. He gazed down the table to where Federov was locked in quiet conversation with a man who looked weathered, like someone who'd seen too much in life and survived to tell the tale.

Akhmet Orazov, another relic of the Soviet era, like so many of the men around this table. He had been invited as an observer to the CSTO proceedings at the insistence of Federov.

Nikolay cast a sideways glance at Karimov. The two of them were the only relatively young men in the room. In the early days of his leadership of the Russian Federation, Nikolay believed that his age was a good thing. Youth—or at least someone under the age of sixty—represented a breath of fresh air in the sclerotic oligarchy his Uncle Vitaly had built.

New ideas. Fresh thinking. A bright future.

The next draught of vodka slid down his throat. His glass magically refilled and he drank.

He had tried for too much on this visit. Relationships with men like Karimov and the rest of them were built over the course of years. But I don't have years, Nikolay thought, not if the Moscow hardliners have their way.

In the aftermath of the Soviet Union's collapse, the Collective Security Treaty Organization had formed to replace the defunct Warsaw Pact. The military alliance protected Russia's near-abroad, using border countries like Ukraine, Belarus, and Kazakhstan as security buffers to the west and south.

But over the last decade, the power of the CSTO had eroded. Russia's failed invasion in Ukraine and the subsequent Western sanctions had bitten deeply into both the economy and the Russian national psyche. As Russian attention to Central Asia wavered, the Shanghai Cooperation Organization, a Chinese-led sister organization in the region, flourished.

Nikolay's path to success for this meeting had always been a narrow one: solidify the support of the CSTO members, then tackle the challenges from Beijing. The economic agreement was his way of showing the leaders of Central Asia that he was serious about a renewed relationship.

And they had shoved the agreement back in his face without explanation.

Nikolay felt the vodka break through his normally even demeanor. His belly was warm and his blood coursed hot in his veins as Karimov spewed more words at him.

I need their support. No, I *deserve* their support.

Another signal. Another glass of vodka rested between his fingertips, gleaming like a jewel in the shitty light of this shitty room. He retreated further into his own thoughts.

He supposed they were worried about the insurgency. The Seljuk Islamic Front had been harassing Chinese infrastructure projects for the past year. How long would it be before those same terrorists came after their oil and gas pipelines? Would the Russian Federation be there to protect their infrastructure?

Their doubts about Russia's ability to deliver on his promises had substance. Despite Nikolay's public expressions of optimism, pressure was on him from all sides. The Ultras—former supporters of Uncle Vitaly—constantly attacked him from the right. The progressives on the left were less bloodthirsty, but no less dangerous. They lived in an economic fantasy-land, expecting him to modernize the Russian economy overnight. They seemed not to understand that their country was a petrostate, and the money to reform the country came from the sale of oil and gas.

Nikolay had worked hard to diversify Russia's economy, but foreign direct investment depended on the rule of law. Three decades of Uncle Vitaly's kleptocracy had left him with little to work with.

Another sip of vodka turned into a long pull. What he needed was this economic agreement signed to give his government breathing room until the next election. He needed a win, if only to build political capital back in Moscow.

Three days. He'd wasted three days gladhanding and politicking these men for an economic agreement that, by rights, was his for the taking.

And he was heading home empty-handed.

Nikolay turned a baleful eye on the prattling Kazakh politician next to him. It took a few seconds for the man to stop talking.

"I apologize. Did you say something, Mr. President?" Karimov asked. He offered up an oily smile that made Nikolay want to punch him in the face.

"Why didn't you sign?" Nikolay asked bluntly, but quietly. "The real reason, not more of your bullshit." He flicked his fingers down the table. "If you signed, they would sign. But you didn't. Why?"

The man shifted in his seat. Even though the room was not warm, he had a sheen of sweat across his forehead. His eyes darted down the table in a plea for assistance, but no one was paying attention to him.

Nikolay thought briefly about letting him off the hook. He was breaking every diplomatic nicety by putting the man on the spot, but he didn't care. What would Uncle Vitaly do? Would he listen to this man's prattle for an hour and smile?

No, President Luchnik would have pressed this upstart into the nearest corner and come away with what he wanted—what he *deserved*.

"Well?" Nikolay demanded. The waitress approached with the vodka bottle and he waved her away. His mind felt clear and sharp. He narrowed his eyes at Karimov and the man wilted under his glare.

The man's submissive response sparked a pleasure center in Nikolay's brain. Was this how Uncle Vitaly felt every day?

"It's not that simple, Mr. President," Karimov said. "There are many factors to consider—"

"Such as?" Nikolay interrupted. "I've increased your revenues by twenty percent. I've offered security guarantees and additional armaments. Yet none of it seems to matter." He leaned closer, his face mere centimeters from the younger man. "I want to know why."

The table felt suddenly silent. Nikolay's gaze locked on Federov. The head of the Federal Security Service, sat very still, his bald pate shiny in the dim light, his crystalline brown eyes luminous. He gave a slight shake of his head, but Nikolay ignored him. He stood and rapped his empty glass on the table.

"Can *anyone* explain to me why the economic agreement is not signed yet? Anyone?"

"It's because your promises are shit." The man who spoke was Federov's conversation partner. He stood now, the scrape of his chair loud in the room. The other faces ping-ponged between either end of the table. Federov, normally unflappable, sported a deer in the headlights look.

"You are an observer to these proceedings, Mr. Orazov," Nikolay replied quietly. "You have no wolf in this hunt."

The man's hooded eyes were lost in shadow. Unlike the rest of the politicians at the dinner, who wore dark business suits or ornamental garb, he was dressed plainly. The sleeves of his shirt were pushed up to his elbows and Nikolay noted the cords of muscle on his forearms. This was no soft politician. This man was a soldier.

"You are correct, Mr. President," Orazov replied. His voice was even and calm. "But the Russian Federation is not the fearsome power that it once was. The foolish war in Ukraine saw to that. Your soldiers are ill disciplined, barely trained, and poorly led. The armaments you promise us are of poor quality. If the shipments arrive at all, they're incomplete. The Russian bear is old and toothless."

Orazov rested his knuckles on the table and leaned in. "As for the economic incentives, if you cannot protect what you have, what good is a piece of paper? These men need security guarantees, not empty promises."

He swept his arm down the table in an expansive gesture.

"For three days, I have listened. Not once has anyone mentioned the real threat to our region." He paused, his gaze clocking the faces at the table, ending on Nikolay.

"China. The Chinese *Belt and Road*"—he spat the words out like a curse —"is making all of you soft. The Chinese plans are grand, but there is a cost: our sovereignty. We are caught between the Russian bear and the Chinese dragon."

His eyes locked on Nikolay. "You want us to choose. Us or them. But that is not the only choice. We can choose our own path. Independence for our region."

When Orazov finished speaking, a chilly silence settled over the room. The waiters stood frozen in position, their backs against the wall, bottles of vodka and plates of food unmoving in their hands.

Nikolay's gaze caught on the face of the young woman who'd poured his vodka. She was looking at Orazov and her expression was something he'd not seen in a long time.

Hope.

"The real answer to your question, Mr. President," Orazov said, his low voice loud in the stillness, "is that these men think they can get a better deal with the Chinese. *That* is why you are going back to Moscow empty-handed."

The very important men seated at the table looked at their empty plates, their wine glasses, or each other—anything to avoid looking at the Russian president.

Nikolay let out a slow breath. He wanted to ask a thousand questions, but instead he just nodded.

"I thank you for speaking plainly, Mr. Orazov." In his mind, he finished the thought: *Which is more than I can say for the rest of these spineless pricks.*

Aloud, he said, "Gentlemen, the hour is late and I have a flight to catch." Nikolay headed for the door. His security detail met him in the hall. They had to jog to match his furious pace as he took the stairs two at a time and pushed through the glass doors into the winter night. Cold, dry air bathed his hot, sweaty face. He breathed in great gulps as if to purge his body of the alcohol and the ill will.

He slid into the back seat of the waiting limousine. The car door shut behind him with the solid *thunk* of a coffin lid. Nikolay rested his aching head against the cool window. He closed his eyes.

The car door opened and shut again as Federov got in. The vehicle pulled away from the curb and Nikolay let the acceleration push him back into the soft cushions.

"What the fuck was that?" Federov said finally. "Mr. President," he added after a beat.

"The truth, Vladimir," he said. "The unfortunate truth."

"You took a bad situation and made it worse," Federov said, his normally calm voice laced with anger.

"Don't hold back, my friend."

The silence continued long enough that Nikolay opened his eyes. Federov sat rigidly in his seat, hands clamped on thighs, staring straight ahead.

Nikolay sighed. "I should have been more tactful. I'll send each of them a personal gift to apologize. Including Mr. Orazov."

Federov's breathing slowed and Nikolay could see him calming down as they merged with traffic.

"What do we do now, sir?" Federov said finally.

"I should think that answer is obvious, Vladimir."

Federov's smile was icy. "Enlighten me, Mr. President."

"We go to see my uncle."

3

Herndon, Virginia

Dusk was falling when Harrison drove his Audi A3 through the Virginia suburbs outside of Washington, DC.

He was over an hour late. He'd managed to leave the office just in time to hit the thick of evening rush hour and then added to his lateness by stopping at a wine store. No worries. He knew Jenny would understand.

She would want to know all about his new job, of course, and Harrison tried to think of ways to talk about it without sounding petty or ungrateful. Since Don Riley had been promoted to CIA Deputy Director of Operations, or DDO, Harrison had been serving—*sentenced* was a better word—as Director of Emerging Threats Group. *Interim* director, he reminded himself. There was no way he wanted the job for good. He'd made his feelings very clear to Don.

Riley had offered up a smug smile. "It's just temporary, Harrison. I promise."

That was four months ago, and the temporary nature of the job had turned disturbingly permanent. The feeling was strong enough that Harrison considered just leaving the Agency. He was single and had saved enough to do whatever he wanted . . .

He dismissed the thought. He loved his job at ETG. Well, not the director job, but his real job as an analyst and occasional field operative. He'd started his career in the field, and he intended to get back in the game if Uncle Sam was of a mind to let him. He told himself that if he just delivered for Don now, then Riley would owe him one.

As he drove past wide, neatly trimmed lawns and brick-fronted houses with butter-yellow squares of lit windows, he could feel the stress of the day melting away. He patted the bottle of Willamette Valley Pinot Noir on the seat next to him. The dinner invitation from Jenny Trujillo had come at just the right time. What he needed was a night with friends and a few good laughs to forget about the office. The management headaches would still be there in the morning.

He pulled up in front of the Trujillo home, a Colonial-style brick front with a columned portico. Even in wintertime the yard was immaculate. The lawn was Tim's obsession and it showed in the exact placement and care of every flower and shrub.

Harrison's breath steamed in the cold as he jogged up the driveway, wine in hand. He pressed the doorbell, feeling his lips already forming a smile at the thought of the evening to come.

When Mark Trujillo opened the door, Harrison did a doubletake. On the shorter side, with heavy shoulders and a tight waist, Mark was the spitting image of his father at that age.

"Uncle H," Mark said, hugging him. The kid was solid muscle. Harrison held him at arm's length and studied his face. He had square features, wide set eyes, and wavy dark hair. The very sight of the young man took Harrison back to a steamy summer day along the Hudson River in West Point, New York. He'd met Tim Trujillo on the first day of Beast Barracks, and they'd been fast friends ever since.

"I know, Uncle H, I look like my dad. You don't have to say it. Again." The kid's brown eyes met his, and Harrison could see they were troubled.

"What's the matter?" Harrison asked.

"I'll let Mom tell you," he said, "but I'm glad you're here. She's really worried."

Harrison made his way to the kitchen where Jenny Trujillo faced the stove, idly stirring a pot of tomato sauce with a wooden spoon. Her curly brown hair, captured in a silver clip at her nape, ran halfway down her back.

He immediately knew something was wrong. Jenny loved music. If she wasn't singing or humming, she was listening to music. But tonight, the kitchen was silent. Her shoulders were set in a rigid line as her hand moved the spoon with a mechanical rhythm.

He put the wine on the table. "Jen," he said softly.

When she turned, he could see she'd been crying. He opened his arms and she rushed at him. Her grip was tight around his ribs as he hugged her back. "Thank you for coming," she said, her voice muffled against his chest.

Harrison made his voice sound like he was choking. "I see . . . you've been . . . working out. That's quite a grip you've got."

Jenny laughed as she released him and wiped her eyes. "I'm being stupid," she said, but her face was still clouded with worry. "Except I know I'm not."

Harrison pulled out a chair for her and handed the bottle of wine to Mark. "You wanna talk about it?"

"I have a feeling, Harrison. About Tim."

"You can't get in touch with him?"

She shook her head and Harrison could see she was close to tears again.

He took her hand. "Talk to me."

"I haven't heard from Tim in three days," she began. "That's not unusual. When he's in the field, he doesn't always have phone coverage. There's the time difference, and sometimes he just forgets when he's wrapped up with work. . ."

Mark placed two glasses of wine on the table. Harrison nodded his thanks.

"But you think it's more than that," he said.

Jenny bit her lip. "I have a bad feeling, Harrison."

"I tried the phone locator app," Mark volunteered. "The last place he was on the network was an airport in Tashkent. Three days ago."

"Email?" Harrison asked. "Text?"

"Nada," Mark replied.

"He's still consulting for that oil company, right?" Harrison asked.

Jenny nodded. "Grand Surfan. I tried calling them and they said he's in the field. The only way they can get a hold of him is by his mobile phone. He was in Tashkent airport to catch a shuttle three nights ago, except the shuttle was cancelled."

Harrison knew what Tim would do if his primary means of transport fell through—he'd find an alternate method of travel.

"He probably rented a car," Harrison said. "Maybe the car broke down in the mountains or something. Maybe his phone is dead."

It sounded lame and he knew it. Jenny's eyes pleaded with him silently.

Harrison squeezed her hand. "Let's do this: You finish making dinner. Mark and I will have a look at his office."

Tim's office was like a memory palace for Harrison. His best friend's "I love me" wall was crowded with framed pictures and plaques from his career in the Army.

A hand-crafted display case held a few hundred challenge coins from various units, senior officials, and foreign military outfits, all neatly arranged in precise rows. A shadow box showed off Tim's promotions from 2nd lieutenant all the way up to colonel, and his rack of ribbons from military operations were set against black felt. Harrison's memories of his own service washed over him as he took in the United States Military Academy bachelor's degree mounted alongside Tim's appointment letter from the President of the United States commissioning his best friend into the U.S. Army. It was all neat and organized, very Tim-like.

He picked up a picture from the desk. Tim and Jenny on the night they'd met. Arms around each other, Tim was dressed in civilian clothes, red Solo cup in hand. Jenny was smiling at the camera, but Tim was looking at her. Harrison had taken it with a disposable camera at a cast party after his last performance in *Man of La Mancha* at West Point.

Harrison had brought Tim, his roommate, to the cast party at the director's house off-post. He remembered Jenny was there as someone's date, but that date was over as soon as the pair saw each other.

Harrison always thought that love at first sight was a Hollywood myth, but that night he saw it in action. When it came time for them to leave, he practically had to put his roommate in a chokehold to get him into the car.

"Memories, Uncle H?" Mark asked in a quiet voice.

Harrison put the photo back on the desk. "Yeah," he said. "Good ones."

Jenny and Tim married right after graduation from West Point, and she followed him all over the world as an army officer's wife. In between having two kids of their own, she became a primary school teacher. Harrison knew Jenny like a sister. She was level-headed and pragmatic. One did not serve a career as an Army spouse and not know how to deal with the stress of separation. If Jenny was worried about Tim, then she deserved to have her concerns taken seriously.

He took a seat behind Tim's desk and powered on the family computer. "Tell me about your dad's job, Mark."

The young man pulled a chair around the desk so he could sit next to Harrison.

"He does security consulting for multinationals," Mark said as he logged onto the family email account. "Oil and gas companies mostly. He gets a lot of work from investment firms that want to make sure the companies they put their money into are secure."

"Your dad liked field work," Harrison said as he scanned through emails. He had no idea what he was looking for. The last email Tim had sent to Jenny and the kids was three days ago, a breezy three-paragraph account of his travels. He scanned the email, noting the cities on Tim's itinerary. Dushanbe, Tashkent, Ashgabat, then Beijing at the end of the week for a meeting with headquarters staff. Harrison checked the date. Tim was supposed to be in Beijing tomorrow.

"Yeah," Mark continued, "he always said the best intel gathering device was your own two eyes."

"That sounds like him," Harrison replied. He used their password manager on the computer to access the family's bank and credit card accounts. There had been no transactions in the last three days.

"What's this?" He let the cursor hover over an icon in the toolbar at the top of the screen. It was a tiny shield with capital letter I superimposed on the front.

"You got me," Mark said. "You know how Dad's always trying out new stuff."

Despite the seriousness of the circumstances, Harrison smiled. Tim was a true-blue gadget head, always trying out the latest piece of electronics or the newest software program. Their room at West Point had the best sound system on campus, and Tim was forever upgrading his phone and laptop.

Harrison clicked on the icon, and was immediately sent to a login screen for an application called Ironclad. Unlike all the other applications on the computer, the login information for the Ironclad account was not in the password manager. He checked the registry and saw the program had only been installed three weeks ago, the last time Tim had been home.

"I guess he was trying it out?" Mark ventured.

"Dinner!" Jenny called up the stairs.

Harrison shut off the computer. "I don't see anything here out of the ordinary."

"What about the phone locator app?" Mark asked.

"I have a better version at the office," Harrison replied. "I'll see if I can turn something up."

"Should we be worried, Uncle H?"

Harrison studied the young man. He could not shake the uncanny sense that he was talking to Tim himself. "I'm on it, compadre. I'll find your dad. No worries."

Mark hugged his uncle. Harrison reflexively embraced him in return, suddenly realizing that even though Mark looked grown up, he was still a boy inside.

"Thank you," Mark said.

"Let's get some dinner," Harrison replied. "I'm just gonna wash my hands."

He closed the bathroom door and splashed cold water on his hot face. He stared at his reflection, water droplets dripping down his cheeks.

"Where are you, Tim?" he whispered.

It was well after eleven when Harrison pulled his car into the ETG parking lot in Tysons Corner.

Dinner with Jenny and Mark had been a forced affair. Harrison felt the weight of Tim's absence shadowing every laugh and story they shared. His rational brain told him that getting lost for a few days in the steppes of

Central Asia was not that unusual—even Jenny admitted that—but somehow this *felt* different.

He cleared away the stacks of paper covering his desk. Don Riley had trained all of his direct reports to provide everything in hardcopy. It was a difficult habit to break. No matter how many times Harrison told people he didn't want paper reports, they just kept showing up anyway.

The activity focused his attention. For this exercise, he needed a clear desk and space to think.

Harrison entered Tim's phone number into his computer and used a commercially available locator app. As he expected, the data showed the phone's last location as the airport in Tashkent.

Harrison dialed a contact at the NSA, a night shift supervisor.

"Annette? It's Harrison." He endured a few minutes of small talk, then got to the point. "I need a favor. Can you run a phone number for me?"

The line was quiet, and he waited. As acting head of ETG, seeking location data on a mobile phone overseas was within his legal purview, but the right way to do it was to file a request. That would take time, especially when the number was owned by a US citizen. Time was a commodity Harrison didn't want to waste.

"It's a friend," he said. "I told the family I'd check up on him."

Annette let out a sigh. "You're going to follow up with official paperwork?"

Harrison winced. "Of course. You know me."

"Yeah, I do know you, and you're a bad influence." She paused. "Gimme the number."

Harrison read off Tim's mobile number.

"Stand by." He heard the muted clacking of a keyboard in the background. "Okay, mobile phone for Timothy Trujillo was located at an airport in Uzbekistan a little over three days ago. I have coordinates if you want them."

"What about after that?" Harrison asked. "Anything?"

More keyboard noises. "Nope . . . well, wait."

Harrison sat up in his chair. "What?"

"Looks like the phone was turned on again right around 0300 local. We got a single ping off a tower, then nothing."

"Coordinates?"

"This data's shit, Harrison. It's a single tower, probably an echo."

"I'll take it anyway." Harrison scribbled down the numbers as Annette read them off.

"That's it," she said. "His phone hasn't touched a network since."

"Thanks, Annette. I owe you one."

"Yeah, you do. File the paperwork. Please."

"You know me."

"That's why I reminded you again, Harrison. Good luck with your friend."

After they hung up, Harrison entered the coordinates into a map program. He stared at the screen.

According to Tim's email, his plans had been to fly into Ashgabat, located southwest of Tashkent. But the cell tower that his phone had pinged at 0256 local was nearly a hundred miles in the opposite direction, northwest of the airport. He zoomed in on the map and read the Cyrillic script: Ugam-Chatkal National Park, on the border between Uzbekistan and Kyrgyzstan.

He zoomed in closer. There were no roads that he could see. Even if Tim had been in a car, there was no way he could have traveled anywhere near that cell tower only an hour.

A plane? Harrison searched a database for any aircraft transponder activity in the area at that time of the morning. Nothing.

He checked for satellite coverage in the area during the time frame. Still nothing. It didn't surprise him. The U.S. interests in the region were negligible, and satellite resources were precious.

Harrison blew out a breath and sat back in his chair. The single data point in the wilderness made no sense. Annette was probably right. The signal must have been an echo off another tower.

So much for technology, he thought. I can sit on my ass in Washington or I can get out in the field to use my best intel-gathering device: my own two eyes.

Harrison logged onto an unclassified browser and looked at plane tickets to Tashkent. He would need to get a visa, and that would take some time. He let his gaze roam over the stacks of paper he had pushed to the side.

First things first, he thought.

He opened his unclassified email program and found Don Riley's name in the directory. The cursor blinked in the subject line.

He typed: *Emergency leave of absence.*

4

Tashkent, Uzbekistan

The black Mercedes-Benz Sprinter van pulled to the curb of the new Tashkent high-speed rail terminal. On the wide sidewalk, a knot of men clad in identical blue business suits waited for the Chinese delegation.

"One moment, General." The makeup artist was young and beautiful with delicate porcelain features. Two tendrils of straight dark hair framed the oval of her face. When she concentrated on Major General Gao's features, brush poised in the air, a tiny furrow appeared between her wide set eyes.

The director consulted with the cameraman in the back seat, then spoke to Gao. "Sir, would you mind leaving your overcoat in the van, please? We want your ribbons to be visible when you go into the entrance hall."

Gao Yichen sighed as if all these petty details were beneath him, but inside he glowed. The Party had chosen to make *him* the centerpiece of their documentary about the Belt and Road Initiative in Central Asia. Without a doubt, it was the most important story of their time, and he, the Hero of Taiwan, was the star. He imagined how proud Mei Lin would be when the documentary appeared on state television. His picture, his personal story, the colorful rack of ribbons on his chest and the scar on his cheek being seen by millions of eyeballs.

Gao coughed gently into his fist and waved away the makeup artist. “If you think that's really necessary.”

He thought he saw a flicker of emotion flash across the director's face. Did he see through Gao’s facade of modesty? Did he secretly think the hero of his film was a fraud?

For Gao, the nightmare was always the same: A crowd of people surround him. A child steps forward, a boy, and points at Gao. “Liar!” the child shouts. “Coward!”

Then Gao wakes up in a cold sweat.

The makeup girl swooped in again and ran a delicate finger along the ridge of his cheekbone. “Perfect,” she said in a breathy voice.

The director leaned forward. “I want to get a following shot of the general exiting the van. Then we set up and do it again from the curb.”

Gao nodded his understanding. He sat up straighter in his chair so his uniform was tight across his shoulders. He was aware of the camera lens behind him.

“Action,” said the director.

Gao reached for the door handle and pulled.

Nothing happened.

“Cut!” The director swore. “Put the car in park, you idiot!”

Their driver was a local man, maybe twenty years old, with heavy brown features. He looked at the interpreter riding in the passenger seat for guidance, who pointed at the gear shift. The young man flushed red, then complied.

“Again,” the director said, his voice dripping with sarcasm.

This time the automatic door slid open smoothly and Gao stepped out onto the patterned concrete sidewalk. He raised his gaze to take in the great vista of the billion-dollar transportation and logistics center, designed and built by the Chinese government for the people of Uzbekistan.

He strode forward to where the delegation waited. A stiff breeze, dry and chill, ran perpendicular to his path and Gao wondered if it ruffled his hair, which he’d grown longer than regulation length for this trip. How would it look on camera?

The man leading the Uzbek delegation was short and squat, and he sweated despite the cool of the late February day. The sun was harsh. Gao wished he'd remembered to put on sunglasses.

With his best diplomatic half smile in place, he extended his hand toward the sweating fat man.

"Cut!" the director called out. But the man had latched onto Gao's hand. His grip was wet and clammy and he held fast as Gao tried to pull away.

"We are . . . glad . . . you are here, General Major Gao," the man wheezed in mangled Mandarin.

"*Salom*," Gao replied. *Hello*, in Uzbek. He extricated his hand and turned back toward the van.

"You are leaving?" the man said, in English.

The interpreter rushed in to explain the situation as Gao walked away. It had been like this the whole day, a mixed salad of languages. Few Chinese spoke the local dialect and fewer locals spoke Mandarin, but everyone seemed to know at least a little English, so it became their fall-back position. He allowed a wry smile. That fact would never make it into the documentary.

The makeup girl assumed his smile was for her. She met his gaze as she examined his face and pronounced him perfect yet again.

They repeated Gao's exit of the van and introduction to the Uzbek contingent. The director made a rolling motion with his index finger to indicate they should keep going, so Gao allowed the sweaty Uzbek man to lead him through the automatic doors into the vast foyer.

Pale sunlight flooded through the domed glass ceiling twenty meters overhead. The floor was a mosaic of different colored marble made up to look like a distant mountain range. The foyer served as the public entry point for the high-speed rail station and a not so subtle symbol of the greatness of Chinese engineering.

Gao stopped to admire the hall. It was immense. It was magnificent. And it was completely empty.

"Cut!" the director shouted. "Where are my extras?"

The man leading the Uzbek delegation looked lost.

The director swung his arm around the empty space. "People," he exclaimed in English. "Where are the people?"

The man's face cleared and he pulled a mobile phone from his inside pocket. Less than a minute later, the double doors at the far end of the space opened and people streamed out.

Gao spent thirty minutes waiting while the director rushed around the hall marshalling his extras like so many mannequins. Few in the crowd spoke English or Mandarin, so the director mimed walking and talking for the assembled actors.

When they started shooting again, Gao followed the fat man through the thronged hall as he babbled on in his native language. Gao nodded and did his best to keep the camera on the side of his body where there was a clear shot of both his ribbons as well as his scarred face.

The walking tour ended on the observation deck. An entire wall of floor-to-ceiling windows looked out over the airport to the barren landscape beyond. Hot, brown earth as far as the eye could see, sloping up into distant, snowcapped peaks. It was dramatic, but not quite real to Gao, like something out of a movie set. He half-expected to see a horde of Mongol raiders on horseback come thundering across the plain.

The makeup girl arrived for a touch-up that Gao was certain he did not need. As the young woman fussed over him, Gao gave himself a stern reminder that Mei Lin was home in Beijing with two young children, one still in diapers. The attention from the clearly infatuated girl was flattering, but would come to nothing. He was a most happily married man.

She stroked his eyebrow with a carefully manicured fingernail and once again pronounced him *perfect*.

The director approached, dismissing the makeup artist with a curt wave of his hand. "We're going to set up in the control room," he said. "We'll get some B-roll. When the train arrives, we'll follow you out to the platform for the ceremony." He lowered his voice. "Just try to be yourself, General. The best acting is not acting."

The director walked away, leaving Gao to stew over this criticism. Was he being too showy? What did the man want—

"General!" the director called. "We're ready for you."

Gao tried "not acting" as he descended the stairs, camera crew in tow, into a subterranean bunker the size of a ballroom.

The operations center for the rail portion of the transportation hub was staffed with at least a hundred people hunched over computer workstations, most of them local men and women, and all of them under the age of twenty-five. The elder in the room was a stoop-shouldered Chinese man in his early thirties with a harried expression and a pair of half-moon reading glasses on a chain around his neck. His face told Gao that a camera crew was the last thing he wanted to see on this very busy day.

Gao walked along the alley at the back of the room, studying the monitors that covered the front wall. The center third of the monitors showed a line drawing of the railyard and the status of all the trains. Only one line was active: the incoming high-speed train filled with dignitaries for the ribbon-cutting ceremony.

Gao's gaze shifted to the left, where a series of monitors displayed video from the interior of the arriving train. Although he recognized none of the faces, he'd seen a list of the VIPs. The President of Uzbekistan was there, as was the mayor of Tashkent, and the Chinese ambassador. He saw a few military uniforms from other Central Asian countries mixed in among the dark suits and colorful dresses.

The bottom of the screen said the train was operating at 260 kilometers per hour and would be arriving at Platform One in 15 minutes. When they arrived, Gao would be there to greet them. Gao, the Chinese ambassador, and the President of Uzbekistan would cut the ribbon to formally open the Tashkent Logistics Hub.

"Cut!" the director called. The camera crew faded away.

Gao found a seat behind an empty workstation in the back row and sat down, still watching the live video feed from the dignitary train. His eyes narrowed in thought. They seemed to be having a good time while he was stuck here in the basement, waiting for the party train to arrive. He watched the director deep in conversation with the camera crew, wondering again what he'd meant by *the best acting is not acting*.

The makeup girl appeared holding a cup of tea. As he accepted the gift, their fingers brushed gently. Gao took a sip. "Perfect," he said, and the girl blushed.

Gao placed the cup on the desk and followed the contours of the young woman's legs as she walked away.

Perfect, indeed. And you're still *a married man, Yichen.*

He shifted his attention back to the video screens. There were security stations at every kilometer mark along both the new highway and rail lines that ran from Bishkek, Kyrgyzstan to Tashkent, Uzbekistan, all captured on video and delivered to the control room courtesy of the Huawei network. By this time next year, a person would be able to take a train or drive a car from Xinjiang province in western China all the way to Tehran, a modern-day Silk Road of steel and asphalt.

Gao leaned his elbow on the desk and posted his chin in his palm. Before the end of the year, the Party would stage a grand celebration in Samarkand to unite the rail lines being built from the east and the west. They were calling it the Jade Spike Ceremony. Gao wondered if he would be invited to that ribbon cutting.

Probably not, he decided. The General Secretary would be at that event. Surely, he would do the honors.

The thought of the most powerful man in the People's Republic of China steered Gao's musings in a new direction. Had he exhausted his opportunities for advancement in the military? Maybe it was time to parlay his connections with the General Secretary and the Minister of State Security into a political career. Nothing too grand, not at first anyway. A mayor of a medium-sized Chinese city to start, then perhaps a governor of a province—

Gao felt a slight tremor under his elbow. The liquid in his teacup quivered. Half of the video screens on the wall of monitors went blank. There was a beat of shocked stillness, then a cacophony of raised voices.

The supervisor shouted over the din and Gao heard the word "reboot." The man obviously thought they had lost their computer connection.

But as a combat veteran, Gao knew this was more than just a simple loss of power or a faulty computer connection. There had been an explosion nearby. An explosion large enough to be felt in an underground, seismically-isolated bunker.

He stood, staring at the screens, comparing location tags. All the video feeds for the railyard were out, so the explosion must have taken out a local control node.

His gaze snapped over to the video from the incoming train. People drank champagne and laughed as the landscape outside the windows passed in a brown blur. The data feed at the base of the screen read: Speed: 256 KPH.

Gao checked his watch. Thirteen minutes until the train arrived.

He strode across the room and seized the floor supervisor's elbow. The man's skin was feverish hot and he was trembling like a kitten. Sweat bathed his face.

"It's not just a computer failure," Gao said. "There's been an explosion."

The man looked at Gao without comprehension. "Explosion . . . ?"

He tried to extract his arm, but Gao held him fast. "Somewhere in the railyard." He pointed at the video monitors. "Look, all your railyard cameras are out. Can you signal the train to stop?"

The man looked, blinked at the wall. Gao watched the color drain from his face. "The train. . ." he whispered.

"Yes, you need to stop the train!"

Gao felt tension in the man's arm and he let him go. The supervisor barked at one of the operators, a young woman who seemed like she was handling the stress of the moment better than her manager. She tapped at her keyboard, then spoke into her headset. Gao saw her shoulders go rigid, then she repeated her actions, taking care with each keystroke.

When she turned back to her supervisor, Gao didn't need a translator. Her face told the story: they had lost communications with the train.

His gaze clocked up to the video feed where the people on the train were still drinking and laughing. 267 kilometers per hour. Ten minutes.

"Remote control?" Gao asked. "Can you stop the train from here?"

The supervisor hurried across the room to a set of workstations set along the far wall. Gao was relieved to see the screen held an image of what looked like a control panel for a train operator. The supervisor spoke to the technician, who nodded his understanding and then tapped the screen. He dragged his finger across a virtual throttle to reduce power. The screen showed the train speed slowing down rapidly.

Gao watched the video monitor of the train occupants. There was no reaction. Speed: 256 KPH. Arrival: Nine minutes.

The supervisor looked like he was about to throw up.

"Not working," he said in Mandarin. "Not working."

Gao's own stomach roiled with fear. Then he realized the camera crew was filming and sweat broke out all over his body. If there was an accident at the grand opening, it would overshadow everything he had accomplished. The documentary would be a farce. He would be shunned in the Party. No one wanted to be associated with failure.

He seized the supervisor by the shoulders and shook him. "Do something!"

The man's head lolled like he was drunk. Gao pushed him aside. There had to be a way to stop that train.

"Show me a map of the railyard," he ordered the young man at the workstation.

It took him only a few seconds. Gao tried to make sense of the lines snaking across the screen. There was only one rail line active, the incoming train inching across the screen as a thick red line. The remainder of the journey showed green, all the way into the railyard and up to the platform. The same platform where an enormous red ribbon was stretched between two concrete pillars and hundreds of reporters and TV cameras were waiting. Gao's stomach spasmed.

Speed: 253 KPH. Seven minutes.

Gao ran his finger across the path of the train to where it passed a yellow line that branched off, ran for a few centimeters, and stopped.

"What is this?" he demanded.

The young man zoomed in. "It's a rail spur. For future expansion."

"What's out there?" Gao stabbed at the end of the yellow line.

"Nothing. It's just open."

Gao swallowed. "Divert the train there."

"But . . ."

"Do it!" Gao shouted. "Now!"

"We don't have control of the rails, sir."

"Use the back-up then," Gao said.

"But we don't have—wait." The young man sat bolt upright in his chair. He switched screens on the monitor, replacing the map view with lines of code. He muttered to himself as he opened a search box and typed in a string characters. The screen scrolled down at a dizzying rate, stopping at a highlighted line of code. He tapped in a fresh line of code, then looked up at Gao, finger poised over the keyboard. "Are you sure?"

Gao felt his breath coming hard and fast. This was not his responsibility, but if he stood by and did nothing... "Do it," he ordered.

The tech dropped his fingertip to the keyboard, then immediately switched back to the map view of the rail network. The green line had shifted from the railyard onto the rail spur to nowhere.

"That section of track is not powered," the supervisor said. He was at Gao's elbow. "Their speed will drop."

Gao turned to watch the video of the train occupants on the wall screen. They lurched as the train made an unexpected turn. He saw mouths open in surprise, champagne glasses tumble to the floor. One woman lost her balance and reeled against the wall.

Gao's eyes were glued on the speed of the train 180 . . . 140 . . . 98 KPH.

He looked at the progress of the red line on the map. It was nearly at the end of the rail spur now.

The brand-new high-speed train was still moving at 38 KPH when it ran out of track. The people on the video feed lurched and careened inside the carriage in a silent pantomime of panic.

But they were alive.

Gao was aware of the camera moving close to his left side—his good side—and he slowly turned to face the gleaming lens.

"Good job, everyone," he said in Mandarin. "You saved the day."

And he smiled for the camera.

5

The White House, Washington, DC

It was just past seven a.m. when Don arrived in the waiting area outside the Oval Office. This was not an early meeting for Don. Since he'd been promoted to Deputy Director of Operations for the CIA, his normal wakeup time was five a.m. and he was in his office at Langley by six.

His new position came with a driver, allowing him to catch up on the overnight intel updates before he dealt with his calendar, which was filled with back-to-back briefings and meetings that usually lasted until seven in the evening. After a quick dinner in the cafeteria, he managed a few more hours of prep for the next day.

Then he did it all over again.

Weekends were the same schedule, except with fewer meetings. Even by his own standards, he'd become a social hermit. His job was his life—at least for the foreseeable future.

The President's executive assistant pointed wordlessly toward the door of the Chief of Staff's office and Don headed in that direction.

CIA Director Samuel Blank sat behind the chief's desk, his face pensive. A paper cup of coffee steamed in front of his folded hands. In one of the matching wing chairs opposite the desk sat Carroll Brooks, the CIA

Director of Analysis. It was unusual for the Director, the DA, and Deputy Director of Operations to all visit the White House for what was supposed to be a routine Presidential Daily Brief.

No matter what the official schedule said, this was not a routine PDB. All of them knew it.

"Good morning," Don said, taking a seat.

The Director nodded and sipped his coffee. He looked outwardly calm, but Don noticed he was sitting forward in his chair.

"Riley," Carroll said in a rich contralto voice.

Carroll Brooks was a handsome woman who wore her shoulder-length silver hair brushed straight back from her forehead. She had strong facial features, penetrating pale blue eyes, and a no-nonsense style that had earned her the nickname of Ice Queen. Despite Brooks's detractors, Don knew her style and work ethic inspired fierce loyalty among her direct reports. She was more than competent at her job and well respected in the Agency. Under better circumstances, they might have been good friends.

The chill in her greeting told Don all he needed to know: Carroll Brooks still didn't think Don was the right man for the DDO position. He also knew there was no shortage of people in the Agency who agreed with Carroll Brooks. He met them every day and felt them watching, and waiting, for him to screw up.

It went with the territory, he supposed. He was in the big leagues now, in charge of hundreds of operations all over the world and thousands of intelligence operatives. Lives literally depended on how well Don did his job. That was what got him up at five every morning and kept him at his desk until late into the evening.

Like Don, Brooks was a rare officer who had cycled between operations and analysis jobs over the course of her career with the Agency. Unlike Don, her assignments were regular placements into existing positions, all part of a carefully orchestrated career trajectory. Don's advancement, on the other hand, was a wild ride of one-off postings and sudden job changes, concluding with the formation of the Emerging Threats Group, an internal Agency startup designed specifically to look for threats the existing intelligence apparatus had missed.

In other words, in Brooks's mind, ETG existed to police the intelligence establishment. *Her* community, and by extension, her.

It was no secret where Carroll had developed that attitude. Since the very start of her career, she'd been close to Dylan Mattias. It was obvious to everyone, including Don, that Dylan was grooming her to take over as his deputy when he ascended to the directorship of the entire agency. Don was sure that Mattias could have pulled it off, too. All over Washington, DC, he had built personal and political alliances over the years. When Sam Blank finally left the Director's chair open, Dylan was the obvious first choice to replace him.

That career track ended in a fiery explosion, when Dylan and Abby Cromwell were shot down over Ukraine.

Brooks was left to pick up the pieces. Shortly after Dylan's death, she had been promoted to Director of Analysis, the position which she still held. As far as Don was concerned, she was damn good at her job. He wished he could find a way to start over with Carroll, but so far, the opportunity had eluded him.

And meetings like this one didn't help his cause.

"I'm not sure why we need Don here, sir," Carroll said. "If we need Ops at all, why not the actual Director of Operations? I'm sure Don has more important things to do than sit in a PDB."

Blank drained his coffee. "It's above my paygrade, Ms. Brooks," he said mildly. The empty cup went into the trashcan next to the desk. "The President requested Mr. Riley by name."

Brooks arched an eyebrow at Don and he felt heat rise in his cheeks. He knew what she was thinking: he was the President's pet analyst, and that's why he'd gotten the job as DDO.

A sharp rap on the door interrupted Don's spiral of self-doubt. "They're ready for you," announced the President's executive assistant.

The Director stood. "Just remember, we're all on the same team." He jerked his thumb toward the Oval Office. "I have no idea what we're going to find in there, so best behavior."

President Ricardo Serrano greeted Don and the rest of the party like they were old friends. When he shook Carroll's hand, Don thought he could see her frosty demeanor melt just a little bit. Serrano's gift of personal connection never failed to amaze Don. He had the uncanny ability to make people feel immediately at ease in his presence, making them believe that he was listening only to them when in fact his mind was a million miles away.

Don turned his attention to the Vice President of the United States, who he knew was the real reason for this "routine" PDB.

Hawthorne was in his mid-sixties, with sculpted gray hair that hugged his skull like a helmet. His family line was the bluest of blue bloods, the polar opposite of Serrano's rags-to-riches immigrant story. There was old money, the running joke went, and then there was Hawthorne money. Name recognition was not an issue for the Vice President. The Hawthorne Foundation was a fixture on public television and with any number of philanthropic efforts around the country.

Despite his money and his family visibility, Lionel Hawthorne's own run for president had been short-lived. He'd thrown in with Serrano early in the last election cycle. As VP, he'd lived out of the public eye, lost in the shadow cast by the larger-than-life persona of President Serrano. But that was about to change. Serrano, coming to the end of his second term, could not run again.

This was the moment Lionel Hawthorne had waited for his whole life, and his eagerness to take the reins of power was plain for all to see.

Of course, the President wasn't finished running the show. The next stage of his plan was to use Hawthorne to secure his legacy. Today's meeting was lesson number one in the education of Ricardo Serrano's handpicked successor to the presidency of the United States.

The group settled in the sitting area of the Oval Office. Serrano took the armchair while the Director and Hawthorne sat on one of the pale-yellow sofas. On the opposite couch, Don sat next to Brooks, who passed out briefing tablets.

Serrano smiled at her and crossed his legs. "Ms. Brooks, I'd like to expand the scope of today's meeting. Let's give the Vice President a broad overview of not only intelligence analysis, but also intelligence operations that are in progress. A lay of the land, if you will. Which is why I asked Sam to include Don in our discussions."

"Of course, sir," Carroll replied. She touched the tablet, which was linked to the others in the room. The Director had prepared her for this change in agenda and she didn't miss a beat in her delivery.

Don settled in. Carroll Brooks was a seasoned briefer, instinctively knowing how much detail to add to a description to keep her audience engaged. Enough to inform, but not enough to overwhelm.

He listened as she described the intel take from an ongoing action in Iran to support the women's movement. She pivoted to three separate direct operations in Mexico and Central America that targeted drug smuggling, arms trafficking, and ransomware operations, and smoothly linked them to similar issues elsewhere in the world. When she transitioned to an influence operation designed to boost the democratic movement in Hungary opposing President Victor Orban, the Vice President raised his eyebrows.

"Don't we consider Hungary an ally?" Hawthorne asked. "Is that legal?"

An uncomfortable silence followed. The question showed a fundamental lack of understanding of covert actions.

Carroll started to respond, but Serrano interrupted. "Why don't you take that one, Don?"

Don could feel the cushions on the couch shift as Carroll's body went rigid with irritation. He cleared his throat.

"Mr. Vice President, an influence operation is a type of covert action allowed under U.S. law. The Intelligence Oversight Act of 1980 frames the rules by which the President can use covert means to further clearly defined U.S. national security interests.

"With regard to Hungary, intelligence suggests that President Orban's party is skewing even further to the right, undermining what remains of the democratic institutions we recognize with NATO. Our goal is to recalibrate Orban's party and urge them back to representative democracy, in line with our European allies."

Hawthorne pursed his lips, then nodded. Carroll touched her pad to move to the next slide when the Vice President interrupted her again.

"I don't see any operations in here against Russia, Ms. Brooks."

"That's correct, sir," Carroll replied. "There are no ongoing covert actions inside Russia at this time."

Don cut a look at the Director. There were no ongoing operations inside the Russian Federation because the President had deemed it so. It was part of his arrangement with Russian President Nikolay Sokolov following the ouster of former President Luchnik and the withdrawal of Russian forces from Ukraine.

"That feels wrong to me," Hawthorne replied. "I mean, I would hardly call Russia an ally."

Carroll cast an ice-blue gaze at Don. "Perhaps you'd like to comment on the Vice President's question, Mr. Deputy Director?" Her smile was brittle.

"At this moment, sir," Don said. "We have no reason to request any covert actions inside the Russian Federation. Our normal channels of monitoring the Russians have proven satisfactory." He concluded with a firm nod that he hoped would put the matter to rest.

Hawthorne's lips twisted as he processed Don's wholly inadequate answer, then turned to Serrano. "Mr. President, being an election year, I think it might be useful if we turned up the heat on the Russkies. They have a proven track record of election interference. Let's show them we mean to play hardball."

Don watched Serrano carefully, realizing just how far out of the loop the Vice President was on foreign affairs. The President nodded as if he was giving Hawthorne's suggestion deep consideration. "I think it's a fair point, Lionel. I haven't pushed the issue from this office, mostly because I have a good relationship with President Sokolov, and he's needed the breathing room to effect his reforms. Still, always good to keep a sharp eye on things. Let's have Mr. Riley take that one as homework and move on, shall we?"

Don saw the Vice President studying him and he didn't like it. The last thing he needed was to get between the competing egos of the current and the prospective presidents. He had enough on his plate already.

Carroll moved to the next slide when Hawthorne interrupted again. "I don't see anything here about the incident in Tashkent," he said. "The Chinese train accident. Was it a terrorist attack or not?"

Carroll said, "I think that question is best handled by the DDO, Mr. Vice President."

Don cleared his throat. "The Chinese are calling it a mechanical failure, sir."

"I can read the newspaper, Mr. Riley," Hawthorne said with acid in his tone. "I was hoping the seventy billion dollars we spend every year on strategic intelligence would yield some more insightful commentary."

"We're looking into it, sir," the Director said.

That was generous, Don thought. The reality was that their intel assets in the Central Asian region were few and far between. The CIA was reading the same newspapers as the Vice President with about the same level of insight.

"The Chinese have been dealing with a terrorist problem for the last year, Mr. Vice President," Carroll said. "The group is known as the Seljuk Islamic Front, or SIF. They're rumored to be affiliated with the Uighurs in western China and opposed to all things Chinese, including Beijing's Belt and Road Initiative."

Hawthorne looked at Carroll with new respect. "That sounds like what I'm after, Ms. Brooks. Tell me more."

Carroll had a slide for that buried deep in her background material. She beamed it to the tablets around the sitting area.

"Although our information on the SIF is *limited*," Carroll said with enough subtle disapproval that Don experienced a flush of embarrassment, "we believe the man running the organization is Akhmet Orazov."

Don's tablet showed a man who looked to be in his mid-sixties with sun-browned features and a cropped gray beard. His hooded eyes, weathered skin, and prominent nose made him look like a bird of prey. The photo radiated confidence and experience.

"Orazov cut his teeth fighting the *mujahadeen* in the Soviet invasion of Afghanistan in the late 1980s. After the war, he maintained his relationships with Moscow and a personal connection to former Russian President Luchnik. For years, he ran the intelligence operations in Turkmenistan after it became independent from the Soviet Union. Through a series of family connections, he's also linked with the hardliners in Iran. He is rumored to have a direct line to the Ayatollah, another reason why he was very useful to Luchnik.

"About ten years ago, Orazov was caught up in a scandal that ousted him from Turkmenistan's intelligence service. His detractors say he was dirty. His supporters say it was a preemptive move by the next President of

Turkmenistan to take a rival off the playing field. Either way, Orazov pretty much disappeared from the international scene."

"And now he runs a terrorist group?" Hawthorne said.

"That's our assumption, sir. In our view, he's one of the few leaders in the region with enough connections to organize a group like the SIF."

Hawthorne looked at the President. "I smell a campaign issue, sir."

"And I don't." Serrano's voice was sharp. "We are running on a platform of peace and prosperity. Domestic stability, not foreign affairs. I have no interest in discussing half-baked theories of anti-China terrorist groups in places most Americans have never heard of."

Hawthorne's face flushed. The unspoken truth hung heavy in the room. It was Hawthorne's presidential campaign, not Serrano's. There was an uncomfortable moment of silence, then Hawthorne said, "All I'm saying is that we need to show strength abroad, Mr. President, a muscular—"

"Enough!" Serrano's face was carved into a scowl. "Mr. Riley."

"Sir," Don said. It was hard to tear his eyes away from Hawthorne. The man looked like he'd been slapped, but Serrano ignored the obvious slight as he spoke to Don.

"You will prepare a briefing on the situation in Central Asia, including a full background on this Orazov character and what, if any, intelligence collection operations you think might be appropriate to initiate in Central Asia. Ms. Brooks?"

"Yes, sir."

"Continue."

6

Sochi, Russia

The well-maintained gravel road climbed through the pine forest. On the hairpin turns, snatches of bright afternoon sunlight flashed down through the tree cover onto the tinted windows of the limousine. Moscow in March was miserable, cold, and gray. But here, just a few kilometers from the Black Sea, spring was in full bloom.

Nikolay had a sudden urge to stop the car and go for a walk in the forest. No security guards, no mobile phones, nothing except nature and his own thoughts.

The car fishtailed on a sharp curve, then burst from the tree cover. A hundred meters ahead, the road dead-ended at a wrought iron gate set in an imposing, three-meter-high stone wall. The two men flanking the gate watched them approach. They'd known Nikolay's car was coming since it had turned off the highway and onto the private road, the only land access to this mountain retreat.

The driver slowed and the two security men took positions on either side of the vehicle. It was a warm day, but they wore light jackets to conceal their handguns. Other than the guards and the cameras posted at intervals along the wall, there was little to suggest that this was one of the highest security areas in the entire Russian Federation.

No one entered this compound without the express permission of Russian President Nikolay Sokolov.

Federov lowered his tinted window. The guard nearest to them snapped to attention. "Good afternoon, Comrade General."

Federov smiled thinly. "Good afternoon, Arkady. Is he at home?"

"Sir?" The joke was lost on poor Arkady. The inhabitant who lived inside the walls of the compound had not left the premises in over three years.

"Let us in," Federov ordered.

"Right away, sir." The gate swung open, and the limo passed through.

Nikolay nodded at the guard as the car pulled through the gate. "One of yours?" he asked.

Federov's lips bent in a humorless smile. "They're all mine, Mr. President."

The courtyard fronting the three-story stone dacha held a working fountain surrounded by a sea of carefully raked pea gravel. Back in the days of the czars, the estate had belonged to a count. The grand edifice wore its history like a royal mantle, its graying stone exterior, copper roof green with verdigris, and tall windows reminiscent of another, more elegant age.

Nikolay studied the face of the building, trying to find the security cameras he knew were recording their approach. His gaze shifted to the crystal blue sky. Somewhere up there, an overwatch drone sent a constant stream of images to Federov's men on the estate.

As the car glided to a stop, a young man appeared and opened the door. He was also armed and wore the same light jacket as the first two guards.

"Good afternoon, Mr. President. He's expecting you, sir."

Nikolay and Federov followed the young man into the house. Immediately inside the front door was the security control room. Nikolay glimpsed a bank of monitors and the open door of a well-stocked armory before he was thrust back into the nineteenth century decor.

They passed a drawing room adjacent to a grand dining room with a long table that could have seated twenty people with room to spare. A grand balustrade covered in bloodred carpet ascended to the second floor.

The library was a two-story room with bookshelves that rose to the vaulted glass ceiling. A rolling ladder on a brass rail reached to the upper stacks.

The whirlwind tour ended at a pair of French doors. Their guide opened them with a flourish and strode across the flagstone terrace to where a lone figure sat facing the Black Sea. The young guard approached the man and bent close to whisper something. The man nodded.

"He'll see you now, sir," the guard reported.

Nikolay shot a glance of annoyance at Federov, who offered a slight shrug in return as if to say: *This was your idea*.

Former Russian President Vitaly Luchnik's close-cropped hair had thinned and grayed since Nikolay had last seen the man. He felt his stomach clench in that particular blend of admiration and fear he always felt around his uncle.

At one time in his life, this man had meant everything to Nikolay. A father figure, a mentor, a counselor, a friend. Even today, he caught himself saying or doing things that echoed his uncle. It was not a stretch to say that he owed everything to this man.

And yet, Nikolay had betrayed him. Led a coup to depose the man he respected and feared more than any other. It had been the right thing to do for his country—Nikolay was as sure of that today as he was the day he'd confined his uncle to this dacha by the sea. Luchnik had taken the Russian Federation to the brink of nuclear war with the West, and Nikolay was still convinced that his uncle would have taken that final step.

But even now, he felt the magnetic pull of the man's personality like the gravity of a planetary orbit.

Luchnik stood and turned to greet his visitors.

Nikolay's first thought was how much his uncle had aged. It seemed as if decades had passed in the space of a few years. His facial features had succumbed to gravity, and his movements betrayed a slowness that Nikolay did not remember. But the old man's eye was sharp as he surveyed his only living relative. Nikolay felt the familiar heat of his gaze.

Luchnik opened his arms. "Nephew, to what do I owe this great pleasure?"

When Nikolay hugged him, he felt a sinewy body beneath the loose clothes. The old man was keeping in shape.

Luchnik released him and turned to Federov. The two men stared at each other for a long moment, faces like stone. Nikolay wondered what they were thinking. The head of the FSB had been Luchnik's most trusted advisor, and the cornerstone of the coup to oust the former president. Without Federov's active participation, Nikolay's plan would have been doomed to failure.

"You look well, Mr. President," Federov said in his gentle tenor voice.

Luchnik cocked an eyebrow. "*Spasibo*." He held out his hand. *Thank you.*

Two valets, also armed, arrived with two chairs and a low table. The staff set up a tea service and departed. The former president made a great show of pouring tea for his successor. He brandished a pair of silver tongs. "Do you still take two lumps, Mr. President?"

"One will do, Uncle. And please call me by my given name."

Luchnik passed him a tea glass in a silver holder. "One lump, Nikolay Vitalyevich," he said to his adopted son.

Nikolay winced inwardly at the implied insult. He knew one of Luchnik's proudest memories was the day that young Nikolay had insisted on using his uncle's given name as his patronymic. He eyed his drink. It was probably laced with polonium.

"It's a beautiful view, Mr. President," Federov said from Luchnik's other side.

And it was. They faced west, into the afternoon sun. An orchard in full bloom blanketed the hill that sloped away from the house. In the valley far below, a thin line of highway snaked along the coast. The sky was cobalt blue and the sea was flat, the color of slate. On the distant horizon, Nikolay noted a wall of thunderheads, a smudge of gray on an otherwise flawless day. Despite the pleasant moment, Nikolay felt tension building in his shoulder muscles.

"Bullshit," Luchnik replied. "It's the same fucking thing every day." He pointed to the horizon. "The highlight of my day is watching a raincloud."

Nikolay's shoulders cinched tighter.

Luchnik turned in his chair. Nikolay could see his face was deeply tanned, as if proof that he spent every day in the sun. "Do you remember when you used to beg me to post you to Moscow?"

Nikolay nodded.

"Take me to Moscow," Luchnik said. "I long for shitty winter weather and cold rain."

Nikolay's eyes cut over his uncle's shoulder to Federov, but before he could respond, Luchnik burst out laughing. "You should see your face."

The old man refilled his tea, leaned back in his chair. He steepled his hands, studying Nikolay. "Now. Why are you here, nephew?" His clipped voice was edged with frost, the laughter gone from it.

"I need your advice," Nikolay said. There was no point in beating around the bush with his uncle. The man surely knew about the disastrous meeting of the CSTO. He had spies briefing him on Nikolay's tenuous political situation in Moscow.

Luchnik sipped his tea. "Honesty," he said "That's a new tactic for you. Tell me what's going on."

Nikolay took a deep breath before plunging ahead. It took him fifteen minutes to relay the complete picture. He told his uncle of the failed meeting in Dushanbe and the increasing pressure from the Ultras in Moscow. Throughout the entire recitation, Federov stayed silent, lips pursed, staring at the water.

When he'd finished, Luchnik sat completely still. A breeze coursed up the hill, releasing a flood of apple blossoms that looked like a cloud of butterflies.

Luchnik smiled wistfully. "Orazov chewed you out, eh? He's a bastard, but don't underestimate him. He was with Spetsnaz in Afghanistan. Fierce fighter and one of the finest intelligence officers I've ever known. A useful man, don't you agree, Vladimir?"

Federov, staring at the horizon, nodded. Luchnik busied himself with the mechanics of pouring more tea, then he settled back in his chair.

"You have a credibility problem, nephew," he said. "These people who make your life difficult—the Ultras, Orazov—they only respond to one thing: fear."

Nikolay started to speak, but Luchnik cut him off.

"You've made your problem worse by allowing it to go on for so long. If you try to establish control now, you'll just look desperate. Your plan to offer higher tariff rates to that upstart fuck, Karimov? Terrible idea. It only makes him greedy. Makes him think he has the upper hand."

"I should offer him less?"

Luchnik shook his head like he was speaking to a slow child. "No. You don't offer him anything. You make him come to you."

Nikolay looked past his uncle to Federov, but the FSB chief's gaze remained fixed on the horizon. "I . . . I don't understand."

"I know. That's because you did not allow me to teach you."

Nikolay's anger flared. Coming here was a mistake. Luchnik was a relic of another time. His inner voice crowded forward to block out the old man.

I am a different kind of leader. I will lead with my head and my heart—

"Are you listening, nephew?" His uncle's voice cut into Nikolay's runaway thoughts.

"I'm listening, Uncle."

"You need to start a war—not a big one, just large enough to get everyone's attention. If you can do it in Central Asia, so much the better."

Nikolay recoiled. He placed his teacup on the table and started to get up.

"Sit down." Luchnik's voice made him freeze in his chair. "I might be here under lock and key, but I hear things. I *know* things. Your friends in Moscow are few and far between. Your enemies smell blood in the water. They would like nothing more than to feed on your bones. You need to change the conversation."

A sudden thought chilled Nikolay. What if the source of the Moscow resistance movement was the man pouring him tea? Was it possible that Luchnik was planning a return to power?

Federov had assured him that the entire staff were his people, but was that the same thing as being loyal to Nikolay? Federov had been a loyal counselor, patient to a fault. But had Nikolay's outburst at the CSTO been the final straw in his patience?

He reached for his teacup and gulped the liquid down. Federov's loyalties lay with the State, they always had. That had been the lever to secure his cooperation with the coup that overthrew Luchnik, but maybe Federov now regretted his action.

"Did I say something that upset you, nephew?" Luchnik's smile was cruel, wolfish.

Nikolay replaced his teacup on the table and stood. "Of course not." He hugged his uncle, kissing the man on both cheeks. The wind had picked up, and Nikolay saw the storm clouds closing in on the shoreline.

The former Russian president escorted his guests through the magnificent house to the front door. He watched them from the portico as they got into their vehicle. He raised his hand as they drove away.

Nikolay did not wave back.

Federov stayed silent until the trees of the forest closed around them.

"Well," he said, "did you get what you came for?"

Nikolay nodded.

"You're going to start a war?"

Nikolay looked out the window at the lovely green boughs of the pine forest and said nothing. A fat raindrop hit the windshield.

7

Samarkand, Uzbekistan

Although she had not yet celebrated her fortieth birthday, Nicole Nipper had lived many lifetimes already. As a special correspondent, she made her living by going wherever the story led her—usually into a war zone. She'd been shot at, bombed, kidnapped, and even poisoned. She'd been around the world more times than she could count.

Her incisive interviews with some of the most dangerous and important men in the world had earned her the ire of their rabid followers. In her email folders, she maintained a special file of the most creative death threats she had received in her career. As of this morning, there were 111 emails in the folder.

But for all her experience, she was not sure what to make of the man before her.

Timur Ganiev was in his mid-fifties, but could have passed as her peer. Tall and slim, with the kind of cheekbones that belonged on a model, she could imagine him as the leading man in a lurid romance novel.

Which is not to say he was all style and no substance. A native Uzbek, Ganiev had earned his medical degree from the University of Moscow and, after the collapse of the Soviet Union, he'd gone on to earn a PhD at the

London School of Economics, where he studied healthcare delivery mechanisms for indigenous populations. After a stint in the World Health Organization, he had returned home to the Central Asian steppes to put his theories into action.

Together with his wife, also a doctor, he established the Tamerlane Foundation, based in Samarkand, to deliver healthcare to the underserved peoples of the region. From the very beginning, the foundation eschewed the nationalist politics used by so many of the leaders in the Central Asian republics. Timur's goal, he said, was to serve the people of the entire region, regardless of ethnicity or arbitrary political borders.

When tragedy struck the Ganievs, it only made news in philanthropic circles. Lala Ganiev, while visiting a remote village on the disputed border between Tajikistan and Kyrgyzstan, was killed in a gun battle between rival militia forces.

For Timur, however, the death of his mate wrought a fundamental change in his life's mission. He became a passionate advocate for a non-violent cultural renaissance in his Central Asia homeland.

At least that was the narrative Nicole had gleaned from her research. From the outside, Ganiev was a human interest story, one of thousands written ever year on every continent. Touching, but local in scope.

As a news veteran, Nicole liked to believe she had a nose for a story about to break into the public consciousness—and to her, Timur Ganiev had all the earmarks of breaking news. There was something here worth investigating. She could feel it.

All these thoughts ran through Nicole's brain as the door to Timur's apartment opened and she met the man face-to-face for the first time.

He smiled, even white teeth in a generous mouth, and held open the door. "Ms. Nipper, welcome to my home."

The foyer of his apartment was warm after the cutting chill of the windy doorstep. The door closed behind her, cutting off the sounds of the street.

Ganiev professed to be a moderate Sunni Muslim. He publicly denounced the violent and regressive tactics of organizations like the Taliban in Afghanistan, or the Islamic State adherents that fought on in pockets around the world. Nicole decided to test her subject's religious sensibilities. She stripped off her headscarf and extended her bare hand. "Thank you for seeing me, Dr. Ganiev."

There was no hesitation. Ganiev enclosed her cold fingers in both of his warm hands and bowed his head. "The pleasure is all mine, Ms. Nipper. Please, call me Timur."

"Nicole," she replied, as he took her coat.

"I've prepared tea." He led the way down a short flight of stone steps into a sitting room.

Nicole followed. The pictures and articles she seen about the man did not do him justice. He was dressed in a tan cashmere sweater that clung to his athletic frame, a pair of gray flannel trousers, and loafers. He had immediately greeted her in English, and he spoke the language with an accent that revealed his London education.

The sitting room was small but well appointed, with a leather sofa and two armchairs gathered around a beaten brass platter fashioned into a coffee table. A silver samovar and tea service sat on the low table. Like the man, the subtle room furnishings suggested a person equally comfortable in the cultures of Central Asia and London. She nodded toward a colorful ikat, a traditional silk wall hanging decorated with diamond-shaped designs. Ganiev's eyes followed her gaze.

"My late wife had a wonderful sense of style." He swept his arm around the room. "This is all her doing."

Nicole doubted that. Lala Ganiev had been dead for years, and the wall hanging looked brand-new. She kept that thought to herself. "Exquisite," she said.

Once they were both seated, Ganiev served tea in the Russian style, in glasses with silver holders. Nicole declined the offer of sugar, but Ganiev added three lumps and a dash of milk to his. "My time in London spoiled me," he said with a smile.

"Thank you for seeing me, Timur," Nicole said. "May I?" She held up a small digital recorder.

"Of course." Ganiev settled back against the sofa, crossed his legs, and adjusted the crease of his pant leg so it lay neatly across his knee. He spread his arms across the back of the chair.

The very picture of openness, Nicole thought. She decided to dispense with warmup questions and see if she could catch this very composed man off guard.

"Timur, tell me your vision for the people of the Central Asian region."

The question seemed to instantly energize the man. He leaned forward, elbows on knees, and spoke with an earnest intensity.

"When you look at a map of Central Asia, it's like a jigsaw puzzle," he began. "The borders make no sense. These are not boundaries based on geography. These are boundaries based on politics, drawn by powerful men from thousands of miles away during a very different time."

He held up four fingers and ticked them off as he spoke. "Turkmenistan, Uzbekistan, Kyrgyzstan, Tajikistan. These are proud cultures with a rich heritage that has been buried under centuries of conquest by outside oppressors. In this country, there is a difference between an Uzbekistani and an Uzbek. An Uzbekistani is a transplant, but an Uzbek has a line of ancestry that has been here for a thousand years."

His eyes, which she now noticed were a deep, molten brown, glowed as he warmed to his topic. "Today in these four countries, we have four people, four languages, four rich cultures, all with a shared heritage. But it was not always so. Once upon a time, long before there was a Soviet Union or the People's Republic of China, this entire region was united under the great leader Timor."

"You're speaking of Tamerlane," Nicole said.

Nicole had visited the famous tomb in Samarkand. She'd waited in long lines and studied how people reacted to seeing the shrine of the legendary fourteenth-century leader known as the "Sword of Islam" who had subjugated most of the known world at the time.

"That is what you call him in the West, yes," Timur agreed.

Her subject was modest enough not to mention the obvious connection between his own name and the famous historical figure.

"I believe it is time for our people to put aside our petty differences and stand together," Timur concluded.

Nicole took a sip of her tea to cover for the fact that she had drifted off in thought. No matter, it was all captured on the tape recorder. Right now, her mind was racing with possibilities, one following on another. How long had it been since she'd had a real scoop?

Timur Ganiev was the full package: attractive, erudite, highly intelligent, passionate, and willing to blow up the establishment for what was sounding like a noble objective.

You're getting ahead of yourself, Nicole. Do. Your. Job.

Nicole consulted her notes. "Talk to me about how climate change affects this region."

Timur's face lit up again and he launched into another lengthy answer. He described the water scarcity in the region, the impact of climate change on the normal weather patterns, and how the lack of water limited crop growth. Then, he pivoted.

"The Central Asian republics are small countries sandwiched between two great powers: Russia and China."

Nicole almost interrupted him to debate whether or not Russia was a great power, but she held off. Great or not, there was no denying the Russian influence here. It pervaded the lives of every person in the region. Even after the collapse of the Soviet Union, their governments, their food, even the common language of the region remained Russian.

"Our countries are rich in natural resources and therefore of great interest to our larger neighbors. But we need partners, not masters. Water, oil, mineral resources, people—whatever Central Asia has to offer—is available, but we must not allow ourselves to be exploited any longer. Foreign direct investment is welcome, but the resources must be controlled by the people who live here. We can build our own industries and the people in Central Asia can all benefit, together."

Timur leaned in. "China and Russia love to pit one country in the region against the other. These are artificial political barriers held in place by nationalistic leaders and greed. No more! The natives of this land have a birthright. Together, the unified people of Central Asia must control our future."

Nipper leaned forward. "What about the United States? Do you see them as a way to balance the Russia–China duopoly in the region?"

Timur shook his head, chuckling. "You miss my point, Nicole. Beijing, Moscow, Washington, they are all the same to us. We are tired of being treated like children who must be protected or disciplined. We must be free to choose our own path forward."

"It's a beautiful dream, Timur, but the reality is that Central Asia is four separate countries with four separate governments and four different agendas. How does your vision of the future work in practice?"

Timur relaxed back into the sofa and spread his arms. "You are asking a political question, Nicole," he said. "I am not a politician. I'm a man of the people. My only goal is to help my brothers and sisters to rediscover our shared cultural roots and stand as one people."

For a man who claimed he was not a politician, that was a damned good political answer.

"Today," Nicole said, "the most active country in the region is China. Beijing is pouring billions of dollars into infrastructure projects for their Belt and Road Initiative. How do you feel about that?"

Ganiev shrugged. "We want a healthy relationship with Beijing, but we reject direct influence in our affairs. The infrastructure projects being built in the region need to benefit my people first and the people of China second."

Nicole noted the use of the possessive.

"It seems that not all of 'your people'—to use your own words—agree with you," she countered. "The Chinese government is becoming increasingly frustrated by the rise of the SIF. Can you comment on that?"

Ganiev's easy manner turned dark. "This is a very serious topic and I want to make sure that we give it the right focus. The Seljuk Islamic Front does not represent the people of Central Asia. They are a small contingent of disaffected zealots who seek to solve their problems through violence. Violence is not the way. Violence is wasteful. Violence has not future."

He leaned back. "You can quote me on the last part. I am a doctor, a healer. I do not wish to see my people destroyed by radicals. And, having lost my wife to senseless violence, I am deeply opposed to it."

A shadow crossed his face, like a mask slipping, then disappeared. Again, Nicole noted the possessive and the intensity of his words. The way he controlled his language and his outward actions told Nicole this was a man who would not allow his personal loss to be part of his public persona. His every answer pointed to a brighter future.

Timur appeared to be at ease again, arms spread, legs crossed. Despite his protests to the contrary, there was no doubt this was a politician who sat across from her. She could not shake the feeling that there were depths here worth exploring.

Pale afternoon sunlight filtered through the window, giving the room and her interview subject a natural glow. Damn, she'd left her camera in the hotel. All she had was her iPhone.

"May I take your picture?" she asked.

Ganiev offered her another wide, model-quality smile and a low chuckle. "Of course."

"Stay right there," Nicole said. She got to her feet and paced the room, looking for the right angle as she snapped pictures. Even now, the light was starting to fade. She put her iPhone on portrait mode and moved close, kneeling before her subject. He looked directly at her, the light shading his cheekbones, his eyes glowing.

Perfect. She took the final photo.

"May I see them?" Ganiev asked.

Nicole sat next to him on the sofa and scrolled through the pictures. Their shoulders touched as he leaned close to see her phone. He smelled like sandalwood.

"The light was perfect," she said. "I only wish I'd had my really good camera."

"You have skill," he replied. "You made me look good."

Nicole wondered who this man was in his most intimate moments. So many of her famous subjects who so publicly cared about the problems of the world were absolute shit when they let down their guard in private.

Not that she had any business judging people. Her own love life had been a string of failed relationships and one-night stands. Nicole was attracted to men like herself: adrenaline junkies who were allergic to commitment. She wondered what the real Timur Ganiev was like.

She returned to her side of the room. If Ganiev had felt anything in the moment, he gave no indication.

Get your head in the game, lady. He's the subject of an article, not your next conquest.

But even as the thought flitted through her mind, Nicole decided she needed to get closer to Timur Ganiev. Years of experience told her this man was destined for greatness and she could be the one to tell that story.

The demographics of Central Asia skewed young, and that meant millions of young people were looking for an identity. The borders of the Central Asian republics were lines on a map, often drawn with little geographical or cultural sense, but protected fiercely by a string of autocrats fully invested in staying in power at all costs.

To the north and west, the failing state of Russia struggled to maintain a grip on the region. Meanwhile, the People's Republic of China invaded from the east with billions of dollars invested in a 1,000-mile juggernaut of infrastructure that would define the region for generations to come.

And at the nexus of all these forces stood a charismatic man with a vision.

Nicole's pulse quickened. Oh, yes, she was on to something here. This was the story of a region in crisis, maybe even the birth of a new nation. This was a *New York Times* cover story, maybe a book. Or even a documentary film series.

"Nicole?" Ganiev interrupted her thoughts.

The light had faded and he was in partial shadow now. He leaned across the table.

"Do you have any more questions?" he asked.

So many questions, Nicole thought. But first, I need to gain his trust.

"Only one, Timur," she said. "Would you have dinner with me?"

His teeth flashed white in the gloom.

"It would be my great honor, Nicole."

8

Tashkent, Uzbekistan

Like everything else about the Tashkent airport, the customs area was brand-new. Harrison could still smell the glue used to lay the carpet as he made his way up to the uniformed official behind a glass partition.

He slid his passport under the glass. The customs officer was a trim young man in his early thirties with dark eyes and an impressive walrus mustache. Harrison glanced around, clocking at least six cameras in plain view, which meant there were at least that many hidden.

Along with their construction capabilities, the Chinese had also imported their security state of mind. Harrison's cynical side wondered if that was for the benefit of Uzbekistan or the Chinese Communist Party. Was his picture being processed by some AI in Beijing right now?

The customs officer fed his passport into a device the size of a small toaster. With one eye on his computer screen, he said, "What is the meaning of your visit, Mr. Kohl?"

His English was heavily accented, so Harrison took a chance. "I am here to see your beautiful country," he replied in Russian.

The young officer looked up, surprised, and replied in the same language. "You speak Russian very well, sir."

"It is a beautiful language," Harrison said, "I'm glad to speak it again."

"Tourism, then," the customs officer said, making a note on his computer. "Where are you staying, Mr. Kohl?"

Smiling to mask the impatience he felt, Harrison gave him the name of the hotel. Instead of expediting his way through customs, his use of Russian—the de facto language of the region—had turned his customs officer into a Chatty Cathy.

Nothing about his investigation into Tim's disappearance had gone well. In the ten days since his best friend had gone missing, there'd been no word on his whereabouts. Jenny's attitude escalated from concern to panic to anguish. She'd contacted everyone from her congressman to the State Department. Nothing had made a difference.

For his part, Harrison had been mired in bureaucratic paperwork. Just to get a tourist visa to visit Uzbekistan had taken the better part of a week—and that was with Harrison calling in every favor he could from diplomatic friends and acquaintances. Just to be sure, he'd used the delay to obtain visas for all the other countries in the Central Asian region as well. If he needed to travel anywhere in this part of the world, he was well-prepared.

His efforts to get answers from the Grand Surfan Oil company had run into the proverbial brick wall. His inquiries were bounced from one company officer to another. Mr. Trujillo was a contractor, so his movements were not monitored by company officials. He was given assignments and turned in his deliverables and his invoices, which had all been paid. As far as Grand Surfan was concerned, Mr. Trujillo's absence from work constituted a breach of contract.

Finally, Harrison was on the ground in Uzbekistan, where he could trace Tim's last known steps and maybe get some answers from the oil company in face-to-face meetings. That was his first move, a trip to the regional Grand Surfan office in Tashkent to pay a call on Li Zhao, the Vice President of Regional Security Affairs.

Harrison had dressed in khakis and white shirt with a dark blue blazer, hoping the business casual appearance would move him through customs faster. His only luggage was his trusty Samsonite roller bag, battered from countless overseas trips.

The customs official frowned at his computer screen. Harrison smiled reflexively, wondering whether they'd figured out he was an American intelligence officer. He'd guessed there was a fifty-fifty shot that he'd get pulled aside for special questioning. Although he'd done nothing wrong and was traveling under his own name as a tourist, former communist countries detecting an intel officer entering their country normally liked to have a chat.

If this had been any airport in Russia, he'd already be in some smelly interview room by now. But one look around this gleaming space was enough to tell him that Mother Russia's influence wasn't what it once was. This was a new ball game. Harrison had never been to this part of the world before and he'd never been involved in an operation against the Chinese. Well, never *directly* involved.

Another minute passed with no comment from the customs official. Harrison smiled at the camera lens a foot from his face and waited in what he hoped was a casual manner. The security feed surely had behavioral analysis built into the algorithm. If he appeared nervous or uneasy, they might pull him in for a few questions to see if anything popped up.

Be calm. It'll all be over soon.

"Mr. Kohl?"

"Yes?"

"What is your occupation, sir?"

Harrison met his gaze without hesitation. "Consultant."

The young customs officer nodded and tapped at his computer.

The machine surrendered Harrison's passport. The official stamped the visa page with an inked pad the size and shape of a silver dollar and slipped it under the glass partition.

"Enjoy your time in Uzbekistan," he said.

Harrison smiled. "*Spasibo*."

Less than a minute later, Harrison walked briskly through the baggage claim area. Like the rest of the massive complex, this level was brand-new and mostly empty. Of the twenty-five baggage carousels, only two were in use. The Chinese designers clearly saw a bright future for Tashkent.

He passed through a set of glass doors to the wide sidewalk outside the terminal. Harrison squinted in the pale sunlight and shivered at the chill breeze that raced down the boulevard.

Welcome to the high plains. His first two local purchases would be a pair of sunglasses and a heavier jacket.

The taxi queue was empty and he took the first one, a dark blue BYD Han sedan. Inside, the electric vehicle was well-appointed. Brown leather seats, soft to the touch. An interior engineered for quiet and a space-age LED screen in the center of the console.

The taxi driver, a bearded man with unruly black hair, immediately divined that Harrison was not his typical fare.

"American?" he asked.

Harrison ignored him and gave his destination in Russian. The car pulled away smoothly, without a sound.

The taxi driver was not fooled by Harrison's fluent language skills.

"I love America," he declared in English as they left the airport and merged onto a four-lane highway. The skyline of downtown Tashkent filled the windshield. "Especially American basketball. LeBron James." He raised a clenched fist. "The King!"

Harrison forced a smile. "*Da*," he replied without enthusiasm.

The forty-eighth floor of the Nest One Tower was the home of the Uzbekistan branch of the Grand Surfan Oil and Gas Company. From his advance planning, Harrison knew it was the tallest building in the country and the second tallest in all of Central Asia.

The Grand Surfan regional office was designed to impress. Harrison stepped from the elevator onto plush royal blue carpet inlaid with the company logo in rich gold. He approached a long, curved reception desk staffed by two very attractive Chinese women.

"English?" he asked.

"Of course, sir," one of the young women replied smoothly. "How may I help you?"

"I have an appointment to see Vice President Li."

"Your name, sir?"

"Tim Trujillo." He spelled the last name.

"Of course, sir. I'll let Mr. Li know you are here." She indicated the sitting area. "Please have a seat."

Harrison perched on the edge of the black leather sofa and waited. By now the receptionist would have contacted Li's assistant and determined there was no appointment. The young woman behind the desk looked up. Her eyes found Harrison and she spoke into her headset.

He focused on the pair of cameras over the receptionist's station where someone was undoubtedly checking him out. They'd know he wasn't Tim Trujillo, so right about now they'd be asking themselves: Who was this guy?

Five minutes passed as Harrison watched the door leading into the private office area of Grand Surfan. His lie was risky, and probably stupid, but he would at least get a response, which was more than he'd managed to get from Grand Surfan so far. Of course, that response might be a jail cell, but nothing ventured, nothing gained. This mission was about Tim, and Harrison was prepared to do whatever it took to bring his friend home safely.

At the sixteen-minute mark, the heavy wooden door opened and yet another attractive twenty-something Chinese woman stepped into the lobby and approached the sitting area.

"Mr. Li is ready to see you, sir." She pointed at his roller bag. "Please leave your luggage at the reception desk."

Harrison did as he was told, sure that his luggage would be thoroughly searched. They would not find nothing of intelligence value.

The door opened onto a sea of cubicles. Harrison was struck by how quiet the vast room was. Behind them, the automatic lock on the door engaged with a heavy *clunk*.

His guide took a left into a wide hallway lined with closed wooden doors to offices that fronted the western side of the building. Through the narrow pane of glass adjacent to each door, Harrison could see people hunched over their computers or talking on phones. Their desks faced away from the window and the magnificent view.

The young woman led him to the corner suite at the end of the hall. Walking into Li's office was like walking into an IMAX theater. Floor-to-ceiling windows occupied two entire walls. The busy city of Tashkent spilled out below them. Where the city ended, the plains began. The steppe was like a sandy brown ocean that stretched to the distant horizon.

Grand Surfan Vice President Li was different than his colleagues. His desk faced the panorama.

The man who stood to greet him could not have been more than thirty-five years old, far too young to be a VP in a Chinese multinational company. He was Harrison's height and build, with pomaded jet-black hair and dark eyes that drank in details with a glance. Politically connected or part of the Chinese security services?

Li extended his hand. "So sorry to have kept you waiting, Mr. Kohl. I trust you had a comfortable flight in this morning."

Question asked, question answered, Harrison thought as he shook Li's hand. Definitely an intelligence officer.

The man's smile was professional. He spoke perfect English and his handshake was firmly confident. Li led them to a pair of white leather couches and waved at Harrison to sit.

"Call me Jimmy," he said. "Coffee?"

Harrison nodded. Li tapped his phone and tossed it on the coffee table between them.

"You speak excellent English, Jimmy."

"Columbia undergrad, then Stanford business school," Li replied. Harrison could feel the man's gaze raking over him, assessing every detail. "I wanted to work for Facebook, but instead I work for a soul-sucking oil company. What can you do, right?"

Harrison looked out the window at the magnificent mountain range. "It's a living."

Jimmy laughed loudly. The door opened and the assistant was back with the coffee service. Jimmy dismissed her with a wave and passed a coffee to Harrison. As Jimmy mixed in cream and sugar, Harrison took a sip of his drink.

It was smooth and rich, hardly acidic at all. Jimmy smiled at his reaction.

"I have it shipped in from Hawaii. I picked up a taste for the stuff when I lived in California."

"Thank you for seeing me," Harrison said.

"My interest was piqued when a man impersonating a missing contractor shows up in our lobby," Jimmy replied evenly. The smile was gone.

"What can you tell me about Tim's work with the company?"

"May I ask your connection, Mr. Kohl?"

"I'm a family friend," Harrison said. "His wife is worried and I offered to help. I speak Russian."

Jimmy's eyes glittered. "A useful skill in this part of the world. What do you do for work, Mr. Kohl?"

"I'm a consultant, like Tim."

Jimmy sipped his coffee and looked out the window.

"I didn't know him personally, but I heard good things about his work from corporate. As far as I know, he was hired to conduct a physical audit of the Grand Surfan field installations. Oil wells, pumping stations, pipelines, that sort of thing. He was assessing their ability to withstand physical attacks." Jimmy smiled thinly. "We have an insurgent problem in the region. So far, oil companies are not a target, but one cannot be too careful."

"Tim's last location was here, in Tashkent, at the airport."

"Really? I didn't know that," Li replied with a straight face.

Harrison ignored the obvious lie. "He was last seen at the private air terminal, waiting for the company shuttle. It was cancelled the night he disappeared."

Jimmy refilled his cup and made a show of mixing in cream and sugar. "How can I help, Mr. Kohl?"

"I want to see the security footage and flight logs from that night."

Jimmy put down his coffee cup and went to his desk. He made a phone call, speaking in Mandarin. When he returned to the opposite couch, he carried a tablet with him. By the time he'd finished his coffee, the device chimed with an incoming message. He logged in, then handed the tablet to Harrison.

"Mr. Trujillo arrived at the airport shortly after eight in the evening. He went straight to the private air terminal." On a video, Harrison watched a car approach a long, low building and stop. Tim got out. He was dressed for field work in cargo pants, a work shirt, and hiking boots. He carried a duffel and a computer bag as he entered the building. In the background was an aircraft hangar adjacent to a concrete apron.

"That's all we have, Mr. Kohl. The private air terminal was housed in a temporary location due to construction. There is no security camera footage from inside the terminal. Mr. Trujillo never left the building."

"I want to see the building," Harrison said.

"I'm afraid that's not possible."

"I insist," Harrison said. "Security camera footage can be manipulated. I think we both know that."

"I'll make you a copy of the recordings. You can have them analyzed."

"That's not good enough." Harrison had no idea what he hoped to find. Hundreds of people might have passed through that building since Tim had last been there. Still, it was all he had. The last tangible clue of Tim's existence.

Jimmy sighed and put down his coffee cup again. Another phone call in Mandarin, then Jimmy retrieved a jacket from a hidden closet behind his desk.

With exaggerated patience, Li motioned Harrison toward the door, "Let's go."

"Now?" Harrison asked.

"No time like the present, Mr. Kohl. I want you to be satisfied that Grand Surfan has answered your every question."

They rode to the airport in a grey Mercedes-Benz EQS 580 luxury sedan. Jimmy was silent during the trip, which was fine with Harrison. They bypassed the public entrance and turned onto a frontage road that paralleled the runway. Harrison consulted the GPS map on his phone where Tim's last known location showed as a red pin. Outside, a fleet of construction equipment prepared the ground for a new airstrip.

They made a left turn onto a gravel road and were stopped by a Chinese worker in a blaze orange vest and hardhat. Jimmy rolled down the window and spoke to the man. The guard carefully wrote on a clipboard and waved them through.

The car moved slowly past a long row of dump trucks waiting to unload. The driver stopped the car.

"Here we are," Jimmy said. Before the driver could get out to assist him, Jimmy popped open his door and stepped out of the car.

Harrison verified their location with the GPS and followed. The air was filled with the roar of heavy equipment and the steady *beep-beep* of trucks backing up.

"I don't understand," Harrison said, looking around.

Jimmy pointed to a cleared concrete slab next to a tower of construction debris. A crane with a claw was taking bites from the pile and swinging them into the empty bed of an idling dump truck.

"This was the temporary private air terminal. I thought maybe you needed to see things for yourself."

Jimmy's lips spread into a wide grin, but the smile never reached his eyes.

"Mr. Kohl, may we drop you somewhere on our way back into the city?"

9

Beijing, China

The street in front of the Great Hall of the People was blocked in both directions, and the huge stone pillars that fronted the face of the building were lit from below, making it seem like the structure extended far into the night sky. From his view in the back seat, Major General Gao watched their driver nose the black Hongqi limousine past a wall of people barely restrained by the crowd barriers on either side of the street.

To his left, across the boulevard from the Great Hall, the dome of the National Centre for the Performing Arts gleamed in reflected light. The curved titanium shell of the building gave it the nickname, The Egg.

Mei Lin gripped his hand as she stared out the window. "Is this all for you?" she asked in a breathless voice.

"I don't know," he said.

Maybe there was a premier at The Egg, some international star, he thought. But there was another possibility, a possibility that his brain had a hard time conceiving.

The Hero of Tashkent had been released only last night. All day, Gao had been fielding congratulatory phone calls and texts, but they were from insiders, people in government and military service, not ordinary people.

He and Mei Lin had watched the movie together, sitting side by side on the couch in the living room of their Beijing apartment. He held two-year-old Lixin on his lap while Mei Lin nursed Bai.

When he recalled that day in the train station in Tashkent, it was all a blur. He remembered the feeling of near panic, but also the urgent need to do *something*. He'd forced out a string of half-conceived orders that somehow worked out in the end. The high-speed rail cars were all damaged, but all of the passengers had survived.

And then the incident disappeared as the Chinese government sought to suppress the terrorist attack. News leaked out in the Western media, but in China, the incident was carefully censored from the public.

Two weeks ago, Gao had received notice that for his heroic actions at the Tashkent train station, he was to be awarded the August 1 Medal at an evening event in the Great Hall of the People. Furthermore, the notice read, twenty-four hours prior to the awards ceremony, the Party would air a new movie about the incident.

Watching the movie from the safety of his couch was an out-of-body experience. Somehow, through careful editing of the footage from the camera crew, Gao's actions did not appear as feckless and panicked as he remembered. He looked decisive, in control, and most of all, heroic. Mei Lin scarcely breathed as she watched the TV with rapt attention.

The limousine stopped before a red carpet that ran down the wide stone steps of the Great Hall. The driver disembarked and held the door open for them. Gao stepped out onto the red carpet and reached back to offer Mei Lin his hand.

It was a rare clear night in Beijing. Stars glittered overhead as he took stock of the unreal scene before him.

Crowd control barriers, set up on either side of the red carpet, held back hundreds of schoolchildren identically dressed in white shirts, dark blue trousers, and dark blue overcoats. They were all screaming and waving at him. A spotlight from the darkness atop the Great Hall beamed down, capturing Gao and Mei Lin in a cone of pure white light.

Gao froze, trapped in a wave of some unidentifiable emotion. Pride? Embarrassment?

Through the sleeve of his overcoat, Mei Lin dug her fingernails into his bicep.

"Wave," she hissed through smiling teeth.

"What?" Gao felt like his brain was stuck in neutral.

Mei Lin's fingers dug deeper. "Wave to the children." As if to demonstrate, she lifted her own hand and waved.

"Now, walk." She hip-checked him to move his body forward and Gao paced ahead as if in a dream. Mei Lin applied pressure on his arm to steer him toward the nearest barrier.

A young girl, maybe eight years old, with a round face and a bobbed haircut thrust out paper and pen.

"General," she screamed, even though he was only a meter away. "Can I have your autograph?"

Gao stared at the child. His autograph? Why did she want his autograph?

Mei Lin intervened again. She plucked the pen and paper from the girl and handed them to Gao. Through smiling, clenched teeth, she hissed, "What is the matter with you, Yichen?"

Gao signed his name automatically and put the paper back into the grasping hands of the child. Another child. Same request, exact same pad of paper and pen. Gao signed again. Then again and again and again, walking slowly along the barrier, shaking hands and smiling, smiling, smiling.

Suddenly, the mental fog lifted and he was in the moment. The night air was sharp and clear. The crowd morphed into a mass of faceless people who were here for one reason: to love him. To adore him. Gao had never taken drugs, but this must be what it felt like to be high.

I am a rock star. I am the Hero of Tashkent.

Mei Lin released his arm and she faded into his peripheral vision.

It took them more than thirty minutes to make their way up the red-carpeted stairs of the Great Hall. The three-meter-high doors swung closed behind them, cutting off the sound of the screaming children.

Gao's heart beat wildly and his face was flushed. He wanted to laugh and dance with sheer delight. In the past, the Party had named him the

Hero of Taiwan for his actions during the invasion, but that title never found favor in the general public.

But this? This was the real thing. He felt the genuine adoration in those children outside.

"May I take your coat, sir?" The uniformed attendant interrupted his thoughts.

"Yes, of course." Gao shucked his uniform overcoat and helped Mei Lin out of her coat.

His wife wore a long, cream-colored gown that left her shoulders bare. Her round face, still plump with weight from the recent pregnancy, showed signs of worry.

"What's the matter?" Gao asked.

"What was that out there?" she whispered. "All those children? And the autographs? What's going on?"

Gao felt a flash of anger. This was his moment in the spotlight. Was she was trying to take that away from him?

Before he could answer, the director of the film crew approached. "We'd like to get some B-roll footage of you and your wife walking in the Great Hall," he said.

Gao turned to Mei Lin and started to explain what B-roll footage was.

She took his arm and started walking. "I know what B-roll footage is, you ass," she hissed through a fake smile.

Since his time in Tashkent, the documentary team had been upgraded from one camera to three, and the director now had two assistants and a rotating cast of producers.

"Cut!" the director called. "Makeup, the general needs a touch up."

It was same makeup artist from Tashkent. "Good evening, General," she said with a brush poised above his face. "Congratulations." Gao closed his eyes, reveling in the gentle brushstrokes.

"Perfect," she pronounced with a slight smile. She cast a critical eye at Mei Lin. "You're fine."

Mei Lin seized Gao's arm and sunk her fingernails into his elbow. "*Perfect, General*," she mimicked in a breathy voice.

Before they could start again, a man in a dark suit strode up to the director and said a few words.

"That's a wrap," the director called. "Set up for the ceremony."

The man approached Gao and Mei Lin. He was short and compact, with a muscular body that filled out his well-cut suit. "Good evening, sir. Ma'am. The General Secretary would like to have a word with you."

Without waiting for an answer, he turned on his heel and started to walk away. He led them past the hall where the medal ceremony was going to take place. Through the open door, Gao saw an audience of hundreds of men and women in evening dress and military uniforms. The sounds of the chattering crowd spilled into the marble hallway. Their guide turned a corner and stopped outside a door guarded by two security men.

The room was small, with a pair of sofas and a muted TV in one corner that showed the stage and the audience. They were in the green room, Gao realized. In the center of the room were three chairs and a round, linen-covered table set with tea service.

The General Secretary of the Chinese Communist Party was a large man with doughy features, but the cut of his suit turned his bulk into solidity and strength. Despite his reputation for impassivity, his thick lips split into a grin when he saw them.

He approached, hand extended. "General," he said warmly, as if they were old friends. "Let me be the first to congratulate you on this great honor."

He shook Gao's hand in both of his, then turned to Mei Lin. "And this beautiful woman must be Mei Lin." He kissed her gently on both cheeks. The color rose in her cheeks and Gao saw her chest rise and fall as she tried to catch her breath.

Gao experienced a similar swell of excitement at this proximity to power. All his previous meetings with the General Secretary had been secret, but this public encounter—in front of his wife, no less—made him feel powerful. The combined effect of the evening, the movie, the limousine, the crowds of people all calling his name, was intoxicating to Gao.

The General Secretary came between them, placed a hand on each of their backs, and urged them toward the table. The great man held Mei Lin's chair for her, then he seated himself and poured tea for all of them.

"I would serve something stronger, but your husband and I have to attend a ceremony in a few minutes, my dear," he said to Mei Lin. Then he looked at Gao. "Your great service to the Party is noted, Yichen."

Gao thought his head might explode with joy. What was happening? The most powerful man in the world was calling him by his first name and serving him tea.

"I am honored to serve the Party, sir," Gao managed to reply through the lump in his throat.

"I'm glad you feel that way, because I may need to call on you again, Comrade Gao."

"Anything, sir," Gao replied immediately. "I want to be of service. I need to be of service to the Party."

The General Secretary sipped his tea, pursing his fat lips on the rim of the cup as if considering whether or not to say something. Gao wanted to scream with frustration.

Tell me, he shouted in his head.

"My husband has done so much already," Mei Lin said tentatively.

Gao stared at her. What was she saying? A public assignment from the leader of the Chinese Communist Party was not a request, it was an order. And when he completed it, his path to promotion would be unstoppable.

"How can I help?" Gao pressed.

"Our security position in the Central Asian region is precarious," the General Secretary began. "You've seen it for yourself. If not for your actions, the grand opening of the Tashkent transportation center would have been a disaster."

Gao inclined his head modestly. It was odd. The way he recalled the incident now merged in his head with the movie version of the events. The fear and self-doubt of those moments in the control room faded in his memory. Now, he was the Hero of Tashkent, his actions bold and certain, not dithering or second-guessing.

"The Belt and Road project is the most significant investment in the history of the Party," the General Secretary continued. "It is the key to our economic prosperity for the next hundred years."

He set down his teacup for emphasis. "It cannot fail. To be successful, our people must feel confident in their safety and the terrorists must fear us. I need a leader, a leader like you, Yichen."

Gao held his breath. The general in charge of the Belt and Road security was a two-star. Was he being offered a promotion right here?

"I would be honored to serve the Party," Gao said.

"My husband has done so much for the Party already," Mei Lin said. "He's been wounded in combat twice. Perhaps a supervisory position in Beijing would be more suitable for such a national hero."

Gao gaped at her. This was a promotion in rank and a chance to be involved in the most important project in Party history. After this, anything would be possible. The General Secretary— indeed, the entire Party— would owe him.

The General Secretary's lips bent into a smile as he studied Mei Lin. Her color was up, but her chin was set. Gao knew what that meant.

"Your wife is a wise woman," he said, "and she loves you." He got to his feet and Gao stood as though he'd been ejected from his chair. He started to speak, but the General Secretary held up his hand. "You and Mei Lin need to talk."

As soon as the door closed behind him, Gao whirled on Mei Lin. "What were you thinking?" he shouted.

"They're using you, Yichen." She waved her arm at the closed door. "All of this. The crowds, the meeting, the ceremony, the movie. You're being set up."

Gao clapped his hands to his head. "A setup? I'm a national hero. Do you know what that means? When this is over, I can get out of the Army, go into politics. I could have *his* job in twenty years!" Gao pointed at the General Secretary's empty chair. "I'm doing this for you."

"You have a family, Yichen."

"I'm doing this for the kids."

Mei Lin's jaw trembled. "You're doing this for yourself." She pressed a finger under her mascaraed eye. "Please. Say no."

There was a soft knock at the door and the director poked his head in. "We have less than five minutes. Can I come in?"

Mei Lin looked away. Gao nodded. "Come in."

As the makeup artist stroked her brush gently across his face for the umpteenth time, the director briefed Gao on where to stand on the stage. When Gao turned around, his wife was gone.

Minutes later, he stood at attention on the dais next to the most powerful man in the world.

Through the glare of the lights, he could just make out the splash of white in the first row, but he could not see Mei Lin's face. A cameraman crouched to his right, the lens pointing up at Gao's face. The noise of the applause from the standing crowd thundered in his ears and Gao felt his heart might burst with pride. Although he could not see her, he imagined Mei Lin's face alight with joy at his success. She was angry with him now, but she would see it his way. When he returned from this assignment and launched his political career, she would say he had been right.

The General Secretary's thick features loomed into view as he pinned the medal on Gao's chest.

"Did you consider my offer, Yichen?" he rumbled in a low voice. "I can announce the promotion right now, in front of everyone."

"Yes, sir." His heartbeat quickened in his chest. "I accept your offer."

10

Rome, Italy

Don Riley trudged after the Secret Service agent. He'd been up since 4:00 a.m. local time and his body was feeling it now. It was times like these, when he went more than two or three nights with too little sleep, that the scar from the bullet wound in his thigh burned.

Over time, he'd come to see the wound as a reminder of why he did what he did for a living. That remnant from a top-secret mission on a North Korean island had proved costly in more ways than just an old scar on his leg. Hardly a week went by that he didn't remember how his friend and mentor Brendan McHugh had died at the hands of an international terrorist.

Brendan McHugh had been an upperclassman at Annapolis when Don started as a plebe. A born leader, Brendan saw potential in the timid, out of shape plebe and encouraged him to stick with the rigorous program. Brendan was there when Don was forced to leave the Academy for medical reasons, and he was there when Don landed at the CIA. They even worked together for a time, including the mission where Brendan lost his life.

Telling Liz Soroush that her husband was dead was one of the hardest things he'd ever done—and something he never wanted to do again.

So when Don was tired and the ache in his thigh started up, he thought of his friend—and then he got back to work. People were depending on him.

"We scouted this place out last week, Mr. Riley," the Secret Service agent called over his shoulder. "It's the perfect spot for a quick meeting—as long as you don't mind the smell."

That might as well have been the theme for this G20 meeting. The Esposizione Universale Roma, better known by the acronym EUR, had been built by Benito Mussolini in the 1930s as the site for the 1942 World's Fair and a celebration of twenty years of Fascism in Italy. The planned exhibition never took place because of World War II, but despite the many expansions and modernizations over the years, there was an unmistakable stench of the building's founding ethos.

Don found it deeply ironic that today, as some of the G20 leaders flirted with autocracy, this meeting was taking place at a monument to Fascism.

The Secret Service agent rounded a corner into a wide hallway where every other overhead light was dark. Don sniffed the air, detecting an undercurrent of mold and damp.

"It's just at the end of this hall," the agent said.

Two floors above them, on the ground level, the twenty-sixth annual meeting of the G20 was breaking up for the day. There was always a crush of confusion as the competing security agencies from the world leaders all arranged to move their principals to their next venue. Tonight was labeled as a free night on the agenda, but everyone's calendar was packed with dinners and follow-up meetings that would undoubtedly go late into the night.

The press was everywhere, hoping to be the first to spot what was known in the diplomatic trade as a "drive-by," the supposedly unscripted moments when world leaders happened to meet in a hallway and exchange a few words. There would be pictures of politicians at opposite ends of the diplomatic polarity shaking hands, each assessing the other with measured gazes meant to send a message.

Don checked his watch. If he was on schedule, President Serrano was about to run into the leader of the People's Republic of China right about now. In the years since the Chinese invasion of Taiwan, ties between the countries had been understandably strained. The President's advisors had decided that a drive-by was just the right amount of contact to let people know that the two countries were slowly working towards normal diplomatic relations.

That was President Serrano's intended message as the next U.S. election approached: normal diplomatic relations. Since he'd negotiated an end to the Ukraine War with the new Russian leader Nikolay Sokolov a few years prior, Serrano had dedicated himself to his domestic agenda. He was determined to go down in history as a successful peacetime president, not the guy who had gotten his country into one international conflict after another.

"Here we are, sir." The Secret Service agent stopped at a set of double doors. The lower half of the white-painted entrance was scuffed and scarred by contact with countless rolling carts.

Inside the room, the smell of mold increased. Judging by the outlets along the wall and the drains in the floor, Don guess this had once been a central laundry area for the facility. The machines were all gone, but in the center of the bare linoleum floor stood a cheap card table and half a dozen metal folding chairs. The overhead light made the room seem dingy.

"It's used as a break room." The agent pointed at a matching door on the other side of the room. "The other entrance leads to a parallel corridor with separate access to elevators, stairs, and multiple surface-level egress points."

Don nodded. Separate entrances and exits for the President and his visitor so no reporter could put them together. He cocked an eyebrow at the agent.

"We also scanned it for listening devices," he said, anticipating Don's question. "It's clean. Say the word and I'll start moving people into position, Mr. Riley."

"Let's do it," Don said. "I'll let the Russians know."

Don pulled a mobile phone from his pocket and sent a text to the number that Vladimir Federov had passed to him in the buffet line at lunch. The scrap of paper bore a phone number in neat block lettering and a message: *Time to call in a favor. 1930h today. Principals' meeting. You choose location.*

Federov had done his homework, identifying a twenty-minute break in the President's evening schedule. It seemed he'd even anticipated the unscheduled drive-by with the Chinese president.

Serrano had not been pleased. His face clouded red when Don showed him the note.

"I don't want anything public, Don," he said. "Ten minutes in a discreet location. That's it."

And that, Don mused, was how he'd ended up in the dank bowels of a building built by Fascists, waiting for two of the most powerful men in the world to join him. He admired Federov's skill not only in picking the time, but in knowing exactly how to get Serrano to show up. Whatever Don thought of his president, the man kept his word. The President owed Nikolay Sokolov a favor, and Ricardo Serrano always paid his debts.

The two parties arrived at the same time, entering through opposite doors. The Secret Service detail entered, scanned the room, and then held the door for the President of the United States. Serrano was dressed in a dark blue suit with a faint chalk pinstripe and a red tie. His face was flushed and he was puffing from the quick walk downstairs. He wrinkled his nose at the smell and cut a quick glance at Don.

President Sokolov entered the room with FSB chief Vladimir Federov in tow. Don and his Russian intelligence counterpart exchanged looks. Federov offered a slight nod in greeting.

Sokolov was also dressed in a dark suit with a dark tie and white shirt. To Don's eye, the Russian president's skin was pasty and his suit fit loosely, as if he'd recently lost weight. Still, his face lit up when he saw Serrano. The President waved away his security detail and the two men embraced. The scene reminded Don of the night in Helsinki when they'd signed the peace accord that formally ended the Russian war in Ukraine and acknowledged Nikolay as the new leader of Russia.

"Mr. President," Don said in a low voice. "We're short on time, sir."

Serrano nodded curtly and led Nikolay to the table. The two men sat down in battered folding chairs and leaned forward, elbows on knees.

"It's good to see you again, Nikolay," Serrano said warmly. He reached across and clapped his hand on the younger man's shoulder. "You look well."

Nikolay barked out a short laugh and shook off Serrano's hand as he sat back in his chair. "You see, Vladimir," he said over his shoulder to Federov. "His first words are a lie."

"Mr. President," Federov replied in his tenor voice. "Mr. Riley—Don—is right. Our time is short and our need is great."

Nikolay sighed. "I need your help, Rick."

"Is this about Central Asia?" Serrano asked. That had been Don's guess, and he saw by the pained look on the Russian's face that he was correct.

"The CSTO meeting was a disaster," Nikolay said. "I needed that economic agreement signed and those bastards just let me twist in the wind."

Don had seen Serrano navigate his own share of tough political situations, and he suspected his president empathized with the Russian leader's plight. "This too shall pass, my friend. Give it time."

"My time is running out, and the only thing that's going to pass is a knife through my ribs." Nikolay looked up. "Unless I can get your help."

"If I can do it, it's yours."

It was the right answer, Don knew. An answer calibrated to the reality of their situation. Although the men were friends and Serrano owed the Russian, neither was going to put his own country at risk for a personal debt.

"I need intel," Nikolay said. "My sources in Central Asia are . . . not what they once were. I need information I can trust."

"We might be able to help," Serrano said carefully, "but I need to know what you're going to do with that information."

Nikolay sat back in his chair. For a second, his expression showed a hint of desperation, then his professional facade fell back into place. "I need that economic agreement signed and my near abroad to the south secured. I'm getting killed by the opposition in Moscow."

"You think the Chinese are blocking you?" Serrano asked.

Good, Don thought. Serrano was following the script. This was a perfect chance to get an outside view on Central Asia.

Nikolay shook his head. "The Chinese are taking it in the ass from the SIF and that makes everyone nervous. The republics want protection and they don't think I can offer that anymore."

"And who's backing the SIF?" Serrano countered.

Nikolay and Federov exchanged a glance. "India."

Don considered the new information. The big news story from the first day of the G20 summit had been the verbal dust-up between China and India. The Indians objected strenuously to what they called "economic coercion" of the weak Central Asian republics by Beijing. Since none of the republics in question were represented on the G20, the Chinese defended their own actions as benevolent efforts in the developing world. To Don, the diplomatic fencing had not rung true. He was missing pieces of the puzzle.

Nikolay's explanation made sense. The biggest economic loser from the Belt and Road infrastructure connecting western China and Tehran was India. Could it be India supporting the SIF as a covert operation against the Chinese?

It was an explanation that answered a lot of questions.

"You're looking for blackmail," Serrano said.

"I'm looking for leverage," Nikolay snapped. "I can't afford to lose Kazakhstan. I need that agreement signed."

Like the United States, Russia also had an election within the year. If the intelligence briefs from the Russia desk at CIA were correct, Nikolay planned to stage a fair election, something that his Uncle Vitaly had not bothered with in decades.

The risk for Nikolay in an actual contested election was substantial, but the risk for the U.S. if the hardliners regained control in Moscow was something Don would rather not deal with.

Serrano leaned forward. "I need your word, Nikolay. You will verify everything we give you on your own. Nothing can be traced back to us."

The Russian president extended his hand. "You have my word, Rick."

Serrano looked back at Don. "Well, Mr. Riley," he said. "How do you feel about sharing intel with our Russian friends?"

Federov's eyes weren't exactly pleading, but his message was clear:

Help me, help you.

Federov had betrayed his own country in order to save it. The FSB chief had given Don the key to taking down the Russian political elite who'd backed Luchnik in the Ukraine War. Together, they'd prevented World War Three. He'd gambled everything on the man sitting across from President

Serrano. Don recalled their chance meeting in Helsinki, at the celebration for peace accord that ended the War in Ukraine.

"I am hopeful President Sokolov will live up to his potential," Federov had said. "We had the right players this time, Donald. Next time, we may not be so lucky."

Was this the next time? Was this the payback Federov expected? Most important, was it the right thing to do for the U.S.?

"Don?" Serrano chided him. "We don't have all night, you know."

Federov's crystalline brown eyes locked with Don's.

Help me, help you.

"I think we should do it, sir," Don said.

Serrano stood and Nikolay Sokolov followed. The two presidents shook hands.

11

Tashkent, Uzbekistan

Harrison could not help but feel a little pang of disappointment when he arrived at the restaurant. When he'd contacted Roger Shalikashvili, the Chief of Station in Tashkent, the man suggested they meet for lunch outside the office. Since Roger was known for his fondness of the finer things in life, Harrison allowed him to select the restaurant.

In his mind, he had pictured linen tablecloths, fine china, a bottle of wine—maybe two bottles. He'd been traveling nonstop for over a month. He was tired and wanted nothing more than a good meal, a stiff drink, and a lifeline to the failing investigation of his best friend's disappearance.

Fronting a tree-lined boulevard in a professional suburb of Tashkent, the glass door of the establishment read *Pita Street Food*. Apart from the starkly Soviet architecture of the surrounding older buildings and the seemingly endless wind, both the street and the restaurant could have been in Washington, DC.

The modern interior did nothing to lessen his disappointment. The narrow room had white walls and blond-wood furniture that looked like something straight out of an IKEA catalog. Young people, professionally dressed and groomed, gathered in groups of twos and threes eating, laughing. And vaping. It seemed like everyone in this part of the world spent half their life blasting out clouds of thick white vapor. Through the grayish haze, Harrison spied Roger at a two-person booth in the back corner. The station chief raised his hand in greeting.

Harrison slid into the booth, acutely aware that his back was to the door.

"When you said you wanted me to take you to lunch, I assumed you meant something a little more upscale," he said by way of greeting.

Roger chuckled. The man never full-out laughed. "Don't knock it till you try it, Harry."

Harrison gritted his teeth. He hated being called Harry, and Roger knew it.

This is not about you. It's about Tim, he reminded himself.

Roger was dressed in a V-neck cashmere sweater over a snow-white dress shirt and carefully knotted silk tie. His suit jacket, which Harrison guessed was from some designer he'd never heard of, was folded on the seat next to him. His upscale clothes, aquiline features, and refined manners made Harrison think of a World War Two–era diplomat.

Still, the man was good at his job, Harrison knew that. If anyone in the region could help him revive his search for Tim Trujillo, it was the man sitting across the table from him.

Harrison forced a smile. "How about you order for both of us, Roger. I want to get the full experience."

If Roger sensed sarcasm in Harrison's reply, he didn't show it. When the waitress came to their table, Roger ordered in flawless Russian. Two special pitas with everything and two glasses of *ayran*, the local drink made from milk. It had taken a while for Harrison to understand the appeal of a drink that tasted like thin, salty yogurt, but he was used to it now.

Yet another sign that he'd been here too long.

Roger was Harrison's age and also prematurely gray, but the similarities ended there. Roger was tall and rangy, with a stylish haircut, while Harrison was of medium height and build and his hair was long overdue for a trim. Although they'd started at the same time in the Agency, their careers were similarly disparate. Roger's next posting after his Chief of Station tour would be an executive position back at headquarters in Langley. Harrison, on the other hand, was doing pretty much the same job he'd had since he'd started at the CIA. Trained as a case officer, he'd taken a risk and his career had suffered for it. Don Riley, by picking him up as an analyst at Emerging Threats Group, had pulled him out of the doghouse and saved his skin—and let him get back out in the field from time to time.

Roger sipped his drink and blotted his lips with a paper napkin. "You're a long way from home, Harry. What can I do for you?"

He had no doubt that Roger knew exactly why he was here, but Harrison played along. "A friend of mine, a good friend, is missing. His last known location was here in Tashkent. The family's asked me to look into it."

Roger sat back in his seat. "Tell me what you know."

Harrison held his irritation in check. If the roles were reversed, he might have compared notes, maybe expressed some sympathy, but Roger was all about control.

Harrison began with the call from Jenny, the visit to the house, the decision to fly halfway around the world and play detective. He described in detail the interactions with Grand Surfan, noting how Roger nodded when he mentioned Jimmy Li, confirming Harrison's suspicion that the man was MSS. He even got a raised eyebrow when he described the demolition of the temporary air terminal.

Harrison recounted how he had spent the last weeks retracing Tim's steps, visiting each oil field and pipeline his friend had been to during his final weeks. Since he didn't have the benefit of a private jet to move him around the region, Harrison's travels had been a combination of delayed airlines, long train trips, and hired cars. All his efforts had led him to the same conclusion:

Nothing. Tim had vanished without a trace.

"I'm at the end of my rope, Roger," Harrison said. "I need help."

The food arrived and Roger used the break to tuck into his pita without comment. Harrison bit into his own and found it was delicious. He knew he was more than likely eating horsemeat, but he pushed the thought out of his mind. He was hungry, and the food was the best he'd had in at least a week.

"I'm afraid it doesn't look good for your friend," Roger said finally.

Harrison's appetite faded. He put down his pita. His rational brain knew Roger was right, but up until this point he'd prioritized action over analysis. Constant motion was one way to keep reality at bay.

"What's your experience with kidnappings in the area?" Harrison asked.

Roger shook his head. "If your friend was kidnapped, you would have gotten a ransom request by now. Besides, kidnappings are rare. They happen, but your friend was ex-Army, not exactly a soft target."

Harrison took a sip of ayran and the drink soured on his tongue. He pushed his plate away.

"I think you've done everything you can reasonably do," Roger continued. "You can go back to the widow with a clean conscience."

Widow. The word hit Harrison like slap. Jenny, a widow. He tried to process the word and failed.

Harrison shook his head. "They deserve more. I'm not going home until I get answers."

"Be reasonable," Roger urged. "You've taken every legal action possible—"

"What about illegal actions?" Harrison interrupted.

Roger stiffened in his chair. "Look, I'm going to level with you, Harry—"

"My name is Harrison, Roger." The change in tone caught Roger by surprise, but only for a moment.

"Harrison, then." The other man blew out a breath of frustration. "I'm getting calls about a crazy American poking around."

"Then help me!" Harrison wanted to shout, but he clamped his jaws together so tightly that the words came out as a hiss.

Roger's eyes flared and he crossed his arms. "What do you want me to do?"

"Call in some favors," Harrison said. "Put out a bounty for information. Whatever the cost, I'll cover it. I'm not leaving until I know what happened to my friend."

Roger rolled his neck in irritation. Harrison knew he was asking a lot. They weren't close friends after all, and if Harrison's inquiry caused a mess in the region, clean-up duty would fall to the chief of station.

Harrison knew he was pushing hard, but Tim's life mattered and Jenny deserved answers. If there was a cost to be paid—and there would be, Harrison knew that—he would take the hit. Tim Trujillo was more than a friend. The lives they had shared made them brothers.

The station chief blew out another rigid breath of frustration, then leaned across the table. "Look, Harrison, I'm sorry, but I can't—"

BOOM!

The next words out of Roger's mouth were obliterated by a devastating noise. The blast rocked the room, knocking pictures off the walls and sending a tray of dishes crashing to the floor. Harrison felt the explosion like the slap of a wave against his body and his head connected with the wall. His eardrums compressed. His hearing dulled, replaced by a high-pitched whine.

All over the restaurant, diners recovering from the blast stared in wide-eyed shock, voices muted. Even the haze of smoke in the air seemed to quiver from the force of the explosion.

Harrison had done time in Iraq and in Syria. He knew what a car bomb sounded like, felt like. This was a car bomb—a big one—and it was close by.

The moment of shock passed, replaced by pandemonium. Screaming. Crying. More glass breaking. As a mass, the diners in the restaurant rose and rushed for the street entrance.

Roger sprang up and headed for the rear entrance. Harrison followed.

The alley behind Pita Street Food was narrow, sandwiched between a pair of three-story buildings and cast in shadow. Harrison skidded into a dumpster as he came through the rear entrance at speed.

He looked up. To his left, a column of smoke rose in the clear blue afternoon sky. Roger was already running in that direction and Harrison took off after him, his boots slipping on the puddled street.

He caught up to Roger at the end of the alley and they burst onto the sunlit street together.

The scene was utter devastation. A hundred meters away, an explosion had obliterated the midday boulevard, carving a bomb crater out of the earth and scattering cars like children's toys.

The front facade of a four-story stone building was gone. Harrison could look into cross-sectioned offices and empty meeting rooms. Loose paper fluttered on the wind like dandelion seeds.

A few meters in front of them, a white Daewoo hatchback lay on its roof, wheels still spinning. Roger ran to the driver's side and wrenched open the door. He helped a young woman crawl out of the car and get to her feet. She was dressed in a wool overcoat and knit cap. Her face was blank and white as bone.

Roger gripped her by the shoulders. He asked in Russian, "Are you hurt?"

As Harrison passed them, the young woman shook her head and Roger moved to the next victim.

Side by side, the pair triaged the casualties of the explosion. Harrison knew what they were doing was very dangerous. A tried-and-true terrorist tactic was to detonate a second bomb once people flooded in to aid the victims of the first explosion.

He pushed the fear aside. That was for the police to worry about.

On the sidewalk outside the immediate blast zone, he came across a man in his mid-twenties with broad shoulders and thick dark hair. He was dressed professionally in a business suit, which was powdered with dust, and he stared stupidly at the stump of his right leg. Thick red blood stained the pavement. Working quickly, Harrison stripped off his belt and used it as a tourniquet. When the flow of blood stopped, Harrison took another turn around the man's thigh then he wrapped the belt around the man's hand.

"Don't let go," he told him. He waited for a nod of acknowledgement, then moved on.

Harrison's mind did not allow him to feel, only to assess and act. Once he reached the outer limits of the bomb crater, he turned left. He paused to search for a pulse in a mangled body and found no sign of life. He moved on automatically. There was nothing to be done for the people who were already dead.

A woman crouched next to a car, shivering. Her hands were wrapped around her knees and a puddle of urine had pooled between her black high heels. Her forehead lay open, the wound so deep that Harrison could see pale bone. The whites of her eyes stared out from the blood sheeted across her face.

He took a handkerchief from his pocket and pressed it over the wound. He unpeeled one of her hands from her knee and lay it over the dressing.

"Apply pressure," he told her. When he took his hand away, her palm stayed in place. He took off his jacket and wrapped it around her shoulders.

He moved on. Harrison had no idea how much time had passed. An EMT toting a medical kit arrived at the side of the next victim at the same time as him. Harrison stood back, recognizing that emergency professionals had arrived in force. His work here was done.

He looked around to find Roger standing a few meters away. His pressed pinstripe slacks were torn at the knee and there was blood on his cashmere sweater. His carefully coiffed hair was mussed, and a fine layer of dust coated his body. Harrison could feel the residue of pulverized cement on his own skin, a gritty reminder of the destruction they had witnessed.

He stood next to Roger, said nothing. The Chief of Station stared at a flag draped over the side of a building. The realization swelled in Harrison's mind that since it was still there, it must have been unfurled after the explosion. Otherwise, it would have been swept away in the blast with everything else.

He stared at the white image on a blue background. A double-headed eagle, wings outstretched, talons reaching. At the bottom, in bold Cyrillic letters, it read:

SIF

Roger's voice was a croak. Harrison had to struggle to hear him over the wail of sirens and shouts of first responders. "Seljuk Islamic Front. They did this."

Harrison wasn't sure if Roger was about to weep or throw up, maybe both. The man clenched and unclenched his hands. He gasped for air, then spoke again.

"Whatever you need, Harrison. I'll help you."

12

The White House, Washington, DC

When Don Riley was in middle school, his parents filed for divorce. Thinking back on that time in his life, what he remembered most were the fights. Even at nine years old, he recognized how petty the arguments were, how small the stakes. It seemed as if his adult parents were just trying to find something, anything, to use against each other.

From Don's seat on the pale yellow sofa in the Oval Office, it looked as if the President and Vice President were headed for a nasty divorce.

"Mr. President," thundered Vice President Lionel Hawthorne, "I tell you, sir, you're making a mistake."

"I didn't invite you into the Oval Office to debate the merits of my decision, Lionel," Serrano snapped in reply.

One cushion to Don's right on the sofa, the Director sat still as a stone, letting the storm rage around him. Don tried not to shift in his seat, but he really did not want to be here.

"Your affinity for Russia is going to come back to bite us in the ass," Hawthorne declared.

To Don, it wasn't so much *what* the Vice President said, but *how* he said it that seemed to irk the President.

"My *affinity* for Russia? Do you care to explain that comment, Lionel?"

The Vice President backpedaled. "I'm just pointing out that you have a soft spot for Nikolay Sokolov, sir."

"I have an obligation as a human being and as the leader of this republic to a man who saved our collective asses when it counted during the Ukraine War," Serrano shot back. "Or perhaps you've forgotten about how the Russian Navy saved our bacon while we were looking for a lost Chinese nuclear weapon in the middle of the Pacific. Sokolov put his forces in harm's way because I asked him to. What you call an *affinity*"—the word dripped with contempt—"I call a debt of honor."

Hawthorne's ruddy complexion took on a deeper hue of red. "I'm not suggesting we abandon them, sir. I just think we need to consider all aspects of this situation a little more deeply." Hawthorne looked over to the Director. "Help me out here, Sam."

The Director pursed his lips. Don could tell he wanted no part of this family spat.

"If what I'm reading about Tashkent is true," the Director said, "then I suggest we apply more resources to the region."

That was about as good a diplomatic non-answer as Don could have come up with on the spot. Hawthorne took it as a win. He turned back to the President.

"Exactly what I'm trying to say, sir. We should be making our own way in the region, not helping the Russians get back on their feet." The Vice President pointed to a copy of the *Washington Post* on the coffee table. "There's opportunity for us there. We just need to seize it, Mr. President."

Hawthorne had skills, Don had to admit. He'd taken the Director's mealy-mouthed reply and turned the conversation to a more productive vein.

The *Washington Post* had reprinted an article by independent reporter Nicole Nipper in the World section of the paper. It was an interview with an Uzbek named Timur Ganiev about a growing indigenous movement in the region. The reporter hinted Ganiev had the chops to unite the fractious ethnic tribes across the nation states of Tajikistan, Kyrgyzstan, Uzbekistan, and Turkmenistan into some sort of unified group.

To Don, the claim seemed long on promises and short on reality. These were post-Soviet states, pseudo-democracies run by entrenched autocrats who specialized in holding on to power. The influence of the great powers in the region was in flux, that much was true, but the Central Asian republics had more in common with the Mafia than with Massachusetts.

More relevant to the current conversation was that Ganiev's vision was in direct opposition to Russia's desire to reestablish control over the region —and, therefore, in opposition with Serrano's commitment to Nikolay Sokolov.

"Enough." Serrano's voice was sharp. "Lionel, there's a difference between running a campaign and making foreign policy."

"With all due respect, sir," Hawthorne shot back, "it's my campaign, and when I win, it will be *my* foreign policy."

As soon as the heated words left the Vice President's mouth, he realized he'd gone too far. Don winced. Serrano's face darkened. He shot out of his chair, glared down at Hawthorne.

"I. Am. The. President," he said in a voice that brooked no argument. "Furthermore, I've won elections to this office. Twice. I suggest you do less talking and more listening, Mr. *Vice* President."

Serrano stalked away from the sitting area, rounding the curved perimeter of the office with angry strides. Don half expected him to step into his private study off the Oval Office, but he kept walking. He paused behind the Resolute desk, crossed his arms, and stared out the window.

Outside, the day was warm and sunny. The trees were a riot of soft pastel petals that from a distance looked like cotton candy.

The President returned, rested his hands on the back of his armchair. He drew in a deep breath and let it out.

"That was unprofessional of me. I apologize, Lionel." His tone was personal, his full attention on Hawthorne. It was as if he'd forgotten Don and the Director were still there.

The Vice President hung his head. "I spoke hastily, sir. It was prideful of me. I'm the one who should apologize."

Serrano broke the awkwardness by taking up the coffee decanter and refreshing everyone's cups.

"Of course, you're right," the President continued as if there had been no break in the conversation. "This is your campaign and it will be your foreign policy once you win. That said, I have obligations that must be met during my time in office. One of those obligations is to support Nikolay Sokolov."

He took his seat and balanced the china cup and saucer on his knee. "With that in mind, I think the first order of business is to lower the temperature in the region." He turned to Don. "Tell me what we know about this terrorist group that is causing so much turmoil, Mr. Riley."

Don fumbled with his tablet to find the correct slide, which he synced to all the other briefing tablets in the room. The other men studied their screens.

Don was acutely aware that their information on the SIF was embarrassingly sparse. He cleared his throat. "The Seljuk Islamic Front has emerged as the primary terrorist threat in the region over the last eighteen months. The organization is believed to be a splinter group of the East Turkmenistan Islamic Front, which has been active in Xinjiang region of China for years."

"They support the Uighurs, right?" Hawthorne asked.

"That's correct, sir. They've been a thorn in the side of the Chinese government for years in support of the Muslim Uighur population. The SIF is focused exclusively in Central Asia. To date, their attacks are low-level sabotage of work sites along the Chinese Belt and Road Initiative."

"I take it from your tone that there's a 'but' in there, Don," the President said dryly.

Don nodded and flipped to the next image. "Two days ago, the SIF took responsibility for a car bomb that exploded outside the Ministry of Defense in Tashkent."

In the photo, tendrils of smoke rose out of the fresh bomb crater. Sunlight, filtered through a haze of pulverized concrete, cast an unearthly light over the devastation. Cars were scattered like toys. The face of an office building had been sheared off. If he zoomed in, Don could make out corpses.

Don paused to let the scene of devastation sink in. Harrison Kohl had taken photos using his phone and sent them to Don along with a personal narrative of the terrorist attack. Don explained Harrison Kohl's presence, and that he and the Chief of Station had been on the scene almost immediately and had acted as first responders. He flashed the image of the SIF flag draped over a building.

"This attack had nothing to do with the Chinese," Don continued. "However, the Uzbek government has been friendly to the PRC. It appears that the SIF is expanding their fight to include regimes that cooperate with the Chinese."

"What do we know about their leadership?" the President asked, still staring at the car bomb photos.

Don flipped to a new page. An unsmiling man dressed in traditional Turkmen garb with a trimmed beard and piercing grey eyes stared out from the screen. Don sketched out Orazov's history, mostly a recap of what they had been briefed on earlier.

"Where does their funding come from?" the President asked. "Throwing sand into gas tanks at a construction site is one thing. Setting off a car bomb in downtown Tashkent takes a different level of sophistication."

Don cut a sideways glance at the Director, who cleared his throat. "The short answer is that we don't know, sir."

"Is there a longer answer?" Serrano asked.

The Director chose his words with care. "Don looked into President Sokolov's theory that the Indians might be behind this. On paper, it makes perfect sense. The Indians have motive, means, and opportunity. There's only one problem."

"Which is?" the Vice President asked.

"We have not a single shred of evidence to support this theory," the Director admitted. "Nothing."

The President broke the long silence. "If it looks like a duck, quacks like a duck, and walks like a duck, why don't we just call it what it is."

Don tried not to wince. This was going too fast on too little verifiable information. They needed to slow down, gather more intel, and figure out what the heck was going on. He had a queasy feeling in the pit of his stomach that there was more to this story than met the eye.

"There is one way we could test the theory," the Director said. "And very quickly."

Don frowned. That was news to him.

"Don't keep us in suspense, Sam," Serrano said.

The Director reverted to careful word selection again. "I have a contact in the Indian Research and Analysis Wing—RAW. That's their version of the CIA. We go way back. I could get a meeting and sound him out on this."

Don watched the two politicians chew on the Director's idea. As a career intelligence professional, Don's mind rebelled against the idea. The Director was proposing a fishing expedition.

"I like it," Serrano said.

Vice President Hawthorne nodded in agreement.

"There is a catch to this plan," the Director said. "Jay Patel is honest and smart as they come. He'll see right through me. I need a proxy, someone who can give us an honest assessment as to how deep the Indians are in this mess."

Suddenly, Don knew were this was going. He started to the open his mouth, but Serrano spoke first.

"No problem, Sam. Send Riley."

13

Dushanbe, Tajikistan

As the Y-20 military cargo plane broke through the cloud cover, Gao peered out the window. Through a thin veil of smog, he got his first look at the city of Dushanbe, Tajikistan.

His briefing book had provided the basic facts about the city, but the view told the real story. Dushanbe occupied the western end of the Gissar Valley, where the open land narrowed to a *V* between two snowcapped mountain ranges. Once no more than a riverside trading post, the metropolis had expanded to consume all the available space in the valley. Densely packed buildings drew a gray line across the steep foothills, reminding Gao of a dirty ring in a bathtub.

The six-hour flight from Beijing had been made very comfortable by the VIP suite that had been installed at the forward end of the military aircraft's cargo bay. In this soundproofed pod of comfort, Gao might as well have been flying first class on a commercial airliner. Leather armchairs, carpeted floors, curtains on the windows, even a private bathroom. His luxurious mode of travel was a far cry from the jump seats occupied by two platoons of soldiers only a few meters aft of the walls of the general's suite.

In fact, the rest of the cargo bay was packed with men, machines, and pallets of war materiel.

The luxurious suite gave Gao satisfying proof that the Party was not sending him out into the wilderness, as Mei Lin had feared. They would be there to support him every step of the way.

The flight attendant, a corporal dressed in a pressed PLA field uniform, approached. He gestured at the half-finished cup of jasmine tea at the general's elbow.

"The pilot has informed me that we will be landing in fifteen minutes, Lieutenant General," the young man said. "May I take your teacup?"

"You may, Corporal." Gao noted how the young man had called him "Lieutenant General" for the entire trip, a subtle but constant reminder of the second star that now adorned Gao's uniform. He sighed with content. Normally, a subordinate used the generic term "General" to address any senior officer of general rank, but this corporal had seen fit to recognize Gao's full title.

The previous evening, Gao had spent time in the bedroom at his apartment modeling his new uniforms, unable to take his eyes off the second star. He could scarcely believe his good fortune. In the space of less than five years he'd moved from a lowly major to a two-star general, an astonishing accomplishment.

Mei Lin came into the bedroom as he was trying on his dress green uniform with the gleaming gold stars. She still wore the same dirty housecoat she'd worn all day. Her lips twisted in a sour expression.

"Yichen, you're leaving in the morning," she said. "You need to spend time with your children."

The Mei Lin he'd fallen in love with might have pouted when she wanted him to do something, or even turned the request into a subtle seduction. But that Mei Lin was gone. The woman who'd replaced her had an edge to her voice, an unspoken anger.

True, he'd taken the security job in Central Asia after she'd pleaded with him not to. Even after he'd said yes to the General Secretary, Mei Lin begged him to reverse his decision. Things were different now, she insisted. He had the children to think about, not just his career.

The old Gao would have held his wife and told her it would be okay. He would have laid out the reasons for his actions in calm, even tender, terms. The opportunity would set them up for a life of elite privileges, the old Gao would have said. One did not refuse a personal request from the General Secretary of the People's Republic of China. It was his duty to serve his country. His honor.

He could have said all those things, but he didn't. Instead, the new Gao snapped at his wife. It seemed that the new Gao was a man who made his wife cry.

They did not make love the night before he left. Instead, Lieutenant General Gao spent his last night at home on the sofa. In the morning, Mei Lin made a show of happiness for the sake of the children, but her lips on his cheek were cold.

The flight attendant interrupted his thoughts with a gentle reminder. "Your seatbelt, Lieutenant General."

Moodily, Gao returned his attention to the window. The clutter of the city gave way to open space as the Gissar Valley widened into gently rolling hills checkerboarded with pastureland and fields under cultivation. Villages dotted the terrain, and gray lines of local roads snaked along the earth.

A raw wound of brown slashed across the landscape, arrow-straight. Contained in the borders of the cut, Gao saw the glint of steel rails and a smooth trail of black asphalt. It was the Road from China, the modern Silk Road, the very thing he was here to protect. Gao blinked at the sudden rush of pride he felt.

The flight attendant was back. "The pilot wishes to inform you that he intends to make a loop through the valley so you can see the area before we touch down at Anyi Air Base."

"Very well," Gao replied, his voice still choked up.

The eastern spur of the Chinese Belt and Road project connected to the new PLA forward operating base. Gao's eyes widened when he saw the size of the military facility that would be his new home. This was more than just an air base, he realized.

The facility was anchored to the south by four runways crossed along the axes of the prevailing winds. The main base was a beehive of activity, with dozens of prefabricated buildings arranged in a grid. Adjacent to the road and rail spur was a large permanent structure next to a field of skyward-facing antennae. That would be the Huawei compound, he thought. The Belt and Road was more than just a collection of physical roads—it was a data highway as well, and this building was the main hub for the entire region.

To the east, facing Dushanbe, was a depot, but Gao was surprised to see it was covered. He estimated the area was the size of a dozen soccer pitches. Why spend the time and money to erect a roof over that much real estate?

The entire base was ringed with cyclone fencing topped with razor wire. Guard towers were erected every half kilometer, and the terrain had been cleared of obstacles for hundreds of meters in every direction.

Gao noted the rail line ended abruptly at an unfinished bridge spanning a river a few kilometers past the western edge of the base.

The Y-20 entered the landing pattern and began to descend. A few moments later, Gao felt a bump as the cargo plane touched down. At the end of the runway, the enormous plane began a wide, slow turn and Gao spied the assembly waiting for him.

As the plane taxied to a stop, Gao unclipped his seatbelt and stepped into the adjoining bathroom. He slid the door closed and inspected his pressed field uniform in the mirror, his fingers lingering on the pair of stitched stars that signified his new rank. The whine of the four jet engines, each the size of an SUV, faded away. He felt the vibration of the rear ramp being lowered.

Gao splashed water on his face, then held his own gaze into the mirror. "You can do this," he whispered. "You *deserve* this."

When he exited the bathroom, the flight attendant had Gao's bags in hand. He opened the door for the general.

The interior of the cargo bay was all steel: exposed steel ribs of the plane fuselage, steel decking with evenly spaced holes for securing cargo. Four rows of jump seats were folded up behind a company of soldiers standing at attention. The company commander, a captain, snapped a salute at Gao.

Gao returned the honor, then strode past the ranks of soldiers toward the square of bright light at the rear ramp. He passed military vehicles and pallets of supplies. The flight crew, already prepping the unloading operation, came to attention as he passed them by.

He paused at the top of the broad steel ramp, blinking in the sunshine. He waited until the assembled troops were called to attention, then he descended to the tarmac, faced the red flag of the People's Republic of China, and delivered his smartest salute. The band played the Chinese national anthem. Gao's chest puffed with pride.

A man and a woman strode forward. The man was a colonel with a blocky physique and a bland expression. The woman, a captain, was tall and lithe with sure movements. Sharp eyes studied him from an oval face.

They both came to attention and saluted.

"Colonel Yan Gong, base commander, sir."

Gao shook his hand. His grip was callused and crushing.

"Captain Fang Xiaomei, your aide-de-camp, Lieutenant General."

Gao blinked at her. He'd been told only that his staff would meet him at his new post but had not been provided with any personnel files. He hesitated a second longer than was necessary, then held out his hand. "Pleasure to meet you, Captain."

She gripped his hand and their eyes locked. Fang Xiaomei was a confident woman, he could see that, but she was a *woman*.

"I look forward to working with you, General Gao." Her voice was husky.

The colonel cleared his throat. "Sir, we have a developing situation that may require your attention."

Gao frowned. "What kind of situation?"

Colonel Yan's face crumpled into a scowl. "Locals." His tone of voice had all the subtlety of a granite block.

"A security issue, sir," the captain added. "You may have seen the unfinished bridge on your flight in. The mayor insists on your personal assurance that the work site is safe from terrorist activity."

Gao didn't like it. He hadn't been on the ground more than five minutes and these underlings wanted him to meet with locals?

"Why do they need to see me?" Gao asked.

"I was there last week," the colonel admitted, "and there was another problem this morning."

"What kind of problem?" Gao pressed.

The colonel looked away, then back to Gao. "An IED was found at the work site this morning."

"The detonator was faulty," Fang said. "It didn't explode, but it has the work crews spooked." She waved toward one of the hangars and Gao noticed a CSK-131 light-armored vehicle speeding toward them. A series of antennae and radomes sprouting from the roof told Gao it was configured as a command post. The vehicle came to a stop next them and the captain opened the rear passenger door. "I'll give you a full briefing on the way, sir."

Gao hesitated, but Captain Fang did not back down. "It's an excellent chance for you to make your presence felt in the local community, Lieutenant General."

Gao climbed into the back of the tactical vehicle. He still had doubts, but somehow Captain Fang's confidence settled his mind. Fang climbed in and lowered herself into the seat next to him. She moved gracefully, like a cat, without a single wasted movement. The colonel stayed behind, glowering as the vehicle door closed.

"Thank you, sir," Captain Fang said quietly enough that the two enlisted operators facing the communications suite could not hear. "Now that we're alone, I can say that the colonel wanted to handle this himself, but he's lost all credibility since the last incident." Her gaze was dark and steady. "This situation requires a more experienced leader."

Gao didn't know what to think. The woman seemed both competent and confident, but he didn't like being rushed into anything. "Perhaps you should give me that briefing now, Captain."

Fang's explanation was as efficient as her movements. The SIF had been active in the area. Two weeks ago, an explosion had killed three workers and shut down the job site. It was only after personal security assurances from Colonel Yan that work resumed on the delayed bridge construction.

A few hours ago, another IED had been discovered. Work stopped immediately.

"Sir," Fang concluded, "if we can restore work before the end of the shift, there would be no need to inform Beijing of the delay." She raised an eyebrow for added emphasis.

Now Gao understood the urgency. Announcing a delay to Beijing on the same day as his arrival in the region was not a good look. The captain was looking out for her general.

Their vehicle joined a waiting convoy of three light-armored tactical assault vehicles, all painted desert brown. The column raced through the base and out the main gate. The security personnel came to attention and saluted the general's car as it passed.

The road outside the gate was flat and wide. Gao caught a glimpse in the side mirror of the trailing vehicles dropping back and staggering their positions to the left and right for optimum fields of fire.

Gao's thoughts cast back to the invasion of Taiwan. He'd dealt with insurgencies before. That, he supposed, was the reason why the General Secretary wanted him for this job. His experience.

Still, the intelligence briefing he'd been given about the Seljuk Islamic Front was long on conjecture and short on facts. It was hard to believe the PLA had not taken a hostage or secured a single spy within the insurgent ranks since the SIF started their attacks over a year ago. He would investigate that right away, Gao decided.

"We're here, sir." Fang's announcement interrupted Gao's train of thought.

The tactical group sped past a row of construction equipment and topped a rise overlooking the work site. It drew abreast of a group of trailers and stopped abruptly. A knot of men, some in business suits and some in work clothes, waited. A cloud of dust from their passage washed over the waiting men.

Fang pointed out the window. "The one on the right, in the yellow hardhat, is the foreman. He's the problem. His boss is in the suit next to him." She looked at Gao and smiled. "They're brothers."

Without waiting for his reply, Captain Fang opened the door and jumped down to the ground. Gao climbed out after her. Fang strode to the man in the suit and introduced Gao in English.

The man's dark blue suit was covered in a fine sheen of tan dust. He shook Gao's hand in both of his and offered an oily smile. The brother in the hardhat glared at Gao when he shook his hand. He refused to look at Fang.

The suit gestured toward the trailer. "Come in, General."

"That won't be necessary," Fang replied. "The general just arrived in the country. He came here immediately to find out why work has stopped."

"The security issue—" began the suit.

"There is no security issue, Mr. Hasanov," Fang interrupted. "What you found was a decoy. The bomb was inoperable." She looked at the other brother. "But I think you both knew that already."

Apparently, the second brother did not speak English well enough to follow the conversation. When his suited brother filled him in, the man flushed an angry red. Gao watched as Hardhat said something to his brother in Tajik. He cut a look at Fang and Gao. Even though Gao had no idea what the words meant, the biting tone was clear.

Then Fang replied, fluently, in the same language.

If the stakes hadn't been so high, the effect would have been comical. The suit's mouth gaped open and he went pale. His brother in the hardhat froze. He glared at Fang.

She let them dangle for a full ten seconds. Then without taking her eyes off the pair, she spoke to Gao in rapid-fire Mandarin, pitched low.

"It's a shakedown, sir. They want to raise their rates. And their remarks about us were . . . unkind. May I handle this, General?"

Gao nodded.

Fang took a step toward the brothers and unleashed on them in a stream of Tajik. Their eyes fell to the dirt and they hung their heads like children called before the school principal. When she finished speaking, they nodded together.

She turned back to her commanding officer. "My recommendation is you agree to overlook this incident as long as they get their crews back to work immediately."

Fang stepped back until she was a pace behind Gao. "Tell them to look at me," he said.

The two men raised their faces. They were beaten and they knew it.

"I am a busy man," he began in Mandarin, allowing Fang to translate. "You have disrespected my time and my staff. However, I will let this incident pass as long as you resume work and make up for the lost half-day of progress—out of your own pockets."

Five minutes later, they were back in their vehicle speeding toward the PLA base. Gao let out a laugh of relief.

"You speak Tajik, Captain Fang," he said.

"Only when required, sir. It's a skill best kept for emergencies."

"Like this one?"

Fang inclined her head modestly, but her eyes twinkled with amusement. "It's my job to make the general look good, especially on his first day in the country."

"Thank you," Gao said, and he meant it. Fang had turned a potential disaster into a political coup.

He looked out the window at the Gissar Mountains and the white peaks. Now, he needed to turn his attention to the SIF.

"Captain Fang?"

"Sir?"

"How did you know that the IED was a fake?"

Her lips peeled from her teeth in a hard smile that had no humor in it.

"I didn't."

14

Moscow, Russia

Nikolay had conflicting feelings about his private residence near the Kremlin. In his mind, he still thought of it as Uncle Vitaly's house, and with that fact came an emotional baggage train.

On the other hand, he'd been coming here for as long as he could remember. In the entire city of Moscow, it was the only place he could call home.

The official residence of the Russian President was in Novo-Ogaryevo, west of Moscow. A palatial estate built by a grand duke in the nineteenth century, it was perfect for state functions and photo shoots. It was exactly what one expected the residence of the Russian President would look like. But it was also old and drafty and a long drive from the Kremlin.

So, Nikolay did what his uncle had done: He lived a quiet, if lonely, existence in a small, unassuming house only a few minutes from work. He kept a low profile in this neighborhood, using only a small security detail, his valet Yuri, and Magda the cook.

Nikolay liked to take his breakfast in the kitchen with Magda. She was a wizened stump of a woman with the round, crinkled face of a peasant and the heart of a grandmother. She'd fed Nikolay since he was a boy.

The abrupt retirement of Uncle Vitaly seemed not to have bothered the old woman at all. Her job was to make nourishing food for great men. What they did outside her kitchen didn't matter a whit.

Leaders came and went, but everyone needed to eat.

Nikolay liked to keep breakfast simple. Coffee and kasha. He ate at the kitchen counter in his pajamas and bathrobe. The windows were still dark, but the dimly lit kitchen was warm and snug. Magda hummed softly as she busied herself at the stove.

Nikolay breathed deeply. It was an early spring morning, with the last bit of winter in the outside air, which made the room seem even cozier. On mornings like this, he could forget he was the President of the Russian Federation and enjoy a few moments of peace.

He thought about how his life might be different if he had a wife. Someone he could confide in, someone to keep him warm in body and soul through the gray Moscow winters. But female companionship had never come easy for him. He'd always been too focused on his career.

Just like your uncle, said an accusing voice in the back of his mind.

Except Uncle Vitaly had created a family by adopting his nephew. The same nephew who years later would depose his adopted father.

Nikolay poured warm milk over his saucer of buckwheat porridge and stirred in a scoop of brown sugar. The first spoonful was halfway to his mouth when his mobile phone lit up with an incoming message. He put the spoon back down and touched the screen.

Breaking News: Bomb explodes in Leninsky Prospekt metro station.

Nikolay blinked at the screen. A subway bombing? In Moscow?

"Magda," he said quietly, "turn on the television please."

The glare of the screen bounced off the dark windows. The sound shattered the stillness of the peaceful kitchen as the announcer, a woman with a severe haircut and a dark business suit, read the news with the grimness the moment deserved.

A bombing during morning rush hour in a crowded subway station. The announcer cut to a live feed of first-responder vehicles, lights flashing, jamming the wide boulevard at Gagarin Square. Smoke poured from the metro entrance.

Magda's thick fingers gripped the gold cross on her generous bosom. Her lips moved in silent prayer.

"Yuri," Nikolay called out to his valet.

No response.

Nikolay slid off the stool, his eyes still on the TV.

"Yuri!" he shouted.

When there was no response the second time, Nikolay shifted his attention to Magda.

"Tell the security detail I want my car outside in five minutes."

As the cook scurried away, he gulped down the rest of his coffee and shoved a spoonful of porridge into his mouth.

He was crossing the foyer toward his bedroom when Magda reappeared. She skidded to a halt, her lined face pale with fear.

"There's no one outside," she said. "The security detail—"

Nikolay didn't hear her last words. He was already running for the private office at the back of the house, fear lending him speed he did not know he had.

No security detail...His mind froze with terror. *They're coming for me.*

He ran. His bare feet slapped against the hardwood floors as he threw himself through the doorway and heaved the door closed behind him. He slammed home the heavy deadbolt and pressed his forehead against the steel reinforced door.

His robe had come undone in the scramble and he'd lost his slippers, but he was safe.

For now.

He breathed a sigh of gratitude for his paranoid uncle who had set up his private office as a safe room.

Panic room was more like it, Nikolay thought as he tried to calm his racing heart. His armpits were soaked in cold sweat and his knees felt rubbery.

He held his breath and pressed the intercom button so he could hear what was going on outside. He half expected to hear the blast of a breaching charge and the rush of booted feet in the halls of his private home . . .

But all was quiet.

Nikolay cinched the belt of his robe closed. Somehow pajamas and bare feet made him feel vulnerable.

Think!

He forced himself into action.

Nikolay crossed to the heavy desk in the corner of the room and sat down. He placed his shaking hands flat upon the surface. White skin on dark wood. He pressed them harder against the desktop and breathed deeply until the tremors subsided. Then he opened the bottom drawer and withdrew the MP-443 Grach. He pulled the magazine, confirmed it was full, slammed it home, and chambered a round.

Then he laid the weapon on the desk and called Federov.

"It's me," Federov's soft voice sounded tinny through the intercom. "I checked the house. It's safe."

Nikolay took a deep breath and threw the deadbolt. He pulled the door open and let it swing back against the wall. He'd found a pair of sweatpants and a T-shirt in the closet that had belonged to Uncle Vitaly. They were too small, but they were better than pajamas and a bathrobe. He was still in his bare feet.

He felt like a fool. An angry fool.

"What happened to my security detail?" Nikolay snapped. "And Yuri, where was Yuri?"

Federov cast a look behind him and made a dismissive gesture. Then he stepped inside and closed the door behind him.

"You need to calm down, Mr. President," he said.

"Calm down? Are you fucking serious?"

Federov walked to the bar, poured a shot of vodka, and handed it to the Russian President. "Drink."

Nikolay did as he was told. Even at room temperature, the vodka hit his empty stomach like a punch. A few seconds later, he felt a warm glow spreading from his belly. He handed the glass back.

"I apologize, Vladimir." He stopped. "How is Magda?"

As he said the words, Nikolay felt a flush of shame creep up his cheeks. He'd left the old woman to fend for herself as he ran for his hiding place.

"Worried about you," Federov replied. "She understands you did what you had to do."

"Of course." Nikolay looked away. The safe room suddenly felt small. Was this what he'd been reduced to? Hiding in his own home?

"Yuri received a text message this morning at 0600, just before you came down to breakfast. Your new shoes were ready. He went to pick them up and got delayed. The text was real, as were the shoes." Federov shrugged his heavy shoulders. "The delay? Debatable."

"And the security detail?" Nikolay demanded.

"They were relieved at 0615 by the day shift. They said they didn't recognize the new team so they called for verification. It checked out. Yuri said he saw the new team outside the door when he left a few minutes later."

"Where are they now?" Nikolay asked.

It was Federov's turn to avert his eyes. "We'll find them, Mr. President. I will rescreen the security personnel and any schedule change will be approved by me. It won't happen again."

Nikolai returned to the desk and sat down. These people, whoever they were, had managed to strip away his security defenses with seeming ease. He'd been left unprotected in his own home.

"Why wasn't there an attack?" he asked.

Federov's shoulders heaved again. "Maybe something happened and they scrubbed the mission. Maybe . . ." His voice trailed off.

"Maybe they were sending a message," Nikolay finished for him.

Federov nodded.

Nikolay had another sensation in his gut now. Warm, but not from the alcohol. "Who?" he said.

The FSB chief's attention was on the muted television.

Nikolay found the remote and turned up the volume.

A popular morning talk show host faced the camera. Valentina Baranova was in her late twenties with a penchant for plunging necklines and short, tight skirts. She had something for every demographic. The women loved her style, the men loved . . . Well, the men appreciated her style in their own way. To add to this devastating combination, she was a brilliant interviewer who always managed to get just a bit more out of her subjects than they'd planned to reveal.

The camera drew back, revealing her guest. Konstantin Zaitsev, leader of the Ultra Faction in the Russian Federation Council, was dressed in a charcoal gray suit and pale blue silk tie. He had stylishly cut blonde hair and a rakish cant to his chin. He was a made-for-TV politician: graceful, charming, and erudite. Somehow, he managed to make even the craziest conspiracy theories sound like reality.

The host crossed her shapely legs and leaned in. Her voice was both probing and seductive at the same time. "Senator Zaitsev, can you tell us who is behind this bombing?"

Zaitsev set his jaw. "You mean the terrorist attacks, Valentina." His gaze swiveled to the camera. "Because that's what these are. Terrorist attacks on the citizens of Moscow. On Mother Russia. Enemies of the state who've been given license to—"

Valentina interrupted his monologue. "Surely you have intelligence briefings, Senator. Can you tell our viewers who has done this to our city?"

Zaitsev sat back in his chair. "That information is classified, and I cannot violate state secrets," he said. "But I can tell you who you should be asking that question to."

Wait for it, Nikolay thought.

"President. Nikolay. Sokolov," he intoned, a clocklike emphasis on each word.

And there it was.

"Under his leadership, every aspect of Russian life has deteriorated. Our economy has struggled, morale among the public sector is in the toilet, and now the safety of our children is under attack. How long are we going to let this go on?"

"You sound like you're making a political speech, Senator," the host said coyly. "Are you?"

"I love my country." Zaitsev's face was grave. "It pains me to see her suffer like this at the hands of a hapless leader who seized power from his own family."

"President Sokolov was elected," the interviewer replied.

"Fake news," Zaitsev countered in a dismissive tone. "We all saw what happened with our own eyes. He deposed his uncle, the greatest living leader in Russian history, then rigged an election, which he won by a landslide. Does that sound possible?" He leaned toward the host. "I didn't vote for him, Valentina. Did you? Did anyone you know? So where did this landslide come from?"

The host smiled at him. "New elections are happening in just a few months."

"We need to save our country from this weak man—"

Nikolay turned off the television. The silence in the room rang with accusation.

"Was it him, Vladimir?" he asked.

Federov shook his head. "I don't know. Yet."

Nikolay struggled to form the words, fearful that if he said them out loud, they might be true. "What about . . . ?"

Federov's features contracted into a scowl. He knew exactly who Nikolay was talking about.

Uncle Vitaly.

"Is it possible?" Nikolay pressed.

Federov met his gaze. "I don't know," he said finally.

Nikolay sat back in the chair, the soft leather of the cushions cold against the bare skin of his arms.

The warmth in his gut crystallized into hot, sharp anger. Whatever his fate, he was not going to meet it hiding in his office behind a locked door.

He stood suddenly, the force of movement slamming the desk chair back against the credenza.

"Have my car outside in fifteen minutes," Nikolay ordered.

Federov met his gaze with steady resolve. They had both been caught unawares this morning. For whatever reason, they'd been handed a second chance.

It was up to them to use it.

15

Bishkek, Kyrgyzstan

Harrison Kohl ordered his second beer before he'd finished his first. When the new glass of Heineken arrived, he drained his first in one long gulp and moved right to the replacement.

It had been that kind of day.

Somehow, he reflected as the level in his glass lowered, he'd forgotten just how lonely life in the field could be.

His gaze stole toward the mobile phone on the bar next to him. Harrison shook off the sense of creeping guilt.

He should update Jenny on his progress—or lack of it—but he dreaded the thought. Every time he talked to her, he tried to think of some way to keep the hope alive.

I'm doing everything I can, Jenny. No leads yet, but I'll keep trying. I won't come home until I find him.

He never actually said "dead or alive" after that last bit, but it hung in the background of every conversation now like a dirty secret. If he never said the words, then they might not be true.

Harrison took another gulp of beer. True to his word, the CIA Chief of Station in Tashkent had made introductions into the shadier side of business in the region. Harrison knew that he was dealing with drug dealers and human traffickers and gun runners, but at this point he didn't care. He needed answers, and if that meant operating outside the lines to get them . . . well, he would do whatever it took.

Without consulting Jenny, he'd settled on a $25,000 bounty for information on the whereabouts of Tim Trujillo. He made sure his contact understood it was cash, U.S. dollars, which made a difference in this part of the world.

Harrison had imagined that kind of money would shake something loose, but so far it had been crickets.

These things take time, the station chief told him. *You must be patient.*

But that didn't make the waiting any easier. He'd exhausted every bit of technology and special access at his disposal to find his best friend. All that was left now was to grind it out.

Harrison made a pact with himself. He would not leave Central Asia until he had gotten to the bottom of Tim's disappearance. If it happened—*when* it happened, he corrected himself—it would be a combination of shoe leather and luck.

There was nothing he could do about the luck part, so he resolved to try harder. Stay on the move and run down every lead, no matter how small. At the very least, the constant action beat the hell out of sitting on his ass in Tashkent waiting for something to happen.

He had returned to Bishkek for two reasons: one, it was the last place Tim had visited before Tashkent, and two, it was at least in the general direction of the last mysterious ping on Tim's mobile.

Harrison had devoted a lot of brain power to that last event. A single ping on a single mobile tower in the middle of the night. Without at least one more tower to localize the signal, it was next to useless. It could have been anywhere inside of hundreds of square miles, most of which was a national park.

The experts told him it was likely just an errant connection. A lucky coincidence of atmospheric disturbance and location. A ghost in the machine.

Harrison had attacked the airport side of the problem multiple times. He'd even paid off an employee to get access to the flight records from the day Tim vanished. No aircraft had been registered in the system as having landed or taken off after 2300 the night of Tim's disappearance.

Harrison studied his beer. He tried to imagine what Tim might have done if his flight was cancelled.

Get a car, he decided. His mission-oriented, Type-A friend would have found another way to get to his next destination. He imagined Tim driving through the mountains at night. When he reached an elevated place on the road, his phone might have connected briefly with a mobile tower hundreds of kilometers away.

Unlikely, but possible, the experts told him.

Harrison paid for his beers. "Quiet tonight, huh?" he said to the bartender.

The young man rolled his eyes. "Crazy Russians. I hate them, but their money is good."

The prior evening, the streets around the Osh Bazaar, where the bar was located, had been flooded with Russian soldiers on liberty.

Harrison had talked to a few of them. The Russian 31st Guards Airborne Brigade was on maneuvers with the Kyrgyzstan 25th Special Forces Brigade. It was mostly for show, the soldiers told him. Their equipment was old and they were chronically short of fuel and ammunition. Like soldiers all over the world, they were convinced that their generals had their heads firmly up their collective asses. They were more than happy to talk to Harrison as long as he kept buying beers—and he was more than happy to listen.

His hangover in the morning had been a timely reminder that he was no longer twenty, and that drinking the night away with Russians was a bad decision at any age.

He stepped outside, mobile phone in hand. If he made the call on the busy street, maybe that would give him a reason to keep it short. Every time he called Jenny, it gutted him. He had no more words to console her and no good news to share.

The evening outside matched Harrison's mood. Gray and drizzly. No matter how many layers you put on, the kind of raw dampness from a night like this one cut through them all.

At least he wasn't freezing his butt off in the field like those Russian soldiers.

Two men, their heads covered by Muslim *tubeteika* skullcaps, pushed by him, nearly knocking him over. Harrison called after them in frustration, but neither turned around. On the street, traffic was stopped and people were getting out of their cars, trying to see what the hold-up was.

Harrison followed their gazes. A block away, at the intersection of the Osh Bazaar, people spilled off the sidewalk into the street in a solid mass.

Harrison snugged the zipper of his rain shell closer to his neck and followed. *A car accident?* he wondered. His mind flashed on the car bomb in Tashkent, the memory suddenly fresh. Harrison stopped, his eyes sweeping the street. The buildings in this part of town were four and five stories high, solid walls that would amplify the effect of an explosion.

Two young women, mobile phones in hand, rushed by him. He caught the Russian word for "army."

"What's happening?" Harrison called.

"They caught him," one of them shouted over her shoulder.

"Caught who?"

But they were gone.

Against his better judgment, he went with the flow of pedestrian traffic. No one seemed to understand exactly what was happening, but they all seemed eager to get there.

When the forward movement slowed, then stopped, Harrison reassessed. Traffic was stopped all four ways, and the crowd had formed a rough circle in the intersection. The headlights from a few cars blazed into the open space and Harrison could make out shadows of people as they walked across the beams of illumination.

He shouldered his way through the crowd, ignoring the muttered curses behind him. When he got to the edge of the ring, he sucked in a breath.

A well-used Land Rover was parked in the center of the open area. A scuffed steel pushbar jutted out from the front of the vehicle.

A young man, stripped to the waist, was bound to the pushbar, his arms spread wide. He had short blond hair and his face was bloody. His feet were bare, bone white in the glare of the headlights. His butt hung two feet off the ground, his body suspended by his bindings.

Harrison focused on the pants. Camouflage, the kind worn by soldiers in the field.

The kid was a Russian soldier.

Facing Harrison, a young woman, maybe seventeen years old, clad in conservative Muslim dress, knelt on the ground. Her hijab had been pulled away and droplets of rain shone in her shoulder-length dark hair. An older man, probably her father, stood next to her, his face dark with anger and shame.

The lights shifted as another man strode across the headlight beams. He was on the short side and stout. He wore the traditional Muslim head covering and the robes of a mullah, and he was shouting.

The words were in native Kyrgyz, but Harrison didn't need a direct translation to get the picture.

There was going to be a lynching.

The holy man raised his arms and shouted, flecks of spittle falling like diamonds in the illuminated vapor of his breath. A mist of rain blew through the open space like a shimmering veil.

Harrison looked around. Where were the cops? He remembered there was a police station a few blocks away. He got out his mobile and dialed 102, the emergency number for the police.

The phone lines were jammed. Harrison looked around. Every person in the crowd had a phone out, ready to record what was coming next. The holy man screamed again and this time the crowd roared in response.

Harrison's mind reeled. If they killed this soldier, there would be an international incident, maybe even a war. The Russians would be forced to respond.

The holy man reached under his robes and produced a long, curved knife.

Holy crap, he was about to see some Russian kid get carved up like a Thanksgiving turkey.

"Let me through!" he shouted in Russian, but no one moved.

The mob screamed again, then the sound died away. When Harrison looked up, he saw the people on the other side of the ring part. A man strode into the circle of light.

The newcomer was tall, with a three-day scruff of salt-and-pepper beard. His head was bare and he was dressed in blue jeans and a puffy jacket.

Although he looked like a tourist, he clearly was anything but. He completely ignored the holy man, who stared at him in amazement as the newcomer crossed to the Russian soldier and knelt on the wet pavement.

The stranger took the young man's pulse and peeled back an eyelid. Then he stood and faced the mullah, who was still holding the knife.

"Let this man go," he ordered in Russian.

The holy man stared back, his face slack with disbelief. The staring contest went on for a full ten seconds. In the silence, Harrison could hear the hiss of rain. Then the mullah broke. He stepped to the truck and cut the kid's bonds. The young Russian slid to the wet pavement.

The man reached out to the kneeling girl. She looked at his hand, then gripped his fingers and stood, trembling. He said something to her and she nodded. The man spoke to the father. "You have been wronged?"

"I have." The father's eyes welled up.

The man nodded as if he was considering the answer. He produced a mobile phone from the pocket of his jacket and offered it to the father. "Call the police," he said. "Report a crime."

The father hesitated, then took the phone.

The police must have been standing by, because they showed up in what seemed like only a few seconds. It was a team of six officers, four of them in full riot gear. They advanced into the circle. Two of them got the soldier on his feet and they left.

The crowd did not move. They stood in the cold rain as if mesmerized by this man who'd just walked in on a mob and stopped the violence without even raising his voice.

Who was this guy? Harrison wondered.

"We are better than this," the man said. His tone of voice was conversational, but it carried throughout the silent throng. He indicated the father. "This man was wronged. His anger is justified. His anger is righteous. But" —he slashed his hand down—"we are not animals."

He paused, casting a glance at the holy man who seemed to deflate before him.

"My name is Timur Ganiev. Like many of you, I am a proud descendant of the first peoples of this land. That man was Russian, an outsider. He was here because a long time ago some politician drew a line on a map and said, on this side of the border, we are one country, and on the other side, we are a different country. They divided us.

"I do not care about their borders. My people—your people—were here first. Our forefathers founded these great cities and they built these great roads. I do not care if you are Uzbek, or Kyrgyz, or Tajik, or Turkmen—you are part of this land, part of this culture, and you deserve better."

A murmur swept through the crowd like a shiver. Harrison felt it, too, like a living presence slipping between the pressed bodies.

Timur Ganiev pointed behind him, the way the police had gone when they took the soldier away.

"That young man, that Russian soldier, I do not know if he is guilty. That is a legal matter. It is not my concern. But his presence here *is* my concern."

He paced now, circling the open space. People reached out to touch him as he passed them.

"I know one thing: this land—our land—is no place for Russian soldiers. That is the real crime here, and the only way we can make it right is by standing together."

The chant started somewhere behind Harrison. It started softly, building until the syllables echoed off the walls of the building and rang in the street.

Ti-mur . . . Ti-mur . . . Ti-mur . . .

Ganiev, smiling in the light of a thousand mobile phone screens, pumped his fist in time to the chanting.

Then he shouted, "This is our land!" and the chants echoed his words, louder and louder.

16

New Delhi, India

Whenever Don had worked in South Asia before, he'd always relied on senior operators or contractors to guide him through the local issues and logistics.

But this visit was different. He was here to deliver a message—alone. For all the technology available to the leaders of the world, at the end of the day, decisions were made by people—and sometimes it took a face-to-face meeting to make things happen.

Don scarcely slept on the long flight from Washington to New Delhi. At first, he'd used the time to prep for his meeting at the Indian Research and Analysis Wing, usually referred to as RAW, the Indian equivalent of the CIA. He was scheduled to meet with the Secretary of Special Operations. Director Blank had set up the appointment personally, assuring Don that Jay Patel was a "good egg," whatever that meant. It didn't matter; Don would form his own opinion of Patel.

As it did on so many nights, sleep eluded him, and he sat for the rest of the flight staring out the window. He watched dawn break over the eastern horizon, then saw the day age into noon as he turned over the bits and pieces of data he had about the situation in Central Asia. There were too many unknowns to even form a hypothesis yet and that frustrated Don.

In his opinion, reaching out to the Indians this early was a mistake. There was no intel to suggest that the Indians were involved with the Seljuk Islamic Front.

But what other option did he have? Building an actionable intelligence network was a long-term investment, and he needed answers now.

By the time they landed in New Delhi shortly after noon, he'd consumed far too much coffee and his eyes felt as if they'd been rubbed with sandpaper. Don left his security detail behind as he climbed into the car provided by Secretary Patel.

Outside the tinted window of his limousine, India was a riot of foreign sounds and smells. The armored sedan was quiet, a welcome shield to the sensory assault outside. The driver and the security man in the front did not engage in small talk.

Don thought he was familiar with bad traffic, but New Delhi took it to a whole new level. Cars choked the road, belching thick black diesel exhaust. It wasn't so much the number of vehicles that alarmed him as it was the free-for-all nature of navigation. Cars snaked through traffic as if the lines on the pavement did not exist. Horns were more common than brakes, reminding Don to make sure his seatbelt was securely fastened.

Don's driver, a young man in a white shirt and dark tie, seemed unperturbed by the chaos. He wound the limousine through the crush of cars, trucks, minibikes, and tuk-tuks, even driving on the sidewalk at one point. He left the highway and descended into a warren of side streets, expertly navigating the heavy car through local traffic without once touching the horn.

They emerged into another world of wide, treelined boulevards lined with orderly multistory office buildings.

"This is the CGO," the driver said. "Central government office complex."

Traffic here was lighter and followed the lines painted on the roadway and traffic signals. The driver used his turn signal to enter the portico of a large office building that bore the insignia of the Indian intelligence service, a pair of olive branches surrounding the country's national emblem. The building was unremarkable, a long rectangle, nine stories tall. The white exterior was dulled by a layer of dust.

A young woman with a thick plait of black hair dressed in a dark blue blazer, matching pencil skirt, and sensible shoes awaited them. She looked up from her smartphone as the car pulled up and opened Don's door.

"Good afternoon, Mr. Riley," she said in English. "My name is Asha. Secretary Patel is expecting you." She handed him a visitor's badge to clip on his lapel as Don got out of the vehicle.

Even though it was still technically spring, it was already in the mid-eighties and humid. Don felt himself perspiring as they climbed the steps. Asha held open the door for him and guided him around the security checkpoint.

Don was impressed by the efficiency of the visit. Asha even had an elevator waiting for them. "Sometimes you have to wait fifteen minutes for a car, but for VIPs, we can reserve one," she explained.

The scene that greeted him when the elevator doors opened was a familiar one. An open floor plan showed rows of analysts at work on computers. Don glimpsed a satellite photo on one screen as Asha whisked him toward a row of offices that lined the walls.

Despite the similarities, Don knew there were key differences between the American CIA and the Indian Research and Analysis Wing. While both had similar missions, RAW was part of the Cabinet Secretariat, which reported to the Prime Minister. Unlike the American CIA, which had oversight from the legislative branch, there was no parliamentary oversight for the RAW. Don wondered how different his job would be if he didn't have to brief Congress on all of the CIA's operations.

Asha took him directly into Secretary Patel's office—no waiting in the lobby—further raising Don's hope for a fruitful meeting.

Jayesh Patel was in his mid-sixties and a few inches shorter than Don. He was on the stout side, but he moved with purpose. His features had a ruggedness that made him seem like a man of action. He greeted Don with a warm handshake and a ready smile.

"How is Sam?" Patel asked. "I know how he hates election season. Who am I kidding? These days it seems like every year is election season. It's the same way here."

Patel laughed at his own joke, but Don was surprised at his willingness to make a political comment to someone he'd just met. The Director hadn't being lying when he described Jay as a man who spoke his mind.

"The Director sends his regards," Don said.

"Does he still live in Annapolis?" Patel asked as a coffee service arrived.

"He does." Don gratefully accepted a cup of black coffee.

"I used to stay with him when I visited the U.S.," Patel said. "I loved the view of the Naval Academy from his back porch. Once upon a time, I wanted to be a naval officer."

"So did I." Don's hackles were up now. Did this man know that he'd once attended the Naval Academy and medically washed out?

But Patel seemed relaxed. He stirred his coffee, then sat back in his chair and crossed his legs. "We could go on about the beauty of the Chesapeake Bay all morning, Don, but I don't suppose you flew all this way to talk about the weather in Annapolis. If Sam sent you, it must be important."

"I have a request, Mr. Secretary," Don said.

Patel's eyebrows raised. "Now I am intrigued. Sam Blank sends his protégé halfway around the world to ask a favor. He must be desperate."

You have no idea, Don thought.

"We want you to back off in Central Asia."

Patel's face did not move. "I think perhaps you should explain that comment."

Don took a deep breath. "We have reason to believe your organization is involved with the Seljuk Islamic Front."

Patel's eyes shifted, but his smile remained firmly in place. "I can see now why Sam sent you. You don't mess around, do you, Mr. Riley?"

Don said nothing.

Patel's eyes narrowed. "It's more than that. You're fishing, aren't you? Show me your proof and I'll do what you ask."

"I can't do that, Jay. Sources and methods."

Patel belly laughed. "Sam always did have a sense of humor. If you pulled that crap with anyone else in this building, they'd make you walk back to the airport."

"But not you?"

"I enjoy a good joke, Don. Even if it's at someone else's expense."

"So, you're not involved with the SIF?"

"The SIF is a godsend as far as I'm concerned," Patel replied. "They're slowing down the Chinese in a part of the world that always seems to be too far down anyone's to-do list to care."

"Does that mean you're not supporting them?" Don asked.

"That's what it means, Don." Patel's voice was matter-of-fact, and Don found himself believing him.

"Nothing at all? What about intelligence? Or third-party funding?"

"My organization has not provided one rupee to the SIF and we don't have any intelligence sharing going on. We're not training any of them, and we're not providing weapons, explosives, or any other support. Is that a clear enough statement for you? I want you to tell my friend Sam those very words."

Don sipped his coffee to give himself a moment to think. Patel's response was not a carefully parsed answer. It was a flat-out denial with no room for negotiation.

Don sifted through other possibilities—none of them good.

The Iranians were always looking to stir up trouble, but to what end? The road and rail projects went through Central Asia to Tehran. The Chinese were offering a welcome economic and influence boost in the region for Islamic Republic of Iran.

The Taliban was always a possibility. The border between Afghanistan and the Central Asian republics was long and porous. Chinese influence meant a loss of control for the more devout brand of Islam peddled by the Taliban hardliners.

"You look troubled, Don," Patel said.

"I am," Don admitted.

Patel leaned forward. "Perhaps I can help."

Don studied the man's face. What did he have to lose?

"You have to admit that India is the most likely supporter for the SIF, Jay."

Patel nodded. "As I said, they are doing God's work, as far as I'm concerned." He paused. "But maybe you're ignoring the most obvious answer."

"Which is?" Don felt the effect of jet lag coming on. His thought processes downshifted and drowsiness set in.

"You're assuming that there's some outside influence at work behind the SIF. That's a very imperialist attitude, Don. Isn't it possible that the movement is entirely homegrown?"

Don looked hard at Patel. He was right. It could indeed be a homegrown terrorist group. Perhaps headed by someone who really understood the region, and understood how insurgencies could be built and run. Someone with intelligence training.

Someone like Akhmet Orazov.

The meeting ended as quickly as it had begun. Asha reappeared as Patel stood, and moments later Don was back in the limo. He mulled what had taken place as his driver plunged through the New Delhi afternoon traffic.

His gut told him that Patel was telling the truth. His mind went back to Patel's statement about the SIF bring entirely homegrown.

Don let his head loll back into the headrest. He kept coming up against the same barrier: lack of data.

There was only one way to break this logjam.

"Road trip," he muttered to himself.

Don pulled out his mobile phone and dialed Harrison's number.

17

En route to Tashkent, Uzbekistan

"The information we have right now is sparse, sir," Don said into the secure phone on the CIA plane.

On the other end of the connection, the Director stayed silent.

Don studied the laptop screen. Calling their intel *sparse* was lipstick on a pig. All he really had were the basic facts: The head of the Tajik Air Force, a man named Farzann Rakhimov, had been assassinated in broad daylight, gunned down only a few kilometers outside the capital of Dushanbe. There were no survivors, and a flag bearing the insignia of the Seljuk Islamic Front had been left behind.

While these facts were bad enough, the political reality of the situation was much worse. Rakhimov was first cousin to the current President of Tajikistan and a vocal supporter of the Russian military. In one bold move, the SIF had not only struck at the heart of Tajikistan's government, but they had also attacked Russia's most reliable ally in the region. The fallout for Nikolay Sokolov in Moscow would be bad.

"I was hoping for more, Don," the Director said. He was on his way to the White House to brief President Serrano.

"I'm landing in Tashkent in thirty minutes, sir," Don said. "I'll get a full briefing from the Chief of Station when I land. I'll call you with anything new."

Don hoped that was the end of the conversation, but the Director shifted topics. "How did the meeting with Jay Patel go?"

Although the meeting had been only a few hours earlier, it already seemed like a long time ago.

"I'm not sure," Don admitted. He sketched out the encounter with the RAW Secretary, concluding with Patel's flat-out denial of having any connection with the SIF.

"Do you believe him?" the Director asked.

That is the question, Don thought. The whole point of him flying halfway around the world to meet with someone for less than an hour.

"I do, sir," Don said finally. "I think he was being straight with me."

"So where does that leave us with the SIF?" the Director asked. "They're escalating. A car bomb in Tashkent and now an assassination of a senior military officer in broad daylight. If we don't do something, this whole region could blow up."

Don let the comment hang in the silence. The President had made it perfectly clear that he did not want to get the US involved. They'd agreed to share intel with the Russians, and that was it.

The Fasten Seatbelt sign flashed on. "I'll call you after my briefing, sir. Maybe the Chief of Station will have something new we can work with."

Don stowed his laptop and turned his attention to the view outside his window.

They approached from the southwest, the afternoon sun behind them spreading golden light across the city of Tashkent. To the east, snowcapped mountain ranges framed the horizon. To the west, it was grassland and cultivated fields as far as he could see.

Although this modern city was home to some three million people, about the size of Chicago, people had lived at this site for over two thousand years. Don saw skyscrapers glinting in the afternoon sun as the jet lined up for its final landing approach.

The CIA Gulfstream touched down with hardly a bump and taxied off the runway. The airport looked brand-new. As they rolled toward the private air terminal, he could see the roofline of the airport's main terminal was constructed to look like irregularly shaped white points poking up. Against the backdrop of the snow-covered Tian Shan range, the effect was one of natural harmony.

When the plane stopped, he saw Harrison leaning against the side of a black SUV.

His friend was dressed in hiking boots and blue jeans. A windbreaker and sunglasses completed the outfit. Even from this distance, Don could see that Harrison was worn out. His shoulders slumped and he seemed to sag against the vehicle.

A stiff breeze greeted Don at the open door, cutting through his thin sport coat. The sun was bright after the dim cabin, and he squinted as he made his way down the steps.

Harrison wrapped him in a bear hug, which surprised Don. Harrison had never struck him as a hugger, but the man seemed genuinely glad to see him.

They climbed into the SUV. Harrison noticed Don studying the airline terminal. "That's the latest Chinese Belt and Road project. Pretty impressive, huh?"

Don nodded. It was one thing to read cold statistics on paper about the size and scope of an infrastructure project, but it was another to see it up close and personal.

"How are things back at ETG?" Harrison asked with an air of forced casualness.

Don sighed. "Honestly, I couldn't tell you. I've got bigger fish to fry." He changed topics. "Have you found your friend?"

Harrison looked glum. He shook his head. "Not a trace. I feel like a dog chasing his tail. I even put a bounty out on the gray market for information. Nothing."

"Sorry to hear that," Don replied. He wanted to ask if that meant Harrison was coming home, but he held his tongue.

"How well do you know the Chief of Station here?" Harrison asked.

"Shalikashvili?" Don answered. "Only by reputation. Why? You've got some advice for me?"

"He's got a hard-on for the SIF," he said. "He's going to push for direct action."

Don digested that nugget of information. A presidentially sanctioned covert action in the region was not in the cards. "I'll hear him out," was all he said.

Harrison nodded at the windshield. "We're here."

The United States Embassy in Tashkent was an imposing, three-story building constructed of tan stone and set on a parklike campus of several acres. A ten-foot-high stone wall ran the perimeter of the property. Don could make out satellite dishes peeking over the roofline. Bollards, fences, and a pair of guardhouses made up the layered defenses at the security checkpoint.

They were immediately cleared through and less than fifteen minutes later, Don and Harrison were seated at a long table in a conference room with a cup of coffee and a briefing book. The Tashkent operation was efficient. He'd scarcely had time to use the restroom and splash some water on his face.

With his bespoke pinstripe suit, polished wingtips, and stylish silk tie, Chief of Station Roger Shalikashvili struck Don as a dandy. Next to this tall, impeccably dressed man, Don felt like a bum.

"Welcome, Deputy Director Riley," Shalikashvili intoned. Even his voice sounded cultured.

"Thank you. This is my first time in Uzbekistan, but I have a feeling it will not be my last."

The chief's patrician features warped into a smile. "I think not, sir. I have a briefing on the latest action by the SIF."

Don was surprised that the Chief of Station delivered the briefing personally. It took a special blend of personality, brains, and skill to run a CIA operation in a remote corner of the world. He was responsible for the lives and actions of his people, and by extension, his country, on foreign soil. A healthy amount of self-confidence—some might say ego—was part of the job description.

Still, in Don's experience, the best chiefs of station mentored their people, pushing them to develop skills, including briefing senior visitors.

Harrison's forewarning about Shalikashvili and his strong opinions regarding the Seljuk Islamic Front were warranted. The briefing was long on anecdote and short on facts. Moreover, the chief was not shy about what he thought the role of the CIA should be in the region.

"How are they funded?" Don asked. "Do you have any evidence of Indian influence in the SIF's operations?"

"No," Shalikashvili said in a dismissive tone, "but it doesn't matter."

"Why not?" Don pressed.

"The SIF will not stop until you stop this man." He flashed a picture on the screen. "Akhmet Orazov," he continued, "is the beating heart of this terrorist group. You stop him, you stop the attacks. Plain and simple."

He said it like a challenge. When Don did not respond, the chief continued.

"Orazov is a double threat. He was trained by Soviet special forces and he has contacts in the highest levels of Russian government, including Vitaly Luchnik himself. He also has an Iranian half-brother who is very close to the ayatollah. Those connections alone put him in the deplorable category. He was thrown out of the Turkmeni government for corruption right about the same time as the Chinese began ramping up their infrastructure investments in the region. A few months later, the first SIF attacks began."

Don frowned. "So far, I haven't heard anything that directly links Orazov to the SIF."

"Deputy Director, I've got twenty years of experience in this part of the world. Not long ago, I was on the scene of a car bomb in downtown Tashkent at lunchtime . . ." Shalikashvili's paused to compose himself. "It was the most horrible thing I've ever seen. And I've seen some bad stuff in my career. The SIF needs to be stopped. Now. And the way to do it is to take out Orazov."

Don rubbed the three-day stubble on his chin, feeling the sharp whiskers grind into his palm. That was never going to work. Even if the station chief was right, Serrano was not going to greenlight a direct action mission. There had to be another way.

"Can I offer a suggestion?" Harrison asked.

"Please," Shalikashvili said in a voice that indicated anything but welcome.

Harrison addressed the young woman running the laptop for the briefing.

"Miriam, can you pull up the video I showed you earlier?" He leaned back in his chair and crossed his arms. "Just watch this."

The video was taken from a mobile phone and narrated in a language that Don didn't recognize. But he didn't need words to understand what was going on.

It was a nighttime scene. A wall of people formed a ring around a circle of wet pavement, the space lit by car headlights. Police were helping a bare-chested young man to his feet and taking him away.

A man dressed in blue jeans and a puffy jacket seemed to hold the attention of everyone in the area. The crowd was deathly silent as the man spoke. The tone of his voice was reasonable, confident, almost conversational.

"This was three nights ago in Bishkek," Harrison said. "I was there. The guy in the puffy jacket is Timur Ganiev. I guess you'd call him an indigenous activist. The guy on the right is the girl's father. He said a Russian soldier raped his daughter and he took his complaint to the local imam. When I showed up, those guys were leading a mob. I thought they were going to kill the Russian kid."

"What happened?" Don asked.

"Timur happened. Just walked in and stopped the thing cold. It was the most amazing feat of crowd control I've ever seen. He saved that kid's life and he had the mob eating out of his hand in about five minutes."

On the video, the crowd started chanting something.

"What are they saying?" Don asked. "Is that Russian?"

Harrison shook his head. "It's the guy's name. Listen . . . Ti-mur . . . Ti-mur."

"What's your point, Harrison?" the chief's tone dripped with sarcasm. "You're saying we should recruit this guy?"

But Don saw it now. "Not recruit," he said. "Promote."

Shalikashvili's forehead creased. "I don't follow, sir."

"An influence operation," Don replied. "We don't have the mandate or the intel to go after Orazov directly, but what if we fight fire with fire? If we promote Ganiev, we're elevating nonviolence. The SIF has turned from attacking the Chinese to bombing their own people—you said it yourself, Roger."

Shalikashvili's expression softened. "It might work."

Don sat back in his chair. *Best of all, we don't get our hands dirty.*

He turned to Harrison. "How would you feel about coming back to work? You'll get all the time you need to continue your search, but in return, I want you to keep tabs on Ganiev."

Harrison's face showed his indecision. Don knew he was offering him what he wanted most—a field operative position—but his allegiance was to his continued search for his friend.

Don played his final card. Harrison's tourist visa would be expiring soon. "The new position comes with a diplomatic passport, and you'll report directly to me."

Slowly, reluctantly, Harrison nodded.

18

80 kilometers northwest of Dushanbe, Tajikistan

Gao tapped Captain Fang on the arm, motioning for her to pass him the map. In the tight confines of the Changhe Z-8 helicopter, he unfolded the laminated paper until he could view the entire country of Tajikistan.

Amazing. The country didn't have a single straight border. Instead, it looked like an ink blot spilled across the page. The Tajik borders were contorted to fit between Kyrgyzstan and Uzbekistan to the north and west, China to the east, and Afghanistan to the south. With the exception of the Gissar Valley, where the capital of Dushanbe and the PLA air base were located, and the smaller Fergana Valley in the north, the entire country was mountainous.

It was a crystal-clear afternoon. Gao peered out the open side door of the helo at a distant mountain, trying to find the peak on the map. Captain Fang must have realized what he was doing. Her slim finger slid into his field of view and tapped a point much farther to the east than where he was searching.

Gao raised his sunglasses to see the fine print on the map. The map was in English and the peak was labeled as Lenin Peak. Elevation 7,134 m (23,406 ft).

He shook his head. The nonsensical borders, an English map with the highest peaks in the country named for Soviet leaders, it all made sense to him now. The country had no identity of its own. It had been warped into being by centuries of conquest.

He smiled to himself. The People's Republic was just the latest in a long string of conquerors.

Fang's finger appeared again, tapping the grease pencil mark on the laminated map. Gao's eye followed the snaking path of Highway M34 through the mountainous terrain to a dot labeled *Takob*. According to the legend on the map, the tiny black dot was the smallest denotation of a human settlement.

And yet, this miniscule dot was the site of another attack by the SIF. The terrorist organization had gotten increasingly bolder during Gao's time in country. It was a constant shuffle of too few security resources trying to cover almost two thousand kilometers of constantly evolving infrastructure projects.

Despite all the promises he'd received of unlimited support, actual manpower was in short supply. Gao had eight battalions of infantry at his disposal to deploy as he saw fit, but he could have used fifty battalions for a job of this magnitude. He was personally responsible for security across four nations, including over one hundred infrastructure projects, some with thousands of workers at a single site. And that didn't include all the kilometers of new rail lines that were being laid out across the region.

Most of his forces were allocated to major facilities in cities. Airports, railyards, major road connections, and Huawei communications towers. He had put far fewer troops in the field and none at a flyspeck of a mountain town like Takob.

That had proven to be a terrible mistake.

The SIF attacked the tunneling project at Takob. Instead of routing over the pass, which was frequently blocked by winter snows, the Belt and Road northwest spur connecting Dushanbe and Samarkand required punching through kilometers of solid mountain rock. Prior to the attack, the project had been two weeks behind schedule. After the attack, the chief engineer on site refused to even provide an estimated completion date for the project. Gao, who needed to report to Beijing weekly, decided the Takob job site deserved a visit from the general himself.

In his headphones, Gao heard Fang energize the private circuit. "The site will be visible in just a moment, sir."

Gao squinted through the sunlight at the mountains below them. It was a beautiful country, rugged and desolate. On paper, the idea of tunneling through a mountain appeared trivial, but out here, flying over these giant natural wonders, it seemed like an impossible task.

"There." Fang mouthed the word, leaning across his body to point out the open door. It was odd, Gao thought. She wore a helmet, sunglasses, combat uniform, and body armor. Yet, even under all those layers of shapeless masculinity, she had an undeniable sex appeal. Her hair passed by his face and he smelled orange blossoms.

Get a grip, Yichen. You have a wife who loves you and two wonderful children. Don't fuck that up.

For her part, Captain Fang seemed to be unaware of her effect on men. She and Gao worked together every day and she'd never even hinted of anything more than a professional relationship.

Gao edged as far from her as his seatbelt allowed, then keyed his microphone. "Tell the pilot I want to see the job site from the air before we land."

She nodded, switched channels, and spoke to the pilot. The helicopter descended until they were two hundred meters above the ground and then made a slow circuit of the valley.

The village of Takob was a collection of small stone buildings clustered next to the highway. The work encampment associated with the job site easily tripled the town's population. At the far end of the valley, there was a growing mound of crushed rock, presumably tailings from the tunneling operation.

Then he saw the damaged job site.

The face of the mountain looked like a collapsed sandcastle, completely filling one end of the valley. The light breeze picked up a haze of dust that looked like smoke from this height.

Gao turned his gaze up, toward the mountain ridges overlooking the job site. This was ambush country. There could be a platoon of armed men up there and his people would never spot them—until they started firing.

Maybe this visit wasn't such a good idea.

He keyed his mic. "Tell the pilot to put us down and take off again. Watch for an ambush. I don't want to be on the ground long, Captain. Let's get what we came for and get out."

Fang was already on it. The helo descended toward an open area adjoining the lone construction trailer. When it touched down, Fang ordered their four-man security detail out, then climbed out herself. Gao followed as the security team fanned out around them. They ducked low as the helo took off again, running toward the small knot of men waiting for them.

As he straightened up, Gao felt the heat immediately. The bowl of the valley seemed to amplify the sunlight. It was bone dry. Dust danced in the air before him. Apart from the chop of the retreating helo's rotors, the valley was silent.

Gao picked out the site engineer immediately. He was a short man with a paunch and owlish spectacles. He wore a pith helmet against the harsh sun and bright red suspenders. His manner seemed gruff even as Fang introduced them.

"Why are you here, General?" he demanded.

Captain Fang flushed with anger at the man's tone, and a thrill of satisfaction rushed through Gao at her protective instincts. But he decided to take the high road. Gao raised his hand to stop her. "Mr. Shu, please tell me what happened here. I want to help."

The engineer's gaze cut between Fang and the general. He seemed to want to engage Fang, but instead, he clamped his mouth shut, turned, and started off at a brisk pace. Gao hurried after him.

The engineer headed for the pile of tailings, climbing a well-worn path with a vigor that defied his body shape. At the top, he came to an abrupt halt. He removed the pith helmet and wiped his sweaty brow with a damp handkerchief. His face was beet red.

From this vantage, Gao had a view of the entire work site and damaged mountainside. It was one thing to see it from the air, but a ground level view offered a new perspective. Loose rock stretched up hundreds of meters. The engineer pointed at the top.

"The explosion was staggered to not only collapse the tunnel, but also to trigger a landslide. To continue work, I need to remove thousands of tons of rock to reach a stable formation where I can start the boring operation again." He dragged his handkerchief across his sweaty, slicked-down hair and clamped the pith helmet back on his head.

"How long?" Gao asked, suddenly anxious. "What is the delay to the project?"

Shu peered at him through his spectacles, blinking like an owl. "I don't know."

"Then give me your best guess," Gao snapped.

Shu screwed up his features. "Twelve weeks. Optimistic estimate."

Gao felt like he'd been punched in the chest. Twelve weeks? They were already three weeks behind. How was he going to explain an additional delay to Beijing?

"Not acceptable," Gao replied. "How can you do it faster?"

"I was being optimistic, but it all depends on you, General."

"Watch your tone, sir." Even Fang seemed to be losing patience with this obstinate man who spoke in cryptic bursts.

"Captain," Gao said, "I will speak with Engineer Shu alone, please."

Even through Fang's sunglasses, Gao could feel the daggers she was throwing at the dumpy engineer. "Yes, sir." She stalked away down the hill.

Shu watched her go. "I don't like her, General."

"I need you to get back to work, Mr. Shu, as fast as possible. Tell me how I can help."

"I need three times as many men, twice the number of dump trucks and earthmovers," the engineer said.

"Done," Gao said. He would reallocate machinery from other sites. "Can you do better than twelve weeks?"

Shu squinted at Gao. "That depends."

"Depends on what?" Gao asked through clenched teeth.

"Security."

Gao said nothing. In that area, he had much less flexibility. All his inquiries to Beijing for additional military resources fell on deaf ears. He had his battalions, he was told. Make it work.

And yet, military transports landed at the Dushanbe base every day. Gao had seen men and equipment being unloaded and moved into the covered depot on the eastern side of the base. When he tried to gain access, he was politely advised by the base commander to mind his own business. When Gao pushed the issue, he was ordered to back off—by a *three*-star general in Beijing. The forces in that part of the base, he was told, were reserved for special military support, whatever that meant.

It was beyond frustrating to Gao, but this emergency might be just the excuse he needed to access those untapped resources. It would require a trip to Beijing, though.

"I'll do what I can, Mr. Shu, but it will take time."

Shu wagged his chin with disapproval as if Gao were a slow child. "You don't see it, do you?" He pointed at the landslide.

"See what?"

"We were lucky, General," Shu said quietly.

Gao looked up at the tons of rock and debris that slid into the valley, narrowly missing the village and the construction camp.

"You mean because no one was hurt in the landslide?"

Shu's chin wagged again and he added a sigh. "No, I mean the project itself." He waved his hand at the debris. "This needs to be cleaned up, but that's just time. It just slows us down."

Time was the thing Gao had too little of. That was a big deal.

"Speak clearly, Mr. Shu, please."

"Whoever set these charges knew exactly what they were doing, General. If they had wanted to close down the project for good, they would have set charges *inside* the tunnel to collapse the entire structure on top of the boring machine. That would have forced me to find an entirely new site and bring in a new boring machine from Beijing. Six months' delay, at least."

"I don't understand what you're saying, Mr. Shu."

The engineer squinted through his round glasses.

"We were just very lucky, General. Extraordinarily lucky."

19

Moscow, Russia

The stage lights blasted down from the shadows over Russian President Nikolay Sokolov's head. He felt sweat prickling on his brow, but he resisted the urge to mop it off for fear it would smear his makeup.

Although the lights in the audience were at almost full strength, they seemed dim when viewed through the white-hot glare of the stage lights. Barely two meters away, the clear glass eye of a camera bore down on him. Nikolay struggled to block out everything except the reporter who was standing halfway up the arena seating.

His question was too long and had multiple parts, but Nikolay had already cued up the answer in his head.

Yes, the Russian economy was strong. Yes, the balance of exports had shifted favorably toward high-tech during the three years since he was elected. Of course, these benefits were the result of his forward-looking economic policies and his ability to negotiate favorable trade deals with the West.

The reporter finished. Nikolay lifted the microphone to his mouth and smiled. First, he thanked the reporter for his excellent question. Then, he unloaded his preprogrammed answer, smiling all the while with practiced confidence.

But there was something missing. He certainly felt it and he wondered if the people in the audience felt it too.

His answer lacked energy. He was tired and it showed.

A few months ago, Nikolay would have attacked the question with gusto. He would have been out of his chair, pacing, hands carving the air as he reeled off a slew of statistics. Exports from five years ago compared to today. He would have name-dropped a few of the more successful new companies, ones run by young entrepreneurs with large social media presences.

But today Nikolay stayed in his chair. He crossed his legs and spoke slowly and clearly into the microphone. His explanation was patient and boring as he told the people in the room how today was better—much better—than three years ago.

It was true, of course, but it didn't *feel* better—and that was the real problem.

Wake up, he ordered himself.

When Uncle Vitaly was the Russian president, he'd held press conferences once a year. In hindsight, Nikolay admired the shrewdness of his adopted father. Scarcity made the President's press conference an annual event. The practice accomplished two major goals: everyone looked forward to it, and everyone watched.

Because he only did it once a year, Nikolay's uncle turned the event into a marathon lasting several hours. This had the added effect of portraying Vitaly Luchnik as a man of stamina and deep knowledge who could speak to whatever topic was thrown at him. Nikolay knew that every question had been screened in advance and his uncle drilled on the answers. For those rare moments when things went off-script, Luchnik wore a wireless earpiece so a group of policy experts could feed him a few relevant details.

Nikolay had promised to be different. Three years ago, when he'd won his special election in a landslide, he made a solemn promise that he would hold a press conference every month.

This, he declared, was the age of openness. The people deserved to have access to those they had elected to power.

Now, as he stared through the white-hot lights at the reporter who was raising a skeptical eyebrow at his flat answer, Nikolay wondered why doing this every month had seemed like a good idea.

"Next question," Nikolay said into the microphone. An attractive woman with shoulder-length dark hair, porcelain skin, and piercing blue eyes stood in the third row. She looked young and inexperienced. He didn't recognize her, which should have raised a red flag. He nodded at her.

The woman smiled, tilted her head. "Svetlana Kulakova, Russian Unity press."

Nikolay felt his gut tighten. Now he knew why he didn't recognize her. Russian Unity was the latest hardline news service on the scene, rumored to be backed by the Ultras and Konstantin Zaitsev. Their tagline was "Russia first. No retreat, no surrender."

Nikolay was half-tempted to end the news conference, but he matched her smile. "Miss Kulakova, how can I help you today?"

"Can you comment on the reason for cutting short the Russian military exercises in Tajikistan?" the woman asked.

How much did she know? Nikolay wondered. The microphone felt extraordinarily heavy as he lifted it to his lips.

"It's not appropriate for me to comment on classified military matters, Miss Kulakova."

Her red lips stretched, her teeth flashed. "I have it on good authority, Mr. President, that the exercises were not cut short. The Russian troops, our troops, are being ejected from the country of Tajikistan. Can you explain to the people how a former Soviet state has the gall to force the Russian military to leave its borders? Have we become so weak that even our allies can push us around?"

"I don't know where you're getting your information, Miss Kulakova," Nikolay replied.

That was a lie; he knew exactly where she was getting her information. It was being fed to her straight from the lips of Konstantin Zaitsev. Pillow talk, if he believed the gossip. "I will say this. We are dealing with a delicate diplomatic situation with a trusted ally. Thank you."

He started to get out of his chair when a shout from the back of the room caught everyone's attention.

"SHAME!"

Nikolay could make out someone walking down the steps toward the stage.

"Shame!" the woman's voice shouted again.

In that split second, Nikolay could have shut everything down. A simple motion to his security detail waiting in the wings would have done the trick.

But Nikolay hesitated.

The entire room was staring at the woman walking down the steps. She reached the last step and stopped. She leveled an accusing finger at Nikolay.

"Shame!"

She was thin and middle-aged, her gray-streaked dark hair pulled back in a severe bun. Her face was gaunt and she wore a plain, dark blue print dress and black walking shoes. Across her breast she clutched a framed picture of man with short hair dressed in a Russian Army uniform. He was smiling and looked very young.

Kulakova appeared at her side. She put an arm around the woman's shoulders. Her grin had all the warmth of a skeleton.

"This is Irina Ditrimova, mother of Private Alexei Ditrimov, who is being held in a Tajik jail, Mr. President. Is this the delicate diplomatic situation you spoke of, sir?"

Nikolay got to his feet. "Private Ditrimov is accused of the crime of—"

Before he could get out the word *rape*, Kulakova interrupted. "We are Russian, Mr. President. We are a powerful country. How could you allow a former Soviet Republic to take this woman's son, a member of the Russian military, into custody?"

"Enough," Nikolay said. "We are in negotiations to bring this soldier home to face charges here in Moscow. Your actions here today, Miss Kulakova, are jeopardizing that diplomatic effort."

Everything Nikolay had said in the last forty-five minutes evaporated as the press seized upon this new story like vultures on a dead moose. Phones, cameras, eyes all focused on the woman, who was now weeping openly. "Please, Mr. President," she wailed, "my son is a Russian soldier rotting in a foreign jail. He is innocent. He is Russian."

Nikolay started to speak, but Kulakova hugged the sobbing mother. "This morning, Mrs. Ditrimova and I met with Senator Konstantin Zaitsev," she announced to the audience, abandoning her facade as a news reporter. She wheeled on Nikolay.

"Senator Zaitsev believes you are failing this woman. He believes you are failing this country. He told us that—"

Suddenly, there was movement along the edge of the crowd. Nikolay saw one of his security team barrel toward the disturbance. "He's got a gun!" someone shouted.

Kulakova's spell was broken. Pandemonium erupted, screaming people streamed toward the exits.

Two of the President's security detail burst from the wings. They seized Nikolay by the arms, propelling him off the stage. His feet barely touched the floor as he traded the white-hot stage lights for the cold darkness of backstage. They didn't stop. A door at the back of the stage showed as a rectangle of bright sunlight. His body, still assisted by a pair of security guards, went through the open door and into a waiting vehicle.

The door slammed shut behind him and Nikolay was pressed back into the seat as the car accelerated away.

"What happened?" Nikolay asked Federov, who was sitting in the passenger seat.

The FSB chief turned. He was wearing black wraparound sunglasses that made his bald scalp look like alabaster.

"I'm sorry, sir. I felt the situation warranted a security exercise. We'll be confiscating all the footage from the reporters in the room as part of the drill."

Nikolay wanted to close his eyes. That's what he'd been reduced to: his own people staging a security breach because their boss bombed his press conference.

I'm no better than Uncle Vitaly, Nikolay thought.

"Who was she?" he asked.

"Kulakova? Zaitsev's latest media darling. Face of an angel, heart of a snake."

"Not the reporter, the woman. Was she really the soldier's mother?"

Federov's shoulders moved. "I don't know. Possibly."

The car turned the corner and Nikolay glimpsed a demonstration in Red Square. Hundreds of people holding signs. He spotted the word STYD in bold letters and an enlarged picture of the smiling Russian soldier that the woman had been clutching to her chest.

Styd. Shame.

A protest. In Red Square. Yet another thing that never would have happened during Uncle Vitaly's time.

How had he come to this?

As he watched the protest from the back seat of the speeding car, he mentally shed the numbness that had so gripped him on stage. He thought about how Kulakova's beautiful face had shifted into anger. That was fire. That was passion. The kind of passion he needed.

He clenched his fists until the knuckles turned white and his forearms shook with the strain.

You knew from the beginning that none of this would be easy. But today, you sunk to a new low, Nikolay. You hid behind your security detail for protection against a grieving mother.

He bit his lip until he tasted blood.

Enough hiding. Seize the moment.

He loved his country, but Mother Russia needed to change and he was the one to change her. Whatever it took, he was up to the task. No more hiding, no more half-measures.

"Vladimir?"

"Yes, Mr. President?"

"Set up a call with Serrano. He's not holding up his end of the bargain."

Federov nodded without turning around.

"At once, Mr. President."

20

Cincinnati, Ohio

It took nearly an hour to travel the six miles from the Cincinnati Municipal Airport to the Fifth Third Arena. Home of the Bearcats, according to the sign Don saw when the building was finally in sight.

The black government SUV navigated through the multiple layers of security associated with a presidential visit until they arrived at their destination: the loading dock at the rear of the building. A Secret Service agent posted at the steel double doors leading into the arena approached the vehicle.

Don rolled down the window. "Don Riley, CIA. I'm here to see the President and Vice President."

The agent checked his mobile and spoke into his throat mic.

"It'll be ten minutes, Mr. Riley," the agent said. "The meeting will be here in the car. Sit tight, sir." He moved back to his post.

Twenty minutes later, Don was still waiting. Through the half open window, he could make out the noise of the packed arena. It sounded like ocean surf surging and falling in the distance.

He checked his watch again. The longer the wait, the more nervous he felt about the whole situation. The Director had insisted the briefing be conducted in person. Don would have preferred to meet the President on Air Force One, but the Director nixed that, too. "Too much press around, Don," the Director had said. "Make the pitch and keep it short."

The Secret Service agent on the dock stepped back as one of the steel doors swung open. Roaring crowd noise surged into the parking lot. President Serrano walked on to the loading dock escorted by two agents. They accompanied the President to the car and opened the door. The driver exited the vehicle, leaving them alone.

Don had seen Serrano in campaign mode before. The man was a born entertainer, someone who knew how to play a crowd like a conductor leading an orchestra. Tonight, he was ready for action in the persona of the Casual President. He wore a blue Oxford dress shirt unbuttoned at the neck, no tie, and a brown leather bomber jacket with just enough weathering to make it look authentic. He wore light makeup and his hair was carefully styled to achieve a tousled and carefree look. Don felt the energy radiating off the man as he slid into the seat.

"We have to stop meeting like this, Mr. Riley," the President deadpanned.

Don forced an obligatory laugh. "Will the Vice President be joining us?"

A shadow of emotion flitted across the President's features, then it was gone again, replaced by a jovial, high-energy grin.

"Nope," he said. "Just me tonight, Donnie boy."

Don reached into his bag and pulled out a tablet. He started to hand it to the President, but he waved it away.

"Just talk to me, Don. You've got ten minutes, by the way."

As if on cue, there was a surge in volume from the arena that captured the President's attention. "It's a great crowd tonight, Don. They had to set up a jumbo TV in the parking lot to handle the overflow. Phenomenal venue."

"Yes, sir," Don said, aware that his allotted time was ticking away.

Serrano looked back at Don and his eyes went hard. "Why didn't we see it coming, Don?" The president's tone was brittle.

All week, the news about Russian forces being expelled from Tajikistan played again and again. Following the assassination of the Tajik Air Force officer, the government of Tajikistan decided that Russian security guarantees weren't worth the paper they were printed on. If the Seljuk Islamic Front was trying to drive a wedge between Moscow and Dushanbe, it was working like a charm. At every press conference, the White House was asked for their position on the growing tensions in Central Asia.

Editorials in leading papers and cable news pundits expounded on whether Central Asia was the next hotspot for the Serrano administration.

Don started to reply, then closed his mouth. It was a rhetorical question; they both knew the answer. The world did not operate according to the American election cycle or fiscal projections. It operated on real life. When politicians diverted focus away from national security issues or held up budgets for their own purposes, it had consequences in the real world. Operations never got off the ground. Intelligence networks withered. Vital information was not there when you needed it—like right now.

"How was your meeting with the Indians?" Serrano continued. "Are they going to cut it out?"

"It's not that simple, sir," Don responded.

Serrano barked out a humorless laugh. "You don't have to tell me twice." Another long look out the window toward the door leading into the arena and the adoring crowd.

"Let's get down to it, Don. How do I contain this situation through the election? I can't have terrorist attacks in Tajikistan showing up on the news when I'm trying to get people to focus on childcare tax credits. Kapeesh?"

"I have an idea, Mr. President."

"You know there's a part of me that cringes whenever you say that, Don." The President sighed. "Okay. Let's hear it."

Don began to explain how boosting Timur Ganiev in the region could serve as a counterbalance to the violence of the SIF, but Serrano stopped him with a raised hand.

"You want to run an influence campaign? I thought I made it clear I will not authorize a covert action. There's too much risk involved, especially this close to the election. She's up in the polls, you know. If something like that got out . . . " His voice trailed off. His gaze went back to the door leading into the arena.

She was Senator Eleanor Cashman, the Vice President's opponent in the race for the presidency. As Senate Minority Leader, Cashman would be briefed on any covert action authorized by Serrano.

"If an operation went public, she would crucify me," Serrano continued.

Don tamped down his frustration. He didn't bother to point out that the President wasn't running for office anymore.

"Sir, we don't have the resources or the intelligence infrastructure necessary to interdict the SIF. If what we are seeing now is a pattern, they're escalating. This has the potential to get much, much worse."

Don saw the President's shoulders stiffen and he knew he was pushing it. But did he really have a choice? He plunged on. "The lowest profile option we can implement in a reasonable amount of time with some chance of success is an influence operation. Yes, it will require a presidential finding for a covert action, but if we act now, we might be able contain this problem."

The Secret Service agent knocked on the window. The President rolled it down a few inches. "Five-minute warning, sir."

"Thank you, Hanson. Tell me when I have two minutes, please." He turned back to Riley. "How bad could it get, Don?"

"The SIF has moved from petty sabotage of Chinese work sites to a car bomb in downtown Tashkent to an assassination of a military officer with sympathetic ties to the Russian Federation." Don shrugged. "It could get very bad, sir."

Serrano's frustration bubbled over. "What about the Indians, dammit? Can't you get them to knock it off?"

"I'm not convinced the Indians are involved, Mr. President. It's . . . complicated."

"It's always complicated with you, isn't it?" Serrano snapped.

Don didn't bother to offer a response.

"Is this truly my *only* option, Riley?" He scowled at Don. "Really?"

"In my opinion, yes, sir."

In the dimness of cabin, the President's white teeth worried at his lower lip. "The Director's looked at this? He's comfortable?"

"Yes, sir."

It was mostly true. Nothing in the intelligence community was without risk. *Comfort* was a matter of personal judgment.

The Secret Service agent knocked on the window, signaling their time was up.

Serrano blew out his breath. He stared out the windshield at the distant lights of the highway traffic. "Write up the presidential finding and I'll sign it. I want you, personally, to brief the Gang of Eight."

He stepped from the car. The double doors leading into the arena were both open, and the sound of wild cheers spilled into the night. The noise of the crowd buoyed the President's mood. His face lit up with a wide grin.

"Great crowd," he said to the Secret Service agent. The agent nodded.

Serrano turned back to Don. "Am I going to regret this decision, Mr. Riley?"

Don forced a confident smile. "Absolutely not, sir."

But the car door had already slammed shut.

21

Tashkent, Uzbekistan

A few blocks from the U.S. Embassy in Tashkent, Harrison stared outside through the plate glass window of a coffee shop.

The day was warm and the tables on the sidewalk were packed with young professionals talking and drinking coffee. Clouds of vape smoke billowed on the patio. A meter down the standing bar along the window, a young woman sucked on a pink vape pen, expelling a wreath of white smoke. The sickly-sweet smell of bubblegum wafted in Harrison's direction.

The cell phone sitting next to his coffee cup on the narrow bar vibrated to life. He flipped it over so he could see the screen.

Jenny Trujillo.

He sighed, then frowned when he looked at the time on the screen. 10:00 a.m. in Tashkent meant it was 1:00 a.m. in Washington. A little burst of hope swelled. Maybe she'd heard from Tim.

"Jenny," Harrison answered.

"Harrison." Jenny's voice cracked, and any hope for good news evaporated. He swallowed hard, tried to make his voice light.

"You okay, Jen?"

No answer. But he could hear her breathing heavily on the other end of the line.

"Where is he, Harrison?"

The crushing pain in her words made him shut his eyes and bow his head. He wondered if he would ever love someone that deeply.

"Why hasn't he called?" she continued. Harrison detected a slur in her words. *Damn it,* he realized. She'd been drinking.

"Where's Mark?" Harrison asked. "Can I talk to him?" He fought to keep his voice light. He'd always thought of Jenny Trujillo as strong. This despair in her tone frightened him.

"Travel team," Jenny replied, her voice flat. "Away for the weekend. I made him go."

"I don't think you should be alone, Jen. Is there someone who can stay with you?"

Did he even have Mark Trujillo's mobile number in his phone? Harrison couldn't remember.

"I don't know what to do, Harrison," Jenny continued as if he hadn't said anything. "It's all a mess."

"What's a mess? Talk to me, Jenny."

"Tim took care of everything. All the finances, all the bills. Ever since we were married. No matter where he was in the world, he always took care of it. He used to say that I had enough on my plate dealing with the kids. He said we were partners in everything, and it was the least he could do handling that mundane stuff"—her voice broke—"but he's not here anymore and I don't know what to do."

Harrison pressed the phone against his ear in concentration. "Tell me what you're talking about, Jen."

The information came out in bits and pieces, interspersed with tearful asides. The Trujillo family was in serious debt. It wasn't an unusual story. High cost of living area with one kid in private school, one at a private college. Tim had bought the house using an adjustable-rate mortgage with a balloon payment that was due in just a few months. His Army pension didn't even cover their monthly expenses.

No wonder Tim took the consultant job, Harrison thought.

"Our accountant called me today," Jen said. "The oil company stopped paying. They say Tim violated his contract. I'm in trouble, Harrison. He says I have to sell the house."

"Let's not get ahead of ourselves now," Harrison replied. "How big is the payment?"

When she told him the number, Harrison winced. "I'll send you the money, Jen."

"No," she snapped. "I don't care about the money, Harrison. I don't care about this stupid house. I just want my husband back."

"Look, Jen, it's just a loan. It's the least—"

"He's dead, isn't he?" Jen interrupted.

Harrison took a deep breath, let it out slowly. "I don't know, Jenny."

"You can tell me. I can take it, Harrison. I just need to know the truth."

Harrison heard a rattling sound, like ice cubes in an empty glass.

"I will find him, Jen. I made you a promise and I intend to keep it."

The silence stretched out long enough that Harrison wondered if she was still there.

Finally, she spoke. "I just miss him so much, Harrison."

He clenched his eyes shut, feeling the sting of hot tears.

"I know, Jenny," he whispered.

"I'm sorry. I'm putting this all on you. It's not fair to you. Not your problem."

"It's okay, Jen," he said softly. "Listen, I need you to give me Mark's mobile number."

He wrote the number down on his hand and repeated it back to her.

"I'm going to call Mark and we're going to find someone to stay with you tonight."

All the fight had gone out of Jenny Trujillo. "Okay, Harrison." Her voice was small, distant.

"In the morning, I'm going to call your accountant and work out something on the mortgage. Okay?"

Jenny mumbled agreement.

"Then I'm going to get back to work finding Tim," he said grimly. "I will find him, Jen. I promise."

"I know you will, Harrison."

He was shaking by the time he ended the call. The girl with the bubblegum vape stick had gone and his coffee was stone cold. He drank it anyway, letting the bitter liquid roll around in his stomach.

Only then did he allow himself to deal with his own sense of desperation.

What the hell happened to Tim? He needed answers, now more than ever.

One thing he hadn't discussed with Jenny was Tim's life insurance. Tim's father had died young, leaving his family with nothing. Even as a cadet in West Point, Harrison knew his friend carried life insurance and had added to his coverage over the years.

If his best friend really was dead and Harrison could prove it, then he could get a death certificate. That would solve the Trujillo family's money problem. Absent proof of death, the Trujillo family would need to wait seven years before they could try to declare Tim legally deceased.

I need answers. Harrison dialed the number for the bounty hunter.

"*Da*," the man answered in a Slavic grunt.

Harrison identified himself. "Any progress?" he asked in Russian.

"*Nyet*."

Harrison took a deep breath. "What if I double the bounty?"

A pregnant pause from his monosyllabic counterpart. "More money, faster service."

Harrison did the math in his head. If he tapped his IRA, he'd have enough money to keep Jenny afloat on the mortgage and increase the bounty in the search for Tim.

He watched a couple dressed in professional clothes walk by holding hands. They laughed together, their shadows merging on the sidewalk. He remembered the night when Tim and Jenny met.

"Triple it," Harrison said.

22

Beijing, China

It was a few minutes before ten on Friday morning when the PLA staff car passed Tiananmen Square and Gao saw the Great Hall of the People come into view.

Last time he'd been here it was at night—and what a night it had been. The memories piled through his brain. The limousine, Gao in his finest dress uniform with Mei Lin at his side. He could almost hear the crowds of children calling to him, begging for an autograph, crying out to be noticed by the Hero of Tashkent.

All that glory felt a world away from the reality of the moment. Today, their vehicle was requisitioned from the motor pool. It smelled of gym socks, and the cloth seat next to Gao had a mysterious stain on the fabric. The woman next to him in the car was Captain Fang, not his wife.

Gao stifled a yawn. To make their 10:00 meeting, their plane had departed Anyi Base at midnight.

There had been no VIP suite on this trip. Gao slept in a jump seat in the cavernous cargo bay of an empty Y-20. Captain Fang occupied the seat next to him. Once they had gone over the briefing materials one last time, Gao slept. When he opened his eyes again, they were over Beijing and the sun was up.

Driving past the Great Hall of the People, Gao felt a sudden rush of homesickness. He hadn't seen Mei Lin and the children in months. He supposed the baby would be doing all sorts of new things—and he'd missed them all.

Never mind, he told himself, he would spend some quality time with his family this weekend. Captain Fang had managed to push their return flight to Tajikistan back to Monday night. He smiled. Three days with his family and three nights with wife.

In the back seat of the car, Gao sipped from a paper cup of tea. The hot liquid scalded his tongue and it tasted like cardboard.

Their vehicle proceeded past the wide stone steps and imposing columns of the Great Hall. A block later, they turned into a narrow entrance that led into the underground car park. The car stopped in front of glass double doors guarded by two plainclothes policemen.

Fang was out of the vehicle before it stopped. She held the door for Gao and they hurried together down the carpeted hallway toward the subterranean committee meeting rooms.

Another set of guards were posted outside the meeting room labeled *Committee for the Belt and Road Initiative: Central Asian Region*. Fang checked in with an assistant seated behind a desk and turned the briefing materials over. The assistant told them to wait and disappeared inside the meeting room.

Forty-five minutes later, Gao and Fang were still waiting in the hall and Gao was feeling the aftereffects of a poor night's sleep. His back ached, his feet hurt, and he needed a shower. There were no chairs for them to sit. Gao eyed the empty assistant's chair behind the desk, then dismissed the idea.

Finally, the door opened and the assistant emerged. "The Committee is ready for you, General," he said.

"Good luck, sir," Fang whispered.

"I'm well prepared, Captain," Gao replied. "I don't need luck."

He felt his energy return as he strode through the doors. Gao just needed to get through the briefing, then he could spend the weekend with his family.

The Committee members occupied leather chairs around a long table of dark wood. The people seated at the table were all but obscured by staffers who buzzed around them like bees around a hive. A murmur of hushed conversation filled the air, and Gao could see the members were studying his slides for the briefing.

There were twelve standing members of the Committee, but as his gaze swept over the table, he counted thirteen seated principals. He moved to the head of the table, next to the large viewscreen. As he waited to be recognized, Gao tried to figure out who the extra committee member was.

He saw him just as the Chairman gaveled the meeting to order. Minister of State Security Yan was seated to the right of the Chairman. He nodded at Gao, smiling thinly.

"The Chair recognizes Lieutenant General Gao for a report on the security situation in the Central Asia region." The Chairman was a rotund man, his belly bisected by the edge of the tabletop. He had thinning gray hair swept straight back and plastered to his skull like lines of ink. His round face was florid. "You may proceed, General."

Gao walked through the presentation just as he'd practiced it with Captain Fang. As he spoke, he gauged the reaction of the Committee—and he didn't like what he saw. Their stern faces scowled as he reported on the latest terrorist attacks and schedule setbacks.

That was okay. He wanted to paint a grim picture, because his last few slides had the solution to the problem. More troops, more equipment, more security coverage of construction sites. He just needed to sell it.

When he arrived at the slide showing the schedule delays, the Chairman spoke.

"You can stop there, General." There was an edge of impatience to his tone.

"I just have a few more comments, sir." Gao tried to advance the slide but the screen went dark.

"I think we've heard enough, General," the Chairman said. "We called you back to Beijing for this meeting because we are deeply concerned about your performance."

Gao started to reply, then closed his mouth. They didn't call him back to Beijing. He had asked to brief the Committee because he wanted more resources. His tired brain tried to make sense of the conflicting signals that he was receiving. Gao had a sinking feeling in the pit of his stomach as he ran his gaze over the stony faces arrayed down the table.

"General?" The Chairman's tone led Gao to believe it was the second time he'd spoken.

Confidence, Gao thought. Project confidence. You can do this.

"Yes, sir," he said crisply.

"How long have you been in your current position, General?" the Chairman asked.

Gao cleared his throat. "Almost six months, sir."

"From what I can tell," the Chairman continued as if Gao hadn't spoken. "The security situation in Central Asia has gotten worse since your arrival. Forgive me, but I thought your appointment was supposed to make things better."

It was a cheap shot, but no one at the table objected. In fact, Gao thought he heard a few snickers of suppressed laughter.

The Chairman glared down the gleaming expanse of the mahogany surface. "This is no laughing matter. The grand opening of the Samarkand Interchange is set for the first of November. The General Secretary himself will be in attendance, as will every member of this Committee. Your poor performance has put that achievement in jeopardy."

The heat of embarrassment and anger flushed Gao's face. They were blaming him for this catastrophe? If they would just let him finish, he could tell them how he was going to fix the problem.

Gao started to speak, but he was interrupted again, this time by the Minister of State Security. "I'm afraid I have new information that adds to the gravity of the situation, Mr. Chairman," Yan said. "My operatives have uncovered evidence that links the SIF to the Uighur insurgency in western China."

Gao's pulse thundered in his ears. He was just hearing about this now? He was so preoccupied with his own thoughts that he almost missed the Minister's next words.

"Not only is the Seljuk Islamic Front a threat to the Belt and Road

Initiative, it is a direct threat to the very foundation of the People's Republic of China and the Chinese Communist Party."

The Committee members cut glances at one another. Gao knew what was going on: the blame game. Linking the SIF to a longstanding domestic threat would mean lots of outside scrutiny.

But in that moment of darkness, Gao saw his salvation. He found his voice.

"Thank you, Minister Yan. In light of this new information, I want to request new resources to deal with the SIF in the region . . . "

Gao's voice trailed off as he saw the Chairman raise his hand for silence. In his other hand, he held a single sheet of paper. He shook his head as if he was disappointed. He looked up at Gao.

"Do you know what this is, General?" he asked, brandishing the paper.

"No," Gao replied.

"This is a list of your movements since you arrived at your new post. Is it true that you've never even visited Samarkand?" His voice held a note of incredulity.

Gao wasn't sure what to say. He was a general. His job was to maintain a strategic focus, make sure he had the right resources in the right places to get the job done, not fly around like some traveling salesman.

"Sir, this conversation really needs to be about the level of resources necessary to combat the—"

"Resources?" the Chairman exploded. "I don't think you need more resources, General. You need to get off your ass and get in the field. It is the expectation of this committee that you will be visible to your troops and to the local population, not holed up in a military base. You must take the fight to the enemy."

Gao was beyond anger. He knew his face must be as red as the Chairman's and he had a hard time catching his breath. He clamped his jaw shut to stop himself from responding.

He was Lieutenant General Gao Yichen, the Hero of Taiwan and Tashkent, and this man was dressing him down like he was some rank private who'd missed roll call. He scanned the faces of the Committee. Did these people not realize that he'd been handed a giant bag of shit for which they were now blaming him?"

No, he realized. And they didn't care. If this project failed, he was the one who would shoulder the blame.

"Do I make myself clear, General?" The Chairman glowered down the table.

Gao's jaw unlocked. "Yes, sir."

"You are dismissed. I expect your next report to this Committee to be better. Much, much better."

Gao stood rooted to the floor, unable to make his legs respond to orders. Outrage rose up in his throat and he wanted to spew bile down the table, but years of military conditioning kicked in. He turned smartly and marched to the door.

Outside, Captain Fang met him in the hallway. "Sir, I—"

Gao cut her off. "Let's go, Captain,"

He marched through the hallway, not seeing the artwork on the walls, not feeling the stamp of his feet on the plush carpet. He punched open the double doors into the parking garage. He was shaking with rage, ready to scream—

Then a woman stepped out of a waiting car. Gao felt the incredible anger boil away.

Mei Lin held baby Bai in her arms as she turned to help Lixin out of his car seat. She was clad in a loose-flowing dress of bright yellow and she looked beautiful.

Gao took three steps forward and swept her into his arms. "What are you doing here?" He kissed the baby, then picked up young Lixin. The toddler clawed at the brightly colored ribbons on his father's uniform, making Gao laugh. It took him longer than it should have to realize that Mei Lin wasn't smiling.

"What's wrong?" Gao asked.

Captain Fang answered. "Since the meeting did not go as planned, sir, I assumed we would be returning back to the theater of operations immediately. I've already made the arrangements."

Gao closed his eyes. "Of course, Captain. Good thinking."

He opened his eyes again and touched his wife's cheek. "I'm sorry."

"I'm sure you are." Mei Lin looked as if she might cry.

"What's wrong?"

Mei Lin lowered her to an angry whisper. "Who is that woman?" she hissed.

"Captain Fang is my aide-de-camp," Gao said.

"That's Captain Fang? The aide you work with day and night?" Mei Lin's lip curled. "Funny how you never mentioned the captain was a woman."

"It doesn't matter." But it did and Gao knew why. Their own relationship had started while they both served in the PLA during the invasion of Taiwan.

"How could you, Yichen?" Her eyes were glassy with unshed tears.

"Sir." Fang's voice was cool. "We need to leave, sir."

"Mei Lin, darling, it's not—"

"Go." She snatched the child from his arms.

23

Washington, DC

Don keyed in the combination to the cypher lock and held the door open for the eight people waiting in the hallway. This basement level of the Capitol building was mostly storage rooms, maintenance areas, and a few private offices for the most junior senators. It was also home to one of the many Sensitive Compartmented Information Facilities that dotted the Capitol.

Don had chosen this SCIF because it was out of the way, far from the areas where most reporters roamed the halls of Congress.

One by one, the congressmembers placed their phones and other electronic devices into a secure box. The Capitol security officer looked at Don. "Is that everyone, Mr. Riley?"

"That'll do it, Marston. I expect we'll be about an hour."

The security guard shrugged and turned the key to lock the box. "I'll be here, sir."

Don stepped inside and let the door swing shut behind him. He heard the magnetic lock engage. The secure room was barebones, a rectangular oak table surrounded by ten office chairs and a large monitor on the wall. A secure laptop waited for Don at the head of the table.

"Thank you all for coming on short notice, ladies and gentlemen," Don began as he took his seat. "I know this timing is inconvenient."

"A covert action briefing on a Friday afternoon," said Senator Eleanor Cashman. She smiled, but didn't bother to hide the sarcasm in her tone. "Of course, when I heard about the briefing, I immediately changed my plans. One must stay informed."

The rest of the room chuckled. Eleanor Cashman was not only Senate Minority Leader but also a candidate for the presidency of the United States. Even Don, who didn't follow politics closely, knew that she had a campaign rally in Texas planned for the following night. Don realized it was entirely possible that he was about to brief the next President of the United States—a fact that did nothing to calm his nerves.

The Director had made it clear that this operation was Don's responsibility. From inception to completion, he owned it lock, stock, and barrel. And that included briefing the Gang of Eight.

"Now, Eleanor," the Speaker of the House said, taking care to emphasize his authentic Texas twang. "Let's not badger the witness before he even has a chance to speak."

Don kept a professional smile plastered on his face. He'd known this would be a tough meeting. The law required that for every presidential finding for a covert action, the Gang of Eight, consisting of the Senate Majority and Minority leaders, the Speaker of the House, the House Minority Leader, and the chairs and ranking members of the House and Senate intelligence committees, must be briefed on the action.

The law required only that the Gang be informed. It did not require their approval of the operation. However, Congress held the power of the purse. They could choose not to fund the operation, and they could also demand regular reports.

Don had held out a slim hope that given the inconvenient timing, some of the players might bow out of the briefing. That had not happened.

Because of the classification of the material, the briefings were conducted in a secure facility without staff present and were not recorded. In these types of closed settings, conversations tended toward openness and differences were laid out in frank terms. He'd seen some shouting matches, but usually, these senior politicians were collegial, even friendly to one another. It never lasted, though. When they emerged from the bubble of the secure room, they donned their political armor again.

This meeting was likely to be different, he realized. Having a candidate for the presidency as a member of the Gang of Eight was a political wrinkle that he'd not had to deal with before. Already, he'd seen light sparring between Senator Cashman and the Speaker, who was a member of Serrano's party, and Don hadn't even briefed the operation yet.

Don tapped the keyboard and the words OPERATION CATBIRD appeared on the monitor.

"As many of you are aware, we've seen an increase in terrorist activity within the Central Asian republics of Tajikistan, Uzbekistan, Kyrgyzstan, and Turkmenistan."

The Speaker pretended to study the map of the region Don put up next. "Remind me again. Isn't Uzbekistan right next to I-don't-give-a-damn-istan?"

Don let the polite laughter fade before he continued. "These activities include numerous attacks on infrastructure projects and the assassination of a high-ranking Tajik Air Force officer with political connections. Because of the destabilizing nature of these attacks, we have obtained a presidential finding for a non-lethal covert action in the region."

The joking air in the room ended abruptly.

"To what end, Mr. Riley?" Cashman asked. "What is the American interest here?"

"Regional instability is not in our national security interest, ma'am," Don replied. "This is a volatile region of nascent democratic republics sandwiched between two great powers."

"I'm afraid I'm not following you, Mr. Riley." Cashman's brow wrinkled. "We have a regional hotspot that ties up both of our global adversaries and we want to stop that?"

"Oh, for God's sake, Eleanor," interrupted the Speaker. "Let the man make his case before you start in on him."

Cashman raised her hands in an "I surrender" motion. "Very well. Continue, Mr. Riley."

Don cleared his throat. "The responsible party in these attacks is an organization known as SIF, the Seljuk Islamic Front. There is limited evidence to suggest that this terrorist group has links with the Uighur resistance in western China.

"The theory of success for this operation depends on the ability of the United States to covertly influence a countervailing social movement against the SIF. We believe we can expand upon existing social pressures to discredit the terrorist organization and thereby reduce tensions in this part of the world. The idea is to isolate the SIF from the population, turn the people against them, and reduce popular support for their violent activities."

The room was silent. Finally, the ranking member from the Senate intelligence committee spoke. "We're talking about four different countries, Mr. Riley. I'm not aware of any political party that spans all four republics."

"Not a party, Senator," Don replied. "A person."

He cued up a video of a rainy street at night. A man dressed in jeans and a puffy jacket walked before a crowd on what looked like a city street. He spoke in a foreign language.

"Is that Russian?" the congressman asked.

"Kyrgyz," Don said. "This man is Timur Ganiev, native Uzbek doctor, Western-educated, and leader of an indigenous cultural movement in the region. On this night, a Russian soldier on maneuvers was accused of raping a local girl. The imam and the girl's father kidnapped the soldier and gathered a mob. Then Timur Ganiev showed up and stopped the lynching."

"He got them to let the soldier go?" the congressman pressed.

Don shook his head. "Turned him over to the police for criminal prosecution."

"He just walked into the middle of a mob and stopped them?"

Don nodded. "By sheer chance, one of my officers was there that night. He said it was one of the most extraordinary, bravest things he's ever seen. The girl's father literally had a knife in his hand when Ganiev showed up."

"He just showed up and talked them out of it?" Cashman asked.

"More than just talked them out of it." Don played the next clip. Sounds of *Ti-mur . . . Ti-mur . . . Ti-mur* echoed from the speakers.

"Are they chanting his name?" Cashman asked. She wore a bemused smile. "I could use that guy on my team."

"He's been all over the region pushing a unity movement over the past year," Don said, killing the sound on the video. "He's gaining traction."

"What exactly does that mean? A unity movement," the Speaker asked.

"I would classify it as a grassroots indigenous movement," Don said. "There's a strong distinction in the republics between people who are natives and those who just live there. There is a difference for example, between an Uzbek and an Uzbekistani."

"That's all well and good, Riley," said the Senate Majority Leader, "but these are tribal people, right? Four countries means at least four tribes, maybe more. You're saying this Ganiev fellow can unite them all together?"

"It's unlikely, but it's been done before, sir," Don replied. "The borders in this region were drawn by outsiders, the Russians, mostly. But if you go back far enough, they all trace their roots to a common culture, ruled by one man."

"Tamerlane," said the House Intelligence Chair. "More correctly, Timur the Lame."

"That's correct, ma'am," Don said.

"I was a history major," she replied with a grin.

The congressman who had pressed Don earlier joined back in. "Won't a unification movement just create a new problem, Mr. Riley? Those republics are run by autocrats. When this Ganiev fella starts rockin' the boat, the politicians are not gonna like that one bit."

"Ganiev's message is cultural, not political," Don said. "He's not advocating for political change, he's seeking an indigenous revival. Sort of a recognition of the people in the region, and their shared heritage. More importantly, he speaks openly of independence from both Beijing and Moscow."

"And you believe this man can pour oil on the troubled waters?" Cashman asked.

"It's more a case of expediency and cost, Senator," Don said. "This movement exists already and seems inherently non-violent. If we can amplify Ganiev's message, we believe it's possible to turn public opinion against the SIF. Best of all, we don't get directly involved."

Cashman narrowed her eyes at Don. "What's your probability of success, Mr. Riley?"

The senator had put her finger on the nub of the problem. Don chose his words carefully. "Our intelligence assets in the region are not as deep as we'd like them to be. Nor is there any wish on the part of the administration to get embroiled in an international conflict. Operation Catbird represents a cost-effective middle path."

"How much?" the Speaker asked.

Don flipped to the slide with the budget numbers. "That's for two years, sir."

"A two-year plan? That's a little presumptuous of the President, don't you think?" Cashman commented.

"Eleanor," the Speaker said, "behave." But both of them were smiling. Don started to relax.

Unfortunately, Cashman wasn't done with him yet. "Just a few more questions, Mr. Riley."

"Yes, ma'am."

"What is the connection between this operation and Nikolay Sokolov? In light of the recent assassination in Tajikistan, is this something that our president has promised to the Russian Federation?"

"This operation has nothing to do with the Russian Federation, ma'am," Don said. "I was in the region last month and this operation grew from that visit."

"How will you run the operation? In-house?" the House Chair asked.

Don went back to choosing his words with care. "The CIA will have overall responsibility, but the bulk of the work will be done on contract by Falchion."

"And you're comfortable with that?" she pressed.

Don understood the concern. Ever since Manson Skelly, the ruthless CEO of Sentinel Holdings, had taken the world to the brink of nuclear war, the Gang of Eight had watched the use of private military contractors very closely.

"I am. Will Clarke has integrated the former Sentinel assets into his own company and has been nothing but forthright in his dealings with us. I would trust him with my life."

Don's thoughts went to an operation in Phuket, Thailand. He *had* trusted Clarke with his life, and the man had not let him down.

"They bear watching, Mr. Riley."

"I understand." Don looked around the table. "Anything else?"

Tick, tick, tick. Cashman tapped her fingernails on the tabletop. "What does the Vice President think of this operation?"

"Eleanor," the Speaker cautioned.

"It's a perfectly reasonable question, Hal." She turned to Don. "Did you brief the Vice President on this operation?"

"I did not, ma'am."

"I think that's enough," the Speaker said.

"You mentioned you were in the region, Mr. Riley," Cashman continued.

Don nodded.

"Was that when you visited India?"

How does she know that? Don wondered. "It was, ma'am," he replied.

"And?"

"I met with a high-ranking official in the Indian Research and Analysis Wing. They assure me that they have no hand in funding or supporting the SIF."

"Do you believe them, Don?" Cashman asked. He felt her eyes studying him, reading his face. Her gaze was penetrating, not unlike the Serrano Stare. Don wondered if Ganiev was the same way. The moment lengthened.

"I'm not sure," Don said finally. "Their denial was unequivocal, but it leaves unanswered the question of who is funding the SIF. That's still a mystery."

Cashman held Don's eye for another second, then nodded slowly. "I appreciate your honesty, Mr. Riley."

"Well?" said the Speaker. "Any more questions?"

"Just one more," Cashman said. "Not a question exactly, more of a request."

The Speaker gave a theatrical sigh. "Yes, Eleanor?"

Cashman fixed her gaze on Don. "I will support the funding for this operation for the full two years as requested, but I would like Mr. Riley to keep us informed of his progress. After all, I might have a vested interest in the success of this operation." She smiled at Don.

"Well, Mr. Riley?" the Speaker asked.

Don matched Cashman's smile. "It would be my pleasure, ma'am."

24

Bishkek, Kyrgyzstan

Nurbek Kulov leaned back into the creamy, butter-soft leather that made up the back seat of the Bentley Flying Spur. Although he'd owned the car for almost three months now, the sheer luxury of the vehicle still amazed him.

Through the tinted windows, he watched the city streets of his native Bishkek slip by. They passed the four-story building that housed the Osh Bazaar. It was summer now, and vendor stalls spilled out of the building onto the sidewalk. The place teemed with brightly colored lights and pulsed with life.

At one time, he might have visited that bazaar three or four times a week, but now? Kulov could not recall the last time he'd walked the narrow aisles and heard the calls of the hawkers.

Those days were long gone. As the owner of the largest mining conglomerate in the region, Kulov's days were spent with bankers and investors. His vast fortune would have been unimaginable to his younger self, like something out of *1001 Arabian Nights*.

The number of zeroes in a bank account were not the point, of course. What mattered was what you did with all that wealth.

And Nurbek Kulov had done much. Brick by brick he'd built a fortress of powerful influence and climbed to the very pinnacle of Kyrgyz society. People called him a kingmaker, and there was not a politician or businessman in this part of the world who did not owe Kulov a substantial favor. If he believed his polling—and his pollsters were the best that money could buy—he would be the next President of the Republic.

From sheepherder's son to President.

His wife Rayna reached into his lap, entwining her slender fingers into his.

"Remind me again: Why are we doing this?" Her voice was pitched low, just for him. He loved the husky way she spoke their native language. Even though she spoke sweetly, there was no mistaking the undertone of distaste for this side trip.

"Call it a debt to an old friend," Kulov kissed the back of her hand. Her skin was soft and perfumed and he could feel her pulse against his lips.

For the Red Crescent charity benefit, they both wore a stylish blend of native dress and Western garb. Kulov sported a bespoke tuxedo with satin lapels and mother-of-pearl studs. A handcrafted *al-kalpak* traditional felt hat embroidered with gold thread completed his ensemble.

Rayna's elegant frame was clad in a flowing dress of creamy silk, complemented by an *elechek*, an elaborately stylized version of the traditional headdress of native married women. The loose wraps of the turban emphasized the delicate features in her oval face.

"You look like a queen, *kimbattim*," he murmured as he kissed her cheek.

"I look like the First Lady to the next President."

Kulov chuckled. Things would be different when he was in power. For years, Kyrgyzstan had exported the natural resources of the land. First to the Soviets, and now the Chinese, under pressure from both due to geography. Under his leadership, things would change. The new Kyrgyzstan would be beholden to no foreign power.

His wife tightened her fingers and she scoffed at him. "He wants money. You owe him nothing, Nur. Your debt was paid long ago."

Kulov turned his attention back to the window. If only it were that simple. She didn't understand, could never understand. Akhmet Orazov was his brother-in-arms. Together, as Soviet Spetsnaz soldiers, they had fought in Afghanistan. Partners with death as their calling card.

How many lives had they taken together, he wondered. A hundred, perhaps? And how many times had Orazov saved his life?

"Some debts are never repaid," he said.

Their shoulders touched as the Bentley took the corner in a smooth curve. The gleaming vehicle came to a halt in front of the lighted exterior of a high-end restaurant. The establishment was ironically called *Navigator*, an English name for a Russian restaurant, but it was trendy. Just the sort of place the future president might stop for a drink with his beautiful wife before they continued on to the charity benefit for the Red Crescent Society.

Kulov waited for their chauffeur to open the car door, then stepped into the soft light formed by thousands of tiny bulbs that lined the entrance to the restaurant like a tunnel. He held out his hand. His wife's slim leg emerged from the vehicle, her high heel touched the ground, and she stood in one fluid motion.

She is so beautiful, he thought. He knew many men his age chased their youth through flings with younger women, but that had never appealed to Kulov. Rayna had always been enough for him.

She slid her hand into the crook of his elbow and they strolled together along the cobbled walk toward the restaurant. Before they reached the entrance, the glass door swung wide to reveal a rotund, flush-faced, unmistakably Russian man. He bowed as deeply as his heavy figure would allow, which was not very far.

"Mr. Kulov," he crowed in loud Russian, "your presence here does me a great honor."

"Grigoriy, it is you who honors me." Kulov bent to embrace the beefy owner. "Is he here yet?" he asked in a low voice.

"In the back, sir," Grigoriy replied. "Private dining area. Second door on the left."

It took Kulov and Rayna nearly a quarter of an hour to make their way through the main dining room. Kulov, flanked by a beaming Grigoriy, paused at every table to shake hands with the politicians and businessmen who made up the wealthy clientele. Rayna extended her hand to be kissed and accepted their lavish compliments with grace. Kulov laughed when a few jokingly called him "Mr. President."

Every one of them owed some part of their career to him—and the time for him to collect was close at hand.

Grigoriy deposited them at a table for two at the rear of the restaurant, slightly elevated so they could see and be seen by everyone there. At a nod from his wife, two women detached themselves from a nearby group and approached.

Kulov rose when they arrived and bowed slightly. "I'll let you get caught up. I'll be back shortly, my dear."

He headed toward the restrooms at the rear of the restaurant, then took a left into the hallway leading to the private dining rooms. He slid open the second door and stepped inside, closing the door behind him.

Akhmet Orazov sat behind a table set for two, surrounded by a sea of small dishes. The food was untouched, as was the glass of vodka sitting in front of him.

Orazov got to his feet. He was dressed in Western-style trousers, a loose white silk shirt, and an embroidered jacket that closed with a gold-threaded sash. Covering his cropped gray hair was a *taqiyah*, a Turkmen skullcap embroidered in the style of his jacket. His friend had dressed up just enough to blend in with the other patrons, but compared to Kulov's evening finery he looked almost dowdy.

The two men embraced. Kulov gripped his friend by the shoulders when they parted.

"How long has it been?" he asked.

The muscles under his fingers were solid and strong. Orazov looked trim and fit. When the shorter man smiled, there was a glint of a gold tooth behind his left incisor.

"Too long, old friend." He pulled out a chair.

"I have only a few moments, Akhmet," Kulov said as he sat down.

The two automatically spoke Russian, the language of their shared past. Kulov studied his friend. The shrapnel scar on his neck had faded with time, and Orazov's jawline had softened beneath his neatly trimmed gray beard.

We're old, he realized. Both of us.

"I'll come to the point then," Orazov said in a clipped voice. "I need money."

In spite of himself, Kulov felt a surge of disappointment. Rayna was right. He bit back a sigh.

"How much this time?"

When Orazov told him the number, Kulov at first wondered if he'd heard correctly. He sat back in his chair and gaped at his companion. "What for? Are you going to start a war?"

"Think of it as a down payment on our future," Orazov said. "The less you know, the better."

It was a fair point, Kulov thought. Ever since his friend had been ejected from the Turkmen government, he'd lost track of Orazov's dealings. With his own election looming, did he really want to know?

"A down payment on our future," Kulov said, not even trying to hide his sarcasm. "You sound like Timur Ganiev now."

Orazov's lip twisted. "Don't joke about that. He's a dangerous man."

"He's a crackpot," Kulov scoffed. "The second coming of Tamerlane, my ass. He says he can unite the tribes. The Soviets tried that, and where did it get them?"

"We're speaking Russian now, aren't we?" Orazov said wryly.

"Ganiev is a fraud and he will not be welcome when I am in charge. Kyrgyzstan for the Kyrgyz, that's what I stand for."

"Nur," Orazov said, his tone taking on a new intensity. "I need the money. As soon as possible. And I wouldn't underestimate Ganiev."

Kulov glanced at his Rolex. He'd been here too long already. "I'll give you half."

He started to get up, but Orazov reached across the table and clamped his hand on Kulov's forearm. Through the fine silk of his jacket, Kulov could feel the strength in the grip.

"This is not a negotiation," Orazov said. "I need your help. It's important."

Kulov shook off the hand, staring back at the other man. As soldiers, they'd lived together, fought together, nearly died together so many times. But Rayna was right: it was time to put his past behind him.

Kulov stood. "This is the last time. Old friend."

He stalked to the door, but as his hand touched the latch, Orazov spoke again.

"Be ready, Nur. They're coming. I can feel it."

The tone was enough to make Kulov turn around. He could feel the ticking clock in his head. He needed to go now.

The lines on the weathered skin of Orazov's face were deep, his hair was gray, but his eyes were intense. He had not changed, Kulov realized. Orazov still lived like he was on patrol in the wilds of Afghanistan where every day felt like a new lease on life.

"Don't call me again, Akhmet."

Kulov turned away from his old friend, stepped through the door, and shut it behind him.

Back in the restaurant, Kulov painted on a smile as he rejoined his wife at the table. Her companions faded away and he sipped the drink that Grigoriy had prepared for him.

When he toyed with the stem of the glass, Rayna slid her hand over his restless fingers.

"How did it go?" she asked softly.

Kulov shrugged. "He wanted money, just like you said."

"Let's go," she said.

Kulov signaled to Grigoriy for their car and after another round of handshaking, they were installed in the back seat of the Bentley. The car pulled away from the curb.

Rayna slid across the seat and laid her head on his shoulder. "Let's go home," she whispered. "You can tell them I wasn't feeling well. I want to spend the night with you. Alone. I don't want to share you with a thousand ass-kissers."

It was tempting. The vehicle turned onto Moskovskaya Avenue, bars of light from street lamps cutting across the darkness of the car's interior. A fresh burst of acceleration from the powerful vehicle pressed his wife closer to him. When was the last time they'd spent an evening alone?

Kulov sighed. "We'll just put in an appearance, my love." He pressed his lips against her forehead. "Then we'll go."

Another turn, this one onto Erkindek Boulevard. The grand street had a narrow park with paved walkways in between the lanes of traffic running north and south. The central green corridor was filled with tall trees, fully leafed and vibrant green.

He rolled down the window, allowing the aroma of the forest in bloom to stream into the compartment. He filled his lungs. Summer, his favorite time of year in his city.

Up ahead, red taillights blazed. The Bentley slowed then stopped. Cars gathered on both sides and behind them. They were stuck.

Through the open window, Kulov heard the purr of a small engine. He tilted his head to catch sight of a motorcycle traveling through the space between the cars. Although the lane was clear ahead, the rider stopped next to Kulov's window.

The rider wore a black leather jacket, black helmet, and tinted visor, giving Kulov the impression of a faceless robot. The helmet turned toward the Bentley window.

Kulov nodded. The motorcyclist nodded back.

The rider unzipped his leather jacket and his gloved hand withdrew a handgun. Part of Kulov's brain recognized the blocky shape of a Glock 17.

The window. He needed to raise the window. His fingers raked at the armrest, but the damned button eluded his grasp.

The muzzle of the gun looked like a cannon.

He threw out his arms, twisted his torso to protect Rayna from what he knew was coming.

Fire. Noise.

Darkness.

25

Bishkek, Kyrgyzstan

Nicole Nipper was determined not to be scooped again. After her profile on Timur Ganiev had run in the *Financial Times*, she'd been spending most of her time trying to raise funds for a documentary. It was slow going. Investors wanted to meet her in person before they wrote a check, which necessitated trips back to London more often than she liked.

She'd been in London the night Timur saved the Russian soldier from a lynch mob. That was *her* story. She found him. She promoted him. Without her, he was just a well-educated doctor with no platform.

But instead of reporting the scoop, she'd seen it on social media like everyone else in the world.

Nicole drew in a frustrated breath and immediately regretted it. The back of the taxi cab reeked of stale smoke and sour milk. There was a plexiglass shield installed between the rear seat and the driver, a scratched, smudged remnant of the COVID era. Nicole rapped on the plastic glass. "Faster," she ordered in Russian. "Drive faster."

No, she thought, Nicole Nipper would not be scooped again. She turned to the man on the seat next to her, slumped over the camera bag on his lap. Nudging Barry with her knee, she asked, "You ready?"

She'd roused him from a sound sleep at the hotel and he looked it. He sat up, rubbed his face with both hands. "Yeah. Ready. Got it."

He rummaged in his gear bag, pulling out his Canon EOS 5D Mark IV, good for both still shots and high-quality video.

The last trip to London had not netted her enough to afford a camera crew, so she settled for Barry. He had the skills to get the job done, but he came with baggage. Still, no one else was going to work for what she was paying him.

When she thought about that night almost ten years ago, she cringed. Nicole remembered it as a drunken fumbling mess in the dark. Barry, on the other hand, recalled it much more favorably. He'd made it crystal clear to her that he was willing to reignite their passion as soon as she was ready —and he was willing to wait.

Before they'd left London, she told Barry that it was not going to happen. His head nodded *Yes, I understand*, but his eyes said, *We'll see.*

On her phone, she flipped from one social media outlet to another. Ganiev had been spotted at the National Hospital over an hour ago, there were no further updates. On the other hand, the updates on the attempted assassination of Nurbek Kulov were flowing thick and fast. She tried to parse through what was fact and what was mere speculation.

As best as she could tell, the prospective President of Kyrgyzstan had been riding in his car when he was gunned down by a passing motorcyclist. Clearly, this was a hit on the most famous man in the country, and his fellow countrymen were responding.

All over social media people were posting images of the Kyrgyz flag, a red field with a yellow sun. Growing from the center of the sun was a *tunduk*, which, according to the internet, was the opening in the center of the roof of a yurt. To Nicole, it looked like someone had plopped a hot cross bun in the middle of flag.

The haters were coming out, too. Kulov was the richest man in the country, his wealth based on the sale of Kyrgyzstan's natural resources. There were already memes circulating about the car he'd been in when he was shot, a pearl-colored Bentley.

Nicole waded through the dreck of the internet, looking for the facts of the case. The driver, when he realized what had happened to his boss, forced the Bentley through the stopped traffic and got Kulov to the hospital in minutes. Without a doubt, the man saved Kulov's life. The future President was in surgery at the National Hospital.

Nicole felt the cab jerk to a stop. She looked up to see a wall of red taillights in front of them. Half a block away, elevated work lights blazed white. The idiot cab driver had taken Erkindek Boulevard and run them straight into the police investigation of the crime scene.

"C'mon," she said to Barry. "We walk from here."

She rapped on the plexiglass shield and stuffed a handful of Kyrgyzstani *som* into the slot for payment. The driver's baleful glare followed her out of the car.

Nicole waited on the crowded sidewalk for Barry. He carried his compact video camera in one hand, his Canon DSLR slung across his chest, and a heavy gear bag over his left shoulder. "Keep up," she warned.

Barry was now a heavy man, and hairy—she remembered that much from their one night together. His full beard was streaked with gray and he was already puffing like a locomotive even though they hadn't started walking yet.

"Right behind you," he replied.

Nicole pushed her way through the crowd, opening a hole for Barry to follow. The big man used his beefy arms to protect his precious cameras.

When Nicole turned the corner, the hospital came into sight, a five story building made of gray stone. Police lights at street level dappled the facade with alternating red and blue. She put on a burst of speed, calling for to Barry to keep up.

The press of bystanders thickened as they drew closer to the hospital, but Nicole elbowed her way forward. She was not going to lose this scoop. Her mind was already sketching out an article for the *Financial Times* as she battled her way to the hospital entrance.

The car park in front of the hospital was packed with people who all seemed to be waiting. The entrance was a pair of sliding glass doors under a canopy that cantilevered out from the front of the building. A ring of policemen prevented anyone from mounting the steps into the hospital.

Nicole fumed with frustration. She needed to get inside. She needed to get some video of Timur in action.

Barry nudged her. “What’s with the evening wear?” he muttered.

Nicole looked around them. Apart from a few men dressed in street clothes, almost everyone facing the hospital was dressed to the nines. Men in tuxedoes, women in long dresses. Some of them wore traditional head coverings as a nod to their heritage and an accessory to their western clothes. Both sexes dripped with jewelry. Rolex and Patek Phillipe watches, diamonds, pearls, elaborately wrought silver and gold necklaces.

“Hey, man,” Barry said to one of the normally dressed people. “You speak English?”

The man was in his early twenties. For Nicole, the iPhone at the ready marked him as competition. He considered Barry, his eyes lingering on the multiple cameras, then he nodded.

“What gives?” Barry asked. “Why are these people all dressed up?”

“Mr. Kulov was going to a charity event when the, um, accident happened.”

“A benefit for the Red Crescent Society,” added a tall woman wearing a mink stole. She had the flawless white skin and green eyes that marked her as a native Kyrgyz. “Nurbek was our most generous benefactor.”

“Thank you,” Nicole said. “Have you seen Timur Ganiev this evening?”

Out of the corner of her eye, Nicole noticed Barry was panning his camera around the area, capturing the incongruous scene of people dressed for the opera standing in a hospital parking lot.

“I don’t know who that is,” the woman replied.

You will, Nicole thought. If I have anything to say about it.

There was movement in the lighted lobby and the automatic glass doors leading into the hospital swept apart. A pair of uniformed policemen walked out and posted on either side of the doors, ensuring they stayed open.

Seconds passed, the crowd fell silent and still. A man and a woman walked slowly out of the building and stopped at the top of the steps. Nicole tried to hide her elation. It was Timur. Barry flashed her a thumbs-up sign to let her know he was recording.

Timur had one arm around a tall, slim woman, as if he was holding her up. His other hand was in front of her, and she gripped his hand with both of hers.

The woman was dressed in a flowing gown of creamy silk and she wore an elaborate turban-like headdress of the same material. Diamonds glittered at her neck.

But no one was looking at her fine dress or jewels. Their eyes were on the blood that stained the front of the beautiful dress, so much that it stiffened the silk, interrupting the smooth flow of the material when she walked.

The crowd drew in a collective breath as Timur moved his arm away revealing the full extent of the bloodstains.

"Rayna has asked me to speak on her behalf," Timur began. He did not shout, yet his voice carried over the still crowd, everyone silently straining to hear what he had to say. His eyes roved over the assembly before lighting on Nicole. He gave her a slight nod and Nicole felt a thrill.

The light from the parking lot slanted down across his face. His eyes filled with tears. His voice cracked.

"Nurbek Kulov is dead."

26

Bishkek, Kyrgyzstan

The whole city is in mourning. That was Harrison's first thought as he walked through the Manas International Airport. The air hub was modern and gleaming, another node in the Chinese Belt and Road. Everywhere he looked, every electronic billboard or empty wall held an image of the late Nurbek Kulov.

Outside, Harrison caught a taxi. It would have been easy enough to ask the local CIA Chief of Station to arrange transportation for him, but he wanted to get the lay of the land before they met in the afternoon.

The taxi driver looked at him in the rearview mirror and raised an eyebrow.

"National Hospital," Harrison said in Russian.

The man did not put the car into drive. Instead, he asked, "Are you a reporter?"

"I have business there," Harrison answered noncommittally.

The cabbie pulled away. Although it was a work day, traffic was light going into the city. Flags stood at half-mast everywhere he looked, and he noticed closed signs on many of the businesses.

"Nurbek Kulov was a great man," the taxi driver said. "He was the best of the Kyrgyz people." There was an air of reverence in his voice.

Harrison did not reply, but his thoughts went in a different vein. Kulov's story was no different than any other strong man in this part of the world. He'd fought in the Soviet military. As a result of Russian favoritism and his own political connections, he'd been awarded mineral leases on vast tracts of land. He became fabulously wealthy by selling his country's natural resources to Mother Russia.

Once you've become the wealthiest man in the country, what do you do for an encore? Become president, of course. For life.

But instead, Kulov ended up dead, another victim of the SIF.

"How much do you know about what happened?" Harrison asked the taxi driver.

"SIF." The man said the word like a curse.

Harrison nodded as if he agreed, but something didn't sit right. The SIF was upping their game in a big way, transitioning from petty bombings to political assassinations. But what was the connection between a Tajik military officer and a Kyrgyz presidential candidate? Both men were nationalists and politically connected, but the similarity ended there as far as Harrison could see.

More importantly, if the SIF was bold enough to assassinate the future president of a country, where was their limit?

"Do you know Timur Ganiev?" Harrison asked.

It was as if he had flipped a light switch on the man's attitude. The cab driver broke into a wide grin and he nodded enthusiastically.

"Timur. Everyone knows Timur. He is the best of us."

Harrison frowned in surprise. That was not the answer he expected. Ganiev was an Uzbek. This man was Kyrgyz. Two completely different tribes, in two different countries, yet somehow Timur had managed to bridge that ethnic gap.

"But he's an Uzbek, right?" Harrison asked.

The cabbie wagged his finger at Harrison. "Timur is one of us," he declared, thumping his chest. "He is a man of the people. He understands who we are. Uzbek, Tajik, Turkmen, Kyrgyz, we are all the same people. He understands *us*."

Harrison had seen Timur's impromptu press conference with Kulov's widow outside the hospital. As always, Timur was on message. Peace, unity, and respect for their shared heritage.

The taxi turned onto a wide street with a narrow park running between the north and south lanes of traffic. Harrison realized this was Erkindek Boulevard, where Kulov had been assassinated.

"The most beautiful street in the city," the taxi driver said proudly. He pointed through the trees to where a group of people had gathered. "It happened over there." He swung the steering wheel and they turned down a cross street.

The parking lot in front of the National Hospital had been converted into a makeshift shrine. A pearl-gray Bentley was parked in the center of the empty lot. Harrison could see the right-side front panel was smashed in and there were scrapes down the expensive paint job. The car was almost entirely covered in flowers, stuffed animals, and dozens of traditional Kyrgyz hats.

The driver stopped at the curb and Harrison paid him. The cabbie pointed to a tall, spare man dressed in a charcoal gray jacket, matching trousers, and a blocky cap like something a train conductor might wear.

"That man was Kulov's driver. Without him, Kulov would have died on the street like an animal."

Harrison surveyed the scene from the curb. He wasn't sure what he'd find here, but lacking a better idea he'd come to the scene of the crime.

Every few minutes, someone would drop off a gift at the makeshift shrine. Kulov's chauffeur stood off to one side, his hands clasped behind his back as if he was standing vigil. People engaged him in conversation when they left their gifts and he seemed open to talking.

Harrison tried to come up with a plausible cover story to approach the man and decided stick with the truth. He waited until there was a pause in the flow of mourners, then walked up to the chauffeur.

"I'm investigating the assassination of Mr. Kulov," Harrison said in Russian.

The man took in Harrison's clothes, his mannerisms. "You are police?"

Harrison shrugged and deliberately allowed his American accent to slip into his Russian. "I'm a friend of Kyrgyzstan. May we talk?"

The driver raised an eyebrow, but nevertheless followed Harrison to the side of the building. He took out a pack of cigarettes and offered one to Harrison. He took it, even though he didn't smoke, and waited as the man went through the lighting ritual.

"My taxi driver said you're a hero," Harrison said.

For a moment, he thought the man might break down. His eyes filled with tears and his hands shook. He took a stiff drag of his cigarette and that seemed to steady him.

"I drove Mr. Kulov for twenty years," he said. "He was a great man."

"Can you tell me what happened?"

Half the cigarette disappeared before the man spoke again. "I was driving Mr. Kulov and his wife from the restaurant to the charity dinner. There was bad traffic on Erkindek . . . Mr. Kulov had the window open . . . It all happened so fast."

Harrison let him talk, prompting him gently with follow-up questions. But it was no use. The driver hadn't seen the motorcycle when it approached Kulov's window and he hadn't seen the gun. When the gunshots exploded into the vehicle, he just reacted.

Harrison put his hand on the man's arm. "You gave him a chance at life. You need feel no shame, my friend. The assassin is the only one to blame."

The chauffeur looked at the damaged Bentley heaped with gifts and said nothing.

Harrison started to thank the man, then he paused, struck by a new thought.

"Why was Mr. Kulov at a restaurant?" he asked. "I thought you said they were going to a charity dinner."

The driver's eyes cut left and right to make sure they were alone. "He had a meeting."

"What kind of meeting?" The way he said it piqued Harrison's curiosity.

The driver lowered his voice. "I heard them arguing. Someone wanted money. A friend. Mrs. Kulov was not happy."

Harrison thanked the man and followed the chauffeur's directions to the Navigator restaurant. The entrance was a cobbled walkway under an arch made from thousands of tiny LED lights, like the kind you might use on a Christmas tree. He supposed it was beautiful at night, but it looked tacky in the light of day. The restaurant was closed and the front door was locked, so Harrison walked to the alley in back.

The door leading into the kitchen was open and he could hear voices. Harrison walked in to find three cooks preparing food. They looked surprised, but instead of waiting for them to speak, Harrison barked out in Russian. "Where is he?"

The cook nearest the door jerked his head. "Grigoriy is inside."

Grigoriy turned out to be a fat little Russian man. He sat at a linen-covered table in the empty dining room with a cup of coffee. Harrison marched to the table, pulled out a chair, spun it around and sat down.

Grigoriy stared at him, his mouth gaped. "Who are you?"

"I'm investigating the assassination of Nurbek Kulov."

The Russian man studied Harrison's face. "You're American."

Harrison shrugged. The silence lengthened until the Russian shifted in his chair.

"What do you want?"

"Who did Kulov meet with last night?"

Grigoriy shook his head and started to get up.

"Sit down," Harrison ordered. The Russian obeyed.

"Who did Kulov meet with last night?"

"Mr. Kulov has been good to me—"

"Kulov is dead," Harrison interrupted. "I want to know if you set him up."

Grigoriy's fleshy face drained of color. "I loved him."

Harrison leaned forward. "Answer my question."

"I don't know his name. A Turkman, that's all I know."

Harrison's mind reeled as he worked to keep a stern face. He extracted his mobile phone and swiped through a series of photos. He turned the screen to show Grigoriy.

The man nodded his head so emphatically that his jowls jiggled. "That's him. I don't know his name, but that's him. I'm sure of it."

The picture was Akhmet Orazov.

Back outside, Harrison walked through the afternoon sunshine to his meeting with the local CIA station chief. He tried to fit the pieces together in his mind.

Kulov goes to meet Orazov at the restaurant. His wife argues with him about the meeting. Orazov wanted money. Kulov is gunned down.

A set-up? It would have been easy enough for an assassin to park down the street from the restaurant and wait for Kulov to leave. It all tied back to Orazov. He had the means and opportunity, but what was the motive?

Harrison shook his head. He was still missing something.

The Bishkek station chief had set their meeting in a coffee shop down a narrow side street. Harrison paused inside, letting his eyes adjust. The place was mostly empty at this time of the afternoon. From a booth at the rear of the restaurant, a young Black woman raised her hand in greeting.

He didn't know Amelia McClintock personally, but she had a good reputation with people that Harrison trusted. Ambitious in the best meaning of the word, competent, and not a gossip. Committed to the mission first, not her career advancement.

She was trim and dressed down in jeans and a leather jacket over a forest green blouse. Her handshake was firm and she seemed like the kind of person who enjoyed a good laugh. Harrison liked her right away.

He slid into the booth and they exchanged small talk while they ordered coffee.

"I would have sent a car for you, Harrison," she said.

He shrugged. "I wanted to spend some time in the city."

"Did you find anything interesting?" She had a great smile and he responded in kind.

Why not tell her? he thought. Two heads were better than one. She listened without interruption as he filled her in on his day.

She raised one eyebrow at the connection to Orazov. "That's new, and I appreciate you sharing," She sipped her coffee. "I'll return the favor."

"Okay." Harrison put down his cup.

"Do you know who Jay Patel is?" she asked, leaning in.

"Indian RAW, Spec Ops. Don Riley paid him a visit. The guy swore up and down that they're not involved with the SIF." Harrison paused, studying her face. "But you think otherwise."

"The night Kulov was killed, Patel was here, in Bishkek."

Click. Harrison felt the pieces fall into place.

27

PLA Forward Operating Base
50 kilometers west of Dushanbe, Tajikistan

Gao desperately wanted an antacid. He'd never had trouble with his stomach before, but these days it seemed as if he was eating the chalky pills like candy. Even so, his stomach never seemed to settle down.

Maybe it's stomach cancer? He turned the thought over in his mind. That might not be the worst outcome. A medical discharge would be better than being dismissed for incompetence.

"Would you like me to run the simulation again, General?" asked the briefer.

He looked up toward the large monitor mounted on the wall at the other end of the table. It showed a map of Central Asia, with cities as black dots and the Belt and Road projects as blue lines that snaked between them. Except it was hard to see either the black dots or the blue lines because they were obscured by a rash of red.

Two rows of faces watched him from the long sides of the table. He was their leader. They looked to their general—lieutenant general, he corrected himself—for answers.

Except, at this moment, he had no answers.

"Yes," he said, playing for time. "I'd like to see it again."

The briefer looked pleased that her brand-new algorithm had been met with his favor. She touched her laptop to reset the program and stepped back.

The screen cleared of red blotches. As the time counter ran in the lower right corner of the screen, a few red dots appeared. Then more, and larger ones. The size of the dots was the new twist the briefer was so pleased about.

Every red dot on the map represented the location of a terrorist attack by the Seljuk Islamic Front. Now, this over-educated, self-satisfied laptop jockey had figured out how to equate the "political and social impact" of an attack with the size of the dot. Bigger dots meant a larger impact. As Gao watched the time-lapse program populate the screen with more and larger dots, he thought about his career trajectory. The red seemed to devour the screen like a deadly rash. It made Gao's skin crawl.

The program ended with a bloodred blotch over the city of Bishkek, Kyrgyzstan.

"Again, sir?" the briefer asked hopefully.

Gao ignored her. "What is the construction status in Bishkek?"

She avoided his gaze. "One rail line is open, but all work on the adjoining lines has ceased."

"For how long?"

She shot a glance at the regional construction manager as if hoping for him to jump in, but he stared resolutely at the opposite wall as if his life depended on it.

"Unknown, sir," she said.

Gao's eyes swept down the table until he found the MSS representative. He was on the young side, which to Gao meant he was politically connected, and therefore even more dangerous. His unnannounced arrival and self-invitation to the general's staff meeting did not bode well for Gao's future.

It was out in the open now. Beijing was watching him, and they wanted everyone to know it.

So far, the man had behaved himself. He had the typical MSS arrogance, and for some reason he insisted on being called "Jimmy." Western-style names were often adopted by Chinese working abroad, but it was arrogant to use that name among your own people.

Yet for all his bravado, Jimmy hadn't said a word since the meeting started. And that irritated Gao more than anything else.

First, he invites himself to my meeting, then he ignores me. It was time to go on offense. "Would you care to comment, Mr. Li?" Gao asked.

Jimmy turned his styled haircut toward the head of the table. "About what?" He paused, then added "sir" as an afterthought.

"This might be a good time for the Ministry of State Security to share intelligence about our terrorist problem," Gao said.

The arrogant young prick actually smiled. "I don't know what you mean, General."

The tone of voice, the way he slouched in his chair, it made Gao's stomach spasm. To cover the pain, he leaped to his feet and rushed to the other end of the table. He slapped his hand against the red-speckled image so hard that the monitor rocked on its mount.

"I mean this!" Gao shouted. "This adversary is gaining in strength. There are resources behind these attacks. Where is the money coming from?"

The MSS officer sat up in his chair and it looked like he might actually contribute something useful. Then, he said, "We have no definitive answer to that question, General."

Gao drew in a deep breath and let it out slowly as he fought for calm.

You are the leader here. These people look to you for guidance. If you panic, they will panic.

He stalked back to his place, carefully pulled his chair out from the table, and sat down. He burped quietly into his hand and felt the taste of acid at the back of his throat.

I would give my left testicle for an antacid right now, he thought.

Gao called out the construction manager's name. The man looked away from his spot on the wall.

"Schedule update," Gao ordered.

The man took his place at the briefing podium and started in on a series of Gantt charts. Gao watched the slides and tuned out the man's droning voice. They were only a few months away from the General Secretary's visit to Samarkand, when the great man was supposed to open the rail line between Western China and Tehran. Beijing called it the Jade Spike ceremony, a not-so-subtle reference to the famous Golden Spike ceremony from United States history where eastern and western rail lines were linked together in Utah in 1869.

The name was the Party's way of poking at the decline of the United States. In the 1800s, the Chinese were immigrant labor working on the U.S. railroad. Today, they were masters of their destiny, driving the future, and they were not about to let the mighty United States forget about this moment. Even the tagline for the Jade Spike event was a subtle poke in the eye: *Linking east and west for the 21st century*.

Once the Belt and Road connected Europe and Asia, the Chinese juggernaut would be unstoppable.

But only if you succeed, Yichen. He thought about the red-splotched map and the presence of an MSS agent in his ranks. Success was far from certain.

"How are the security arrangements for the Jade Spike ceremony progressing?" Gao asked.

The security officer manned the podium and gave a textbook presentation on the layers of security they intended to place around a building that was not yet complete.

It was a little *too* textbook, Gao thought, which meant it was probably bullshit.

"Captain Fang," he said, "make a note that I would like to visit Samarkand next week to inspect the progress."

He waited for Fang's crisp "Yes, sir," but nothing happened. She normally sat behind him, against the wall, taking notes. He swung around to find her chair empty.

"She left a few minutes ago, General," the security officer said in a deadpan voice.

The door opened and Fang entered. She crossed to Gao's side and bent down to speak in his ear. Her warm breath whispered against his cheek. "You have an urgent call, General."

Gao cocked his head. This close, her subtle perfume was noticeable. "Who is it?"

Out of the corner of his eye, he thought he saw a smirk flit across Jimmy's face and he got a chill.

Please don't let it be Beijing, he thought.

Fang's voice dropped even lower. "It's your wife, sir. She said it's urgent. A matter of life and death, those were her exact words."

Gao stood immediately. "Submit your written reports to Captain Fang and we'll reconvene this council in one week."

He strode across the hall to his office and crossed behind his desk to pick up the receiver. Fang started to back out, but he motioned for her to stay.

Heart pounding, he pressed the receiver to his ear. "Mei Lin, what's happened?"

He could tell by the throatiness of her voice that she'd been crying. "I can't do this anymore," she said.

"What's happened? My aide said it was a matter of life and death."

"I told that bitch to say it to get your attention. When was the last time you called me, Yichen? When was the last time you saw your children?"

Gao turned to face the window. The view of the snowcapped mountains of Shirkent National Park was stunning. He lowered his voice and adopted a rational tone. "Mei Lin, this is not the time or the place for this conversation."

"When *is* the time?" she screamed, and he had to hold the receiver away from his ear. He cut a look at Captain Fang. Her face was impassive, but Gao knew she could hear his raging wife.

"You haven't been home in months," Mei Lin continued. "Then I found out this morning that you were back in Beijing two weeks ago and you didn't even call me." Her words were running together now and clouded with sobs.

"It's not like that, Mei Lin," Gao replied.

"So, you weren't back in Beijing?" Her sobs lessened.

"Well, yes, I was, but it was only—"

"I knew it! You bastard, it's her, isn't it? Your *aide*. Remember when I was your *aide*? Remember how we used to *work* late at night?"

"It's not like that," he said, but even he thought his words sounded flimsy. He'd been back to Beijing for a meeting, but his time on the ground was only going to be a few hours. He reasoned that it would be easier on his family if he never told them.

"I love you, Mei Lin. I'm doing this for us."

"Us? *Us?*" Her voice cracked. "Are you fucking her?"

Gao flinched. There was no way Fang hadn't heard that.

"No, darling," he said. "I love you."

Mei Lin hung up.

He should have called back, but instead Gao pretended for the benefit of Captain Fang that his marriage was not an evolving trainwreck.

"Good . . . I'll call you tonight, darling. Please don't worry. I love you, too. Kiss the children for me."

He hung up the phone and blew out a breath he hadn't realized he was holding.

Gao closed his eyes. How had he gotten to this place? His career was on the verge of failure, and his marriage was a disaster. But he was stuck here. If he resigned now, they'd take away his second star. Any gains he'd made in the Party would be overwhelmed by the stink of failure. The Hero of Tashkent would become the Failure of Central Asia.

No, he was in too deep. The only way out was forward.

"General?" Fang's soft voice was right next to him. "Yichen?"

Gao stiffened. His eyes snapped open.

Fang stepped back. Her eyes dropped to the floor. "I'm sorry, sir. I overstepped. I just . . ."

Gao's frustrations bubbled to the surface. He lashed out, his tone sneering. "What is it, Captain? Do you find it ironic that your commanding officer has marital troubles?"

Fang seemed to shrink within herself. She blinked, and her chin trembled.

I'm an asshole, Gao thought. *Now I've made two women cry in the space of five minutes.*

Gao lowered his voice, reached for her arm. "I'm sorry, Captain. That was unprofessional of me."

"No, sir, I was the one who acted unprofessionally. I never should have said that, it's just . . ."

"Just what?" Gao urged. He squeezed her arm gently.

"I broke up with my boyfriend," Fang said, her words tumbling out. "We were together for almost five years. He broke my heart." She raised her eyes and Gao saw the anguish in them.

Without thinking, he hugged her. The combat uniform she wore did a fine job of hiding the contours of the lithe body beneath layers of heavy material. She pressed against him, and for a moment, Gao's quivering stomach eased. Her hair rested against his cheek and he smelled her perfume again.

What am I doing? He broke the embrace and they stepped apart awkwardly.

"I need to get back to work, General," Fang stepped around the desk and headed for the door.

"Captain Fang."

She stopped, did an about-face. He could see her cheeks were flushed and her eyes gleamed with unshed tears.

"Sir?'"

Gao swallowed. "In private settings, I would like you to call me Yichen."

A smile broke through Fang's tears.

28

Vladivostok, Russia

Russian President Nikolay Sokolov jogged off stage, propelled by the roar of eleven thousand voices from the supporters packed into the Dynamo Stadium.

This is more like it, he thought. Everything had gone exactly as planned. His speech, the fireworks, even the call and response at the end—flawless. Finally, *finally* he was getting a boost in the polls over Zaitsev. It was only a few points, but it would be enough to put him over the top.

Backstage, he accepted a towel from a woman wearing a headset and he mopped his face. When he handed it back, the white cloth was streaked with tan-colored makeup.

"Sorry," Nikolay said, but she just smiled at him.

He heard the *pop* of a champagne cork and someone passed him a glass of the bubbly. He downed it in one go. Behind him, the crowd was a torrent of excited voices.

He had to admit, the new campaign manager Federov had hired was right. *Get out of Moscow*, she'd said. *Take your message to the people.*

Vladivostok was about as far from Moscow as you could get, and she was right. They *loved* him here. So different from the poisonous backbiting and head games of Moscow. This city on the Pacific Ocean was connected to the rest of the world by maritime trade. People here were just as likely to travel east to Canada or the United States as they were to visit faraway Moscow. They understood what democracy meant. They believed in him and his message of reform.

Tonight, when he came to the line in his speech about his vision for a free Russia, he felt the connection with the people. They were with him.

A stunning young woman in a dark business suit with her blonde hair in a French braid approached. "Can I take you to your dressing room, Mr. President?"

The stage noises faded as they passed through the swinging door and into the warren of dressing rooms. The painted cinder block walls were covered with signatures of past performers. Nikolay had a sudden urge to add his name to the mix. It might be a historic monument one day, he thought. The day Nikolay Sokolov saved his presidency.

The woman opened a door at the end of the hallway and met his eye without hesitation. "If there's anything else I can do . . ." She let her voice trail off suggestively.

"What is your name?" Nikolay leaned against the door jamb.

"Svetlana, my friends call me Lana."

"Lana." Nikolay extended his hand. Her grip was warm and firm. "What a beautiful name."

"Thank you, Lana," said a voice from behind Nikolay. "That will be all for now."

Nikolay tried to watch her walk away, but Federov urged him through the doorway and closed the door.

The dressing room was large, with a well-lit mirror taking up one wall. A separate sitting area had two leather armchairs and a low table laid with tea service and a plate of chocolates.

"You never let me have any fun, Vladimir." Nikolay pretended to pout as he dropped into a chair and popped a chocolate into his mouth. Nothing could ruin his mood tonight.

"If you want to see her later, I'll have her checked out," Federov replied in a curt voice.

Nikolay looked up at the severe tone. "What's wrong?"

"We have a problem, Mr. President."

Nikolay felt the euphoria of the moment evaporate. He crossed to the dressing table and used a wet towel to scrub the remaining makeup from his face.

"Just one?" he said. "I was on stage for an hour. Usually, that's enough time for at least three or four crises to erupt." He looked at Federov in the mirror. The big man's expression was more grave than usual. "Is it the Ultras again? A new hit piece out on me?"

"The Chinese want to meet, sir."

Nikolay balled up the towel and lobbed it into the trash can. "Okay, when?"

"Now."

"Now?" Nikolay repeated.

"Now. Here."

"You mean in this room?"

Federov nodded.

"What do they want?"

Federov shrugged.

"There's something you're not saying, Vladimir."

When Federov told him who was waiting to meet with him, Nikolay stared at his reflection in the vanity for a full minute. "Do I have a choice?"

"My recommendation is that you take the meeting, Mr. President."

Nikolay forced a laugh. "Look on the bright side, Vladimir. At least I don't have to prep for it."

Federov did not respond.

Nikolay blew out a breath. "Let's get this over with."

Federov dipped his chin in a curt nod. "Right away, Mr. President."

Chinese Minister of State Security Yan Tao was a slight man with angular features. His thinning gray hair was the color of dishwater and he wore it slicked down tight against his scalp. At first glance, one might have guessed he was an accountant or a scientist, but Nikolay knew better. Minster Yan was a dangerous man, a skilled politician, and a close confidante of the General Secretary of the Chinese Communist Party.

He'd taken over the post after an ill-conceived invasion of Taiwan, which had been prompted by the machinations of his predecessor. Yan's mission had been to clean up the MSS, to ensure it served the Party and not the other way around.

The Minister was accompanied by only one security man who posted outside the door. Whatever he wanted to discuss, he was taking pains to ensure a low-profile visit.

Nikolay and the Minister occupied the armchairs while Federov stood behind his president.

"This is an unexpected pleasure, Minister Yan," Nikolay began.

"I don't care for small talk, Mr. President." Nikolay detected a smugness in the man's thin smile.

"Fine," Nikolay replied, matching the Minister's curt tone. "What can I do for you?"

"I traveled here tonight to offer you a choice."

Nikolay raised an eyebrow. "That sounds ominous."

"It doesn't have to be, Mr. President. It could be to your benefit."

Nikolay did not reply, so the Minister continued. "I am here to inform you that the People's Republic of China has formed a new security alliance with Kazakhstan. Within the next 48 hours, the People's Liberation Army will begin to relocate troops along the border of our two countries. The People's Republic must deal with the internal threat of the Uighur movement, and Kazakhstan has chosen to assist us in exchange for certain benefits."

Nikolay's fingers gripped the arm of his chair. In the silence, he heard Federov shifting behind him.

The Minister's tone was matter-of-fact, but the statement was explosive. Kazakhstan was Russia's oldest ally in Central Asia, the very definition of *near-abroad* for the Federation. Not to mention the oil and gas resources and the space program. When word of this got out, the Ultras would crucify him.

Nikolay cleared his throat. "You can't do that."

"I think the French term is *fait accompli*, Mr. President. It is already done."

"According to the Shanghai Cooperation Organization, the movement of military forces requires approval before the full body. You are violating your own military alliance."

The SCO was a Eurasian defense and security alliance styled loosely after the North Atlantic Treaty Organization. Like NATO, which relied on the United States for leadership and funding, the SCO was heavily dependent on China.

"And that is where your choice enters the picture, Mr. President. May I?" He gestured at the tea service.

Nikolay nodded, then watched as the man took his time preparing a cup of tea. Finally, the Minister settled back in his chair and sipped his tea. He smacked his lips in satisfaction.

"Where was I?"

"You were about to offer me a choice," Nikolay said in a flat voice.

"Of course, forgive me. You could protest this move and elevate it to the SCO leadership. That is your right as a member in good standing. However, I believe that would create a public issue for you during your upcoming election. We consider this a bilateral arrangement, separate from the broader SCO collaboration."

"I can handle my own public relations, Minister," Nikolay snapped.

"I'm sure your campaign is in good hands, Mr. President, but social media can be heavily influenced by outside entities, yes?" He showed teeth when he smiled this time. "Some people will believe anything if they see it on the internet."

"Blackmail," Nikolay said.

"A recognition of reality, Mr. President," Yan countered in a cool tone. "Your inability to provide the necessary security guarantees has left Kazakhstan open to alternative arrangements. Russia has failed. It is up to the People's Republic of China to step into the breach."

He drained his teacup and placed it on the table.

"All hope is not lost, Mr. President. There is no reason why Chinese troop movements near the border with Kazakhstan cannot be concealed until after your election. Should the need arise, we have means to deploy a fitting cover story about the ongoing issues in western China. Your campaign will not be troubled by this issue. I guarantee it."

"How thoughtful," Nikolay said.

Minister Yan allowed Nikolay to connect the dots on his own. There was no way he could challenge China militarily. If he protested the troop movements publicly, Zaitsev and the Ultras would roast him as weak on national defense. If he did nothing, he was ceding Russian leadership in Central Asia to China.

Check and mate.

The Minister gently cleared his throat. "The influence of public opinion works both ways, Mr. President. If we are able to reach an understanding today, I can assure you that Beijing will be most appreciative."

For a second, Nikolay allowed himself the fantasy of leaping across the table, grabbing Yan by his scrawny neck, and punching him in the face. Instead, he smiled. "Please give my regards to the General Secretary."

Yan smiled and stood. "Thank you, gentlemen."

Nikolay shook the Minister's hand. His grip was light. The bones of his fingers felt as fragile as if they were made of balsa wood.

Yet those scrawny fingers held Nikolay's future in their grasp.

29

The White House, Washington, DC

When Don received a call to brief the President on the progress of Operation Catbird, he was not concerned. In fact, he welcomed the opportunity.

For once, he had good news to share. The influence operation to boost Timur Ganiev's public profile in the Central Asian republics had far exceeded Don's expectations. He could not recall the last time he'd seen an operation this successful in such a short amount of time. He was considering having Harrison write it up as a case study for future reference.

Even the unexpected presence of National Security Advisor Valentina Florez in the Oval Office could not dampen Don's mood. He was bulletproof on this operation. That very morning, just before he left the office, Harrison had reported that there was a rapidly growing movement to form a Central Asian Union with Ganiev as the leader. To Don, just the idea of a cross-border political union showed the power of Ganiev's unifying message on the hearts and minds of his countrymen.

The movement had strong grassroots support in all four republics. Across the region, people circulated petitions and held rallies to demand that their governments recognize the CAU as a legitimate entity. Not since the Arab Spring in 2010 had the world seen so much political change so quickly.

Don nodded good morning to the Vice President and to Florez. The woman's luxurious dark hair hung loosely around her shoulders. She wore a bloodred blouse, black pencil skirt, and a pair of high-heeled shoes with soles that matched her blouse.

"Good morning, Donald," she said in a curt voice.

The President seemed preoccupied, but Don attributed that to the morning headlines. Leading all the news channels was a new poll showing Vice President Hawthorne and Senator Eleanor Cashman locked in a statistical tie in their run for the White House. The talking heads chattered on about swing states and how a few thousand votes out of the millions cast would decide the next election. Don assumed that his summons to the White House was to assure the President that there were no international situations waiting to spring into the public consciousness. In the weeks before an election, even a minor news story, if poorly managed, could leave the votes with the wrong last impression. It could mean the difference between winning and losing.

"The Director was called away at the last minute, Mr. President," Don informed him. "It's just me this morning, sir."

The President took his seat without comment and waited while coffee was served. When the door to the Oval Office closed, he turned to Don.

"Let's have it, Don," he said heavily.

Don adopted a positive tone. "I'm pleased to report, Mr. President, that the influence operation we've constructed around Timur Ganiev is succeeding even better than we'd hoped."

He spent a few moments describing the nuts and bolts of Operation Catbird. He covered this part quickly—the President was not one for operational details.

Don kept an eye on Vice President Hawthorne's reaction, trying to gauge if he was giving the potential next president enough detail to satisfy his curiosity. Hawthorne nodded along as Don spoke. Another positive sign in what was shaping up to be a very good day.

"The best news, sir," Don concluded, "came in just a few hours ago.

We're seeing a concerted push across the region for the formation of a new multinational governing body with Ganiev as the leader."

"Multinational governing body?" Serrano asked. "What does that mean exactly?"

"It's a concept that's been floating around on social media circles for a while now," Don replied. "Think of it as their version of a European Union. Sovereign countries with common borders, a common currency, that sort of thing."

"A Central Asian union," Serrano said, his tone brighter. "I like the sound of that."

"Why now, Donald?" Florez spoke for the first time.

"We see it as a reaction to the increased violence of the SIF, ma'am. The political assassinations in Tajikistan and in Kyrgyzstan have woken up the public. The constant drumbeat of violence is taking a toll on the people's willingness to accept the status quo. Ganiev, on the other hand, has been a consistent voice for peace and unity. It seems as if the people are hungry for that kind of leadership."

"And you see this Central Asian movement as a result of the CIA's influence operation?" Florez pressed.

Where is she going with this? Don wondered. He chose his words carefully. "The goal of the operation was to reduce the influence of the SIF, so I think we can claim success. We were in the right place at the right time to give Ganiev a push."

"It feels like it's all happening very fast to me," Florez said. "It makes me wonder how real the effect will be."

"We're talking about governmental change," Don agreed. "It's unclear how much power a non-governmental body will have in the region, but it aligns with our interests all the same."

Florez did not seem to want to concede the point. "Don't you find it convenient that the death of Nurbek Kulov, a confirmed Kyrgyz nationalist, would be the springboard to Ganiev's ambitions for a Central Asian union?"

"I would use the word ironic," Don replied. "The SIF overstepped, and we reap the rewards."

"This all sounds positive to me," Hawthorne weighed in. "Good job, Riley. Keep up the good work."

"Thank you, sir." But when Don looked at the President, he saw that Serrano had a brooding expression.

"What about the Russians?" the President asked.

"We've been sharing regional intel with the Russians, sir," Don said. "That was what we agreed to do."

Serrano's lips pressed into a thin line. "Agreement or not, the last six weeks have been a disaster for Nikolay Sokolov. Both of the assassinated men were strong Russian allies."

Don shifted in his seat until his back was firmly against the sofa cushions. He was missing something in this conversation, and from the look on the Vice President's face he wasn't the only one.

Serrano toyed with his coffee cup. "I asked Valentina to give me an independent assessment of the operation. She has some questions for you."

Don was stunned. Operation Catbird was a huge success, and now the President was second-guessing his work? "Sir, I think—"

"It's not a reflection on your work, Don." The President's tone was not unkind, but it was firm. "I just want some options."

Don sat straighter in his seat, trying not to let his irritation show. He noticed that Florez had produced a yellow legal pad and a Montblanc pen. "Tell me about your interaction with the Indian Research and Analysis Wing," she said.

Don quickly recounted his visit to RAW, including Jay Patel's clear denial of any connection to the Seljuk Islamic Front.

"And you believed him?"

"I did," Don replied. "At the time."

"What about now?"

Don hesitated. "There's a new possible interaction between the SIF and the Indian covert operations branch."

"Explain," Serrano said tersely.

"The night that Kulov was assassinated in Bishkek, the head of Indian special operations was in the city."

"Doesn't that seem a little too convenient, Don?" Florez asked. "Here's what I think happened: Orazov, the leader of the SIF, used his relationship with Kulov to set him up for an assassination by the Indians."

"That's circumstantial, ma'am," Don replied. "The Director has been in touch with the Indian government. Patel's visit was planned well in advance. His presence there was a coincidence."

"Timur Ganiev was also in Bishkek," Florez pressed. "Was that another coincidence?"

"Ganiev has been to Bishkek multiple times." Don's annoyance was like an itch he could not scratch. He willed himself to be still. He would not allow Florez to see that she was getting to him.

But Florez had a valid point: there were a lot of coincidences in this story. Too many.

"Bishkek was where Ganiev stopped the lynching of a Russian soldier, right?" Florez asked. "That was where you got the idea to use him as the focal point of an influence operation."

"Correct," Don replied. "That's in my report."

"Doesn't it seem odd that Ganiev would support the wife of a confirmed nationalist?"

It was a fair question, Don thought, and one that he'd wrestled with. "Timur Ganiev has always positioned himself as a cultural and spiritual leader, not a politician. Supporting a grieving widow seems on brand to me, especially since he's a doctor by training."

Florez nodded, tapping her pen against the pad of paper. Don shifted in his seat. He didn't see where this was going, and it annoyed him that they were missing the headline: The operation was working as planned.

"Look," he said, leaning toward Florez. "The goal of our operation is to promote Ganiev's influence as a positive counterweight against the SIF. We're doing exactly what we said we wanted to do. It's working."

He tried to think of this situation from Florez's point of view. She was known to be fiercely loyal to Serrano, but the President had cut her out of the loop on Operation Catbird. If Florez's feelings were hurt, that wasn't Don's fault.

Tap-tap-tap went the Montblanc pen.

"Is there anything else?" Don said, not even bothering to hide his peevish tone.

"You've been played, Riley," she said.

"Excuse me?" Don snapped back. "This operation is one of the most successful—"

"And that's the problem, Don," Florez replied. "It's too successful, too fast. Almost like someone wants us to stay on the sidelines."

Irritation was in the rearview mirror now. Don's face flushed hot with anger.

But Florez was not about to let up.

"We're employing half measures, Mr. President," she said. "It will come back to bite us in the ass."

"Half measures?" Don replied hotly. "This is a by-the-book operation yielding stellar results."

"Stellar results for whom?" Florez said. "Ganiev is a joke. The SIF is a real terrorist organization killing real people with real-world consequences."

Too late, Don saw where she was going.

Florez turned to the President. "We can't allow this state of affairs to continue, sir. My analysis says the SIF is alive and well."

Serrano raised an eyebrow.

Good lord, Don thought. He's falling for her bullshit.

Don went on the attack. "What do you propose, Valentina?"

"Cut the head off the snake." She punctuated her point by rapping her pen on the legal pad. "I say we take out Akhmet Orazov."

"A kinetic operation?" Don realized his voice had gone up an octave, but he didn't care. This was madness. "Sir, our goal was a low-key covert action. Nothing to destabilize the region."

Serrano's teeth worried at his lower lip, a sure sign to Don that he was considering the unthinkable. Desperate, Don tried to think of another way to approach the argument and came up blank.

"Don't do it, Mr. President," Hawthorne said. Everyone turned to the Vice President as if they'd forgotten he was still in the room. Hawthorne cleared his throat and plunged on. "I agree with Riley on this one, sir. With all due respect to Ms. Florez, her option sounds risky to me."

Don tore his gaze from Hawthorne back to the President—and felt a little surge of hope.

"I realize you're the President, sir," Hawthorne continued, "and this is one hundred percent your call. But I wanted you to have my thoughts on this matter. Seeing how when we *win*"—he smiled when he said the word —"this is going to be my policy as well. I would prefer that we not start out my administration with an assassination."

Opposite Don, Florez sat up so straight that it seemed like she was levitating. Her handsome features were flushed and her dark eyes flashed, but she kept her mouth shut.

"Mr. President," Don pressed, "I strongly recommend against a kill operation. It's too risky, sir."

Serrano sat back in his chair and sighed.

"All right, Riley, you win. For now."

30

Samarkand, Uzbekistan

Nicole set up for interviews on the upstairs terrace of the Hotel Dilshoba. From that vantage point, there was an excellent view of the azure dome of the Gori Amir, the Tomb of the King, as the mausoleum of Tamerlane was known. Located only a few blocks away, the fifteenth-century tiled structure rose like a royal presence above the roofs of the surrounding houses.

Working with Barry, she tried a series of camera angles to put the dome in the background of their interview subjects while avoiding the unsightly clutter of the power lines. Barry was a master when it came to framing and lighting, and Nicole was pleased with the result. If he kept up this level of work, she might have to sleep with him after all.

For her camera angle, Barry arranged it so that the scene behind her was a backdrop of low-slung houses with the Pamir Mountains looming in the distance.

Timur Ganiev had invited her to the conclave he was hosting and connected her with interview candidates for her documentary. All of the men she'd contacted—and they were all men, she noted—agreed to meet with her. She and Barry had taped three interviews already and were getting ready for their final meeting of the day.

The dome was beautiful in the late afternoon sun, the weathered features softened by the low-angle light. It was hot on the covered terrace, but through the use of fans and misters they kept the temperature to a manageable level.

Firuz Sharipov showed up five minutes early. Unlike the other politicians she'd interviewed, he came alone. As Nicole looked over her list of questions, he allowed Barry to hook up the lapel microphone to his white dress shirt and check his light levels.

Sharipov was Kyrgyz, a native of Bishkek. A relatively young politician, he was known as a rising leader and a voice of the younger generation. She noted that he had been a vocal supporter of the late Nurbek Kulov, but since the assassination, he'd switched his alliance to Timur Ganiev.

Interesting shift, she mused, from autocrat to populist. She'd try to draw him out on that point.

Sharipov was in his early thirties, with a close-cropped beard and thin face. Like many Kyrgyz, his skin was pale and his eyes were deep green. According to her notes, he spoke English, but this was his very first interview with Western media. She decided to test his language skills before they started.

"I'm just going to ask you a series of questions about the conclave," she said in English. "I'd also like to discuss the current political situation in Kyrgyzstan and your relationship with Timur Ganiev. Is that okay?"

The man nodded. "Absolutely," he replied in excellent English.

Nicole sighed with relief. Her other interviews had all been in Russian. While it was perfectly acceptable to translate answers and dub them in on the finished film, the language barrier introduced an extra layer of distance for American viewers. A subject who could speak directly to the question in English would help immensely when she showed clips to potential donors, who at this point were her main audience.

She cut a glance at Barry, who gave her a thumbs-up to let her know that both sound and cameras were ready.

"Can you tell me what the Ashura Conclave means to you, Mr. Sharipov?" she began.

He was an interviewer's dream. Calmly and clearly, Sharipov explained that although Ashura was a holy day for the Islam religion, it held special meaning this year.

"What kind of meaning?" Nicole asked.

"Different sects of Islam mark the day in different ways, but this year, a group of us were asked to come together at the Tomb of the King for a unique celebration."

Perfect, Nicole thought. This guy was so measured, she doubted she would need to edit a single thing.

Sharipov settled into his chair. Behind him, the afternoon sunlight gilded the azure dome of the mausoleum.

"My fellow leaders and I," he continued, "are not here just to celebrate a religious holiday. Over the past three days, the members of the conclave have fasted and prayed together. But mostly we talked about our future, and we listened to a man who has a lot to say about unity for the native peoples of this region."

"And that man is Timur Ganiev?" Nicole asked.

Sharipov nodded. "It is fitting that we are at the tomb of the original Timur, a man better known in the West as Tamerlane. At the height of his power, Timur created an empire that encompassed the known world at the time. Central Asia was the heart of that world.

"We have always been a land of tribes. Some lived on the steppes, some in the mountains. But in Timur's time, those tribal bonds were transcended. The tribes were unified under one man and we ruled the known world for centuries."

"And you think that can happen again?" Nicole asked. "That the Timur of our time can reunite the tribes of Central Asia?"

Sharipov's expression softened. "Timur would not say that."

"What do *you* say?"

The man paused. "I say our borders were drawn by outsiders. They are political boundaries designed to keep us apart. Arbitrary lines, designed to pit us against one another, to keep us unfocused and off balance. While we bicker amongst ourselves, these outside powers have taken over our lands, stripped them of our rich natural resources, and left the people poorer than we started."

"You're talking about Russia," Nicole said.

"I am saying that our past is a path to our future." Sharipov twisted in his seat to regard the azure dome. "Seven hundred years ago, the first Timur united the people of Central Asia into the most powerful society in the world. We can have that greatness again. We are a people with a rich heritage. We deserve to be treated as such by our neighbors."

Nicole shifted gears. "Can you talk about the current political situation in Kyrgyzstan? How has it influenced your thinking?"

Sharipov frowned as if the question caused him physical pain. "This is a very personal question for me. Not long ago, a terrorist hate group took the life of a great leader in my country."

He pressed his lips together in resolve. "That tragedy was a personal turning point for me. Nurbek Kulov was a great man, but he was also a fierce nationalist who looked to promote the interests of Kyrgyzstan over those of our neighbors."

"And you see that as wrong?"

"Timur preaches that to become one people again, we need to transcend the bonds of our own nationalities, to embrace the brotherhood of our shared past."

Timur preaches? Nicole thought. The religious overtones were obvious. She decided to pull that thread.

"Do you see Timur Ganiev as a religious leader or a politician?"

Sharipov shook his head firmly. "Neither. Timur seeks to unify, not divide. The word of Timur transcends the divisions of politics and religion. He preaches a vision of future greatness that is rooted in the power of a people connected by a shared culture, where our different ethnicities are a strength, not a weakness."

There was that word again—*preaches*. "What is Timur's vision?" Nicole pressed.

The man's lips parted and his eyes shone. Nicole felt a shiver go up her spine. She was looking at a true believer. Whatever Timur Ganiev was serving up, this guy had taken a double helping.

"Unity," Sharipov said, his voice hoarse with emotion. "Pride. Single-minded purpose in our future. I struggle to find one word to say what I feel."

"Destiny?" Nicole asked.

The man's face cleared and he broke into a radiant smile. "Yes, that's the word I was searching for. *Destiny*." He said it like he was tasting the word on his tongue for the first time. "Timur Ganiev will lead us to our destiny."

When Sharipov had left, Nicole helped Barry pack up the cameras so they could relocate to the mausoleum for the evening ceremony. "Can I ask you a question?" Barry asked.

"Sure."

"Do you believe this stuff?" Barry asked. "Destiny, unity. I'm getting a messiah vibe here. Kinda creepy."

"I'm here for the story, Barry," she said. "Do I believe it? I don't know. You saw Timur at the hospital in Bishkek. What do you think?"

Although she avoided his question, she'd been wrestling with the same idea ever since the last interview.

Barry hoisted a camera case. "I've covered a lot of politicians and they all have one thing in common: they have the *gift*. They can connect with people on a gut level and make them do stuff that they wouldn't normally do."

Isha, the evening call to prayer, sounded over the city, cutting him off. They both waited until the last notes of the amplified voice faded.

"Ganiev's got the gift with a capital G," Barry continued. "They all keep saying he's not a politician, but he sure looks like one to me. That's what I think."

Nicole nodded, but said nothing. In the United States, when someone wanted to run for President, they started to show up in places like Iowa and New Hampshire. They all claimed they weren't running for the highest office in the free world, but everyone knew the truth. Nicole was getting the same feeling here.

"That's why I'm doing this," she said. "Maybe that's the story here."

By the time they'd gotten something to eat and traveled the two blocks to the mausoleum, the evening prayers had concluded. They set up the cameras in front of a small stage that had been erected in the courtyard. From this close, Nicole could see that the fifteenth-century mausoleum, while beautiful, was actually not that large. She guessed the domed tower was about the size of a small grain silo. In the darkening evening, the structure was artfully lighted, lending an air of mysticism to the setting.

The courtyard was packed with people, and the name of Timur was on everyone's lips. *The Timur she'd met that first day in his apartment or Timur the leader of the Central Asian Union?* Nicole wondered as she helped Barry set up his cameras. It was hard to believe they were the same man.

A line of men dressed in long white robes filed out of the mausoleum. The Tajiks and Kyrgyz wore round *tubeteika* embroidered skullcaps. Timur, the last in line, wore a square *doppa* traditionally worn by Uzbeks.

There was just enough room on the stage to accommodate all the members of the conclave. The crowd hushed when Timur stepped to the microphone. Nicole drew in a breath. The lighting on the stage was perfect. Just enough illumination to allow the men in the background to be visible, but not enough to make them distracting.

Timur was dressed in a white robe, belted at the waist. His face looked gaunt and his eyes burned with an unnatural light. He held out his hand and the people stilled.

"I am a man who has been given much in this life." His voice was low but powerful, and the amplification was spot on, allowing everyone within earshot to hear him clearly. "I had educational opportunities, I had a wife that I loved more than life itself, and I had a purpose. At least, I believed I had a purpose."

He looked down as if lost in thought. Nicole felt the people around her breathing in unison. When Timur looked up again, his lips traced a wistful smile. "Many of you know the story of my wife's death. But the part of the story that you do not know is what her death did to me as a man. How her passing changed me.

"I believed that my purpose in this world was to bring healthcare to the poorest areas of this land. To *our* land. But I came to realize how many of the problems we face today are of our own design. We erect borders, we build walls of nationalist identity. We do these things to keep *them* away from *us*. I realized that I was working so hard to help so few. I came to see how the walls we had built up between us would never let me truly help people."

He turned to cast a long look at the lighted dome.

"It is fitting we are here at the tomb of Timur. There is a story often told, of when Timur questioned his life's purpose. He was in a battle as a young man and losing badly. Injured, he took refuge in the ruins of an ancient structure like this one. It was said he was waiting to die, and he was afraid.

"As he sat there, he watched an ant carrying a grain of rice twice its size try to climb a hill of dirt. Every time the ant tried to take the hill, the dirt would shift and it would fall back down. Fascinated, Timur watched the ant try again and again. Twenty times the ant tried. Thirty times. Timur was convinced the ant would never achieve his goal."

Present-day Timur's eyes focused on the horizon as if he'd forgotten about the audience. "And then it did. The ant overcame the hill and proudly carried his prize back to the colony. In that moment, Timur found inspiration. He said to himself: If an ant can persevere like this, then surely a man can do the same thing."

The crowd was like a field of statues, collective breaths held in unison.

"And in the depths of my personal despair, I resolved to be like that ant from Timur's story. I resolved to persevere until I achieved my real goal: to unify my people. Unity is our destiny. Through unity, we can avoid senseless bloodshed. We can build our region into an economic powerhouse, give our children and grandchildren the future that too few of us have had, and enjoy the freedoms we deserve."

The people around Nicole stirred, whispering, chanting. She felt the energy like a live thing passing through the crowd and she shivered with involuntary delight.

"On this night, I say to you that we are stronger together. One tribe, one people. We no longer accept the artificial borders placed on us by outsiders and politicians. I ask you to follow me in this destiny . . . "

His voice faded out of hearing. Not because the sound system failed, but because his words were lost in the din of thousands of screaming voices.

Nicole found herself leaping and shouting. She clutched at Barry's arm and he grinned back at her.

As the crowd raged with joy around her, Nicole had her own moment of exultation.

This is the story of a lifetime.

31

Samarkand, Uzbekistan

The automatic glass doors whooshed open as Gao followed the PLA colonel from the air-conditioned comfort of the private air terminal into the late afternoon heat. Sunlight reflected off the colonel's dark glasses. He came to attention and saluted.

"I hope you found the inspection to your satisfaction, Lieutenant General Gao," he said crisply.

Gao returned the honor, then held out his hand. The colonel's square jaw slackened in surprise at the personal gesture. He gripped Gao's proffered hand with enthusiasm.

"Excellent progress, Colonel. Keep up the good work."

"Yes, sir." The colonel, who was actually older than Gao, beamed like a schoolboy.

Behind him, Gao heard the Harbin Z-20 helicopters start their engines. Ever-efficient Captain Fang was keeping them on schedule. "I'll return in two weeks for another update, Colonel."

The grin widened. "We'll be ready, sir."

Gao released the man's hand and turned. A hundred meters away, the pair of Z-20s crouched on the tarmac like prehistoric beetles ready to spring into the air. The overhead rotors were a blur of motion. He looked around for Fang and spied her in the lee of the building, a mobile phone pressed to her ear. She saw Gao watching her, spoke a final few words into the phone, and slipped it into her pocket.

She hurried over to Gao and saluted. "We're ready, sir."

"Very well, Captain."

She signaled for their security detail, a squad of eight armed soldiers, to follow. When they got closer to the helos, Fang divided the soldiers into two groups. Two in Gao's chopper, and the remaining six in the second bird.

Gao removed his barracks cap, holding it tightly to his chest, and ducked his head as he followed Fang under the five whirling rotor blades. She leaped into the open door of the aircraft with the grace of a gazelle. Gao gripped the handhold and hoisted himself up into the seat next to her.

The Z-20s were capable of carrying a max of twelve combat soldiers in three bench seats. Two rear seats faced each other, while the third bench, forward-facing, formed a row behind the pilot and copilot. Their security detail manned the Type 67 machine guns mounted near the doors on either side of the craft.

Gao knew they could have fit his entire security detail into one helo, but Fang had added a second chopper. For security reasons, she said.

Under normal circumstances, they wouldn't have flown the three hundred kilometers at all. Even accounting for the mountainous terrain and turns, it was only a four-hour drive from the PLA base near Dushanbe to the massive new Chinese-built Samarkand International Commerce Center.

But ever since he'd seen the landslide that had buried the road in Takob, the thought of driving through the mountains terrified Gao. The peaks were the stronghold of the SIF. In Taiwan, he'd fought in the mountains against motivated men who knew the land, and he wanted no part of that scenario ever again.

Whether Captain Fang felt the same fear or just intuited it in her general, she never brought up the idea of driving to Samarkand.

Gao slipped on a pair of headphones and turned the selector switch so he could hear Fang talking to the pilots.

"We're ready to go when you are, Captain." Fang's steady voice filled

Gao's ears. "Lieutenant General Gao would like to be back to base before dark."

"Not a problem, ma'am," the pilot replied. Gao heard him contact the other pilot and the two aircraft levitated off the ground in unison. They made a wide circuit of the Samarkand International Commerce Center.

It was an enormous structure, a combined hub for the international airport, the high-speed rail lines, and the nexus for all buses and trucking in the region. The colonel who had given them the tour had taken great pleasure in reeling off the statistics of the facility. Even by the standards of large Chinese infrastructure projects, this was big.

Gao leaned back and let out a deep sigh of satisfaction. This day could not have gone better.

There were still the schedule issues, of course, but the colonel had shown him how even if the construction was not fully complete, it would be a simple matter to conceal the remaining work from the visiting dignitaries. The Jade Spike ceremony, he assured General Gao, would happen on schedule.

The venue of the ceremony was to be the great concourse between the airport and the high-speed rail hub. The concourse itself was a magnificent piece of architecture, with high soaring ceilings and skylights that allowed soft light to flood into the space. The floors were dark stone, quarried from the nearby mountains, and the columns were clad in stainless steel textured to look like tree bark. The center of the concourse, where the Jade Spike ceremony was to be held, was open and airy like a clearing in a forest.

Gao had spent nearly an hour walking the great hall and listening to the colonel's detailed explanations of the project. He'd watched the craftsmen put the finishing touches on a circular mosaic in the floor. Two flags—the national symbols of Uzbekistan and the People's Republic of China—were being inlaid into the stone in tiny colorful tiles. At the base of the flags was a thick glass capsule where the ceremonial Jade Spike would reside.

Just thinking about it made Gao's spine tingle with anticipation. This venue would impress even the General Secretary. And that would reflect positively on Lieutenant General Gao Yichen. He felt the months of stress and doubt start to melt from his muscles.

It had been the perfect day, he decided. The venue, the positive progress, the colonel's description of the layered security arrangements. He looked out the window at the golden sunlight flooding into the helicopter cabin. Even the weather was perfect.

For the first time in months, he allowed himself to think about the future.

Mei Lin was worried about nothing. His lucky star was once again on the rise. All the carping and backbiting that he'd experienced in Beijing would be forgotten when the Jade Spike ceremony went off without a hitch on November first.

And it was all because of his guiding hand.

The Hero of Tashkent delivers yet another victory for the Middle Kingdom.

He smiled to himself as he peered out the window. From this height, the rugged mountains looked like silken folds fanned out beneath them. Cattle and sheep dotted grassy hillsides. White snow fringed the tops of the tall peaks and the slanting sun cast shadows across the valleys.

When he came home in triumph, Mei Lin would forgive him. She would have to forgive him. After all, he'd done nothing inappropriate with Captain Fang. His conscience was clear.

Gao eyed his aide from his peripheral vision. She was silhouetted in the afternoon sun, the curve of her slender neck dark against a golden background. His mouth went dry as he recalled the afternoon of his argument with Mei Lin and their shared moment of intimacy. That had been a close call, but he'd stayed strong and true to his wife.

Still, he couldn't help but recall Fang's trembling nearness, her enticing scent, her vulnerability. Although they had offered their first names to each other in that moment, neither had exercised that intimacy yet.

Gao sensed that she might be willing to take their relationship to a deeper level. All he had to do was ask. But he held back.

He turned to the window, pushing thoughts of infidelity from his mind. His reflection ghosted in the glass as he offered himself a smug smile.

Gao Yichen, you are a good man.

The escort helo hung in the sky a few hundred meters away, its rotors a blur of motion. He dropped his gaze to the mountains below them, trying to recall the names of the passes and the peaks.

Suddenly, a pinpoint of light burst from the shadow of the mountain below. The spark evolved into a lancing corkscrew of smoke. Gao's mind locked with panic.

A missile! Someone was firing a missile at them!

The escort helo exploded in front of his eyes. A burst of fiery light, then the craft tilted and drifted downward, trailing thick black smoke.

In front of him, the cockpit erupted into action. The helo slewed violently to the right, snapping Gao's body tight against the safety harness. He heard a *pop*. Out the window, he saw a great cloud of silver block his view of the ground as the pilots deployed chaff countermeasures.

He cranked the channel selector to the air crew setting and listened to the pilots' terse interchange.

"Evasive maneuvers!"

"Missile at two o'clock!"

"Deploying flares!"

Gao saw a string of white-hot flashes trail out behind the aircraft like exploding light bulbs. Somewhere behind them, Gao heard another explosion.

The helo angled down. Icy fear gripped Gao's guts as his body went weightless, restrained only by the harness.

"I'm putting us on the deck," the pilot yelled. "It's our only shot!"

The freefall ended abruptly as the g-forces of the arrested dive slammed Gao downward, grinding his backbone into the hard plastic of the seat. The helo slewed right, then left. Gao felt the contents of his stomach rise and he clamped his mouth shut.

Out the window, brown landscape rolled by in a blur, so close it seemed like he could touch the sides of the narrow canyon. The helo banked hard and he saw a racing river below them.

Gao sat frozen with fear. There was nothing he could do. His life, his entire existence, was in the hands of the two pilots.

Hands . . .

He looked down and saw Fang's fingers entwined with his own. He squeezed, and the action somehow made him feel more in control.

She looked at him. Her eyes were deep brown and he lost himself in their depths. The cabin of the helo was chaos and movement and panic, but in her eyes was . . . peace. He saw her lips move.

"Yichen," she said. He couldn't hear it, but he knew the shape and sound of the voice in his ear.

"Xiaomei," he whispered back. "I—I . . . " Feelings swelled in him. There was so much he wanted to say to her.

"I know," she mouthed and held his hand tighter.

The helo raced out of the gorge into a burst of golden sunshine. Below them, green grasslands stretched as far as Gao could see through the windscreen.

The helo powered forward. The pilot came on the shared channel.

"We're safe, General."

Xiaomei gave his fingers one last squeeze, then let go.

32

The White House, Washington, DC

The National Security Council meeting was limited to principals only. To Don, who was used to the background buzz of staffers packed two deep along the wall, it made the room seem empty and abnormally quiet.

But Don wasn't nervous at all. In fact, he was looking forward to briefing the full Council on Operation Catbird. How often did you get the chance to brief an operation that had exceeded expectations beyond any possible measure? He wanted to use words like *brilliant* and *astounding*, but he held himself back.

Still, the descriptors fit. The progress was nothing short of phenomenal. Social media across the region overflowed with mentions of Ganiev, and the Ashura conclave had only added to the buzz. The video of his speech, with the tomb of Tamerlane in the background, had gone viral. The talk of a united Central Asia progressed from if to when. An online group even sponsored a contest to create a Central Asian Union flag.

Don used the latest tranche of data from Falchion to populate the final slide of his presentation, a classic hockey stick curve that showed no signs of slowing down anytime soon. Often, Don knew he was his own worst critic, but even he had to smile at results like these.

"As this last chart shows, Operation Catbird is a great success," Don concluded. "The presence of Timur Ganiev on social media has severely blunted the impact of the Seljuk Islamic Front in the public conversation. The conclusion we draw is that bright hope for the future of the region is outpacing the chaos and fear generated by the SIF."

The room was quiet when Don finished, another side effect of the reduced attendance. He left the slide with all the latest statistics up as a backdrop when he asked for questions.

"Have you been able to correlate these results with a drop in SIF violence in the region?" National Security Advisor Valentina Florez asked. Today she was wearing a powder blue pantsuit, a splash of soft pastel among the dark business suits and military uniforms at the far end of the table.

"That's not an easily measurable statistic, ma'am," Don replied. "The SIF's activities are sporadic events. The point of an influence activity is to bend the curve of public opinion. The numbers tell us we're on the right track."

"Are we, Don?" the President asked. He toyed with his pen as he formed a question. That was not like him, Don knew. Serrano's questions were normally sharp and to the point.

"Sir?" Don said.

"I understand there's increased activity on the border between Kazakhstan and China. How does that fit in with this operation?"

"I'm not sure what you mean, sir." Don looked at the Chairman of the Joint Chiefs for backup, but the man kept his eyes on the table. "My understanding is that Beijing is calling any PLA troop movements on the border with Kazakhstan part of an internal exercise."

"I agree with Mr. Riley on that one, sir," the Secretary of State chimed in. "We've had no pushback from Kazakhstan. Our intel says that the Chinese are projecting a show of force aimed at an internal audience. We don't see the Kazakhs ramping up their military to counter the PLA activity, which means they aren't concerned."

The President appeared unsatisfied. He chewed his lip as he cast his gaze around the room. "Anyone else?"

"I disagree with Mr. Riley's rosy outlook," said Florez. She rapped a red lacquered nail on the tabletop. "What is the goal of this operation?"

Don tried not to let his frustration show. He'd been down this path with Florez before. "Operation Catbird is an influence operation, pure and simple. We're trying to win hearts and minds. No American lives on the line and very low cost."

"Hearts and minds?" Florez's tone was dismissive. "This is a part of the world where honor killings are still considered to be acceptable."

"Valentina," the President said sharply. "That's out of line."

"Mr. President," Flores said, "we're missing the forest for the trees."

The Vice President entered the conversation. "I supported this operation because it was the lowest risk, highest reward option. Look at these numbers." He pointed to Don's last slide. "If our goal is to influence the people to move toward democracy, then it's clearly working."

Florez looked at Hawthorne with something akin to pity. "With all due respect, Mr. Vice President, if we risk nothing, we gain nothing. It's not the success of the operation that I have an issue with, it's the premise. These are half measures. In my opinion, this path will lead to a very nasty surprise for the United States."

"Explain yourself," the Vice President snapped.

"There's another explanation for the increased PLA troop movement on the border between China and Kazakhstan," Florez said.

"You're saying the Chinese are preparing for an invasion of Central Asia?" Don asked.

"I'm saying the Chinese are looking for an excuse." Florez directed her comments at the President. "And when they act, what will our response be? An angry post on social media? It will be an embarrassment to this administration. This is Taiwan all over again."

To this room of senior advisers, the Taiwan comment was a scathing indictment. The Chinese had misled the United States national security apparatus and President Serrano for the better part of a year, driving them into one international quagmire after another. While US forces were engaged all over the world and far from the South China Sea, the PLA launched a surprise invasion of Taiwan.

It was effective. It was embarrassing to the US. And it almost succeeded.

But this was a completely different set of circumstances. Don waited for the Chairman to weigh in with a military assessment of the Chinese troop movements. To his surprise, nothing happened.

Then the penny dropped for Don. This entire conversation had nothing to do with Central Asia. This was about politics. Domestic politics. Florez was worried about something happening to embarrass the Vice President's campaign.

"Don't you think we're overstating the risk here?" Don said. "The Chinese have spent years investing in these countries. Why would they upset the applecart with a military action?"

"The SIF has links to the Uighurs in western China," Florez replied. "I don't think it's a stretch to say that Beijing sees the Uighur movement as an existential threat."

"Even if that's correct," Don said, "what we're doing with this influence operation makes a Chinese action *less* likely. Timur Ganiev is pushing a Central Asian union as a counterbalance to the SIF. That makes the Chinese position more secure, not less."

Don could see he was losing the argument. He made one last push. "The Chinese would need to justify any action on the world stage. They would need an excuse, a really good one."

Don saw the Director wince, and his heart sank. He'd walked right into a trap.

Florez said, "I agree with Mr. Riley. The PLA would need a bulletproof excuse to justify an invasion into Central Asia. In the Presidential Daily Brief this morning, I was informed of a SIF attack on the PLA general in charge of regional security. An escort helicopter was shot out of the sky. The general himself barely escaped."

"Is this true?" The Vice President directed his question at the Director.

"It's single-sourced intel, but it has the ring of truth," said the Director. "If it checks out, it means the SIF have gotten their hands on shoulder-launched anti-aircraft missiles, and they're not afraid to use them."

"Good lord," Hawthorne sat back in his chair.

"I think the Chinese are on a hair trigger, Mr. Vice President," Florez said. "The next high-profile attack might be successful. What then?"

Don didn't need a degree in psychology to read what was going on inside Vice President Hawthorne's head. And one look at Serrano told him that the President had already made up his mind.

Don tried one last time. "An unsuccessful assassination attempt only means that the Chinese brass is on full alert now. If anything, they're going to be *more* aware of security than they were before. The SIF took their shot and failed."

Don gripped the lectern, leaned forward. He met the President's eye and held his gaze. The President had told him—encouraged him, even—to speak his mind, to tell the truth.

"Mr. President, I'm an intelligence officer. I furnish you with the facts so that you can make the best possible decision. Here are the facts, sir: Operation Catbird is working. If we take a more aggressive approach now, we risk upsetting a very delicate balance of power."

Florez sniffed. "Riley is talking about hope. Hope is not a strategy, Mr. President. We should be playing offense, not hoping that we can win hearts and minds with Facebook posts and Telegram messages."

Election politics had no place in national security, but it was there. Don sensed it was sitting at the table right next to the most powerful leaders in the country.

The Vice President broke the silence. "What do you recommend, Ms. Florez?"

"Sir," Florez's voice was calm and cold. "I recommend we establish a lethal finding against the leader of the Seljuk Islamic Front, Akhmet Orazov. With Orazov off the board, everything improves. We take away China's excuse for an invasion, we reduce the political pressure on the current Russian administration, and we minimize India's influence."

Don's mind raced, trying to marshal all the arguments against Florez's recommendation. But as started to speak, the Director caught his eye and shook his head. It was a tiny move, but the message was clear.

Cut your losses. This decision was made before we walked in the room.

At the other end of the table, the military members of the NSC remained silent, as did the Secretary of State, confirming the Director's unspoken conclusion.

"Everybody wins?" Serrano asked Florez wryly.

The National Security Advisor nodded firmly. "Everybody wins, sir."

The President's gaze shifted to the Vice President. "Lionel? This is going to be your baby, after all."

The Vice President pursed his lips, then nodded his mane of thick gray hair. "Reluctantly, I agree, sir."

Don looked down at the lectern. The laptop screen mirrored the last slide of the presentation. The hockey stick curve, which he'd considered such good news only a few minutes earlier, mocked him.

"Mr. Riley," the President said.

Don looked up. "Sir."

"I direct you to establish a lethal finding against Akhmet Orazov, leader of the Seljuk Islamic Front. Orazov is a clear and present danger to American national security interests and must be removed."

33

Ugam-Chatkal National Park, Uzbekistan

Harrison's day started long before the sun was up. Breakfast was a single cup of coffee served in a tin mug. The drink tasted like dirt sweetened with condensed milk, but at least it was hot.

His breath steamed in the morning chill. Although he was dressed for the weather in a heavy shirt, down vest, and a watch cap pulled down over his ears, he still shivered. It was cold at this elevation, even in early fall.

The four men piled into a white Lada 4x4 towing a horse trailer. Harrison sat in the front passenger's seat next to their driver, a gregarious Uzbek park ranger. He wore a camouflage uniform with a patrol cap and a shoulder patch that read *Uqam-Chatkal National Park* in Cyrillic lettering. He was in his early thirties with a ready smile and endless energy. The fact that none of his passengers responded to his unceasing chatter didn't seem to bother the young man. Harrison supposed that being a park ranger was a lonely job, and the guy was used to the sound of his own voice.

The two men in the back seat remained silent for the car ride. The short, stout one with a surly attitude and mustache like a dustbrush was a member of the Uzbek national police force. Harrison knew the second man by voice only. The bounty hunter recommended by Shalikashvili was the biggest surprise of all for Harrison. On the phone, the man's voice was deep and gravelly, but in person he was slight of build, past middle age, and bald as an egg. He had a nervous disposition and reminded Harrison of a songbird always ready to fly away.

They didn't need four men for their early morning expedition. The only one Harrison really needed was the ranger, but he understood why the other two were there: they wanted to make sure they got paid.

They drove for over an hour on a winding dirt road as the sky lightened above them. The ranger got out twice to open locked gates that blocked their path. Each time, he carefully relocked the gates behind them using a ring of keys on his belt. The terrain on either side of the road grew steeper as they moved further up into the Western Tian-Shan Mountains and the ruts of the dirt track grew deeper.

The road ended in a cul-de-sac with enough room to turn the Lada around. The mountains loomed in front of them like a fortress. Sunlight flooded over the peaks, lighting the slopes on the opposite side of the valley. The terrain was mostly rocks and brown dirt, broken by a few low-slung trees and patches of brush.

The ranger made short work of unloading and saddling the horses. Harrison's mount was a scrappy brown-and-white mare who bore the unlikely Russian name *Malysh*. Nicknamed "Baby," she eyed him warily as Harrison swung into the saddle. He patted the horse's neck and wished he'd thought to bring a lump of sugar or an apple for her. It had been years since he'd been on the back of a horse, and he would require all of her understanding.

The park ranger settled himself in his saddle with practiced ease. The bounty hunter seemed to know what he was doing, but the cop struggled to find his seat. Once aboard his mount, his dour expression deepened.

"How far?" he asked the ranger. It was the first thing he'd said all morning.

The ranger shrugged. "Two hours, maybe more." He smiled. "It's a beautiful day for a ride. Enjoy it."

He set off at a bone-jarring trot and the three fell into line behind him. Harrison stuck close to the guide, and the bounty hunter was not far behind. The cop brought up the rear guard.

The ranger kept up his banter, but shifted into a running commentary of the natural wonders around them. He explained that they were on the edge of the area known as the Lake District, and Harrison noted pools of still water in many of the low-lying areas. High overhead, the ranger pointed out a soaring bird, proudly telling Harrison in English that it was an eastern imperial eagle.

Their progress slowed to a walk as the trail grew steeper. In Harrison's mind, the term *trail* overstated their path through the scrub brush up the mountainside, but the ranger seemed to know where he was going.

They paused on a ridge. While the ranger consulted a GPS receiver and the cop caught up to them, Harrison was treated to a spectacular view of the Tian-Shan Mountains. From this vantage point, he could see where the range abutted the Pamir Mountains as they marched south toward Pakistan. The white peak of Tomur gleamed like a tooth in the autumn sunshine. At a height of almost 7,500 meters, the mountain anchored the western edge of the Tian-Shan range.

"Beautiful?" the guide asked in English.

"Beautiful," Harrison agreed.

The ranger pointed to the slope on the other side of a narrow valley below them. "Not far now. Just over there."

They descended from the ridge with the horses bracing their legs as they half walked, half slid down the rocky slope. At the bottom of the valley was a small lake clear enough for Harrison to see the bottom. Next to the lake, a ring of thick green brush formed a small pasture.

The guide dismounted and let his horse drink from the lake. Harrison followed suit, then watched as the man produced short loops of rope from his saddle bag. He slid them onto the front legs of his horse at knee height, then did the same for Harrison's mount. He explained in Russian that the ropes were hobbles, designed to prevent the horse from taking a full stride. The beast could amble around and graze but would not be able to run or climb out of the valley.

"It is a long walk back if our horses run away," he said with a grin.

The bounty hunter arrived and dismounted stiffly. The three of them waited another ten minutes for the cop. His face was a mask of discomfort and he cursed as he got off the horse.

He looked around. "Where is it?"

The ranger grinned again, pointing up the slope. "Now, we walk."

The cop closed his eyes and let out a deep sigh.

The sun was straight overhead and hot. Harrison swapped his watch cap for a floppy sunhat and dark glasses. He unzipped his down vest. His boots bit into the loose gravel of the trail as he worked hard to match their guide's brisk pace.

The ranger paused, consulting his GPS. Harrison caught up with him, breathing heavily. Rolling his shoulders, he realized that this was the most relaxed he'd been in months.

The guide pointed down the slope to a cluster of scrubby trees about ten meters away.

"There," he said. "Next to the wild apple trees."

Harrison followed the ranger's pointing finger but saw nothing. Then a flutter on the ground caught his eye and he realized he was seeing a scrap of tan cloth. The guide started to walk forward, but Harrison held him back.

"Let me go first," he said.

He made his way down the gentle incline and squatted down a meter from the edge of the trees.

There wasn't much left of the body, and what clothing remained was torn and dirty. Harrison could make out a tattered pair of cargo pants, hiking boots, and the remains of a T-shirt.

Time, weather, wild animals, and insects had done their work on the corpse. Harrison got to his feet and walked slowly around the body, studying the scene from all angles. He heard the heavy breathing of the cop and the bounty hunter as they approached. He put up his hand to hold them at a distance.

Harrison motioned the ranger forward. "This is how you found him?" he asked.

The ranger nodded, suddenly at a loss for words.

"How did you know it was a Westerner?" he asked.

The ranger bared his lips and tapped his teeth. "Fillings in his teeth. Westerner."

"Did you move him?"

The ranger shook his head.

"Are you sure? Did you check for a wallet? A watch?"

The ranger shook his head with more emphasis. "I heard about the money. I was afraid to disturb the body."

Harrison nodded. He might be lying, but the story had the ring of truth to it. He looked at the cop. "Do you need to do anything before we move the body?"

The police officer pulled out a mobile phone and spent the next few minutes doing what Harrison thought was a surprisingly thorough photo documentation of the corpse.

The cop motioned that Harrison could proceed. He squatted down next to the body and searched the pockets.

Nothing. Empty pockets, no wallet.

Gently, he rolled the body to one side and saw the hands were zip-tied behind the back of the corpse. His eyes scoured the arms of the dead man for the Tissot Seastar dive watch. His friend had loved that watch, a gift from his wife. If the watch was there, this was Tim.

The bones of the forearms were intact, but the wrists were bare.

Harrison sat back on his heels. It didn't prove anything, he told himself. The body was about the right size and shape for his friend, and what clothing remained were certainly items that Tim might have worn. The ranger might be lying about the watch or someone else might have happened onto the scene and helped themselves.

The bounty hunter came up to Harrison. "Is it him?" he asked bluntly.

Harrison blew out a breath. "Maybe. I'll need to identify him with dental records, maybe DNA."

The other man's face soured. "Do I get my money?"

Harrison pushed down a surge of anger. "If it's him, you'll get your money."

The cop unrolled a black body bag next to the corpse. With Harrison at the head and the cop at the feet, they prepared to move the body.

As soon as they started to lift it, the head came loose. Harrison called a halt and inspected the skull for bullet holes. Massive blunt force trauma, but no bullet holes that he could see. They tried to move the rest of the body intact, but the legs separated at the ankles and the left hand was pinched between two rocks.

While the cop worked on the feet, Harrison moved to free the arm. He brushed away some loose rock and worked his fingers under the pinched limb. What little skin remained was dry and leathery, like a mummy. With a gentle push, he managed to free the hand in one piece.

Harrison froze. There was a glitter of gold on the third finger. He turned the hand over.

His breath caught in his throat. He felt himself wanting to cry and retch at the same time. His own fingers shook as he removed the ring from the dead man's hand. He rubbed it against his shirt and held it up to the light.

A globe superimposed on the breast of an eagle, crossed swords, and the words "Never falter, never quit."

The motto for their West Point class.

Harrison wrapped his fingers around the golden ring, his knuckles white with the strain. He pressed his clenched fist against his forehead and closed his eyes.

Memories crushed him. The sweaty heat of Beast Barracks summer, a crisp fall morning as they walked to class, the biting cold of winter on the Hudson River. In every moment, he saw Tim and his smile. No matter the setting, the smile was always there . . .

And Jenny . . . *Dear God, how am I going to tell Jenny—*

"Is it him?" The harsh voice of the bounty hunter broke into his thoughts. "It's him, isn't it?"

Harrison forced himself to breathe.

In and out. Once, twice, three times. He wiped his fist across his cheeks.

"It's him," he said. He gently placed the broken remains of his best friend into the black body bag and slipped the ring into the plastic bag for personal effects.

He got to his feet and turned in a circle, studying the landscape. They were hours from the nearest road. Tim had disappeared in the winter. This place would have been covered in snow. How had his best friend died here? Was he kidnapped and somehow managed to escape only to die alone in the wild?

"Sorry," the bounty hunter said. He did not sound sorry. He sounded pleased.

A sound above Harrison, a distant whine, drew his attention. He looked up and shaded his eyes. The tiny outline of an airplane inched across the cloudless blue sky.

And he saw the answer to his question.

He looked down on the remains of his brother-in-arms. The ravaged corpse, the missing watch, the hands bound behind his back. He swallowed down the sickness that threatened to erupt out of him.

He breathed in. He breathed out. The feeling subsided, replaced by an icy numbness. That would do for now.

The airplane crossed the sun. Its shadow raced across the valley.

I know how Tim died, Harrison thought. *Now I need to find the why.*

34

Moscow, Russia

The scene at the All-Russian Exhibition Center was a made-for-TV event. In a normal year, Agriculture and Processing Industry Workers' Day, which fell on the second Sunday of October, would have been an unremarkable holiday.

But this was not a normal year. Nikolay badly needed a public boost, and the holiday was a convenient way to inject some positive campaign momentum into the bloodstream of the ever-changing news environment.

If Uncle Vitaly was watching, he would undoubtedly be cursing at his television set, Nikolay thought as he surveyed the crowd gathered in the space before the Worker and Kolkhoz Woman's Pavilion. The name was a mouthful in any language, but the picturesque venue was worth it.

The narrow building behind him was shaped like the prow of a futuristic ship. At the very top, like the actors in the iconic *Titanic* movie, stood a pair of bronze statues. A twenty-four-meter man brandished a hammer over his head. He was muscular and square-jawed. At his side, a similarly fierce-looking woman thrust a sickle at the sky. The pair lunged into space, their rippling muscles and flowing robes giving them the impression of both forward motion and strength.

It was vintage Soviet, but it was also achingly beautiful and the perfect backdrop for Nikolay's speech. The late afternoon sun turned the statues into a pair of golden twins leaping into the future.

Nikolay waited as the museum director introduced him. He noted the positions of the cameras and mentally rehearsed which angles to use for which lines.

The crowd of several thousand waited patiently. They had been carefully screened and herded close to the stage. The exhibition grounds around them were not blocked off, but there would be no protestors today. The security cordon around the venue was as tight as Federov's security team could make it. There would be no unplanned demonstrations this time.

Even the weather was on his side for a change. Though it was October, the last hours of a sparkling fall day felt warm, a rarity for Moscow.

It was, Nikolay realized, perfect.

As if on cue, the director finished his introduction on a high note. He turned to Nikolay and held out his hand in greeting. The crowd roared approval of their president as Nikolay strode to the podium.

Even though he knew the attendees had been painstakingly curated by Federov's team, the cheers were a tonic to Nikolay's spirits. He smiled and raised his arms in victory. The crowd shouted even louder.

Finally, Nikolay held his palms flat. "*Spasibo*," he said. "*Spasibo*."

The trained audience quieted down. Nikolay allowed his expression to turn thoughtful.

"I come to you on this glorious afternoon at this beautiful venue to enter into a serious discussion."

New camera angle, tuck your chin, squint your eyes just a bit.

"Russia is a great country with a bright future, but we cannot ignore our past. For too long, our leaders have relied on violence and manipulation to shape our politics and our economy. Politicians have used fear to divide us, and once divided, we are weak."

The unspoken truth in his statement was that Uncle Vitaly had been one of the worst offenders. Nikolay pushed past the unbidden thought and pressed on.

"When you elected me, I vowed to change that destructive pattern. I removed the gag levied on the press and allowed them to question my administration freely. I have nothing to hide."

When he said these brave words before a friendly audience, they felt real and right. His eyes strayed over the crowd to the Moscow skyline. But how did those words play out there, in the real world?

He saw now how carefully staged all of Uncle Vitaly's public events had been, and he understood why. Even amongst his most fervent supporters, there was always doubt. Nikolay could feel it, like a scent that fouled every meeting. The smell of defeat.

It was all he could do to hold his stage smile in place. There were so many reasons to doubt him. Zaitsev and the Ultras poisoned the news stream every day with half-truths and outright lies.

Their strategy was obvious: Contaminate the population, make them apathetic, make them believe that it didn't matter who won the election. Nothing was going to change. Ever.

Nikolay snapped himself back to the moment and he drove toward his conclusion.

"Once, Russia was the greatest country in the world. She was both feared and respected as a great power. Join me, and together we will reclaim our place in the world."

Cheers erupted, campaign signs sprouted from the crowd like daffodils in spring. Nikolay took a victory lap across the stage, bending down to shake grasping hands.

The enthusiasm reflected back at him felt genuine. His spirits soared.

He would prove the naysayers wrong. He would win reelection and he would do it the right way. The legal and fair way. He would win a truly honest election.

The reception that followed was invitation-only, the attendees even more carefully vetted by Federov's men. The FSB chief seemed to be everywhere. He had assured Nikolay there would be no mistakes this time.

For an hour, Nikolay shook hands and kissed powdered cheeks. He laughed at bad jokes and smiled until his face ached. He nursed the same glass of champagne through a score of toasts.

Federov materialized at Nikolay's side. He bowed to the ring of supporters around the President. "I am sorry, ladies and gentlemen, but I must escort my President to his next appointment."

He waited patiently as Nikolay accepted another round of farewell kisses and hearty handshakes, then led him to a door at the back of the room. Dusk was falling as they emerged onto the loading dock at the rear of the building. Nikolay's armored limousine idled in the yard.

Federov's phone rang just as they were about to enter the vehicle. He stopped to answer the call, while Nikolay slid inside and relaxed into the soft cushions.

"Well?" he asked as Federov took the seat next to him.

"It was good," the FSB chief replied. "Better than good. It played well, and the crowd was with you."

The sedan pulled away smoothly. With armor, it weighed over six thousand kilograms and rode like an oligarch's yacht on a custom suspension system.

"Was it enough?" Nikolay pressed.

"It was good, sir."

"We're running out of time, Vladimir."

Traditionally, Russian elections were held in March, but Nikolay had shifted the presidential elections to the fall, allowing candidates to campaign more easily during better weather. He wondered now if that had been a mistake.

"Yes, sir, time is always a concern." Federov's agreement spoke volumes. He had won elections for Uncle Vitaly. Both men knew there were actions that could be taken if Nikolay gave the word, actions that would increase his chances of success.

Nikolay looked out the window. He would not do those things. He was a different man from his uncle.

Their sedan joined the motorcade. Two cars in front of the President's vehicle, two behind, and a pair of motorcycles in the lead. The convoy made a right turn onto a wide boulevard and their vehicle accelerated. Through the bulletproof glass, Nikolay made out the thin whine of a siren.

Federov's phone rang. He answered it, listened, then rang off with a curt "*Da*."

"There's a water main break ahead, slight detour."

Nikolay nodded, then rested his head back. He sighed to himself. A water main break. On top of everything else, Zaitsev would probably find a way to blame him for that, too.

Still moving at speed, the motorcade turned right. The streets here were narrower and had cars parked on both sides. The last light of the day brightened the tops of the four-story residential buildings, leaving the sidewalks in shadow.

The sedan suddenly braked. Through the windshield, he could see a garbage truck had rolled across the intersection in front of them. The security team in the front seat shouted back to Federov.

"Get us out of here, now!" Federov roared. "Put on your seatbelt, sir," he ordered Nikolay.

He saw armed security agents pile out of the car in front of them and race for tactical positions along the street. They ran with their faces turned up, looking for threats.

The oversized sedan was too large to make a U-turn in the narrow street, but the experienced driver had other ideas. He slammed the car into reverse. Nikolay lurched forward against his seatbelt, then was thrown back abruptly as their heavy vehicle crashed into parked cars behind them. The driver cranked the wheel and aimed for a space that would allow him to drive the armored limo onto the sidewalk.

There was a brilliant flash of light, then *WHUMPF*. The explosion registered on Nikolay's body not as a sound, but as a physical trauma.

His ears popped, his chest compressed, and his head flopped like he had lost all muscle control. He felt his body go weightless, restrained only by the three-point safety belt. The entire cabin turned, hanging in midair for what seemed like an eternity. Federov, who was not restrained, floated through Nikolay's field of vision.

The armored vehicle crashed into the facade of a building, then rolled, coming to rest on its roof.

The quick action of the driver had shifted the blast zone of the explosion from broadside to nose-on. The driver was in a coma and the security man in the front seat had been decapitated. Eight other members of the presidential security detail, the ones who had been in the open, were dead.

Nikolay had a minor concussion and a persistent ringing in his ears that the doctor assured him would go away in twenty-four hours. Federov had his left arm in a sling. He stood at rigid attention while Nikolay pulled on his shirt. His fingers fumbled with the buttons.

"Mr. President—"

"Don't," Nikolay said.

"Sir, I—"

Nikolay wheeled on him. The intense pain in his head made his eyes water. Bitter anger washed over him like a wave.

What was the use? His enemies would stop at nothing. There was no price they would not pay to see him defeated.

He drew in a deep breath. God, it even hurt to breathe. Every muscle in his body seemed to spasm into knots at the slightest movement.

Nikolay looked at Federov, who was clearly not only in physical pain, but in emotional anguish. The Russian president forced his anger to subside. Whatever admonishment he might deliver paled in comparison to what this man was putting himself through. Vladimir Federov had risked everything for Nikolay to lead his country—and he had asked for nothing in return.

Nikolay placed his hand on Federov's uninjured shoulder. "What do we do now, Vladimir?"

"We go to see your uncle."

Nikolay sighed.

35

Sochi, Russia

The air in the study was stifling hot and dense with humidity. The tall windows stood open to a breeze, but the sheer white curtains hung limp. From Nikolay's armchair, the Black Sea looked like a silver plate in the afternoon sun. His sweaty back stuck to the leather of the chair.

Under different circumstances, Nikolay might have welcomed a break from the cold, rainy weather of Moscow, but at this moment the unseasonable warmth felt more like slow suffocation.

Uncle Vitaly looked well, deeply tanned and a few kilos lighter than on Nikolay's last visit. He moved with the grace and vitality of a younger man.

In contrast, Nikolay felt old and fat. He hadn't had a good night's sleep in what seemed like forever, and his brain functions lacked sharpness. He felt like his body was betraying him.

Along with everything else in his life.

Luchnik strolled to the window, hands clasped behind his back, head bowed as if deep in thought over the state of affairs as Nikolay had just laid them out. Boxed in politically by Zaitsev and the Ultras, hemorrhaging influence in Kazakhstan, and powerless to deal with this new wave of cultural unity weakening the political borders in Central Asia, Nikolay was under pressure from all sides. The assassination attempt was the final straw. They had not managed to kill him, but the bold attempt had been enough to make him look weak, vulnerable.

Luchnik squinted out at the Black Sea. The sheen of sweat across his forehead glowed in reflected light. "You're a fool, nephew."

A flicker of anger sparked inside Nikolay. He wanted to get to his feet and storm out, but that would solve nothing. He had nowhere else to turn.

"Because I didn't do what you told me to do, Uncle?" He soaked his reply in bitter sarcasm.

Luchnik spun on his heel, his head cocked as if Nikolay had spoken in a foreign language. "Yes, that's exactly what I mean. I told you how to deal with your situation and you ignored—"

That did it. Nikolay shot to his feet, interrupting his uncle. "You told me how *you* would deal with the situation." He leveled a finger at the older man. "I am my own man, Uncle. I need advice I can use." He turned for the door.

Fuck the old man. I never should have let Federov talk me into coming here.

Behind him, he heard clapping. Nikolay whirled around.

"What?" he shouted at his uncle. He felt like he was eleven years old again, getting a lecture about his grades at school.

"We all make our own mistakes, nephew," Luchnik replied. He dropped into his armchair, crossed his legs. The former President of the Russian Federation was wearing Bermuda shorts, a white polo shirt, and the air of a man with not a care in the world.

"Sit," Luchnik said. "Please," he added.

Nikolay's emotions warred in his head. He did not have time for this bullshit. Federov was wrong. This old man had nothing to teach him.

I am everything he is not, Nikolay thought. There is nothing here for me.

"Please," Luchnik said again, and his voice was gentle. "Sit. Give me ten minutes. For your mother's sake."

Nikolay poured himself a measure of his uncle's best vodka. "Five minutes."

Luchnik steepled his fingers, narrowed his eyes at his nephew. "You're surrounded. Outmaneuvered."

"Tell me something I don't know."

Luchnik continued as if he hadn't spoken. "Zaitsev is a paper tiger. He is able to blame everything on you. Why? Because you allow him to do it. You have taken away all the levers of power that I put in place. If you still controlled the media outlets, you could ignore Zaitsev." Luchnik waved his hand. "It's too late for that now. You have to fight the war you're in. Zaitsev has to go."

Nikolay stared at him. "That's your counsel? Eliminate my opponent? You don't get it, do you?"

"Get what?"

"The new Russia has a free press, Uncle. The new Russia has real elections, and those real elections have real consequences for the politicians. It is the only way to create the future that we want."

Luchnik stared at him, a bemused smile on his lips. "Never mind. You'll deal with Zaitsev when the time comes."

"What does that mean?"

Luchnik pressed ahead. "Your real problem is the near-abroad. For all Zaitsev's bullshit, he's right about Kazakhstan. China has outmaneuvered you and that leaves you weak. Add in this Timur movement in the poor-as-fuck-istans and you have a big problem in the south. How do you plan to deal with that?"

Nikolay looked at his hands. "I don't know."

"You need to take action, nephew."

Nikolay said nothing.

"I told you what you had to do, Nikolay."

"You told me to start a war."

Luchnik leaned forward. "Exactly. There is opportunity in chaos. When the world is off balance, *that* is the time to strike."

"You're insane," Nikolay responded.

"I led this country successfully for thirty years, nephew. You're about to lose it after three. Who's the insane one?"

Nikolay found himself on his feet. For the first time in his life, he wanted to strike his uncle. Not just hit him, but beat him until his smiling lips were a mass of bloody red pulp.

Luchnik's grin widened. "You're angry with me." He flopped back in his chair. "Good."

"Good?" Nikolay's hands were fists, his knuckles white. He wanted to scream and throw up at the same time. "Good? How is this good?"

Uncle Vitaly's eyes bored into him. "Because it shows you haven't given up. That you still have some fight in you. That you have the will to win."

Nikolay heard a buzzing in his ears. He felt hollow inside as he dropped back into his chair. His mind finished his uncle's sentence: *the will to win...at any cost.*

"You can fix this, Nikolay."

"How?" His voice came out as a croak.

"Start in the Central Asian states. Protect the near-abroad. To do that, you need Orazov on your side."

Nikolay shook his head. "I told you the last time I was here. Orazov led the opposition against me at the CSTO meeting. He wants nothing to do with Mother Russia."

Luchnik laughed. "He wants nothing to do with *your* version of Russia, nephew. Akhmet Orazov is a man of honor, but he is also a man from another time. My time."

"You want me to make peace with Orazov? The President of the Russian Federation goes hat in hand to a disgraced Turkmen rebel and humbly begs for his help?" Nikolay could feel the heat rising up his neck.

"And what are you doing now?" Luchnik asked in a cold voice. "I am the deposed leader of a broken country, and yet you show up in *my* house and ask for *my* help. How is that any different?"

Nikolay stared at his uncle. How was it different?

The anger and frustration that had so consumed him only moments before disappeared, replaced with icy resolve.

This is my country. My responsibility.

He saw his uncle with fresh eyes. Vitaly Luchnik had never really given up power. True, he did not sit at the head of government, but his legacy was at work behind the scenes even now.

Nikolay was fighting thirty years of history. Zaitsev and the Ultras, Orazov and the former Soviet allies—they were the old Russia. Uncle Vitaly's Russia.

"Forget the Americans, Nikolay, you need Orazov," Luchnik urged.

Nikolay smiled—for real, this time. "Thank you for your counsel, Uncle. It has been enlightening."

Back in the hallway, Federov got to his feet and followed Nikolay. The two men strode through the front doors and down the steps. Pea gravel crunched under Nikolay's shoes. The humid air made it seem like he was swimming toward the limo.

Inside the car, the air conditioner was running. The chill air made his sweaty skin prickle. The opposite door opened and Federov settled in beside him.

"Drive," Nikolay said. He looked back at the house, but his uncle did not emerge to see them off.

Federov remained silent as they rounded the circular drive and sped through the open gate. A few seconds later, the limo entered the deep shade of the pine forest.

"Was it a fruitful visit?" Federov asked.

Nikolay did not answer right away. He stared at the greenery flashing by the window.

He knew what he had to do now. The answer was so obvious he couldn't believe he hadn't seen it before. Or maybe he just hadn't wanted to admit it to himself before.

"Your contact in the CIA. Riley. That's his name, right?"

"What about him?" Federov asked.

"Bring him to Moscow."

"Can I ask why?"

The forest looks so peaceful, Nikolay thought longingly. When was the last time he'd spent even an hour in a forest alone? He did not turn from the window.

"We're going to change the rules of the game, Vladimir."

36

PLA Forward Operating Base
50 kilometers west of Dushanbe, Tajikistan

Lieutenant General Gao scowled at his laptop, where the screen displayed his weekly update to the Committee. Fingers poised above the keys, he tried to think of a creative way to report no progress in stopping the attacks by the SIF.

Hoping for inspiration, he spun his chair to gaze out the window at the picturesque Pamir Mountains. He'd been doing a lot of that recently. One way or another, with the Jade Spike ceremony only two weeks away, his time in this job was winding down.

And then what? he wondered. He hadn't spoken to Mei Lin in weeks. And since the helicopter attack, Gao found his thoughts straying to Xiaomei more and more.

Captain Fang, he corrected himself.

There were two sharp raps at the door and the object of his inappropriate thoughts entered the room. Behind her was a boyish-looking second lieutenant who Gao did not recognize. The young man wore the insignia of the signal corps on his shoulder patch and his uniform looked new.

Gao sat up in his chair. Fang's normally stoic features showed the trace of an excited smile. "General Gao, pardon the interruption, sir, but I have news."

Without waiting for Gao's acknowledgment, she turned to the lieutenant. "Tell him," she ordered.

The young officer, whose name was Wei according to his nametag, perspired freely. "I may have discovered an SIF defector." The kid's voice was breathy with nervousness and he looked as if he might hyperventilate.

Gao cut a glance at Fang, then came around the desk, took the young man's elbow, and guided him to a chair. In the weeks since the attack on Gao's helicopter, the SIF's offensive tempo had increased. They'd destroyed military aircraft in Kyrgyzstan, blown up an army barracks in Uzbekistan, and taken out four different radar installations. Any way he looked at it, Gao was losing the war with the SIF.

He sat down across from the young officer and put on his best encouraging smile. "Start at the beginning, Lieutenant. And leave nothing out."

Even with the combined gentle urgings from Gao and Fang, it took an excruciating ten minutes to get the outline of the story.

Second Lieutenant Wei had only arrived at the base a few weeks ago. He had a difficult time making friends, but was an avid gamer and spent all of his free time online. His gamer clan ran a closed chat group.

Gao wasn't sure where this was going, but Fang urged Wei to continue. "Tell him what happened last night, Lieutenant."

The previous evening, Wei found himself on the chat with only one other player. When the other player mentioned that he could see a mountain peak IRL with a peculiar spherical cloud formation around it, Wei got excited.

Gao raised an eyebrow at Fang.

"In real life," she explained.

Wei responded that he could also see a mountain with an odd cloud formation. He snapped a photo and dropped it into the chat.

The two players were looking at the same mountain. Wei was excited. Maybe this was another soldier on base and a potential friend. He paused his story then.

"Well?" Gao asked.

Wei cut a look at Fang who nodded. "It's okay."

"The other player is a local, a Tajik, sir," Wei said. "When he found out I was a PLA soldier, he told me he wants to defect."

Gao was confused now. "Defect from what?"

"The Seljuk Islamic Front," Fang said.

Gao swallowed. For months, the MSS and PLA military intelligence had been trying to infiltrate the SIF with no success. Was it possible this kid had done what the professionals had not been able to achieve? Through online gaming?

Fang's hand landed on Gao's shoulder and the general felt a shiver of intimate delight. "That's not all. Tell him the rest," she ordered Wei.

"He says he has information about the ceremony in Samarkand, sir."

Gao's mouth went dry. "What kind of information?"

"He wouldn't say anything specific, sir," Wei replied. "At least not online. He says he has valuable information about the ceremony to trade."

Gao studied the young man. "Who have you told about this?"

Wei looked up at Fang with something like adoration in his gaze. "Only the captain, sir. She told me to keep it quiet. For security."

"Good." Gao got to his feet. "Lieutenant, please wait outside. I need to speak with Captain Fang for a moment."

Gao waited until the door shut behind the young man, then he turned to Fang. "Do you believe him, Xiaomei?"

To his surprise, Fang blushed. "The lieutenant doesn't have many friends, sir. I met him as part of the intake process and I was kind to him. I think he has a crush on me."

Gao nodded. Captain Fang was a very desirable woman in a male-dominated environment. He guessed half the men on the base had a crush on her.

Fang hesitated. "I fear I may have overstepped, General. When the lieutenant told me about the contact last night, I encouraged him to arrange a meeting."

"Good thinking," Gao said. "We'll bring the defector in and do a full debriefing."

"Is that the best course of action, sir?" Fang said. "I don't trust the MSS and . . . " She hesitated again. "I overstepped. The asset insisted that he wants to speak to the man in charge. I—I agreed to the meeting." Fang covered her face with her hands. Gao had never seen her so upset.

"This is all my fault, General. I'll take this to the MSS right away—"

Gao put his arm around her shoulders. "It's okay, Xiaomei. You did the right thing." She leaned against him for just a moment, then pulled away.

"Are you sure?" She seemed on the verge of tears.

Was he sure? Taking a meeting with an unknown informant was risky, but if it gave them intel about a possible attack on the Jade Spike ceremony, it would be worth it. Gao looked at his open laptop. How many more times could he submit reports to Beijing that said *no progress*?

Gao nodded decisively. "We can't waste this opportunity," he declared, as much for his own benefit as for Fang's. "Where is the meeting?"

Gao tried to ignore the butterflies the size of eagles that fluttered and flapped in his stomach. From behind dark glasses and the tinted windows of the Range Rover, the dry mountainous landscape flashed by. Afternoon shadows were just beginning to creep down the western slopes.

They were less than a hundred kilometers from the PLA base, a little more than an hour away. With luck, they'd be back inside the security perimeter before dark. He imagined a triumphant return, flush with fresh intel. Despite their months of effort and millions of dollars, he alone had done what the vaunted Chinese security services could not: found a spy inside the ranks of the SIF.

It's all up to me, he thought. This is why the General Secretary selected me for this job.

He was the Hero of Tashkent. He had vision. He had agency. He knew how to seize an opportunity and spin it into pure gold. His heroic efforts would ensure the security of the Samarkand ceremony.

Gao cast a glance at Captain Fang on the seat next to him. He supposed every hero needed a sidekick. He and Xiaomei would save the day. Together.

Like him, Fang was dressed in civilian clothes. She wore blue jeans that hugged her figure and a sand-colored sleeveless shirt that showed off her toned arms. With sunglasses and her hair pulled back into a ponytail, she looked young, carefree, and absolutely gorgeous.

Her only acknowledgment to local customs was a royal blue headscarf with silver threads running through it. For now, she'd tied it loosely at her throat. It made her look like a model on an exotic photo shoot.

Dressed in khakis and a polo shirt, Gao felt dowdy and old. He was thick around the middle and his thinning hair was more gray than black now. Stress, he told himself when he looked in the mirror. Not age, stress. He was still a young man.

As they were getting into the car, Xiaomei took his arm and whispered, "You're doing the right thing, Yichen. I can feel it."

The words thrilled him, made him feel decades younger and eager to go on this dangerous mission with this beauty by his side.

In the front seats, Wei and their driver also wore civilian clothes. For the afternoon, they would play Chinese tourists. Gao realized that during his entire tour in the region, he'd never been off base without a security detail, and certainly not in civilian clothes. The feeling was somehow terrifying and exciting at the same time.

They were on their own. Gao had told no one at the base where they were going. They couldn't risk intel getting out. His stomach churned afresh.

Wei's head bowed over his tablet and his mobile phone, monitoring communications with their asset. The driver looked up from the GPS map on the dashboard. "Five more minutes," he announced.

The sense of lightness in Gao's guts threatened to erupt. He had trained as a special operations soldier, and at one point in his career, an operation like this one would have been almost routine. But when was the last time he'd led a field operation? It had been a long time—a *very* long time.

The Range Rover climbed a rise in the road and rounded a bend. Before them lay the Gissarak Dam. The driver pulled to the side of the road and stopped. Golden dust whirled around the car.

Sunlight gleamed off the reservoir that stretched away to the horizon. The two-lane highway ran down to the dam and across the top, then disappeared into the brown hills on the other side.

From the passenger seat, Wei spoke. "Drive to the dam and stop in the center."

The driver frowned. "I don't like it."

Fang looked at Gao. He tried to interpret her expression, but failed. He leaned forward between the seats. "Do it," he ordered.

The driver coasted down the hill and onto the road that crossed the dam. To their right was a spillway, where a mist of silvery spray floated in the air. To their left, the flat blue of the reservoir reflected the afternoon sun. Except for a meter-high concrete barrier on either side of the road, they were wide open, exposed on all sides. Gao imagined an RPG rocketing down from the hills, and his stomach did a fresh series of somersaults.

When they reached the center of the dam, the driver applied the brakes. "I'm turning the car around," he announced and executed a three-point turn.

"What now?" Fang asked Wei.

"The general gets out," Wei said. "The asset is on his way."

"I'm coming with you," Fang announced. When Gao started to protest, she waved him off. "It's not an argument, sir. I got you into this. Besides, you might need a translator."

"Tell him there will be two people, a man and a woman," she ordered Wei.

Gao's knees felt like jelly and he worried they might not support him when he stepped out of the car. He pulled on the door latch anyway. When the seal of the air-conditioned cabin was broken, warm air scented with moisture rushed in.

Gao placed one foot on the cement roadway and tested his weight. His legs trembled, but held. As he stepped away from the car, Fang joined him. To his surprise, he felt her hand sneak into the crook of his bare elbow. Her grip tingled against his skin and his legs felt suddenly stronger.

Wei called through the open window. "That's him."

On the other side of the dam, a car came into view. An ancient Toyota sedan, faded yellow with patches of rust. It approached them slowly and stopped ten meters away.

A man got out of the car, but left the door open and the engine running. He was in his mid-thirties, with a close-cropped beard and sunglasses. He wore blue jeans, a long-sleeved denim shirt, and a blue *tubeteika* on his head. He walked toward them.

"You are General Gao?" He had a soft voice and spoke in halting English.

"I am. You have information for me," Gao said.

The man nodded nervously. He looked to his right and left where wide-open space stretched for kilometers, as if suddenly aware of how vulnerable he was. His Adam's apple bobbed as he swallowed again and again.

"Well?" Gao demanded.

The man opened his mouth and closed it again. Gao shifted his feet. This was wrong, so very wrong. What had he gotten himself into?

Fang stepped forward and spoke in Tajik. Instantly, the young man's face cleared. Fang turned to Gao. "He says he's more comfortable speaking in Tajik. I can translate, sir."

Relief flooded through Gao. He listened as Fang and the source went back and forth.

"He says he wants 10,000 U.S. dollars or equivalent in Euros," she said.

Gao kept his face impassive, but in his mind, he was throwing a massive party. If this guy could get them inside the SIF, he was worth a hundred times that amount.

"Find out what he knows," he ordered Fang.

Ten minutes passed. Gao could not understand a word of the conversation, but he could read Fang's expression. Her face showed surprise, then her eyes narrowed and she questioned the young man intently. His voice rose as if he was angry and his hand gestures became sharp and forceful.

Finally, Fang turned to Gao. She leaned close and spoke in a low voice.

"This is very serious, sir. He says the SIF has a plan to attack Samarkand during the Jade Spike ceremony. He claims they've infiltrated the facility—"

She broke off suddenly and turned back to the young man, launching another volley of questions at him. He answered in short, clipped replies.

Fang turned back to Gao. "He says he won't give me details until he has the money."

Gao folded his arms. Getting that much money would take time. He would need to involve the MSS, and they were a territorial bunch. As soon as they found out about his asset, those greedy bastards would fall all over themselves taking credit for the operation. He and Xiaomei would be lucky to be a footnote in their report.

No, Gao decided, I need something valuable, intel that no one else has.

He shook his head. "Tell him I need specifics to get the money."

Fang tried again, pressing the young man harder.

Gao's eye roved over the landscape. This was taking too long. He turned back toward the Range Rover. "Tell him no deal," he called over his shoulder to Fang.

"Yichen, wait."

Gao turned. Walking away, he thought. Works every time. He was the Hero of Tashkent and he took no shit from terrorists.

"He says the attack is focused on one person," Fang reported. "An assassination."

Gao faced the Tajik man. In very deliberate English, he asked, "Who is the target? If you tell me now, I will give you more money."

The man listened, then nodded his head that he understood. He opened his mouth.

Then his mouth opened wider, gaping larger than Gao would have thought possible. Through the yawning space where the man's mouth had been, Gao could see the other side of the dam.

Gao felt a splash of something warm across his face. He stared stupidly as the man's body crumpled to the warm concrete. His brain registered that the man had been shot, but Gao's body stood frozen in place.

Fang tackled him. He hit the ground on his back, his head bouncing off the concrete. She pushed him hard against the roadside barrier.

"Sniper!" she screamed in his face.

Their driver threw the car into reverse and backed to their position. Fang sprang to her feet, wrenched open the rear door, and hauled Gao's body into the car, pushing him to the floor. She leaped on top of him.

"Go, go, go!" she shouted.

The driver needed no encouragement. The rear door slammed shut from the force of the acceleration.

The Range Rover jinked back and forth across the roadway as the driver tried to evade the sniper. A window exploded in a shower of glass shards. A spray of red painted the ceiling of the car. The car weaved again and Wei's body flopped between the seats.

Gao saw a flash of shadow pass over the car as they reached the safety of the hills. The Range Rover screamed up the incline, catching air as it crested the hill. Gao and Fang's bodies levitated, then slammed back down to the hard floor of the vehicle.

Fang's face was only a few centimeters from his. She cradled his face with her hands. Her eyes were wild with fear, her cheeks flushed. Gao saw she had a streak of red blood across her cheekbone.

"Yichen," she whispered, "I thought I lost you."

Then she kissed him.

37

Moscow, Russia

It was cold, windy, and raining hard at Sheremetyevo Airport.

When the door of the jet opened, the cabin filled with the smell of wet asphalt and jet fuel. The pilot handed him an umbrella.

"Good luck, Mr. Riley."

Don muttered his thanks and stepped into the cold downpour. His shoes were soaked before he covered the thirty meters to the private air terminal.

A young man dressed in a dark suit and overcoat waited inside the door. He watched Don shake the rain from his umbrella and said, "Mr. Riley, I'm your driver." He looked behind Don. "Do you have luggage, sir?"

"I'm not staying." Besides his overcoat and umbrella, Don carried only a burner phone and a wad of Euros. The less he took into a meeting with the head of the FSB, the better. It's not that he didn't trust Vladimir Federov, but the intelligence officer was a professional who would take advantage of every opportunity to collect information. It was a sign of respect. Don would have done the same thing.

He followed the young man to a covered portico where an Aurus Senat luxury limousine idled. Don settled warily into the heated back seat. He was acutely aware that he was deep in enemy territory and his defenses were on high alert.

For the last three weeks, Don had been essentially living at the office. The team searching for Akhmet Orazov were some of the Agency's best, but Don couldn't help managing—some would say micromanaging—them. It finally got to the point that the Director ordered Don to take a night off.

His refrigerator was empty, so Don ordered Chinese food, then opened a beer and hit the shower. The doorbell rang just as he shut off the water, so he threw on a bathrobe and ran to the door.

A man in a FedEx uniform smiled when he opened the door. He handed Don a padded envelope and thrust an electronic pad at him for a signature. Inside, Don ripped open the package to find a prepaid mobile phone. And the device was on.

He put it on the kitchen counter and looked at the package again. The return address said it had been sent from the United Nations Building in New York City.

The phone rang, startling Don.

He let it ring three times before he pushed the button to answer the phone on speaker.

The voice was male, but a high-pitched tenor. Don recognized it immediately.

"Do you know who this is?" said Vladimir Federov.

Don swallowed. He took the phone off speaker and pressed it to his ear. "Yes."

"We need to meet. In person."

"About what?" Don tried to wrap his head around the fact that he was having a conversation with the head of the Russian FSB wearing nothing but a bathrobe.

"We have mutual interests, Donald."

"That seems a little vague."

"Come to Moscow," Federov said. "It will be worth your time."

The line went dead.

Don got dressed before he called Director Blank from a secure line. He put the mobile phone from Federov in his refrigerator before he made the call. One could not be too careful.

"You have to go, Don," the Director said immediately.

Don had not expected that response. "You *want* me to go to Moscow, sir?"

"Absolutely. You've seen the intel about the upcoming election. Sokolov is going to get pummeled. This is a cry for help. If we ignore it, Serrano will skin us alive."

"But . . . " Don fumbled for words. "We don't know what he wants."

"We know he went to great lengths to make a personal appeal for you to come to Moscow. We can't ignore that. Whatever he wants, he's decided he can trust you--and only you."

"Do you want to run it by the President first, sir?"

The Director considered that a long time. "No," he said finally, "I think this is one of those times where it's better to beg forgiveness, Don. I hear Moscow is beautiful in late October."

"But what about the Orazov operation?" Don said.

The Director let out a sigh that spoke volumes. "That operation is in good hands. Anne Hart is experienced, and you looking over her shoulder isn't going to help her find the target."

Don heard the rebuke implicit in the Director's remark. They'd had a version of this conversation twice already.

"Still, sir, I'd feel better if—"

"Dammit, Riley, do I need to draw you a picture? You've just been contacted by the highest-ranking security officer in the Russian Federation asking for a personal meeting with you. Get your ass on a plane. Pronto."

Now, as he sat in the back of a Russian luxury limo with wet shoes and jet lag, he knew only one thing for certain: Moscow in late October was not beautiful.

This meeting was not Don's first unusual interaction with Federov. During the Russian invasion of Ukraine, the head of the FSB had fed Don invaluable intelligence that brought a swift end to the conflict. The war could have ended much, much worse. Before he was removed from power, Luchnik had been prepared to use nuclear weapons against an American amphibious force headed into the Baltic Sea. Federov had prevented the attack.

On the other hand, there was no denying that Federov had used Don.

Yes, he'd supplied valuable intel to Don, but he did it for the sole purpose of supporting his own plot to overthrow Luchnik and place Nikolay Sokolov into power.

As Don peered out the rain-streaked window at the sodden Russian streets, he wondered what Federov had in mind this time.

He called up the map function on his phone and checked their location. After forty-five minutes, he realized where they were going.

The Lubyanka Building.

The Moscow landmark, originally built for an insurance company in the late nineteenth century, had a dark past. Starting with the Bolsheviks in 1919, the neo-baroque yellow brick structure had been transformed into a prison and the headquarters of the secret police. Today, it was still a prison, as well as headquarters for the Russian Border Guard and a small contingent of FSB senior officials.

As soon as he spotted the famous building from the main road, Don imagined the limo pulling up to the front steps. He, a high-ranking CIA officer, would stride confidently through the front door of an enemy intelligence service. He'd read somewhere that the main entrance hall had a hammer and sickle inlaid into the floor not unlike the CIA seal in the floor of the headquarters building at Langley, made famous by countless movies.

His fantasy evaporated when the car pulled up to a nondescript side entrance. The driver looked in the rearview mirror. "We're here, Mr. Riley," he said, making it clear that he had no intention of getting out in the rain to open the door for his passenger.

Don grabbed the soggy umbrella and struggled out of the car. The six paces through the rain to the glass door only succeeded in soaking his shoes for a second time. Inside, a woman waited. Late forties, graying hair pulled back into a bun, and shod in sensible shoes. By way of greeting, she nodded, then turned and started walking. Don followed, his shoes squelching in the silent hallway.

Vladimir Federov's office was on the sixth floor overlooking the square. Silver rivulets of rain snaked down the dark glass as the head of the FSB stood up from his desk.

Although Don was the one coming in from the rain like a drowned rat, he thought Federov looked worse than he did.

The man's bald head was the color of wallpaper paste, and the lines on his face looked like they were carved into his skin. Still, his brown eyes glittered with energy.

"Thank you for coming, Donald." He guided Don to a pair of armchairs set close to a gas fireplace and took Don's coat.

Probably taking it so he can plant a bug in it, Don thought bleakly. Coming here had been a terrible idea. He resolved to burn all his clothes as soon as he left Russian soil.

"Can I get you a drink?" Federov asked.

Don spied a silver samovar. "Hot tea?"

"Of course." As Federov fussed with the tea service, Don moved his sodden feet next to the fireplace. He wondered what his host would think if he took off his shoes to let them dry.

Federov set a silver tray between them with two steaming glasses of tea in elaborate silver holders, a pitcher of milk, and a bowl of sugar cubes. The FSB chief put two lumps into his own glass and cocked an eyebrow at Don, who held up two fingers.

This whole thing is a show, Don realized. The emergency trip to Moscow, the meeting at FSB headquarters, even the tea. There was a big ask coming, Don could feel it.

"Vladimir," Don asked, "why am I here?"

Federov cradled his tea glass between his palms.

"Our situation in the south is very delicate," he began. "You know this already, I presume?"

The Central Asian republics. That made sense.

Don nodded, but said nothing. He was here to listen.

"What do you know of Timur Ganiev?" Federov asked.

Don sipped his tea to give himself time to think. Was it possible the Russians had discovered Operation Catbird?

"Just what we've shared with you," Don said. "He preaches a message of cultural unity and he supports the rule of law. Those ideas align well with American values."

"He's a destabilizing force," Federov replied. "His presence makes it very difficult for the Russian Federation to reestablish the status quo in the region."

"Maybe it's time for the status quo to change," Don said.

"Is the CIA involved?" Federov asked flatly.

"You know I can't answer that."

"We have a saying in Russia," Federov said. "A leopard cannot change its spots. The same in America?"

Don nodded, hoping that he hadn't flown five thousand miles to hear a Russian proverb.

"Has the United States learned nothing from your history?" Federov continued. "Regime change is a myth. Afghanistan, Iraq, Pakistan, South America, this is a lesson you still have not learned."

"I'm not sure what you're driving at," Don said.

"A country is the sum of its history. Like the skin of a leopard, it cannot change. People and their customs, their way of life. We are who we are. You cannot change these things."

"I imagine Nikolay Sokolov would disagree with that statement," Don said.

Federov frowned, then his brow smoothed again. "Perhaps, but that is for another time. Tonight, I need you to stop supporting Ganiev."

"You're making a big assumption about America's involvement, Vladimir. I'm sorry, I can't help you."

The lines around Federov's lips deepened. "The Eurasian countries are the Russian near-abroad. Our influence there is a national security priority. These are lands rife with ethnic conflict. They will never be unified."

"I understand your skepticism—"

"No, Donald, you do not." Federov leaned toward Don, his eyes hard. "I need you to hear me. This path you are on will destroy us both."

Don's fingers tightened on his glass, suddenly angry. "I need *you* to hear *me*. There is no CIA involvement."

Federov studied him for a long time. Don did not look away.

"I brought you here for a reason, Donald." He gestured at the room. "This place, the things that have happened here, are the old Russia. President Sokolov is working for a different future, a better future, but he cannot do it alone. He needs help. He needs your trust, the trust of your President."

Don wondered where this monologue was headed.

"My words may not be enough to convince you, but I want you to meet someone. He will convince you to stop this meddling in—" Don started to protest, but Federov held up his hand. "He will help you see that American involvement in Central Asia needs to change."

Don finished his tea and set the empty glass on the tray.

"Who did you have in mind?"

"Akhmet Orazov."

If Don had still been holding his tea glass, he probably would have dropped it. It took every bit of composure he possessed to keep his expression neutral.

"I don't see what that would do for us," Don said finally. His heart galloped in his chest even as he feigned lack of interest.

Federov's voice turned earnest. "Orazov is a longtime Russian ally. He will convince you that supporting Ganiev is not in the best interest of the United States."

"May I have some more tea, please?"

Don used the interruption to think. The CIA had been hunting Orazov for weeks without success. Was this the opportunity they'd been waiting for?

"Well?" Federov asked, handing him a fresh glass of tea.

Don pretended to be considering the proposal. "You have a lot of faith in Mr. Orazov."

"His ties with Mother Russia go back decades. He's an honorable man. All I ask is that you listen to what he has to say."

Don sipped his tea. The liquid was sweet and hot, the taste of victory.

"I'm always willing to listen, Vladimir. Please. Set up the meeting."

38

CIA Special Activities Center
Langley, Virginia

In her twenty-year career with the CIA, Case Officer Anne Hart had surreptitiously entered sovereign nations at least a dozen times. She'd jumped out of airplanes, planted listening devices in the home of a Russian FSB officer, and run an influence operation inside a South American country to sway a close election. For the most part, she'd avoided violence, but she did have a scar on her right side from a knife fight in Bulgaria.

At her rank, Anne didn't do as much field work these days, but she had a reputation as a solid operator with excellent attention to detail who got results.

She supposed that was the reason she'd been assigned to lead this kill operation in Uzbekistan. Deputy Director of Operations Don Riley had offered her the assignment in person.

She said yes, but now she was thinking that maybe she'd been a little too hasty.

On the face of it, the operation was simple. A CIA case officer on the ground in Uzbekistan would lure a target to a meeting location. With the terrorist positively identified, her team would track the target when he left the meeting and eliminate him with a drone strike once the CIA friendly was in the clear. The meeting site was outside major population centers, which minimized the risk of collateral damage—always a factor in these types of operations.

While the mechanics of the kill chain were simple, the logistics of the operation were brutally complex. To get armed drones on station, she needed to violate the sovereign airspace of at least a half dozen countries, none of which were especially friendly to the United States. The kill operation was taking place only fifty miles away from a major Chinese ceremony in Samarkand. She didn't know exactly what the Jade Spike ceremony was and she didn't much care. What she *did* care about was the dramatically increased security profile of PLA forces in the area, which amplified the possibility of detection of her assets to an uncomfortable degree. To aggravate matters, there was a contingent of Americans at the Samarkand event, including Don Riley and the U.S. Secretary of State.

Once she moved the drones on station, she was on the clock. There was no way to refuel the UAVs while they were inside enemy airspace.

You play the hand you're dealt, she thought. Success in this case was all about logistics and timing—and a whole lot of luck.

Her handpicked team was small, only twenty people, with five operators on duty at any given time. They sat in a row behind six workstations facing a configurable wall screen.

From left to right, she had a comms stack that could put her in touch with anyone on the planet in the space of a few seconds, two stations each monitoring one of the advanced MQ-9 Reaper drones, one stack on the RQ-180 White Bat UAV, and a final workstation devoted to monitoring local EM traffic such as social media, news sites, and police scanners, for anything unusual. That system employed a CIA proprietary AI program that continually searched the full spectrum of human communication for anything related to their operation. The sixth workstation served as a configurable backup that could mirror or supplement any other operator.

"God's Eye has a link with Hornet One, ma'am," reported the operator on the White Bat UAV station.

The RQ-180 was called God's Eye for a reason. The Air Force's latest UAV surveillance drone was a platform of astounding capabilities. The stealthy flying wing design, loitering thirteen miles above the country of Uzbekistan, maintained continuous laser communications with a satellite network, providing Anne a constant tactical picture over a link that was not susceptible to detection or jamming. In addition, the RQ-180 had both optical and synthetic aperture radar which could see through even the densest cloud cover. Although God's Eye had enough onboard computing power to maintain communications with hundreds of ancillaries, Anne needed only three nodes for this operation: Hornets One and Two, the MQ-9 Reaper drones, and their man on the ground, Case Officer Harrison Kohl.

The entire operation had begun some twenty hours before, when Anne ordered the God's Eye launched from Thumrait Air Base in Oman. Although the Royal Omani Air Force base was over five thousand kilometers south of the target, it was still the closest and most secure point from which to launch this high-value air asset.

The UAV flew east, then turned north making landfall over Pakistan and refueling over Afghanistan before arriving in Uzbekistan airspace. Hours later, the MQ-9s, each carrying two StormBreaker smart bombs, launched from a forward air base in eastern Turkey. Normally, she would have staged the Reapers from their home base in Incirlik, Turkey, but the added flight time would have limited their time on station or added a refueling evolution. She'd made the call that the added security risk of launching from an FOB was worth the operational flexibility.

The Reapers, Hornets One and Two, separated shortly after takeoff. Hornet One flew north, passing over Armenia and Azerbaijan. It now loitered over the northern end of the Caspian Sea. Hornet Two took a southern route and was in a holding pattern at the south end of the Caspian.

These were the G variant of the MQ-9 Reaper family. They carried external fuel tanks for extended range, the latest sensor package, and radar-absorbing skin for added stealth. Anne wanted every possible advantage on her side for this operation.

All the logistical pieces were in place. There had been no mechanical failures, no sensor outages, no jammed communications, no detection by hostiles. Everything was working exactly as planned and the clock was running . . .

And now she was waiting on the human element.

Anne hadn't touched a cigarette in over ten years, but she experienced a sudden craving for one. She paced behind the row of workstations, using the cadence of her footsteps to calm her nerves.

"Ma'am," reported the God's Eye operator. "Gandalf is approaching the meeting point."

39

40 kilometers west of Bukhara, Uzbekistan

Harrison unclenched his right hand from the steering wheel of the Chevy Captiva and shook his fingers out. He placed his right hand back on the steering wheel, then repeated the process with his left.

It did absolutely nothing to lessen his stress level.

He cast a glance to the screen of the mobile phone clipped into a holder at eye level. The red pin that marked his destination was ten kilometers away. The kill team back at Langley had reported that the location was a gas station with an attached bar positioned at a crossroads. The place had zero social media presence, so there were no interior pictures available. Since the geo-location pin for his meeting with Akhmet Orazov had arrived in his phone less than an hour ago, that was all the prep he was going to get.

His gaze snapped up to the rearview mirror. Over the course of the last hour, he'd done everything he could think of to discover a tail. He'd changed his speed, gone around blind curves, and pulled off to the side of the road, all for nothing. If Akhmet's people were following him, they were good.

He knew there was a drone miles overhead watching his every move, but all it could do was watch. If something happened, he was on his own.

His mobile reported he had five kilometers to his destination.

Harrison tried to steer his thoughts back to Akhmet Orazov.

You have a job to do, he told himself. Focus. When this is over, you will take Tim's body home. Be with his family, grieve with his family. Just this one last thing to do.

Sunlight glared on the dusty dashboard and his mind wandered back to a broken corpse on a remote hillside. What sort of person threw another human being out of an airplane?

Harrison tried to imagine Tim's last moments on this earth. The animal fear that must have consumed his best friend as he fell to his death. What were his last thoughts?

The car tires shuddered on the rough berm and he swerved back into his lane. His knuckles were bone white and he gripped the steering wheel so hard that he could hear the plastic cover cracking. Worse yet, he couldn't remember any landmarks from the last five kilometers of road. Harrison controlled his breathing and shook out his fingers again.

Focus, dammit.

He hadn't told Jenny how her husband died. He couldn't bring himself to do it. Instead, he made up some bullshit about a robbery gone wrong and Tim getting shot. He didn't suffer, Harrison assured Jenny. It was a quick death, but the killers had buried the body. That's why it took so long to find him.

His mobile reported he had one kilometer to his destination.

Harrison wasn't sure whether she believed him or just wanted to believe him, but it didn't matter. Dead was dead. In another twenty-four hours, he'd be on a plane headed home with his best friend's remains in the cargo hold.

He'd fulfilled his promise to Jenny. Somehow, he'd put this all behind him and get back to living. He owed Tim that much.

He topped a rise in the road and saw his destination ahead. Harrison let the car coast into the cracked asphalt parking lot.

The place had seen better days. The gas station was abandoned, but the bar had lighted neon signs in the window and two cars parked in front. The highway he'd driven might have been a major travel route in the past, but he hadn't seen another car pass him in the last thirty minutes. The crossing highway didn't look any busier. All this place needed was some tumbleweeds to complete the picture of desolation.

He backed into a parking spot, shut off the engine, and sat there.

Outside, he could hear the wind sighing against the car. Another thing he wouldn't miss about this damn country. He breathed in a four count and blew it out. He cracked his knuckles and let the rage bubble in the pit of his stomach.

You can do this, he told himself. Meet Orazov, listen to whatever bullshit he wants to tell you about the SIF, then you make the phone call that wipes him off the face of the earth.

Bada-bing, bada-boom. Another piece of human terrorist filth departed from this earthly place, courtesy of Uncle Sam. Don was worried about blowback from the Russians, but that was all background noise to Harrison. He'd seen firsthand what the SIF had done to this part of the world. The best way to stop that kind of terrorist organization was to take out their leader. Orazov had to go. There was no other option.

Harrison popped open the car door. Loose asphalt ground under his feet. In the distance, the snowcapped mountains gleamed in the sun and a bank of angry-looking storm clouds rolled across the open grasslands.

He paused for a minute. There were some things he would miss. Despite the circumstances, he'd grown to love this region and the people. They had a complicated history of invasion and reinvasion, partition and subjugation. But that was changing. Men like Timur Ganiev were making a difference, while men like Akhmet Orazov were losing their grip on power.

Today, he was going to make that transition go a whole lot faster.

He pushed open the door to the bar and stepped inside. He paused, letting his eyes adjust.

The interior continued the story of decay that he'd seen outside. The sheet metal bar had probably been modern once upon a time, but now it was scarred and dented. The half-dozen metal and Formica tables scattered over the checkboard floor looked sad, the seat cushions worn and cracked. The decorations were all neon signs: Sarbast beer and three different

Russian vodkas. The collection of bottles on the shelf behind the bar was meager.

The only life in the place was a muted TV in the corner, tuned to a Samarkand channel.

Two men rose and approached Harrison. Neither of them was Orazov, but they were both armed and looked like they knew how to handle themselves.

"Where is he?" Harrison asked in Russian.

They ignored him. One hung back, while the other searched Harrison. Harrison did not resist. All he had on him were the car keys and a burner phone.

When the searcher nodded that Harrison was clean, the second man pulled a mobile phone from his pocket and made a call that lasted only a few seconds. He hung up, pointed to a table, and said, "Sit."

40

Samarkand, Uzbekistan

The United States delegation to the Jade Spike ceremony at the Samarkand International Commerce Center consisted of Secretary of State Henry Hahn, four members each from the Senate and House Foreign Relations committees, and the U.S. ambassador to Uzbekistan. Including security and staff for the VIPs, the total visiting contingent from the U.S. numbered more than thirty people.

Don Riley was in charge of security.

He hadn't planned it that way. After he'd accepted Federov's offer to meet with Orazov, the whole operation nearly went off the rails when the Director forbade Don from taking the meeting himself.

"You're not a field officer, Don," the Director had said. "With the knowledge you've got in your head, I can't risk putting you in that kind of situation. Send one of your case officers, or tell the Russians no deal."

Don was at a loss. He needed to be involved, as close to the center of action as possible. In the end, Federov solved the problem for him when he set the meeting with Orazov to take place at the same time as the Chinese Jade Spike ceremony.

And that gave Don an idea. After all, he hadn't spent a quarter century in Washington without learning a thing or two about politics. He convinced Secretary of State Hahn that the CIA's Special Activities Center was the best choice to handle security for the U.S. visit to Samarkand, and Don should supervise the security personally.

Personal was the right word for it, Don thought. If the President insisted on continuing with the kill operation against Akhmet Orazov at the same time as the U.S. delegation was on the ground in Uzbekistan, that was the White House's call. But Don wasn't about to sit in the Washington ops center while his people strolled into the lion's den. He owed them that much.

With everything on the line, Don put his best team on security for the Samarkand visit.

Tom Stellner and Andy Myers were a package deal; they only worked together. Both veterans of the 5th Special Forces Group, then Special Forces Operational Detachment Delta, they were known across the Agency as S&M. They were also two of the most effective operators Don had ever worked with. He would trust them with his life—and had, on several occasions. If things went sideways in Samarkand, Don wanted S&M in his corner.

The United States delegation arrived on two jets. A Boeing C-40 Clipper, the U.S. Air Force's version of the Boeing-737, could have seated the entire party, but Don had also requisitioned a CIA Gulfstream V for the trip. Flexibility was key. If they needed to depart quickly, Don wanted to have options.

The jets taxied into the newly completed private air terminal at the Samarkand International Airport at a few minutes past ten in the morning. The tarmac was crowded with aircraft carrying visiting dignitaries from all over the world. The U.S. planes parked nose-out and side by side, sandwiched between jets from France and South Africa. The U.S. delegation, led by Secretary Hahn, disembarked into a small fleet of black SUVs, all driven by experienced CIA field operators, handpicked by S&M.

The plan was to keep the delegation together until after the Jade Spike ceremony—and hopefully, the completion of Harrison's mission. Don did not want members of the group separated until he was sure the kill operation had gone undetected by their Chinese hosts.

Again, Don's plan was helped by outside forces when Timur Ganiev asked to meet with the US delegation before the official ceremony. With that as his excuse, it was easy to keep the Secretary of State and members of Congress in a group.

The sudden popular rise of Ganiev and his Central Asian Union had blindsided the autocratic leaders in the region. It seemed on any social media site or news outlet the name of Timur was everywhere. The people were demanding change in a way that had not happened in centuries.

Although legally it meant nothing, politically it was a huge issue. One by one, the autocratic leaders met with Ganiev and made noises about breaking down political barriers between the Eurasian republics.

Outside the region, the pressure was mounting as well. In the United Nations, the Secretary-General wasted no time in endorsing the CAU as a "shining light of freedom in Eurasia," even inviting Ganiev to speak at the next meeting of the General Assembly. The European Union, which saw itself as the model for the CAU, was especially vocal in its support. Only the week before the Jade Spike ceremony, *The Economist* featured Ganiev's picture on the cover of the magazine.

The U.S. convoy, led by a pair of Chinese-made Humvee knock-offs flying crimson PRC flags, made their way slowly out of the private air terminal.

"Looks like we're taking the scenic route," Stellner said to Don. The exit from the private terminal led onto a highway where it seemed as if their PLA escorts were parading the U.S. vehicles through the city streets.

They passed an electronic billboard and Stellner jerked his chin at the three-story image of Timur Ganiev looming over them. "The guy's everywhere. You'd think they were crowning him or something."

It was true. Ganiev's face was on billboards, newspapers, even a mural on the side of a building. The caption on the mural read in Uzbek, Russian, Mandarin, and English: *Unity is not a dream. It's our future.*

"Catchy slogan," Stellner observed.

"Yeah," Don checked his phone. Nothing. He'd expected to hear from Harrison by now, or at least an update from Anne Hart. He blew out a breath and counted to ten.

After another few blocks of scenery, the PLA vehicles turned back toward the airport. They entered the brand-new four-lane highway for a few kilometers, then took a long, curving drive toward the grand entrance of the commerce center.

And it was grand. Soaring at least five stories in the air, the sheer cliff of glass looked like a crystal waterfall. On the broad stone sidewalk in front of the entrance, a wide red carpet had been rolled out for visiting dignitaries. On either side of the red carpet, ropes held back members of the press corps. The President of Uzbekistan was on hand to greet the U.S. Secretary of State and members of Congress. Hundreds of cameras and other recording devices waited to capture the moment.

Don cursed. There was no way he was going through that. Stellner was already one step ahead of him, ordering the convoy drivers to separate the vehicles containing dignitaries and staff. Secretary Hahn and the congressmembers pulled up next to the official entrance, while the rest of the U.S. contingent rallied a short way past the red carpet media frenzy.

Over the radio, Myers acknowledged and moved an advance team of U.S. security to meet the U.S. dignitaries on the other side of the red carpet.

Don was breathing heavily when he and Stellner rejoined the group at the security screening area. Immediately he knew something was wrong. The U.S. delegation was off to the side, and Myers was engaged in a heated discussion with a PLA colonel. When he saw Stellner and Don, he waved them over.

He jerked his thumb at the colonel. "Dude says we have to surrender our weapons."

Don shook his head. There had been careful negotiations with the Chinese prior to agreeing to a visit by a U.S. Cabinet official. "That's not our agreement," he said to the PLA officer. "Our security team has approval to carry sidearms."

The colonel pressed his lips together and shook his head. "Not possible."

The ambassador joined them, clearly rattled that there was a visible disagreement in full view of the press. "I think our recalcitrance has been noted. Perhaps we can find a compromise, Mr. Riley?"

Don ignored the diplomat, keeping his eyes on the colonel. There were two possibilities: either this guy was out of the loop, or the Chinese were testing his resolve. Well, two could play at that game.

Don crossed his arms. “I want to speak to General Gao. Immediately.”

The officer narrowed his eyes at Don. He shook his head.

Don had counted at least a dozen cameras around him, and he had no doubt that everything they’d said was being monitored. He turned to the ambassador.

“I’m sorry, sir,” Don said briskly. “You need to return to the vehicles until we get this sorted out. We had a security agreement with General Gao. Please go back out the main entrance.”

Apparently, the thought of the U.S. delegation walking back down the red carpet and leaving before the ceremony even started was enough to electrify the Chinese chain of command.

“What is the problem, Colonel?”

Don turned. He’d never met Lieutenant General Gao Yichen in person, but he’d read the man’s dossier multiple times. The chest of his dress uniform was crowded with brightly colored ribbons. As far as Don knew, Gao was among the very few Chinese officers for whom the failed invasion of Taiwan was a boost to his career. In fact, Gao’s meteoric rise from the rank of major to two-star lieutenant general would be a remarkable feat in any military, let alone the PLA.

Don could also see that the picture of Gao in the CIA files was out of date. Although his uniform was carefully tailored, the man before him had gained weight. He had bags under his eyes and his complexion was sallow, making the scar on his chin stand out as a jagged red line.

Don realized the man’s use of English to address the PLA colonel was for his benefit. He extended his hand. “General Gao, I am—”

“I know who you are, Mr. Riley, and I know what you do.” Gao’s English was thick. “Is there a problem?”

“No problem,” Don replied, annoyed that he’d been cut off. “My security team needs to be armed. Those were the terms of our attendance.”

“I can assure you that the highest level of—”

Now it was Don’s turn to be rude. He cut in. “I have the Secretary of State in my delegation. Are you going to abide by our agreement, or do I escort the Secretary back to our aircraft?”

Gao reddened. Clearly, this was a man who did not hear *no* very often. A female PLA captain stepped forward and placed a hand on his arm. When she whispered in his ear, he leaned toward her.

Don thought the gesture had a hint of intimacy. He watched the two interact. There was definitely something there. He made a mental note to find out more about the female officer.

Gao adopted a strained smile. "Captain Fang has refreshed my memory on the details of our agreement. Your security personnel are free to retain their weapons. She will escort your team through the security process to ensure that you are not late for your meeting with Mr. Ganiev."

"Excellent," the ambassador said. He bowed to Gao. "My sincere thanks for your assistance, General."

Gao's smile was brittle.

41

CIA Special Activities Center
Langley, Virginia

Anne paused her pacing behind the God's Eye stack. Raymond, the operator, had longish brown hair that curled at his collar.

"Put the visual on the big screen," Anne ordered.

The video feed was a combination of sensors: optical, SAR, and infrared. It showed a gas station at a crossroads on the far outskirts of an Uzbek town called Bukhara. She could see that the roads were lightly traveled. Perfect for their operation. Less civilian traffic meant less potential for collateral damage and less chance of immediate discovery once she gave the kill order.

There were three vehicles outside and three IR signatures inside the building. One vehicle belonged to Gandalf, the operational code name for Officer Harrison Kohl. The other two vehicles were linked to the other two men inside the building.

So far, so good, she told herself. *The difference between a successful operation and a failure is the prep. You got this.*

"Anything from Gandalf?" she asked.

"No, ma'am," comms reported. "Nothing yet."

"Someone in the building is making a call," her comms operator said.

"Track it," Anne said. "Get audio if you can."

"It's gone," the operator reported. "The call was all of three seconds."

Anne stared at the screen, willing something to happen. The urge for a cigarette resurfaced. She felt a ripple of doubt surface in her mind.

This is madness, she thought. Less than fifty miles away from that lonely gas station in the middle of nowhere, the General Secretary of the Chinese Communist Party is cutting a ribbon for their latest project. And we're about to fly armed drones into the country.

Play the hand you're dealt. You got this.

She focused on her next call: moving the Reapers into position.

Since Harrison hadn't reported an ID yet, she had to assume that either Orazov was coming to the meeting separately or they were going to move Harrison to another site.

If she waited to move the Reapers into position, she might lose her window of opportunity. On the other hand, once she moved them into Uzbek airspace, the likelihood of detection by the Chinese forces went up dramatically.

She blew out a long breath. And made the call.

"Transfer operational control of Hornet One and Two to God's Eye," she ordered. "Move them into position. Stay at maximum altitude."

She got repeat-backs from both operators.

"Hornet One will be in position in forty-eight minutes," one operator reported.

"Hornet Two is thirty-nine minutes out," said the second.

The waiting was always the hardest part. Fifteen excruciating minutes passed by in which she had nothing to do except stare at the wall screen and worry.

She narrowed her eyes as if just concentrating hard enough would offer her an answer. Harrison Kohl was in that building with two of Orazov's men, and so far they showed no signs of leaving. Did that mean Orazov was en route?

Five more minutes dragged by and she fantasized about a cigarette. A Marlboro. No, a Camel.

"Ma'am," announced the God's Eye operator, "we have vehicles inbound to Gandalf's position."

Without prompting, the operator expanded the field of view on the wall screen.

Two vehicles in close formation approached from the south.

"Twenty klicks out, coming fast," the operator reported. "I've got three men in the lead vehicle and two in the chase car. Three mobile phone signatures between them."

Anne did the mental math. They'd be at the gas station in less than ten minutes. The Reapers were still inbound, but they'd be within weapons range with time to spare.

It was all coming together—assuming these cars held her target.

"Please let it be Orazov," she whispered to herself. "Please."

The minutes ticked by as she watched the moving vehicles on the screen.

"Ma'am . . . " the God's Eye operator said. "They're slowing down. They're stopping at the gas station."

Anne let out the breath she hadn't realized she'd been holding.

"Let's look sharp, people," she said. "We will do this by the numbers. Positive ID from Gandalf, track the outbounds, take the target with the closest Hornet. Any questions?"

There were none.

Anne went to the signals intel stack. She scanned the items the AI had pulled from the infosphere. Nothing caught her eye. Her doubts melted away.

You got this, she told herself. *Do the deed and get the assets as far away from the scene of the crime as possible.*

By the time the PLA figured out what happened, the drones would be long gone. With any luck, Harrison would be enjoying a well-deserved cocktail on a diplomatic flight out of Samarkand.

Anne went to the communications stack. The comms officer was a young woman with a long blonde ponytail that twisted halfway down her back. She put her hand on the operator's shoulder.

"Amelia, get me Director Riley on the phone. Tell him I need a final kill authorization."

42

Samarkand, Uzbekistan

The International Commerce Center was even more impressive inside. The U.S. delegation moved as a group in a vaulted space the size of a football pitch and ringed with stainless steel pillars. Huge flags from all the Central Asian republics and the People's Republic of China hung down like banners. Sunlight streamed in through skylights, turning the red PRC flag into a river of crimson fire.

A stage occupied the center of the space, with tiered seating for the highest-ranking dignitaries. Two platforms bristling with cameras flanked the stage and a security area rose on scaffolding above the crowd about fifty meters back from the stage.

Tables of food surrounded cooking stations where Uzbek men and women served up plates of *plov*, the regional rice dish. Waiters in bright traditional garb maneuvered through the attendees with trays of drinks. Teams of uniformed PLA soldiers patrolled the fringes of the crowd, encouraging people to remain in the waiting area.

"Wow," said Stellner, "these guys know how to throw a party."

Captain Fang flashed her badge to one of the security patrols and led them past the stage to a conference room. "Mr. Ganiev will be with you shortly," she said. "In the meantime, please enjoy the refreshments." She pointed to a table laden with bottles of water, a samovar of hot tea, and coffee service.

Don stepped away to check his phone. He had a strong signal, but there was still no word from either Harrison or Anne. He checked his watch. Harrison should be at the meeting by now. Things should be happening. He fretted that maybe Orazov had switched the meeting venue at the last minute.

He heard a disturbance behind him and turned to see Timur Ganiev enter the room. Except for a blonde woman and a cameraman, he was alone, which Don thought was odd. Where was his security?

Because he'd seen the man's face so many times, on billboards, newspapers, and murals, Don had an uncanny feeling that he already knew Ganiev. But the images did not do justice to the man's presence.

Timur Ganiev was tall, with an athletic build and a slight dusting of gray in his hair. He was dressed in a conservative dark blue suit and dark tie, with a matching traditional *tubeteika* skull cap embroidered with gold thread. The camera crew tracked his movements like they were stalking a rare wild animal.

Ganiev made a beeline for Secretary of State Hahn. Without waiting to be introduced, he held out his hand and said, in excellent London-accented English, "Mr. Secretary, it is a great honor. My name is Timur Ganiev."

"The honor is all mine, President Ganiev," Hahn replied.

Don hid a smile. It was a little funny that both men spoke with British accents while neither was British.

Ganiev waved his hand. "You flatter me, sir. The Central Asian Union exists only in the hearts of the people, and I am not their president."

"Yet," Hahn countered.

Ganiev put a hand on his heart. "Inshallah."

God willing, Don thought, *and maybe with a little help from Uncle Sam.*

And maybe Timur didn't need any help. Beneath his understated personality and self-deprecating manner, Timur Ganiev had a blend of charisma and personal magnetism that Don had seen among the most successful politicians. Based on the reactions as he worked the room, Timur also knew how to form instant personal connections.

The camera crew passed in front of Don. The woman was handling sound as the cameraman prowled beside their target.

Ganiev made his way through the members of Congress and then to the U.S. ambassador. He knew everyone's name and rank without prompting, and his smile was warm and inviting to each.

Don hung back from the impromptu receiving line. He was not part of the official delegation. He was the help. Also, he did not want to be on camera.

But he wasn't fast enough. Ganiev reached Don and held out his hand.

Don accepted the greeting and stammered out, "Mr. Ganiev, my name is—"

"Donald Riley," Ganiev finished for him. "Deputy Director of Operations for the Central Intelligence Agency. I know who you are, Mr. Riley."

His grip was firm, his gaze penetrating. Don realized that Ganiev had signaled the camera away. This guy was as savvy as they came.

"I hope you have a very pleasant stay in my country." Ganiev cast a sidelong glance at Stellner, who hovered a few meters away making no effort to hide his sidearm. "But please do not stay too long."

Ganiev turned to the woman who was part of the camera crew.

"Have you ever met someone from the CIA, Nicole?" he asked her.

Nicole regarded Don coolly. "Unfortunately, Timur, I have."

Ganiev laughed. "Mr. Riley, this is Nicole Nipper, a very famous journalist who has chosen to waste her time making a documentary about me, of all things."

Nipper's expression made her opinion of the CIA plain. "Timur, we're behind. The French delegation is waiting."

Ganiev gave an exaggerated shrug. "I must leave you, I'm afraid."

Don's phone buzzed. He stepped away to take the call.

"Hello."

"I'm calling from the clubhouse." Anne Hart's voice came through the receiver. Even though he was using a secure satellite phone, their conversation was scripted.

"Your bill is due," she continued. "Would you like me to charge it to the credit card you have on file?"

Don's mouth went dry. Orazov had shown up to the meeting with

Harrison. The operation was a go. Because of the unusual logistics of having the U.S. delegation only fifty miles from the scene of the assassination, the final kill authorization had been designated to Don.

He had three codeword options: "I'll review the charges when I get home" meant abort; "I'll call later with a new credit card" meant stand by; and "Charge it to the card on file" meant proceed.

"Sir?" Anne said.

Don's mouth was dry. This was it, the moment of truth. He didn't agree with Serrano's plan to assassinate Orazov, but that wasn't his decision. His responsibility was to make sure the kill operation did not impact the safety of the delegation.

"Sir?" Anne prompted. "How would you like to handle the charges?"

"Charge it to the card on file, please."

"Very good, sir. Have a nice day." Anne disconnected the call.

When Don rejoined the group, Timur Ganiev was gone.

43

40 kilometers west of Bukhara, Uzbekistan

Harrison sat at one of the chipped Formica tables. His foot tapped a nervous tattoo on the worn linoleum floor.

Calm down, he told himself, but it was no use.

He crossed his legs to stop his tapping foot and tried to focus on the TV. There was special coverage of the Jade Spike ceremony.

The subtitles were in Uzbek, but the TV images were easy enough to follow. Harrison caught a glimpse of a stage built inside of the huge concourse. Crowds of well-dressed people milled about. He spotted the U.S. Secretary of State seated in a box with an American flag draped across the front. He saw no sign of Don Riley, but he guessed his friend was pulling his hair out running security for a Cabinet member sitting inside a Chinese facility in Central Asia.

The buzz of an incoming text startled Harrison.

When he'd given up his personal mobile device, Harrison had insisted that all his calls and texts be rerouted to the burner. Don had objected, but Harrison stood his ground. He was still worried about Jenny. The compromise reached was that any incoming communications would be stripped of any identifying data before being relayed to Harrison's new device.

Looking at the text now, he didn't need a phone number to know it was from Jenny.

Got an email from the Ironclad service Tim was using. It said the files have been released. Not sure what that means. I fwded it to you. When ru coming home?

Harrison clutched the phone harder. He knew what she was really asking him: When are you bringing my husband's body home?

He cut a look at the two guards, but they were absorbed in the TV. He tapped out a reply:

Just need to finish one thing here, then I'm on a plane. I'll check out the email.

He sent the text, then shot another look at Orazov's men before he logged onto the internet. He quickly navigated to his personal email service and found the forwarded message from Jenny. The subject line read: *Iron-Clad final release of data files.*

Harrison scanned the text. After a set period of time with no activity, the service automatically gave the account holder's designated survivor full access to all files. The default setting was 250 days.

Had it really been that long? A sudden pang of loss swept over him. Two-hundred and fifty days. His best friend in the world had been dead for 250 days.

Harrison clocked another look at the guards, then clicked on the link in the email.

Tim Trujillo's life was summed up in icons. Email, text messages, USAA bank accounts, photos, all backed up on the IronClad file system.

Harrison clicked on the email icon and scanned the list. He'd seen all of these before. The same was true of the text messages. As he read through the last few texts between Tim and Jenny, he felt his heart break all over again. And he felt the anger bubble up, too.

He clicked on photos. The most recent photo was a video. Harrison frowned. He didn't remember a video in Tim's photos. He checked the time stamp.

For a second, Harrison forgot where he was or what he was doing here.

The time stamp was 0113 on the day Tim was killed.

His finger shook so badly that he had to press the screen twice to get the recording to start.

The picture was jerky, but well-lit. It appeared as if Tim had recorded it from a hiding place. Harrison squinted at the screen. Inside a lighted airplane hangar, two men were standing in front of a Gulfstream. One man was facing the camera, a Chinese man.

Harrison paused the recording and zoomed in on the face. He sat back in his chair.

Impossible. It couldn't be him.

Harrison looked away, blinked, and cleared his mind. Then he looked at the phone screen again.

Yan Tao, the Chinese Minister of State Security, was in a video saved on Tim's phone. From the night Tim died.

Harrison checked the data associated with the file. He stared at the latitude and longitude. He didn't need to look them up. Harrison had seen them so many times, he'd memorized the coordinates for the Tashkent International Airport.

He restarted the video. The Minister was arguing with someone, but the man was facing away from the camera.

"Turn around, damn you!" Harrison whispered.

When the man turned, Harrison all but dropped the phone.

He blinked, struggling to process what he was seeing with his own eyes.

The puzzle pieces in Harrison's mind tilted, shifted, rearranged—and fell into a new pattern.

He'd known all along that the Chinese had the ability to erase all records of a private aircraft landing in Tashkent after hours. But here was proof that a Chinese jet had been in Tashkent the night of Tim's death. Moreover, the flight back to Beijing would have taken them right over Tim Trujillo's final resting place.

His mind reeled. His mouth was dry.

His best friend was dead because of what he saw that night. A secret meeting between the most powerful intelligence officer in China and someone Harrison would never have suspected of being in bed with the Chinese.

Then a new thought hit Harrison like a hammer blow.

Everything about the Orazov kill order was based on a lie. The intel was wrong, dangerously wrong. He had to stop this—now.

Quickly, Harrison attached the video to a text and fired it off to Don Riley.

Then, he powered down his phone, took a deep breath, and stood up in one sudden movement.

The guards startled to their feet, reaching for their weapons.

"Call Orazov," Harrison said. "Tell him the meeting's off."

The weapons came out now. The guards separated so it was hard for Harrison to track both of their movements. "Why?" one said.

Harrison blinked, unsure what to say.

When in doubt, tell the truth.

"This meeting is a setup. They're going to kill him."

44

Samarkand, Uzbekistan

The seating layout for the Jade Spike ceremony reminded Don of the way the inaugural platform was arranged on the steps of the U.S. Capitol.

A stage, raised about two meters off the ground, had been constructed at one end of the concourse in the Samarkand International Commerce Center. It was semicircular in shape and tiered upwards away from the main dais. At the focal point of the fan shape stood a massive plexiglass lectern that looked like an ice sculpture.

Seating on the dais was reserved for only the most important officials in attendance. Seating went by rank: the higher your perceived worth, the closer you were to the speakers on the main stage.

Don watched all this from the raised security platform set back fifty meters from the stage. Security chiefs from different organizations all over the world circulated among long camera lenses. The floor space between the security platform and the stage was packed with a standing audience of thousands.

Immediately in front of the podium was an open area roped off from the standing audience and guarded by uniformed PLA soldiers. It held the now-famous Jade Spike for which the ceremony was named.

Don studied it with field glasses. The emerald-green ceremonial spike was about a half meter long, displayed on a bed of crushed red velvet. Next to the spike lay a sledgehammer coated in gold leaf.

A vault with a thick glass cover had been built into the floor in front of the display. Don had read that the spike would be entombed in the vault at the end of the ceremony as a tribute to this great day.

That's if the ceremony ever ends, he lamented. For the past forty-five minutes, he'd been listening to political speeches in foreign languages. He could have used the in-ear translation device he'd been issued, but he didn't really want to know what the President of who-cares-istan had to say about the New Silk Road.

The only thing worse than listening to a political speech was listening to a political speech in a language he did not understand. Besides, he had other worries.

For the umpteenth time, he checked his mobile phone for an update from either Anne back in Langley or from Harrison.

Nothing.

Back on the stage, it sounded like the President of Kyrgyzstan was wrapping up his remarks. On the large monitors that flanked the stage, the man's trimmed beard reflected the light as he spoke. His tone became more strident. He leaned forward and cocked his head to address his last few words at the General Secretary of the Chinese Communist Party seated to the right of the podium.

When the speaker finished, the Chinese leader nodded sagely, his fleshy face immobile. There was polite clapping from the crowd.

Don watched U.S. Secretary of State Henry Hahn through the glasses. Hahn sat ramrod straight in his seat behind a small American flag in the first row just to the right of the podium. The Secretary's face might have been carved of stone and his lips were pressed together. Hahn had not wanted to make this trip. He'd advised President Serrano that the U.S. would be giving tacit approval to the Chinese Belt and Road Initiative by attending what was essentially a Chinese Communist Party ceremony in Uzbekistan. Don had been in the room when Hahn called the Chinese event "economic colonialism."

But Serrano had another agenda. Don was not a politician, but after working with the President for eight years, he wasn't a fool, either. Serrano was using Hahn as political cover, an alibi for the U.S. presence in Uzbekistan in case the assassination of Orazov was exposed. Hahn was also there to send a message to the Central Asian republics that the United States was still available as an economic alternative to the Chinese.

The President of Kyrgyzstan moved back to his seat, crossing in front of the most important guests that lined the edge of the stage. The presidents of all four Central Asian republics were on one side of the stage. On the other side, the General Secretary of the Chinese Communist Party was seated next to Timur Ganiev, representing the future of a unified Eurasia. Next to Ganiev was Lieutenant General Gao.

It seemed odd to Don that Gao was on the dais at all. He sat rigidly on the edge of his seat, his face impassive, his perfunctory clapping mechanical. His PLA dress uniform stood out among the business suits of the rest of the speakers, and he was the only one who was not a politician. Over the general's shoulder, Don could make out the face of Secretary Hahn.

Don lowered the field glasses and checked his phone again for updates.

Nothing.

The announcer started speaking again in Mandarin and Don made out the words *Timur Ganiev*.

As Ganiev stood, a ripple swept through the crowd like a breeze through tall grass. He stalked toward the podium and mounted the gleaming lectern.

Less than a year ago, Timur Ganiev had been a grieving doctor running a tiny non-governmental organization in backwater Central Asian communities. Now, he was a celebrity. His face was everywhere and the Central Asian Union was a reality in the minds of millions of his countrymen.

Don studied the handsome face on the large monitors that flanked the stage.

I made this happen, Don thought. Operation Catbird plucked a nobody from obscurity and turned him into a force for good. Ganiev's positive message had overpowered the hate-filled rhetoric of the SIF.

Don's influence operation was even responsible for putting Ganiev on the stage. The leader of the CAU hadn't been invited to the ceremony until

Don's people put their influence machine behind a petition to make him the keynote speaker at the Jade Spike ceremony. Grudgingly, the Chinese relented. Another win for the CIA.

But even that success had not been enough for President Serrano, Don mused bitterly. He wanted Orazov dead and buried.

It was ironic. The SIF and Ganiev both wanted the same thing—to be independent—but they took opposite paths. The SIF took the path of violence. Ganiev chose to raise people up, to appeal to their better angels.

Don raised his glasses again and swept across the crowd. He was able to pick out Stellner with ease. Everyone in the audience was facing the stage except for the tall white guy prowling the edge of the gathering. He watched the audience.

Don shifted his field of view and found Myers on the opposite side of the stage doing the same thing. Both were in excellent position to protect Secretary of State Hahn, if needed.

Ganiev stood behind the ice sculpture podium, looking every inch a man of the future.

He gracefully acknowledged the previous speakers and thanked the General Secretary for the opportunity to "address my people."

The choice of words was not lost on the room. Another whisper of excitement swept through the audience.

He paused, his hands finding the edges of the lectern.

"But most of all I wish to thank the people of the Central Asian Union for awakening to their power."

Spontaneous applause crackled. Like everyone else, Don found himself leaning forward to catch each nuance of the man's words.

"We are at a time of great change in our region," he continued. "A once-in-a-millennia reordering of power. I have traveled these republics from one end to the other. I have met the people whose ancestors were born on this land, who farmed this land, who tended herds on this land . . . who gave their lives for this land. What I found may surprise some of you: We are more alike than we are different."

His face creased into a stern frown. "Today, you heard from four separate governments. These leaders represent political structures that have kept us apart for the last hundred years. These political structures were designed for one purpose: to keep us apart. Stop us from recognizing our shared humanity, our shared strength."

A buzz from Don's mobile phone interrupted his concentration.

He stared at the screen. He'd expected a coded update from Anne Hart, but instead the text was from Harrison. All it contained was a video attachment. The text read:

Tim sent this the night he was killed.

As Don opened the video, Ganiev continued. "But the message I bring you today is one of unity. While we appreciate our tribal heritage, we also recognize a singular fact: We are stronger together—"

The screen on his phone showed a video of a Chinese man standing in front of a jet in a lighted hangar. Don looked closer.

The man was the Chinese Minister of State Security, and he was talking to someone, a second man with his back to the camera.

"We are not pawns to be divided up amongst the so-called Great Powers," Ganiev thundered. "We are a great people, a proud people, and this is *our* land."

The man in the video turned around. Don looked from his tiny phone display to the massive screens flanking the dais, then back to his phone.

The man in the video was Timur Ganiev.

Don's thoughts cascaded.

The video showed a secret meeting between the highest-ranking intelligence officer in all of China and Timur Ganiev. A video recorded months before he showed up on the CIA's radar as a champion of democracy in a land of autocrats.

That same man was now on a stage speaking to millions of people using words like "unity" and "progress." Everything about the last year snapped into focus. Every misgiving, every stray detail, every odd premonition clarified in Don's mind.

Timur Ganiev was a Chinese agent.

I put him there, Don thought. *They dangled him in front of me like a dog treat and I bit hard. I fell for it.*

Cold sweat broke out across his face. He felt dizzy.

His eyes snapped around the space. Cameras, armed guards. They were cocooned in a PLA security bubble.

It was a set-up. Don could see it as clear as day now.

His earpiece crackled to life.

Stellner's voice: "I've got suspicious movement in the crowd. Something's happening."

45

Samarkand, Uzbekistan

It was the way the man moved that caught Stellner's eye. Smooth motions, deliberate progress.

Everyone in the audience had their faces angled up, toward the dais. They alternated between watching Timur Ganiev at the podium and watching his enlarged image on one of the screens that flanked the stage. Their faces, lit softly by reflected light from the dais, went back and forth, like spectators watching a tennis match.

Except this guy. His eyes were turned toward the stage, but he ignored the large screen. He eased forward in the audience.

Stellner followed his line of vision. He wasn't looking at the speaker, he was looking to the speaker's right. The Chinese General Secretary was there, and seated in the row behind him was Secretary of State Hahn. The Secretary sat upright in his chair with his features set in resting grandpa face, eyes vacant, a bemused smile.

Stellner cut a look at the PLA security team only ten paces away. No one seemed to notice the man making his way slowly toward the stage.

"I've got suspicious movement in the crowd," Stellner whispered just loud enough for his earpiece to pick up his voice. "Something's happening."

He threw another glance at the PLA team. The pair stared straight ahead, gently cradling the QCQ-171 submachineguns that hung from tactical slings attached to their upper bodies.

How could they not see this guy?

The target stayed on the fringes of the audience where the density of people was less. He moved forward another step.

"I see him." Myer's voice on the net. "Medium height, ponytail, glasses."

Stellner swore under his breath. *Dammit, there's two of them.*

"No," he replied. "My bogey is short hair, no glasses."

The PLA security team stared straight ahead.

Stellner took a step forward, hoping to attract their attention. His rules of engagement were that the Chinese initiated all security actions unless Stellner believed his principal was in immediate danger.

If he let this guy move any farther away, he'd be giving up his ability to take action. There was no rule against just following someone, Stellner reasoned. He was allowed to patrol.

"Papa bear, this is Sierra," he said. "I think we might have a roach problem. I'm mobile."

"Same here," Myers said. "I'm going on walkabout."

Stellner pushed off the stainless steel–clad column that had been his post.

Riley had not replied yet.

"Papa, did you copy my last?"

No reply.

Stellner's awareness went up a notch. Had they lost comms?

He turned back to the PLA security team. They were gone.

"Two, this is One, radio check."

"I'm here, buddy," Myers said.

Don Riley's voice came on the net. Stellner had worked with Don for years. He wasn't a field operator, but Riley knew how to keep his wits about him in a tactical situation.

"All units, this is Papa." Don's tone held a note of panic. "All non-essentials proceed to evac point now. No sudden movements, just withdraw now."

A slew of acknowledgments filled the net. Stellner was in the fringes of the audience, his gaze locked on the back of his target's head.

Riley's voice sounded in his ear. "One and Two, I'm on a private channel. Stay on your targets. You are authorized to act, if necessary. As soon as this is over, I want you to evac Eagle."

Eagle was the code name for the Secretary of State.

"What's going on, boss?" Myers asked.

"I don't know," Don said. "Use your judgment, guys. I'll meet you at the stage. Papa, out."

In his long career, Stellner had attended too many political events to count. Rallies, fundraisers, demonstrations—he'd seen it all. Most of the time, when politicos spoke, people fidgeted, checked their phones, talked to each other and took selfies.

But not with this Ganiev guy. People were riveted on the man. Even Stellner, who couldn't understand a word the man said, felt an emotional connection.

He slid past a woman wearing a poofy headdress and a long flowing gown. She gave him a dirty look, but Stellner ignored her.

The target was about ten feet ahead, making his way slowly, methodically toward the stage. He was smooth. He'd step around someone, then pause and check the stage before he moved again. The way he zigzagged through the crowd was like a slow-motion waltz.

Stellner's style was not as refined. He jostled past a beefy guy in glasses. The man grunted at him in Russian.

"Pardon," Stellner muttered.

Six feet away now, close enough to see the guy had a mole on the back of his neck just above his shirt collar. Two ranks of people separated them.

Ganiev was wrapping up his speech, the final words coming fast with a cadence, energy building as he landed each word and pumped his fist.

The audience responded. Clapping, raising their hands, cheering—and blocking Stellner's view of his target.

He cursed, elbowed his way forward.

Only one person separated them now.

The target was not cheering, did not have his hands raised. But his face was turned up to the stage and Stellner followed his line of sight.

Timur Ganiev, both fists raised in the air. He stepped down from the podium and moved to the right. The target's eyes tracked Ganiev.

Stellner saw his right shoulder dip as the man reached across his chest toward his left armpit.

A handgun appeared. The man's arm lengthened, extended toward the stage.

But Stellner was already in motion.

"Gun!" he shouted. He heaved aside the woman separating him from the gunman, lunged forward.

Everyone on the stage was standing, moving, applauding.

The weapon tracked right, passing Ganiev. Then it passed the General Secretary and Stellner saw it come to bear on the Secretary of State.

He was almost there, his right hand raised like a hook to smack down the gunman's arm and spoil his shot.

Almost, but not quite.

The muzzle of the weapon moved a fraction of an inch further right. The gunman pulled the trigger a split second before Stellner hit him.

The crowd reacted like a living thing, instinctively drawing away from the source of the gunshot. The woman he'd knocked down scuttled away on all fours like a sand crab, screaming.

All Stellner's focus was on the gun. He locked one hand on the barrel, the other on the gunman's wrist and twisted, pointing the weapon skyward.

The gunman pulled the trigger again, and then again, but the rounds went straight up.

Stellner headbutted him, then swept his legs to put him flat on his back. He landed on the man's chest with both knees, knocking the wind out of him, then he posted up on one leg to better position himself on top of the shooter.

He punched the guy in the throat and the weapon came free in his hand. Stellner put two rounds in the guy's chest and one in his face.

BOOM.

The explosion knocked Stellner on his ass.

46

Samarkand, Uzbekistan

Although the translation of Timur Ganiev's speech sounded in his ear, Gao's thoughts were elsewhere. So far, the Jade Spike ceremony had been a flawless production. Gao felt the tightness in his chest loosen. It was going to be all right.

His cheeks tightened as he suppressed a self-satisfied smile. Just like in Taiwan and with the lost nuke, he'd gambled everything—his career, his reputation, even his life—and he'd come out on top. Already he was the youngest two-star general in the history of the People's Liberation Army.

The smile leaked out. The elation he felt was like the fizz of champagne bubbles in his head. There was no limit to his career now. All doors were open to the Hero of Tashkent—

Ganiev's voice echoed in the great hall, bringing Gao back to the moment. The man's cadence took on a new urgency as he drove toward a climactic oratorical finish.

He was good, Gao thought. He cast a sidelong glance at the General Secretary. Maybe too good. Would the General Secretary feel upstaged by the new leader of the Central Asian Union?

His thoughts spiraled. If the great man felt slighted, that might reflect badly on Gao. In the original plans for the ceremony, Timur Ganiev wasn't even supposed to be on the dais, much less a featured speaker. But there had been the public appeal and the petition. Normally, Gao would have brushed those aside as not in keeping with Party policy, but Xiaomei had intervened.

The Jade Spike ceremony was not just a celebration of Chinese progress, she insisted. It was a celebration of Gao's ingenuity in outwitting the Seljuk Islamic Front once and for all. Allowing the popular leader of the new Central Asian Union to speak was a stroke of genius.

What better way to show the SIF who's boss? she'd whispered into his ear.

Gao had doubts about the strategy, but Xiaomei was very persuasive—and it didn't hurt her cause that they'd had this discussion while in bed.

Since the incident at the dam, Gao had redoubled his scrutiny of the security arrangements for the ceremony. Xiaomei was at his side as he ran through every possible security scenario. There would be no mistakes. The Jade Spike ceremony would be a triumph. His triumph, but one he would share with Xiaomei.

Gao shifted in his chair. His brain slipped into neutral at the muscle memory of her silken skin pressing against his body. His flesh shivered with desire for her. They'd been sleeping together ever since that day on the dam when he'd almost lost his life. It was as if the brush with death had unleashed their shared desire.

He bit his lip. It reminded him of his first days with Mei Lin. The stolen moments of electric passion, the relentless hunger for each other—

He mentally slammed on the brakes. There was a lifetime ahead with Xiaomei. As for dealing with his wife . . . He put the thought out of his head for now.

Ganiev's amplified voice rose to a fever pitch. Gao watched the audience lean in, eyes alight, lips parted. Hands were raised and a buzz circulated through the crowd like a tidal flow. Anticipation sizzled in the air. Any second now, when Ganiev finished, the room would erupt in applause.

His eye snagged on an anomaly in the audience. The absence of movement, like a dead pixel on a screen, a dot of black in a sea of color. He squinted through the glare of the stage lights.

It was a man. He was in the third rank of the crowd, just on the edge of

Gao's vision. Everyone around him pulsed with energy, hands up, eyes wide, mouths agape.

But not him. He stood still, staring at the stage. His right hand slipped into the left breast of his suit jacket.

Ganiev finished with a hoarse shout, both arms in the air. The crowd sounded like thunder. Everyone on stage, including Gao, stood.

He saw the man's hand emerge, arm extend, the muzzle of a gun pointed at the stage. Gao tracked the shooter's aim.

Ganiev, Gao thought. *He's going to shoot Timur Ganiev.*

The weapon tracked back, leaving Ganiev.

Gao's heart stuttered.

The General Secretary! He's going to shoot the General Secretary.

Gao gathered himself to leap.

But the weapon continued moving. And stopped—

On him.

Instinct kicked in. He checked his forward progress, twisted his torso to present a smaller target.

It was too late.

He heard the *boom* of the weapon, saw the spit of bright fire beyond the glare of the stage lights.

Something hit his right shoulder with the force of a sledgehammer, whipping his body around. His forward momentum carried him to the floor. He landed face down.

Another gunshot, but nothing hit him.

Gao screamed in agony as he rolled over. He could not move his right arm. It felt like his body was pinned to the floor by a white-hot poker.

BOOM. An explosion rocked the stage. Gao saw a swath of the audience fall back as if a wave had swept over them. The bright stage lights went out with a pop, drenching him in shadows.

Screaming filled the void left by the explosion. Pain, fear, panic.

The heavy boots of security teams swarmed the stage, seizing their principals, rushing them to safety. Four men encased the General Secretary in a security bubble that whisked past Gao.

Gao raised his good hand. "Help me."

They did not even look down at him.

He tried to lever himself up to a sitting position, but failed. His head was swimming, his vision darkening at the edges.

Xiaomei appeared above him. For a second, he thought she was a vision.

From his vantage point on the floor, she looked very tall. He thought of her long slender legs wrapped around his body and he smiled.

He lifted his good hand. "Help me, Xiaomei."

She did not bend down or kneel next to him. She did not even extend her hand. Instead, she cocked her head, frowning down at him.

"Darling," Gao tried again. "Help me." He could feel his voice getting weaker.

Her lip curled into a sneer. It was ugly on her face.

I'm hallucinating, Gao thought.

Captain Fang drew her sidearm, leveled it at Gao.

"I'm always cleaning up after you," she said.

The muzzle of the gun consumed all the remaining light, all his attention.

Mei Lin, what have I done?

Fang Xiaomei's head exploded in red mist and pulp. She teetered on her long slim legs, then toppled.

Gao swung his head to look at the audience. A man advanced toward the stage, handgun extended. He was a white man, with a crew cut streaked with gray.

Gao Yichen passed out.

47

Samarkand, Uzbekistan

Don was halfway to the stage when Timur Ganiev finished his speech. As Ganiev pumped both fists in the air, the audience erupted—

And a gunshot rang out. A second later, an explosion. The lights went out.

Don managed to stay on his feet, but his path filled with panicked bodies rushing away from the violence. He dropped a shoulder and plowed through the scrum.

The crowd passed by him, leaving a clear view of the stage. Security teams swarmed, rushing their principals to safety.

Stellner rose to his feet, but the body of another man stayed on the floor. He gripped a weapon in his hand, his eyes focused on the stage.

Don followed his gaze to see a man down.

Who was it? Ganiev? The Chinese General Secretary?

Don realized the downed man was wearing a uniform.

General Gao.

"Stellner!" Don shouted.

But Stellner did not respond. He did not turn around. His full attention was locked on the stage.

A woman in uniform, a PLA captain, had advanced on the fallen general. She stood over him.

The general raised his arm, clearly a plea for help, but the captain did not try to help him. Instead, she pulled out her sidearm and aimed at the downed man.

Stellner raised his weapon and fired. Don saw a spray of red, and the PLA captain fell.

"What the hell is going on?" Don roared.

Stellner ignored him. He advanced to the stage with deliberate speed, weapon forward, both hands on the grip. He climbed the steps and knelt to check the PLA captain's pulse.

Myers and two more of the U.S. security team pulled the Secretary of State up from his shelter on the floor.

"What the hell happened?" Don demanded.

"She was gonna execute him, Don. I acted on instinct." Stellner's voice was calm, matter-of-fact.

Don looked around the rapidly clearing stage. Nothing made sense. Was the general the target or had Stellner spoiled the shot? The aide was going to kill the general. Why? What was he missing?

Myers called out to Don, breaking his train of thought. "Our comms are down. We need to go, sir. Now."

The general stirred, then slipped back into unconsciousness.

Don reached down and grabbed the general's lapel, hauling him up to a sitting position.

"Help me," he said to Stellner. "We're bringing him with us."

"Have you lost your mind?"

"I'm acting on instinct," Don replied.

48

CIA Special Activities Division
Langley, Virginia

Anne Hart had a hollow ache in the pit of her stomach. It could have been that bean burrito she'd wolfed down on a break, but twenty years of experience told her that uneasy feeling was not indigestion.

"C'mon," she whispered at the screen. "Move, dammit."

Two cars had arrived at the gas station bar ten minutes ago. Ancient Toyota Land Cruisers, white with rust-spotted roofs.

When the cars arrived, no one got out of either vehicle and no one came out of the building. From a mobile phone inside one of the Toyotas, a text was sent. From inside the bar, a mobile phone made a call lasting less than ten seconds. They were not able to get audio capture or a trace.

Then, nothing.

Were they waiting for Orazov to arrive or was he inside one of the Toyotas?

Anne's stomach rumbled.

"Nothing from Gandalf?" she asked the comms operator. Even as the words left her mouth, she regretted them.

"No, ma'am."

"Hornets One and Two are in position, ma'am," the God's Eye operator reported.

"Copy," Anne said. They were truly on the clock now. Mission parameters gave her a ninety-minute window on station, but in reality, every second she spent in PLA airspace was a risk.

"Why are they just sitting there?" she asked out loud.

No one replied. Anne moved to the intel workstation. "Anything?"

"No, ma'am. Lots of social media from the event in Samarkand, but the PLA comms volume is tracking inside normal parameters. We're clean as far as I can see."

But that twisty feeling in her gut was still there.

"Ma'am?" the comms officer spoke up. Anne was at the young woman's workstation before her voice slid into the second syllable. She frowned at the screen, tapped on the keyboard.

"I've lost Gandalf's signal."

"Define *lost*," Anne snapped.

"He turned off his mobile—"

"We've got movement," the God's Eye operator reported.

On the wall screen, the two Toyotas pulled up close to the entrance of the bar. Three men exited the bar and piled into the Land Cruisers. Two into the first vehicle; one into the chase car.

The Toyotas spun around in the parking lot, spraying gravel and dust. They reached the crossroads and went in opposite directions.

"Shit," Anne said. "Run back the video. Show it in slow motion."

The operator put the last minute of activity up on the screen. They watched it at half speed, then quarter speed, then frame by frame. A wooden awning overhung the door of the establishment blocking all but a glimpse of the men leaving the bar. All three men wore hats and kept their heads down. It was impossible to tell which was Harrison Kohl.

"There's no heat signatures remaining in the building, ma'am," the operator told her. "Gandalf left with the bad guys."

Anne cursed to herself. Somehow Orazov had smelled the trap and they'd taken Harrison hostage.

"Track both vehicles. Comms, get me Director Riley on the phone now."

"Yes, ma'am." The comms operator tapped her keyboard. She frowned. "I can't reach him."

"Go to his backup then," Anne said, letting the frustration edge into her voice.

"I tried that, ma'am. They're both offline."

"Whoa." The intel operator pushed his chair back from the workstation. His mouth gaped open.

"What?" Anne snapped.

"Everything inside the Samarkand event center just went dead. Gone. It's like . . ."

His voice trailed off, but Anne's brain finished the thought for him.

Like a bomb.

49

Samarkand, Uzbekistan

The room had a metal table and a single chair. Both items of furniture stood in the center of the room and they were bolted to the linoleum floor. The air smelled of fresh paint and plastic.

Timur Ganiev looked up at the dome of smoked glass that protruded from the ceiling. *An interrogation room*, he realized. *They put me in an interrogation room.*

He clasped his hands together to keep them from shaking. His whole body jangled with nervous energy as if he might jump out of his own skin.

His keynote speech at the Jade Spike ceremony was magnificent. Never before in his life had he felt so connected to an audience. How he had held them! A visceral connection—physical, emotional, spiritual. A mere touch of his finger and they might have fallen to their knees.

Even now, just the thought of that moment triggered a rush of endorphins in his brain. When he dismounted the podium, everyone was on their feet, everyone was focused on *him*. Adoring *him*, elevating *him*. Even the powerful people on the stage reached out to take his hand. Even they wanted to share in his glory.

And then it all went horribly wrong. An explosion of brilliant white out of the corner of his eye, like the flash-pop of an old-fashioned light bulb.

And the gunshots. He remembered the gunshots.

It was like an out-of-body experience after that. Strong hands gripped his arms and his feet left the ground as they rushed him off the stage.

They brought him here. They dumped him in this room, this interrogation chamber reserved for . . . criminals. And they left him. Alone.

How long had he been in here? Five minutes? Thirty? Timur wasn't wearing a watch and there was no clock on the wall. His nerves were so fried that he'd lost all track of time.

He looked up at the glass dome protruding from the ceiling. A camera. They were watching him.

Timur turned away, trying to calm his nerves. Whatever was happening, he would need all his wits. He clasped his hands behind his back and paced the six steps to the wall. A sharp turn, six steps back. As he walked, he dug his heels into the linoleum floor. Each footfall made a *pock* sound in the silent room and left a scuff mark on the pristine linoleum. It was a juvenile gesture, but it felt good.

He made four circuits of the room before his thoughts caught up with him again. How long were they going to leave him here? Why hadn't anyone come to see him? When he neared the entrance, his anger erupted. He hammered the steel door with his fist.

"You can't hold me in here," he shouted, hearing the frustration color his voice. "You have to let me go."

As if in response, the door swung open. The Chinese Minister of State Security stood in the doorway. Behind him were four security guards, all of them armed. Timur took a step back. Yan Tao entered the room and closed the door behind him.

He looked at Timur with a bland expression. "How are you holding up?"

Timur blinked. The man acted as if gunshots, explosions, rough handling by the security team, and getting locked in an interrogation room were things that happened every day. He was responsible for this debacle. His incompetence had ruined Timur's big moment.

"How could you let this happen?" Timur raged. "You're supposed to be the most security-conscious nation on the face of the earth. You told me you had a surveillance state second to none. You told me I'd be safe. There were guns in there, and bombs. People died . . ."

Timur paused for breath. Sagging back against the interrogation table, he welcomed the solidity of the surface.

The Minister studied Timur as if he were a bug pinned to a piece of cardboard. "Are you finished, Mr. Ganiev?"

Timur swallowed, nodded.

"Good." The Minister reached into his breast pocket and extracted a folded sheet of paper. He handed it to Timur. "This is your statement. Read it. Memorize it. I don't want you to use a teleprompter. I want the words to flow naturally."

As Timur scanned the page, phrases jumped out at him. *Attack on the sovereignty of the Central Asian Union . . . tough choices must be made . . . formally request the People's Liberation Army—*

He thrust the paper back at the Minister. The forward end crumpled against the man's pressed lapel. "I can't read this. It goes against everything I stand for."

Minister Yan smoothed the crumpled edges. "Don't be a child." He tried to hand it back.

Timur retreated to the other side of the table. He gripped the back of the chair. "I have a vision for the future and it does not include a Chinese invasion of my homeland."

Minister Yan's lips bent upwards at the corners, but his gaze still had the same clinical expression.

"A *vision*?" The open derision cut like steel. "You have no vision, Mr. Ganiev. You are what you are because I made you that way. Do you really believe the Central Asian Union just sprang out of your imagination? I put it there.

"You are a gifted orator—I'll grant you that—but an orator with no audience is just a man talking to himself. I put the people in that hall. I told those people what to think before you ever walked onto that stage. You are my creation."

"They tried to kill me," Timur snapped.

"Who?" Again, the dismissiveness in his voice made Timur angry.

"The SIF."

The Minister laughed. "There is no Seljuk Islamic Front. Just like you, they are my creation."

Timur gaped. "But the bombings, the people killed . . ."

Yan's expression tightened into irritation. "You cannot have light without darkness. In order to elevate the good"—he pointed at Timur—"I needed to create the evil. The SIF was an evil that I could control. It was a necessary part of the plan."

Timur's mind raced through the terrorist acts of the last year. In the stark clarity of hindsight, it was easy to see how the Minister had cleared the path ahead. The violence by the SIF repelled people, made them receptive to Timur's message. The culling of the strongest nationalist voices left people hungry for a new leader. And into the cultural bloodstream came the Central Asian Union promising a bright future...

It was brilliant. Brutal, but brilliant.

The Minister's voice broke into his thoughts. "Now, Mr. Ganiev, it is time for my investment in you to pay off." He placed the sheet of paper on the table between them. "Memorize these words. Make them your own. Your press conference is in thirty minutes. I expect you to be ready."

"And what if I refuse?" Timur demanded. He heard the back of the chair crack under the strain of his grip.

"The Americans have a saying that seems appropriate in this case," Yan said. "We can do this the easy way, or the hard way. Your choice." He nodded at the paper on the table. "That's the easy way."

"Then I choose the hard way," Timur said.

The Minister sighed. "How much do you remember about what happened at the ceremony? At the end, I mean. Do you remember a bright flash of light and the explosion?"

"Yes."

"That was the discharge of an EMP device. An electromagnetic pulse kills every piece of electronics in a two-hundred-meter radius. There are no cameras, no mobile phones, nothing to record what actually happened in those moments between when you finished your speech and disaster struck. Do you know what that means?"

Timur shook his head.

"It means that what I say happened is what happened. The story up to this moment is that the SIF made an attempt on the life of the General Secretary of the Chinese Communist Party. The attack might have been successful except for the brave actions of one Chinese officer who stepped in front of the bullet."

Yan raised his eyebrows. "I can change that story. The new story could be that the Seljuk Islamic Front launched an assassination attempt against Timur Ganiev. Unfortunately for you, they were successful."

Despite his best efforts, Timur's gaze fell to the paper on the table. The Minister noticed.

"It's not really a choice, Mr. Ganiev. I made you. I can destroy you. It makes no difference to me."

The Minister turned toward the door. "I'll be back in twenty minutes. I expect you to be ready."

Timur needed to do *something*. He needed to retain some vestige of power in this relationship.

"Wait," he said, his tone sharp, almost pleading.

The Minister let out a theatrical sigh. "What now?"

"I want my own camera crew at the press conference," Timur said. "I insist."

Instead of answering immediately, Yan walked around the table and approached Timur. Although the Minister barely reached to his chin, Timur tried not to shrink away. He could smell the oil in the man's hair and see the sprinkling of blackheads at his hairline.

The smaller man's gaze pinned him in place, but Timur held his ground. He raised his chin as Yan reached out. The Minister slipped a finger inside the collar of Timur's shirt and gave a sharp tug. Timur felt the material tear.

"What are you doing?" Timur stepped back now.

"We don't want you looking too pretty for the camera." Yan smiled. "Mr. President."

50

Bukhara, Uzbekistan

"Untie him."

Because the words were said in English, Harrison assumed they were meant for him. Rough hands tugged at the ropes binding his wrists and then he was free. He raised his hands tentatively toward the blindfold, then paused.

"Go ahead," said the voice. "You can take it off."

Akhmet Orazov was medium height with a wiry build. He had deep set eyes which gave him a strong resemblance to a bird of prey. The sleeves of his shirt were pushed up to the elbows, revealing corded muscles and dark leathery skin on his forearms. Although he knew Orazov was in his late sixties, Harrison could see the man was still fit.

He drew out a chair and sat across from Harrison. His movements were deliberate and smooth, efficient. Harrison's mobile phone, the battery removed, occupied the center of the table between them.

Harrison scanned the room. In addition to the two guards who had tied him up back in the bar, there were now two more men, looking equally as well-armed and capable.

I'm going to die, he told himself.

"Do you know who I am?" Orazov's English was pretty good, despite the Russian accent.

Harrison nodded. There was no point in lying.

"You came here to kill me."

Harrison did another scan of the guards. Surely Orazov knew Harrison spoke Russian. Maybe he was speaking in English so that the guards wouldn't know what he was saying.

"Look at me," Orazov demanded. One of the guards moved toward Harrison, but Orazov stayed him with a hand gesture.

Harrison forced himself to meet the older man's gaze. His dark eyes were hard, but also curious. "Why are you trying to kill me?" Orazov asked.

Why? Harrison thought. Now that was a great question. His head hurt from where the guards had taken him down in the bar. He was damn lucky they hadn't shot him on the spot. The truth was he'd acted on instinct. He'd seen that the operation was flawed and he did the only thing he could think of: he blew it up.

And now, as he peered into those cold, black eyes, Harrison knew he was going to die.

"Why?" Orazov repeated.

Harrison broke eye contact. An overwhelming sense of shame pierced his fear. He had carried water for the Chinese intelligence service. Willingly. But it was worse than that. Not only had he been duped by the Chinese, he'd roped Don Riley into his fantasy.

Tell him the truth, Harrison, he thought. You might as well die with a clean conscience.

Harrison sucked in a breath and looked at the man on the other side of the table. "The CIA thinks you are the leader of the SIF. There was—is—a kill order on you."

Orazov's eyes clouded with anger, his lips tightened.

"How?"

Harrison looked up at the ceiling.

"A drone strike." Orazov shook his head in disgust. "And your role in this scenario?"

"My job is to identify you. As soon as I'm safely out of the way, they strike."

Orazov's eyebrows went up. "This is dangerous for you."

"I volunteered," Harrison said.

Orazov seemed to like that answer. "But something changed, Mr. Kohl. You told my men the meeting was a trap. Why?"

"I found out new information."

Orazov said nothing, but he leaned in. Harrison took that as a good sign.

"Timur Ganiev," he said. "He has a . . . relationship with the Chinese. He's not who we thought, which means you're not who we thought."

"For this you put your own life at risk?" Orazov asked. "I don't understand."

Harrison swallowed. He wasn't sure he understood. "We were wrong." He paused, then said in a smaller voice. "I mean, I—I was wrong."

The admission of guilt seemed to surprise the other man. "*You* were wrong?"

Harrison nodded.

Orazov rotated his finger in the air. "This is all because of you? The drones, the secret meeting brokered by the Russians, it's all your doing?"

"It all started with me," Harrison countered. "So, yes, I'm responsible."

Orazov got to his feet, pacing. He cut a look at Harrison. "I can't make up my mind about you. Either you are a very honorable man or a very stupid man."

"Maybe I'm both."

Orazov laughed and resumed his place at the table. "Tell me your story, Mr. Kohl."

"My story?"

"Tell me how we ended up in this room together."

Once Harrison started talking, he found it hard to stop. Under Orazov's cold gaze, he unloaded everything. The disappearance of Tim Trujillo, Harrison's promise to Tim's family, Don's arrival in the region, and Harrison's experiences with Timur Ganiev.

He held nothing back. It was his confession—hell, maybe even his last rites.

As he spoke the words, he felt the burden of his responsibility. In the devastating light of hindsight, he felt like a fool. He started all of this. Don made Ganiev the centerpiece of a covert action based on Harrison's recommendation. Because of him, they'd been played by the Chinese. Because of him, his country's position in this region was damaged, maybe beyond repair.

When he finished, Orazov scowled at the table for a long time.

"Do you know how I started my career? Fighting for the Russians in Afghanistan. Fighting the mujahadeen, who were supported by your CIA. I was young and stupid, but things were simple then. Communist versus capitalist. Good versus evil. Pick a side.

"Now the world is all about influence. Lies designed to make you forget yourself. Forget who you are, what you stand for. The SIF is a fiction of Chinese intelligence. There was never a resistance, just Chinese special operations personnel carrying out terrorist attacks on their own people. Now you tell me that Timur Ganiev is a Chinese agent and thanks to the CIA, he is now the most powerful man in Central Asia. Congratulations."

"No," Harrison said, "we can—"

"If the next words out of your mouth are *we can fix this*, then you are a fool and a dead man, Mr. Kohl."

Harrison's jaw snapped shut. Orazov's hooded eyes stared him down, but Harrison did not look away. He didn't dare.

Orazov pushed his phone across the table. "Show me this recording."

Harrison put the battery back in the phone and powered on the device. He called up Tim Trujillo's last moments on earth and passed the phone back. Orazov watched it, his face muscles impassive. He watched it a second time. Then he put the phone down.

"How do you know it's not a fake?" he asked.

Harrison explained the IronClad app and the security protocols around it. "It's genuine," he concluded.

"Your friend was a brave man," Orazov said.

Conflicting emotions roiled under Harrison's skin. Shame at being duped, pride at Tim's bravery, anger at the situation he'd created.

"My friend was a good man," he replied. "And now he's dead."

The door opened. Another armed man crossed the room to Orazov's side and whispered in his ear. Orazov closed his eyes and sighed.

"Turn on the television," he ordered.

51

Samarkand International Airport, Uzbekistan

"Get me a secure line to Langley," Don shouted as he mounted the steps into the CIA's Gulfstream. All he could hear was his own breathing and the thunder of his own pulse. Chest heaving, he collapsed into a leather chair.

"Eagle One is off the ground," Stellner reported. "We've got four F-35s from Incirlik inbound as escorts. They'll pick them up at the Turkmenistan border in ten minutes."

"Good work," Don said. He stripped out the earpiece and dumped the phone he'd been carrying inside of the commerce center. They were both dead.

An EMP device, he thought. That was the only possible explanation. The Chinese wanted the assassination attempt to happen and they didn't want a record of it anywhere. Not even on their own sensors.

Don looked toward the back of the plane where the CIA medical team was working on the unconscious General Gao. Maybe that guy had the answers.

The door of the jet closed. Relative silence settled on the cabin. In addition to the two-man flight crew, the only people on the plane besides Don and Stellner were a tech, the three-person medical team, and the patient.

Don heard the jet's engines increase in pitch. The aircraft rolled forward a few meters, then stopped. He looked out the window. There was a traffic jam on the private air terminal apron as a line of jets queued up to depart.

Rats fleeing a sinking ship, he thought.

"Director Riley," the tech interrupted his thoughts. "I have Officer Hart on the line."

Don took the receiver. "Anne, what's the status?"

"I scrubbed the mission. I'm clearing the lethal assets, but leaving God's Eye in place for now."

Don closed his eyes with relief and let out a sigh.

"Thank God," he said. "Is Harrison at the exfil point yet?"

Anne's voice tightened. "Harrison's MIA, Don. His phone went offline and he was taken from the meeting point. When your entire team fell off the grid, I pulled the plug. What the hell is going on over there?"

Don shot a glance toward the rear of the plane. Someone was checking Gao's pupils with a penlight. "You wouldn't believe me if I told you. Right now, I'm more worried about Harrison."

"They left the meeting in two cars and then split up. One is almost into Turkmenistan and the other is in Bukhara. We think he's in the second vehicle." She paused as she received a report from someone in the room. "His phone just came back up on the network. I can try to patch him in."

"Do it." Don put his hand over the receiver. "I need a map," he said to the tech who handed him a tablet. Using two fingers, he enlarged the map to show details of the area around Bukhara. There was an airport there. Not a big airport, but big enough to land a Gulfstream.

Don beckoned to Stellner. "Tell the pilot I want to land in Bukhara. Do whatever it takes. Fake an emergency, stop for fuel, whatever. We need to be on the ground long enough to pick up a passenger."

Stellner looked past Don to the PLA general at the back of the plane. "Are you out of your mind, boss?"

Anne came back on the line. "I have Harrison."

"Don?" Harrison's voice.

"Are you okay?"

"I'm fine. Just sitting here with my new best friend, Akhmet."

Don froze. “Orazov is there with you now?”

Harrison gave a shaky laugh. “We’re talking current events. Planning our next steps.”

“Your next step is to get to Bukhara airport. I’m going to land the jet there and—”

“No.”

“Okay, you're right. That’s a stupid idea.” Don’s mind blazed ahead. “Get to the embassy and then—”

“No.”

“Harrison, what are you—”

“Turn on the news, Don. Pick a channel, anything local. They’re all carrying it.”

Don turned to the tech. “Get me a local news channel.”

Timur Ganiev’s image filled the screen on the tablet Don was holding. His face was gaunt, his eyes haunted. The collar of his shirt was torn and his salt-and-pepper hair was in disarray. He was the same man Don had seen only an hour ago, but his movements seemed brittle and his words lacked the conviction of the fiery speech of the Jade Spike ceremony.

“More than ever,” Ganiev was saying, “we need the Central Asian Union to fill the leadership vacuum in the republics. There will be a time to grieve and a time to rebuild, but in this moment, I need to ensure the safety of our citizens. The SIF is responsible for this heinous attack and we cannot defeat the SIF on our own.”

Ganiev paused, swallowed hard. “Therefore, I am requesting military assistance from the People’s Republic of China. I have authorized them to secure key installations within the Central Asian Union to protect the infrastructure that will be so vital to our shared future and to protect us from the terrorists . . .”

Don stared at the screen. He felt winded, as if someone had just punched him in the gut.

“Harrison,” he began. “What is—"

“We bet on the wrong guy, Don. We did this.”

Don sucked in a big breath. He wanted to throw up, but he swallowed the bile.

“We need to get you out of there, Harrison.”

"I'm not leaving, Don," Harrison said. "I caused this, and I need to fix it."

He hung up.

"Harrison!" Don said.

"His phone is offline again, Don," said Anne. "I've got his location in Bukhara."

The jet made a sweeping turn and Don heard the engines whine. He peered out the window. The runway ahead of them was clear.

The pilot released the brakes and the jet leaped forward.

52

Samarkand, Uzbekistan

Nicole Nipper wanted to throw the knockoff Chinese laptop out the window.

Every piece of electronics they'd possessed, from her personal phone to Barry's cameras, was gone. They'd been taken by the Chinese security team that now occupied the hallway outside her hotel room. Not that it mattered. The electronics were dead. Fried in some kind of electrical surge.

In return, she and Barry were given these Huawei laptops, which she was sure were riddled with spyware.

She tried not to think about what she'd lost. Scattered across those digital devices were years of consolidated work. She had backups, of course, but it would take her weeks, maybe months, to get back to where she'd been just a few hours ago.

It didn't matter. Right now, she had a story to file, and it was a doozie.

"This thing is a piece of shit," Barry muttered from behind his own laptop. He was seated at the rickety circular table next to the window in Nicole's hotel room. His bulky sides strained against the wooden arms of the narrow chair. He looked like a giant sitting in a dollhouse.

Nicole did not respond. She kept her attention on the transcript of

Timur Ganiev's televised speech she'd scrawled onto a yellow legal pad. She still had a hard time believing the words. The champion of Central Asian independence was asking the Chinese to invade his country. Nicole had followed him for the last year. She thought she knew him...

The details of what happened inside the Samarkand Commerce Center were sketchy. The SIF was behind the attack, that was what the Chinese press release said. According to unnamed sources on the internet, two of the four presidents from the Central Asian republics had been either killed or gravely injured.

The SIF? How was that possible? A car bomb or a drive-by shooting was one thing, but infiltrating PLA security at an event where both the General Secretary of the Chinese Communist Party and the American Secretary of State were in attendance was an entirely new level of boldness and sophistication.

Her journalistic instincts told her everything about this day smelled rotten. She considered the transcript of Ganiev's words. The Timur Ganiev she knew had principles. This man was a sellout. Nothing made sense.

"How are you coming on finding us some footage of the PLA forces?" she asked Barry.

He spun his laptop screen around. "This is from the PLA base near Dushanbe. They're loading tanks onto special trains to move them across the region. One already left fully loaded. This is the second one."

Nicole studied the screen. There had to be at least a hundred tanks organized in ranks. When the camera panned over, she saw columns of uniformed soldiers filing onto train cars. She was not a military expert, but this operation did not look like something that the PLA just threw together in the last few hours.

Yet another fact that didn't fit with Timur's story.

She focused on the legal pad where she was drafting her final report before she was thrown out of the country. "What's another word for *traitor*?" she asked.

Barry grinned. "How about asshole? Prick? Needle-dick bug fucker?"

They shared a laugh, but it was bittersweet for Nicole. She had trusted Timur. She had believed him.

Her eyes burned with unshed tears. Tears of frustration, hurt, anger.

And shame, too. She'd allowed herself to become emotionally invested in the subject at the center of her story. She'd lost her objectivity, not to mention her credibility.

You should've seen this coming, she told herself. Now you get what you deserve.

There was a knock at the door. Nicole and Barry exchanged glances, then Barry got up. He peered through the peephole and turned around with a cocked eyebrow.

"It's him," he mouthed, his eyes wide.

Nicole looked around. Her room was a mess, and her reflection in the wall mirror was not her best self.

Who cares? she thought. According to their Chinese captors, she and Barry were going to be on a plane in three hours. She'd never see Timur again—and that was fine with her.

Nicole stood, brushing the crumbs off her blouse from the bag of pretzels she snagged out of the minibar. She started to finger-comb her hair and gave up. "Let him in," she said.

Timur had changed his shirt since the press conference. He was now wearing a button-down blue Oxford and a tweed jacket with blue jeans and loafers.

Barry made a show of crowding him at the door so that Timur had to angle his body to get past. Nicole almost laughed at the show of male bravado.

Timur came straight to her and took her hand. "Nicole, I'm so glad you're safe."

She pulled her hand away, and she could feel her face bending into an angry scowl.

Timur looked surprised, but he recovered quickly. He turned to Barry. "Could you give us a moment in private, please?"

With his unshaven jowls and curled lip, Barry channeled his inner Rottweiler.

Nicole summoned up a reassuring smile. "Give us a minute, Barry. It's okay."

When the door clicked closed, Timur gave her a tentative smile. "He seems more protective than usual."

Nicole wasn't going to play this game. "What do you want, Mr. Ganiev? I have a story to file before I'm ejected from the country."

Timur reached for her, but she slipped her hands into her pockets. "I think that phase of our friendship is over, sir. I don't consort with traitors."

The remark struck home. Timur kept his hands to himself, but he held his ground. His eyes found hers. "You don't understand the big picture, Nicole."

She crossed her arms. "Then explain it to me."

"You're acting like this is easy for me. Power requires allies. Politics is a game of—"

"Politics?" Nicole sneered at him. "*Politics?* I thought you were above politics. I thought you were all about the cultural affirmation of the indigenous peoples and all that other bullshit you were slinging."

"Grow up," Timur's voice hardened. "You know the saying: Campaign in poetry, govern in prose. You of all people should understand the power of words."

"Oh, I understand words." Nicole snatched up the legal pad from the bed and read out loud, "Timur Ganiev, the once principled and respected leader of the nascent Central Asian Union, showed his true traitorous colors today when—"

He took the pad from her grip and tossed it onto the bed, the canary yellow pages fluttering. "Is that what you think of me?"

"I ran out of synonyms for traitor." Her eyes burned, but she was not about to shed a single tear in front of him. He was never going to see how much he'd hurt her.

"Do you think this is easy for me?" he asked gently.

"Stop it." Nicole cinched her arms tight across her chest.

"We are a good team, Nicole," Timur said in a soft voice. "Don't leave. Stay with me, and I'll show you everything. I'll make sure you get access behind the scenes—nothing off-limits. You thought you had a story before? That was nothing compared to what is about to happen."

Color rose in his cheeks and he reached for her. Nicole twisted away. Timur paced the room.

"Today, we have the Chinese keeping the peace," he continued, "but tomorrow? Tomorrow, we'll have new elections. I'll be the legitimate leader of the Central Asian Union and I promise you that I will be the leader by which all others are judged. I will be the man that you saw when we first met."

He came back to her and gently peeled her hands away from her elbows.

Nicole resisted, but not too much. His hands were warm, his face flushed, his eyes flashing with intensity. She knew that look.

"And you will be there to document it all," Timur said. "The only Western reporter with the inside story. An exclusive."

Nicole's head swam. He was right about one thing: it was the story of a lifetime. The perfect capstone of a career that she'd spent fighting for recognition. She could see her byline on a series of long-form articles, a book, a documentary, maybe a memoir or even a movie.

Timur moved closer, whispered, "You are a reporter, Nicole. I am a story. You are the only person I trust. Please, do this for me."

Nicole swallowed. Her gaze lighted on the yellow legal pad splayed on the bed. She'd written those words in anger. Traitor, treason, liar . . . Maybe there was more to the story.

Her voice seemed to stick in her throat. "What about Barry?"

"Don't worry," Timur whispered. "I'll handle Barry."

53

Sochi, Russia

Shafts of morning sun filtered through the tops of the pines as the limousine carrying Nikolay and Federov approached the gates of Vitaly Luchnik's compound on the Black Sea.

Nikolay had rolled his window down, letting the cool November morning air bathe his face. It had been a long night. A night he would not soon forget. A night his country would not forget.

But necessary, he told himself. You did what you had to do.

The security guard at the gate stiffened to attention when he saw the car emerge. He snapped a smart salute as Federov rolled down his window.

"Good morning, Arkady," the FSB chief said, his voice cheerful but thick with exhaustion. "How did you get stuck with the morning shift?"

"Good morning, Chief." Arkady triggered the remote and the heavy wrought iron gates parted. Nikolay noticed he did not answer Federov's question.

The gravel in the circular driveway crackled and popped under the tires of their car, loud in the morning stillness. When the vehicle drew to a halt, Federov started to get out, but Nikolay placed a hand on his arm.

"I'll do it," he said.

Federov's pale skin stretched across his features like parchment paper, giving him a haunted, skeletal look. Nikolay noticed there was a gap between the FSB chief's collar and the flaccid skin of his neck, as if he'd lost weight recently. He was an old man, Nikolay realized.

When Federov's crystalline brown eyes locked with his, Nikolay saw a flash of emotion cross the other man's face. There and gone in an instant.

Relief? Regret? Nikolay couldn't say.

The old man sat back in his seat.

Nikolay opened the car door and stepped out. He filled his lungs with the cool morning air. Damp with dew, laced with salt from the sea, and pregnant with the smells of the nearby orchard at autumn harvest. The only sound was the fountain bubbling cheerfully in the background.

He trod across the gravel and mounted the stone steps of the three-hundred-year-old building. Nikolay turned the knob on the grand front entrance and the door swung aside on well-oiled hinges.

Inside, the house was quiet as a tomb. There was no movement because the staff had already departed. Federov had seen to that.

Nikolay did not hesitate as he passed the grand staircase with the crimson carpet. At this hour of the morning, a man in retirement might still be in bed, but not Uncle Vitaly. He was an early riser. On a morning like this, his uncle would be taking his coffee on the terrace.

He walked past the drawing room and the library to the back of the house, where the French doors stood open.

Vitaly Luchnik's chair faced the Black Sea. There was enough light to see the horizon, a sharp line of dark water against a lightening sky. The terrace was in shade and the former Russian President wore a heavy cardigan against the morning chill. The sweet smell of the orchard was stronger here.

Luchnik did not turn around at the sound of footsteps on the terrace. Nikolay came to a stop next to his uncle. Under the sweater, the older man was dressed in gym shorts and a T-shirt for his morning workout. He cradled an empty coffee cup in his lap.

Luchnik kept his gaze fixed on the horizon. "It's beautiful here in the mornings," he said quietly.

Nikolay did not respond. As with Federov, Nikolay was suddenly aware of his uncle's advanced age. His feelings seesawed on a knife edge of emotion.

The old man gave a low chuckle. "I heard about Zaitsev. Using the woman was a nice touch." He looked up at Nikolay for the first time. "Federov's idea?"

"Mine," Nikolay replied.

Luchnik was as well informed as ever. By now, the news was blazing across the headlines and consuming the daytime talk shows back in Moscow. In the early morning hours, Konstantin Zaitsev had been gunned down by his lover, Svetlana Kulakova, lead reporter for the Russian Unity Press and longtime mouthpiece for the Ultras. The poor woman had been so distraught by her actions that she'd thrown herself out of a seven-story window.

"What will you do about China, nephew? Do you have a plan?"

The Chinese threat was a problem for another day. On this glorious autumn morning on the Black Sea, he had other business to attend to.

Nikolay ignored his uncle's question. "How did you do it? All those years?"

Luchnik reached his arms toward the sky in a luxurious morning stretch. Nikolay tensed—his uncle was a resourceful man—but he held his ground. Luchnik placed his empty coffee cup on the low table next to his chair.

"I did what I had to do," Luchnik said. "Nothing more, nothing less. Russia has been a great country for a thousand years. We will be so for the next millennium, but we do not change. We do things our own way. Hard, but effective."

Nikolay felt his tongue like sandpaper in his mouth. Was the old man taunting him?

Luchnik twisted in his chair to face Nikolay.

"Weakness has no place in our world, nephew. I think you see that now, but you still have much to learn."

Nikolay licked his lips. Somewhere on the limit of his hearing, came the cry of raven.

"I can teach you," Luchnik continued. "We are a dynasty, you and I. You've stopped the bleeding, that's the important thing. You took out Zaitsev, which will stop the Ultras for now. Throwing the woman out the window will shut the press up for a while—that was good thinking. Well done, nephew."

"But it's not enough, Uncle," Nikolay replied. "I think you know that."

He was surprised how calm his voice sounded. How the gun was steady in his grip. His breath came easily, smooth and measured. Confident.

"Weakness has no place in our world," Nikolay said. "Your words, Uncle."

Luchnik spread his hands in a gesture of disbelief. "But why kill me? I had nothing to do with any of it. I can help you."

"You didn't finish your lesson, Uncle. You forgot the most important thing."

Luchnik lowered his hands. "Tell me."

"Power is perception and perception is power. As long as you live, there will be some who will believe that you tried to betray me, and I let you live. That I was too weak to do what was required of me. You know I can't have that."

Luchnik's lips twitched, and a smile crept across his features. Slowly, like a rising sun, it grew into a grin that went all the way into the old man's eyes. Nikolay saw something else in his uncle's face.

Pride, he realized.

Luchnik's voice was throaty with emotion.

"You have become me, nephew."

Nikolay raised the weapon and pulled the trigger.

54

The White House, Washington, DC

Don was midway through his second cup of coffee when the meeting invite showed up in his inbox. The clock on his computer screen read 0530.

He accepted it immediately. Meeting requests from the White House weren't actually requests, they were orders. Then he studied the details.

Oval Office, 0800 for thirty minutes. There were no other invitees noted and no agenda.

He pulled a freshly pressed suit from his closet and shut his office door to change.

When he arrived outside the Oval Office at 0745, he immediately noticed changes in the White House. It had been two weeks since the election, and President-elect Eleanor Cashman's staff seemed intent on hitting the ground running. Every meeting room and office was full as outgoing personnel and their replacements operated in tandem. In the hallways, staffers sat on folding chairs, hunched over laptops, speaking into their mobile phones in low tones.

The atmosphere was rife with conflicted emotions. Don sensed how Serrano's people were reacting to the political defeat, ranging from resignation to anger. This was balanced by the brightness and exhilaration of success emanating from the newcomers. The riptide of emotions was oddly comforting to Don. He was witnessing the peaceful transfer of power.

The attack in Samarkand and the subsequent PLA move into Central Asia were the final nails in the coffin of President Serrano's ambitions for his handpicked successor. For all his gifts as a tireless campaigner and billions of dollars in donations, yet another international conflict in the last week of the Serrano administration proved too much for the electorate.

In the end, the vote wasn't even close. Senator Cashman became President-elect Eleanor Cashman well before the late-night talk shows hit the airwaves.

To Don's mind, the unfolding situation in Central Asia was a fitting bookend to President Serrano's two terms in office. He'd been baptized by fire in the first months of his time in office and it had never really stopped.

Different chapters of the same book, Don thought. Serrano was the victim of a rapidly changing world. And the changes were not complete yet. The United States was no longer the only superpower. Despite their setback in Taiwan, or maybe because of it, China's challenge to the post–World War Two international order was not going away.

The door of the Oval Office swung open and a stream of people filed out, among them the outgoing and incoming vice presidents. Hawthorne's gaze locked on Don for a split second, then he moved on without acknowledgment.

An assistant entered the Oval and closed the door behind her. Five minutes later, she was back. She held the door for him. "You can go in now, Mr. Riley."

Don looked around. It was just him after all.

Morning sunlight drenched the empty Resolute desk. The incoming and outgoing presidents waited for him in the sitting area of the Oval Office. Serrano occupied the armchair at the head of the table with Cashman on one of the couches. Their conversation paused when Don came in, and they looked up in unison.

Serrano got up. "Good to see you again, Don." The President's smile was warm and friendly. If he was angry about losing the election, Don couldn't see it. In fact, Serrano looked more relaxed than he'd seemed in a long time.

"Eleanor, this is Don Riley."

Cashman's handshake was cool, dry, and surprisingly firm.

"Mr. Riley and I are acquainted from his briefings to the Gang of Eight."

Don wasn't sure if that was a vote of confidence. He forced a polite smile. "Congratulations, Madam President-elect."

"Join us, Mr. Riley," Cashman replied in a tone that left Don wondering where he stood with her.

Serrano poured fresh coffee for the three of them. Don accepted his, but immediately set the cup and saucer on the coffee table. The last thing he wanted was for Cashman to see how nervous he was.

He tried to figure out the dynamic in the room. While Serrano maintained a relaxed demeanor, the President-elect positively glowed with energy. She looked eager to take on the challenges ahead.

Cashman spoke first. "The President and I wanted to have you in for a chat." She sipped her coffee. "I'd like to hear your assessment of how we handled the situation in Central Asia."

Don cut a look at Serrano, but his expression was unreadable.

Honesty is the best policy, Don, he told himself.

"We tried to operate in a region where we've underinvested for the last twenty years. Insufficient intelligence led to running an influence operation to prop up Timur Ganiev, a man who now appears to be a Chinese agent."

"Who bears responsibility for that mistake?" Cashman pressed.

"I do," Don said. "I made the recommendation to the President that an influence operation was a cheap, low-profile way to change the regional dynamic."

Cashman's brow creased as if she hadn't expected him to fall on his sword so willingly. "Continue."

"The expanded mission to take out Akhmet Orazov was a mistake," Don said. "We had no direct intel linking Orazov to the SIF. As we know now, that's because it didn't exist."

"Do you take full responsibility for that, too?" Cashman asked.

Don willed himself not to look at Serrano. "Yes, ma'am. It happened on my watch."

"What about the Russian connection?" Cashman said.

Don blew out his breath. "I think it was a setup, but if we hadn't met

Orazov face-to-face, we'd be much worse off today. Whether they meant to or not, the Russians did us a favor."

"You're saying we got lucky?" Cashman's voice sounded doubtful.

"Sometimes things work out, ma'am. If my officer hadn't met Orazov under the conditions he did, we would have made a terrible mistake. Instead, we have a trusted ally in the regional resistance movement. Trust is not something that happens, it has to be earned—and thanks to Harrison Kohl, we earned it."

"You trust Kohl?"

"He's one of the best officers I've ever worked with."

Cashman looked at Serrano and sat back in her chair. She was done with this witness.

"What's your take on Russia, Don?" Serrano asked.

Don knew what the President was really asking: What happened to Nikolay Sokolov?

"It appears President Sokolov has made a choice, sir. The opposition candidate met an untimely end, which almost certainly guarantees him the election next week."

"You think that was him or Federov?"

"I don't think it matters, Mr. President. President Sokolov has made a choice to retain power through force."

"I have a hard time believing that, Don. I know the man. I think Federov is pulling the strings."

"Mr. President, we have intelligence that says Nikolay Sokolov flew to Sochi and murdered his own uncle. He pulled the trigger, sir. Personally. In my estimation, Nikolay Sokolov has gone to the dark side."

Don let the fallout from that knowledge bomb settle. His hands were steady now. He was pretty sure he was about to be fired and that felt somehow freeing. He picked up his cup and took a sip.

"Thank you for your honesty, Donald," Cashman said. "I find it refreshing."

The comment didn't seem to warrant a response, so Don took another sip of coffee.

"I wanted you to know," Cashman continued, "that I've asked the President to accept Director Blank's resignation, effective immediately. His last day is today."

Don put his coffee down.

Here it comes, he thought. Let the housecleaning begin.

"I've asked Carroll Brooks to step in as acting Director until I can get her confirmed by the Senate."

Don peeled his tongue off the roof of his mouth. "Carroll will do a fine job, ma'am."

"She will need a trusted partner, Donald. I hope I can count on you."

"Ma'am?"

Serrano chuckled. "Riley, you're such a goddamned Boy Scout. You were railroaded into the Orazov kill operation. By my team, I might add. When asked, you could have thrown Florez under the bus, but instead you took the fall."

"Sir, I—"

"Can it, Don. The influence op was a mistake. You got sucked in along with the rest of the world, so shame on you. But the Orazov thing? You tried to tell me, and I wouldn't listen. That's on me, not you."

"I'm not interested in the blame game, Donald," Cashman said. "I need people I can trust to tell me the truth—even when I don't want to hear it. We're in the middle of a proxy war in Central Asia and we cannot afford to wait until I'm inaugurated to take action. President Serrano and I have an understanding. We want you to spearhead a covert operation to resist the Chinese invasion force. You tell me that your best man is on the inside with Orazov. Good, put him to work. I want the PLA to regret the day they ever rolled tanks inside the Central Asian Union. Do I make myself clear, Donald?"

Don swallowed. "Yes, ma'am."

He risked a look at a Serrano. This was almost the same speech he'd gotten from Serrano at the beginning of his first term. History might not repeat itself, but it sure as hell rhymed right now.

Cashman settled back in her chair. "Now tell me about this PLA general you rescued."

55

Undisclosed location
Northeastern Pennsylvania, United States

Gao Yichen had been at The Ranch for about three weeks. At least that was his best estimate. It was difficult to say for sure since there was no television, no radio, and no calendars at the facility.

Although the people around him called it The Ranch, Gao was pretty sure he was not in the western part of the United States. When he'd first arrived, it was late autumn. The remaining leaves on the trees were brilliant oranges, yellows, and reds. Since that time, all the leaves had fallen and it had snowed twice. There was wildlife here, mostly deer who waved their white tails when they fled, and rabbits and squirrels.

The geography was another clue. The Ranch was located in a narrow valley between two hills. Not big enough to be called mountains, definitely hills. A single dirt road led into the valley, but Gao never got to see a license plate. All outside cars parked in a garage at the far end of the property and the personnel moved around in golf carts.

Given all the available information, Gao guessed he was somewhere in the northeastern United States.

The Ranch was managed by a couple in their mid-sixties. Sam and

Martha lived in the farmhouse with Gao. Martha cooked and cleaned and Sam took care of the chickens and goats and the farm upkeep. There were also two armed security personnel near Gao at all times and he had seen cameras stationed around the property. More security people walked the perimeter.

Gao considered himself a prisoner of war. In his People's Liberation Army training, he'd been shown films and given briefings on the barbaric ways the Americans treated their captives. Sleep deprivation, waterboarding, psychedelics, Gao was prepared for all of these things when they moved him from the hospital to The Ranch.

But none of those things happened. On the contrary, the Americans seemed determined to kill him with kindness and boredom.

His days melted into sameness. He got up at 7:00 a.m., washed and dressed and ate breakfast in the kitchen. Martha cooked while he and Sam ate together in silence. After breakfast, he followed Sam outside as the man tended to the chickens and milked the goats.

At 0900, Ling arrived. His physical therapist was a chirpy twenty-something Chinese-American who spoke to him in fluent Mandarin and taught him English as she stretched and massaged his arm. She was pretty and unflaggingly cheerful, but she was also skillful at deflecting his questions. Gao was certain her ultimate goal was to seduce him, but the only thing that happened was his English language proficiency improved.

He was now able to hold a basic conversation with Sam as they did the chores. Sometimes Gao waved at the security guards and said things like, "It's a beautiful morning," and "Have a great day." Ling taught him how to say those things with an American accent.

As a member of the People's Liberation Army, Gao knew it was his responsibility to resist and escape. But first he needed to heal from his injuries. His arm was getting better. The bullet wound in his chest had turned into a thick red button of scar tissue and he was able to take off the sling for a few hours each day.

Soon, Gao told himself. But first he needed to be strong—one hundred percent, as Ling liked to say—to make his move.

And so the days slipped by.

The only part of his routine when Gao was reminded of his status as a prisoner came in the afternoon. Every day at 1400, after he'd lunched with Sam and Martha, one of the duty guards escorted him to the Studio. That's what they called the outbuilding behind the garage. He supposed that it might once have been an artist's studio, but they weren't fooling Gao for a second.

The Studio was an interrogation room. Yes, it had overstuffed armchairs and a big stone fireplace and a small bar in the corner, but it was still an interrogation room.

His interrogators came in all shapes, sizes, ages, and nationalities. Some of them spoke to him in Mandarin, others in English. Some of them were men, some women, some young, some old.

Gao resisted them all. He was a proud member of the People's Liberation Army and the Chinese Communist Party. He would not betray that trust. Lieutenant General Gao Yichen was not a traitor.

The security guard who escorted Gao this afternoon was named Peter. It was cold and their breath steamed in the air as they walked from the house to the Studio.

Peter studied the leaden sky. "Snow coming. I can smell it."

Gao didn't know what snow smelled like, but he said, "Yeah, I know what you mean," like Ling had taught him.

Peter held the door open for Gao. "See you in an hour, General."

"Catch you later, Peter," Gao replied, another Ling-ism.

The interrogator was new. He was in his fifties, and he had a belly. His face was careworn, his reddish hair streaked with gray. It took Gao a few seconds to place the face and remember where he'd seen him before.

The man got to his feet and ambled across the room. "General Gao, you probably don't remember me. My name is—"

"Donald Riley," Gao replied. "We met in. . ."

Samarkand, the day of the Jade Spike ceremony. The day he'd been taken captive.

He did not shake Riley's hand. Gao walked to a chair and sat down. He tried to stay calm, but inside he seethed with nervous energy. The presence of a high-ranking CIA officer meant that Gao's life was about to change, and not for the better. The real interrogation would start now, with all the tactics he'd been warned about in his training.

Riley noticed the change in Gao's demeanor. He said, "Are you okay, sir?"

The man was good, Gao thought. It actually sounded like he cared.

"I'm not going to tell you anything," Gao replied. "You can do whatever you want to me, but I will not betray my country."

Riley sat down on the edge of his chair. He leaned forward, put his elbows on his knees. "I think you have it backward, General. Your country betrayed you."

Gao looked out the picture window. Fat flakes of snow drifted down.

"No response to that?" Riley asked. "Fair enough. Let's make this a dialogue. If you answer one of my questions, I'll answer one of yours."

Gao considered the man. Behind that unassuming exterior, this guy was very good. Why not? Gao wondered. After all, if he was going to escape, he needed some intelligence.

"Deal," he said, another idiom he'd learned from Ling, "but I ask the first question."

Riley sat back in his chair. "Fire away."

Gao assumed that meant yes. "Where is this place?"

"You're in northeastern Pennsylvania, General. The closest large city is Scranton and the mountains you see around you are called the Poconos."

Gao was astonished at Riley's willingness to disclose that level of detail.

"My turn," Riley said. "Why did your government try to kill you?" He asked the question in a matter-of-fact way, as if he was inquiring about the weather.

Gao felt his mouth go dry. He didn't remember a lot about the day of his accident, but he had a recurring dream. Captain Fang stood over him, her face in shadow. She had her sidearm out, pointing her weapon at his chest... and then her head exploded.

It was horrible, but Gao took comfort in the fact that it was just a dream.

"I don't know what you're talking about," Gao said. He could hear the anger in his own voice, but he knew he was more angry at himself for being drawn in by this American spy. He needed to be more careful.

Riley laced his fingers across his stomach and settled deeper into his chair. "I think you do. As a matter of fact, General, the only reason you're still alive is because I saved you."

"That is a lie," Gao snapped.

But was it? He remembered being carried onto a plane, and the next time he woke up he was in a hospital and everyone around him spoke English. That must have been when they kidnapped him. But how did they get him out of Samarkand? There had been hundreds of PLA security personnel that day.

"How much do you remember about the Jade Spike ceremony?" Riley asked in that same neutral voice.

"I remember . . ." Gao's voice trailed off as he concentrated. "I remember there was a man in the crowd with a gun. He was going to shoot the General Secretary, then . . ."

"Then he shot you instead," Riley finished for him. "The gunman had a clear shot at the General Secretary, the United States Secretary of State, and Timur Ganiev. He bypassed all those targets and he shot you." Riley leaned forward now. "Why?"

"It didn't happen that way." Gao's heel went *tap-tap-tap* on the polished wood floor and he willed himself to stop it. Riley was obviously an experienced interrogator. He must not show signs of nervousness.

"That's not everything, is it, General?" Riley pressed. "After the gunman shot you, you weren't dead. The female captain, your own aide-de-camp, came over and tried to finish the job. My security team stopped her. They shot her in the head."

Gao froze in his chair. How did they know about his dream? Did the Americans have a mind control device that could read his thoughts?

"I want to know why they tried to kill you, General."

Gao looked out the window again. There was no mind control device. There was a far simpler explanation. It wasn't a dream at all.

Captain Fang. Xiaomei tried to kill him. The Americans stopped her.

Riley went to a wall cabinet and opened the doors to reveal a television. He used a remote control to turn on the screen and start a recording.

"This is eight hours after you were shot at the Jade Spike ceremony," Riley said.

Gao saw a satellite image of PLA tanks and personnel being loaded onto trains. There were far more vehicles than he'd believed even existed at the PLA base near Dushanbe. The image changed to a young Chinese woman seated at a desk with the PRC flag behind her. Gao recognized her as a popular news anchor in Beijing and he felt a pang of homesickness.

A brutal terrorist attack in Samarkand, Uzbekistan, has claimed the life of People's Liberation Army Lieutenant General Gao Yichen. The popular officer, known as the Hero of Tashkent, died protecting the General Secretary. His killing has sparked outrage across China and the leader of the Central Asian Union has asked for Beijing's help in quelling this highly dangerous and cold-blooded terrorist movement . . .

Riley shut off the television and returned to his seat. He stared at Gao.

"Your country is using your death as a pretext to invade Central Asia. I think that was their plan all along. You were a blood sacrifice."

Gao shook his head. "Lies. All lies. The SIF—"

"The Seljuk Islamic Front was a covert operation run by the Ministry of State Security, General. I would be willing to bet that your aide, Captain Fang, was an MSS operative."

Gao stood.

"Sit down, General," Riley ordered. "Please," he added in a softer tone.

Gao hesitated, then sat back down.

Riley pointed at the dark television screen. "Your own country announced your death and vowed retribution. Yet, you are very much alive."

Gao felt as if insects were crawling all over his body. He wanted to scratch away his skin and scream with rage.

"What do you want from me?" he shouted.

Riley's face was composed, calm. "I am in charge of the U.S. response to the invasion of Central Asia. I need all the help I can get, including yours."

"I won't help you."

Riley continued in his annoyingly calm voice. "There's different ways you can help. For example, I could announce to the world that you are very much alive and living free in the United States. Beijing would be embarrassed and they would have to assume that you were cooperating with us."

Gao licked his lips. The MSS would hunt him down for the rest of his life. Mei Lin and the children would be thrown in prison.

"On the other hand," Riley continued, "your own country says you're dead. We can go along with the lie and say nothing. If you cooperate."

Gao tried to breathe normally. "I need something from you first."

"Name it."

"I want you to get my family out of China. I want them here with me and I want them to be safe."

Riley chewed his lip. "What do you have to trade, General?"

Gao's mind was already racing. He could see now that entire areas of the operation in Central Asia had been compartmented from him. It all made sense now. The starring role in the movie, the promotion, Xiaomei . . . From the beginning, his death was to be the excuse for the invasion. It was all a lie. They had manipulated him, the Hero of Tashkent, at every turn using his own greed and vanity against him.

Gao felt like a fool.

But he wasn't a fool. He was Gao Yichen, the youngest general in the history of the PLA—even if they took away his second star. He was an experienced operative, and he knew how the PLA and the Party worked.

What did he have to trade? What little he knew about the PLA forces in the region was already out of date.

Think, Yichen. Think like the general you are.

Then it hit him.

A force of the size and complexity required to invade Central Asia would prize one thing above all.

Information.

"I can get you access to the Huawei network," Gao said.

Riley's expression shifted and Gao knew he'd struck gold.

56

Karakum Desert
50 kilometers south of Turkmenabat, Turkmenistan

Harrison Kohl shrugged deeper into his jacket, but he left the window of the battered Land Cruiser open.

He loved the desert at night, especially in winter. Quiet, cold, and still. It was a new moon and the stars overhead seemed close enough to touch. They gave off a soft light that turned the landscape darkly silver. A few meters away, a high-wheeled truck with a covered bed was parked on the sand, its engine giving off ticking sounds as it cooled.

The resistance against the Chinese invasion of the Central Asian Union was only a few weeks old, but already the fighting had settled into a depressing pattern of one step forward, two steps back. It was easy to blame the lack of progress on the PLA's overwhelming logistics advantage. With their Belt and Road infrastructure network strung across the region like pearls on a necklace, the Chinese could move troops and war materiel anywhere in the region within twenty-four hours.

But their biggest roadblock, Harrison knew, was the Huawei network that ran parallel to the road and rail lines. The lightning-fast 10G connection fueled a vast surveillance network of cameras, drones, signals intelligence, and satellites that expanded every day.

The Chinese strategy was painfully simple and effective: using the Belt and Road corridor as a beachhead, they expanded their surveillance footprint by adding to the infrastructure and tying it all back to the Huawei network. In Harrison's estimate, Orazov's resistance effort had six months to stop the Chinese. As soon as the surveillance network was complete, the once independent republics of Central Asia would essentially be Chinese provinces.

The Chinese had learned from their failed attempt to invade Taiwan. This time, they had put political cover in place. Timur Ganiev, the leader of the Central Asian Union, had begged for Beijing's help to quell the violence in his country.

The Chinese weren't invading Central Asia. They were saving it.

Harrison winced every time he saw one of Ganiev's broadcasts. The man was a gifted communicator who seemingly had no trouble twisting his message to suit his Chinese masters.

I did that, Harrison reminded himself every day.

The fiction of the Central Asian Union still played well in the Western media, further slowing a worldwide recognition of the Chinese threat to the region.

Harrison turned up the collar on his jacket, welcoming the bite of the night air on his skin.

By the time the world wakes up, it'll all be over.

The flow of arms to Akhmet Orazov's resistance fighters was slow and mostly inadequate. Vintage small arms and ancient ammunition were smuggled across the Iranian and Afghan borders sporadically by truck. Orazov tapped his connections with organized crime syndicates, but criminals didn't work for free.

Hopefully, tonight was a sign of good things to come. The CIA was sending a cargo plane with a weapons shipment. For security, Orazov cleared a landing strip in the desert inside a predesignated fifty-square-kilometer zone. At precisely 0230 local, the ground team would energize a homing beacon that would be picked up by the flight coming across the Afghan border to the south. The CIA cargo plane planned for ten minutes for unloading, then Orazov's team would head for the foothills of the Pamir mountains. By sunrise, the new weapons would be safely stashed inside a cave, ready for distribution to the resistance fighters around the region.

At least, that was the plan.

Harrison shifted in his seat. He should close his eyes for a few minutes. His body was achy and tired, but he knew where his mind would end up if he allowed himself to drift off.

Tim Trujillo. Even after all this time, his best friend's murder at the hands of the Chinese Minister of State Security was still sharp in his memory.

Unfinished business, Harrison supposed. The earthly remains of Tim Trujillo were still in a warehouse in Samarkand, firmly within Chinese control. When the terrorist attack went down, there was no time to clear a coffin through customs and load it onto a U.S.-bound plane.

Harrison picked out a star in the sky and stared at it until he saw double.

That was his one regret about staying behind. He'd abandoned Jenny and her sons to a circle of bureaucratic hell.

Without a body, Jenny could not declare her husband legally deceased. Until he was legally dead, she could not access his death benefits. Harrison thought about their beautiful home and all the family memories inside those four walls. He thought about college tuition and car maintenance and the hundred other expenses that Jenny had to deal with on her own. He thought about the funeral that his best friend deserved and would not receive.

In the seat next to him, Akhmet Orazov stirred. Like a seasoned soldier, Orazov took every opportunity to restore his strength with a short nap. It was a skill Harrison had yet to master.

Harrison heard footfalls in the sand and the form of a man blocked the starlight beside Orazov's window. He murmured to his commander in Turkic. Harrison was just picking up the language. He heard the word for *airplane*. Harrison checked his watch. 0230.

Orazov responded in Russian. "Turn on the beacon." To Harrison, he said, "Did you nap, my friend?"

"No."

Orazov stretched like a cat. "Too bad. I think you need your beauty sleep."

Then he laughed and opened his car door.

Harrison's relationship with the older man was an odd one. Less CIA officer and rebel leader, more like father and son. He realized how the circumstances of their first meeting had shaped everything between them.

Before he even met Akhmet Orazov, Harrison had saved the man's life at the risk of his own. Men like Orazov did not forget such things.

Harrison got out of the car and followed Orazov. In Harrison's experience, it could take months, or even years, to build up the kind of trust he already shared with the leader of the resistance.

"They've locked on to the beacon, Commander," one of the men reported.

"Turn on the lights," Orazov responded.

A string of ultraviolet lights defined the landing strip for the incoming aircraft. Since the UV lights were invisible to the naked eye, the pilots wore night-vision gear. Harrison's ears picked up the drone of a twin-engine propeller aircraft. He searched the night sky, finally picking out a dark shape blocking the stars. The sound deepened as the incoming aircraft reduced power on the glide slope.

At the far end of the makeshift airstrip, the plane touched down in a cloud of silvery dust, then roared toward them. It came to a stop ten meters away from the beacon and executed a turn. The pitch of the rotors lessened, but the pilot did not shut down the engines. They were in enemy territory and they did not intend to stay long.

A cloud of dust rolled over them as Orazov's team advanced. Harrison recognized the blocky fuselage and twin tail configuration of a C-23 Sherpa. The rear loading ramp lowered and red light spilled across the sand.

A man called out in American-accented Russian, "Special delivery."

Orazov's men lined up beside the ramp. The two-man crew inside the plane moved six pallets down a roller-conveyor. Harrison noted the labels as the men hefted them off the ramp.

Night-vision gear, MANPAD shoulder-fired surface-to-air missiles, Javelin anti-tank weapons, small arms and lots of ammunition.

Real weapons. Finally, they'd be able to get into this fight.

The man on the plane watched the last crate get carried away. He looked down at Harrison. "Are you my passenger?"

"What?"

"I'm supposed to pick up one outgoing container and a passenger," the crew chief said. "Hustle up. We're on the clock, man."

"Harrison." Orazov's voice.

He turned to see the rebel leader followed by four men bearing a sealed six-foot-long metal case.

A coffin, Harrison realized.

Orazov held out his hand and pressed something small and round into Harrison's palm. He held it up to the light where he could just make out the inscription on the ring.

Never falter, never quit. Tim's class ring.

Orazov gripped Harrison's arm. "Take your friend home. This is your chance."

As Orazov's men carried Tim's coffin up the ramp, Harrison wrapped his fingers around the ring. The edges dug into his palm.

Home, he thought. I can take Tim *home*.

The crew chief reappeared. "The meter's running, my friend. You comin' or not?"

"No," Harrison said. "Please make sure that package makes it home, but I'm staying."

The crew chief chuckled. "He said you'd say that. Told me to give you this." He passed a black plastic case down to Harrison.

The case was heavy in his arms. "Who?"

"DDO Riley. Said that he's working on a plan and he'll be in touch. Good luck, buddy. We're outta here."

Harrison had a hundred questions, but the ramp was already going up. The pitch of the engines increased and propeller-driven dust whipped past him. The aircraft jerked as the pilot released the brakes and the plane leaped forward. It roared down the runway and lifted off into the night sky.

Tim Trujillo was going home. Finally.

Harrison hugged the case to his chest as the sound of the aircraft drifted away. He closed his eyes, letting the quiet cool of the desert night surround him.

You're doing the right thing, he thought. You are the right man for this job.

Behind him, the sound of a diesel truck engine shattered the stillness. His eyes snapped open.

Time to get to work.

Proxy War
Command and Control #6

In the upcoming global showdown, the U.S. confronts a new enemy on the battlefield: Artificial Intelligence.

In the heart of Central Asia, a strategic power play unfolds as the People's Republic of China extends its military might. Under the pretext of protecting their Belt-and-Road projects, the People's Liberation Army (PLA) gains a stronghold in the region. Against this invasion, a courageous band of freedom fighters is the only challenge to the PLA forces.

On this geopolitical chessboard, the newly-elected U.S. President wants to make a bold statement against Chinese expansionism. Don Riley, recently appointed CIA Director of Operations, is chosen to spearhead the critical mission.

Don launches a clandestine CIA operation to aid the freedom fighters, but as the losses pile up, he realizes they are fighting a new enemy. The PLA harbors a secret weapon – Foresight, a quantum-powered battlefield AI. This advanced system anticipates and counters the resistance's moves with chilling precision, pushing Don to the edge. With each passing day, as Foresight's surveillance net widens, the window for effective resistance narrows.

Don and his team put everything on the line. As the resistance draws the PLA into a decisive final battle, he launches a covert team. Their mission: neutralize Foresight.

ACKNOWLEDGMENTS

Behind every successful book is a Fleet of supporters. This novel is no exception.

Covert Action is our fifth book with Severn River Publishing. We continue to be impressed with their professionalism and their commitment to our work. We write the stories and let them handle the thousands of details that go into the publishing side of the business. Special thanks to Andrew Watts, Amber Hudock, Mo Metlen, and Cate Streissguth, especially to Cate!

We were privileged to work with a new editor for this book. Thanks to Cassie Gitkin for her hard work in getting our manuscript in shape—and for putting up with our idiosyncrasies. Only in our books is the Minister considered a proper noun and always capitalized.

In *Covert Action*, we continued our fraught practice of naming characters after real people. In real life, Tim Trujillo is a good friend of JR's brother and a senior counsel in the health care field. In *Covert Action*, he died in the first chapter . . . sorry about that, Tim.

Will Clarke, a retired US Navy captain and friend of the authors, made a return cameo in this book as well as the CEO of the private military contractor, Falchion.

Jennifer Schumacher, David's favorite sister and First Reader, lent her name to Tim's wife, Jenny Trujillo.

Lastly, as the Bruns-Olson writing team approaches a decade of collaboration, we'd like to thank our families. Melissa, Christine, Cate, and Alex, we love you.

ABOUT THE AUTHORS

David Bruns

David Bruns earned a Bachelor of Science in Honors English from the United States Naval Academy. (That's not a typo. He's probably the only English major you'll ever meet who took multiple semesters of calculus, physics, chemistry, electrical engineering, naval architecture, and weapons systems just so he could read some Shakespeare. It was totally worth it.) Following six years as a US Navy submarine officer, David spent twenty years in the high-tech private sector. A graduate of the prestigious Clarion West Writers Workshop, he is the author of over twenty novels and dozens of short stories. Today, he co-writes contemporary national security thrillers with retired naval intelligence officer, J.R. Olson.

J.R. Olson

J.R. Olson graduated from Annapolis in May of 1990 with a BS in History. He served as a naval intelligence officer, retiring in March of 2011 at the rank of commander. His assignments during his 21-year career included duty aboard aircraft carriers and large deck amphibious ships, participation in numerous operations around the world, to include Iraq, Somalia, Bosnia, and Afghanistan, and service in the U.S. Navy in strategic-level Human Intelligence (HUMINT) collection operations as a CIA-trained case officer. J.R. earned an MA in National Security and Strategic Studies at the U.S. Naval War College in 2004, and in August of 2018 he completed a Master of Public Affairs degree at the Humphrey School at the University of Minnesota. Today, J.R. often serves as a visiting lecturer, teaching national security courses in Carleton College's Department of Political Science, and hosts his radio show, *National Security This Week*, on KYMN Radio in Northfield, Minnesota.

You can find David Bruns and J.R. Olson at
severnriverbooks.com